*For Eduardo, as with everything I do.*

*For my aunt Angela and all the proud women in my family, who have always done what had to be done.*

*And above all, for Ainara.*
*I cannot bring you justice, but at least I shall remember your name.*

'It is never too late, Dorian. Let us kneel down, and try if
we cannot remember a prayer.'
'Those words mean nothing to me now.'
*The Picture of Dorian Gray,* Oscar Wilde


'All things that have a name exist.'
A popular Baztan belief, recorded by José Miguel de
Barandiarán in *Brujería y brujas*

# 1

The lamp on the bedside table cast a warm, pink glow over the room, taking on different tones as it shone through the fairy patterns on its glass shade. From the shelf, a collection of stuffed toys gazed with beady eyes at the intruder silently gazing at the sleeping child. The intruder could hear the murmur of the television in the adjacent room, and the heavy breathing of the woman asleep on the sofa, lit by the screen's cold light. The intruder's eyes slid over the room, captivated by the moment, drinking in every detail, as though wanting to preserve that instant, transform it into a memento to be cherished forever. Eager but calm, the figure memorised the gentle pattern of the wallpaper, the framed photographs, the travel bag containing the little girl's nappies and clothes, and then focused on the cot. A feeling akin to intoxication overcame the intruder, accompanied by nausea in the pit of the stomach. The baby was lying on her back, dressed in a pair of flannel pyjamas, a flowered bedspread drawn up to her waist. The intruder pulled the bedspread back, wanting to see all of her. The baby sighed in her sleep; a tiny thread of saliva trickled from her pink lips, leaving a damp patch on her cheek. The chubby hands, splayed out either side of her head, quivered a few times then relaxed once again. Reacting to the sight, the intruder sighed, overcome by a fleeting wave of tenderness. Picking up the soft toy sitting at the foot of the cot like a silent guardian, the intruder was vaguely aware of the care someone had taken to place it there. It was a polar bear, with small black eyes and a bulging stomach. An incongruous red ribbon fastened about its neck hung down to its hind legs. The intruder stroked the polar bear's head, enjoying its softness, then, nose pressed into the furry belly, inhaled the sweet aroma of the expensive new toy.

Pulse racing, skin beading with sweat, the intruder began to perspire. Suddenly infuriated, the intruder held the toy at arm's length, then thrust it down over the baby's nose and mouth. After that, it was simply a matter of pressing it.

The tiny hands flailed in the air, one of her little fingers brushing the intruder's wrist. An instant later, she fell into what seemed like a deep, restorative sleep. Her muscles relaxed, and her starfish hands lay on the sheets once more.

The intruder pulled the toy away and looked at the little girl's face. There was no sign that she had suffered, apart from a red mark between the eyebrows, caused by the polar bear's nose. The light in her face was snuffed out, and the sensation of gazing upon an empty receptacle intensified as the intruder raised the toy, and inhaled once again the little girl's aroma, now enriched by her escaping soul. The scent was so powerful and sweet that the intruder's eyes filled with tears. With a sigh of gratitude, the killer straightened the polar bear's ribbon before replacing it at the foot of the cot.

Seized by a sense of urgency, as though suddenly aware of lingering too long, the intruder fled, turning only once to look back. The glow from the lamp seemed to gleam in the eyes of the other eleven furry animals as they peered down in horror from the shelf.

# 2

Amaia had been watching the house for twenty minutes from her car. With the engine switched off and the windows closed against the steady drizzle, condensation had formed on the windows, blurring the contours of the building with the dark shutters.

Presently, a small car pulled up outside the front door. A young man stepped out, opened his umbrella, and leaned over the dashboard to pick up a notebook, which he glanced at before tossing it back in the car. Then he went to the boot, retrieved a flat package and walked up to the house.

Amaia drew level with him just as he rang the doorbell.

'Excuse me, who are you?'

'Social services, we deliver this gentleman's meals every day,' he replied, indicating the plastic tray in his hand. 'He's house-bound, and has no one else to take care of him. Are you a relative?' he enquired hopefully.

'No,' she replied. 'Navarre police.'

'Ah,' he said, losing interest.

He rang the bell again, then, leaning close to the door, shouted:

'Señor Yáñez. It's Mikel. From social services. Remember me? I've brought your lun—'

Before he could finish his sentence, the door swung open, and Yáñez's wrinkled, grey face appeared.

'I remember you, I'm not senile, you know . . . Or deaf,' he replied, irritated.

'Of course not, Señor Yáñez,' said Mikel, smiling as he brushed past him into the house.

Amaia fumbled for her badge to show Yáñez.

'There's no need,' he said, recognising her and moving aside to let her pass.

Over his corduroy trousers and woollen sweater, Yáñez wore a thick dressing gown, the colour of which Amaia couldn't make out in the gloomy house. She followed Yáñez down the corridor to the kitchen, where a fluorescent light bulb flickered before coming on.

'Señor Yáñez!' the young man exclaimed in an over-loud voice. 'You didn't eat your supper last night!' He was standing by the open fridge, exchanging food trays wrapped in cling film. 'I'll have to log that in my report, you know. Don't go blaming me if the doctor tells you off,' he added, as if speaking to a child.

'Log it wherever you want,' muttered Yáñez.

'Didn't you like the fish in tomato sauce?' Mikel went on, ignoring his reply. 'Today you've got stewed meat and chick-peas, with yoghurt for pudding, and soup, omelette and sponge cake for supper.' He spun round holding the untouched supper tray, then crouched under the sink, tied a knot in a small rubbish bag containing only a few discarded wrappings, and started towards the door. Pausing next to Yáñez, he addressed him once more in an over-loud voice: 'All done, Señor Yáñez, *bon appetit*, until tomorrow.' Then he turned to leave, nodding to Amaia on the way out.

Yáñez waited until he heard the front door close before speaking.

'What do you make of that? And today he stayed longer than usual. Normally he can't get away quick enough,' he added, turning out the kitchen light, and leaving Amaia to make her way to the sitting room in semi-darkness. 'This house gives him the creeps. And I don't blame him, it's like visiting a cemetery.'

A sheet, two thick blankets and a pillow lay partially draped over the brown velvet sofa. Amaia assumed that Yáñez not only slept, but lived in this one room. Amid the gloom, she could see what looked like crumbs on the blankets and an orangish stain, possibly egg yolk. Amaia studied Yáñez as he sat down and leaned back against the pillow. A month had gone by since she'd interviewed him at the police station. He was awaiting trial under house arrest because of his age. He had lost weight, and his hard, suspicious expression had sharpened, giving him the air of an eccentric hermit. His hair was well kept, and he was clean-shaven, but Amaia wondered how long he'd been wearing the pyjama top showing beneath his sweater. The house was freezing, and clearly hadn't been heated for days. Opposite the sofa, in front of the empty hearth, a flat-screen TV cast a cold, blue light over the room.

'May I open the shutters?' asked Amaia.

'If you insist, but leave them as they were before you go.'

She nodded, pushing open the wooden panels to allow the gloomy Baztán light to seep through. When she turned around, Yáñez was staring at the television.

'Señor Yáñez.'

The man continued gazing at the screen as if she wasn't there.

'Señor Yáñez . . .'

He glanced at her, irritated.

'I'd like to . . .' she began, motioning towards the corridor. 'I'd like to have a look round.'

'Go ahead,' he said, with a wave of his hand. 'Look all you like, just don't touch anything. After the police were here, the place was a mess. It took me ages to put everything back the way it was.'

'Of course.'

'I trust you'll be as considerate as the officer who called yesterday.'

'A police officer came here yesterday?' she said, surprised.

'Yes, a nice lad. He even made me a cup of coffee.'

Besides the kitchen and sitting room, Yáñez's bungalow boasted three bedrooms and a largish bathroom. Amaia opened the cupboards, checking the shelves, which were crowded with shaving things, toilet rolls and a few bottles of medicine. The double bed in the main bedroom looked as if it hadn't been slept in recently. Draped over it was a floral bedspread that matched the curtains, bleached by years of sunlight. Judging by the vases of garish plastic flowers and the crocheted doilies adorning the chest of drawers and bedside tables, the room had been lovingly decorated in the seventies by Señora Yáñez, and preserved intact by her husband. It was like looking at a display in an ethnographic museum.

The second bedroom was empty, save for an old sewing machine standing next to a wicker basket beneath the window. She remembered it from the inventory in the report. Even so, she removed the cover to examine the spools of cotton, recognising a less faded version of the curtain colour in the main bedroom. The third bedroom had been referred to in the inventory as 'the boy's room', and it was exactly that: the bedroom of a ten- or eleven-year-old boy. The single bed with its pristine white bedspread; the shelves lined with children's books, a series she recalled having read herself; toys, mostly model ships and aeroplanes, as well as a collection of toy cars, all carefully aligned, and without a speck of dust on them. On the back of the door was a poster of a classic vintage Ferrari, and on the desk some old school textbooks, and a bundle of football cards tied with a rubber band. As she picked them up, she saw that the degraded rubber had stuck to the faded cards. She put them back, mentally comparing the cold bedroom to Berasategui's flat in Pamplona.

There were two other rooms in the house, plus a small utility area and a well-stocked woodshed where Yáñez kept his gardening tools and some boxes of potatoes and onions. Over in a corner, Amaia noticed an unlit boiler.

She picked up one of the dining chairs, and placed it between Yáñez and the television.

'I'd like to ask you a few questions.'

He used the remote beside him to switch off the TV. Then he stared at her in silence, waiting with that same look of anger and resentment he'd directed at Amaia the first time they met.

'Tell me about your son.'

The man shrugged.

'What sort of relationship did you have?'

'He's a good son,' Yáñez replied, too quickly. 'He did everything you'd expect a good son to do.'

'Such as?'

This time Yáñez had to give it some thought.

'Well, he gave me money . . . sometimes he did the shopping, bought me food – that sort of thing.'

'That's not what I've been hearing. People in the village say that after your wife died, you packed your son off to school abroad, and that he didn't show his face around here for years.'

'He was studying. He was a good student, he did two degrees, and a masters, he's one of the top psychiatrists at his clinic . . .'

'When did he start visiting you more frequently?'

'I don't know, about a year ago.'

'Did he ever bring anything other than food? Something he kept here, or that he asked you to keep for him somewhere else?'

'No.'

'Are you sure?'

'Yes.'

'I've looked over the house,' she said, glancing about. 'It's spotless.'

'I have to keep it clean.'

I understand. You keep it clean for your son.'

'No, for my wife. Everything is exactly the way it was when she left . . .' Yáñez's face twisted into a grimace of pain and grief. He remained that way for a few seconds, not making a sound. Amaia realised he was crying when she saw the tears roll down his cheeks.

'That's the least I could do; everything else I did was wrong.'

Yáñez's eyes danced from one object to another, as if he were searching for an answer hidden among the faded ornaments standing on doilies and side tables, until he met Amaia's gaze. He grasped the edge of the blanket, lifting it in front of his face for a few seconds, then flinging it aside, as though disgusted with himself for having cried in front of her. Amaia felt certain the conversation would end there, but then Yáñez reached behind the pillow he was leaning against and pulled out a framed photograph. He gazed at the image as if spellbound, then passed it to her. Yáñez's gesture took Amaia back to the previous year, when, in a different sitting room, a grieving father had handed her the portrait of his murdered daughter, which he also kept hidden under a cushion. She hadn't seen Anne Arbizu's father since, but the memory of his pain had stayed with her.

A woman no older than twenty-five smiled at her from the picture. Amaia glanced at her, then handed the photograph back to Yáñez.

'I thought we'd live happily ever after, you know? She was a young, pretty, kind woman . . . But after the boy was born she started acting strangely. She grew sad, she never smiled, she wouldn't even hold him, she said she wasn't ready to love the boy, and that he rejected her. Nothing I said did any good. I told her she was talking nonsense – of course the boy loved her – but she only grew sadder. She was sad all the time. She kept the house tidy, she did the cooking, but she never smiled; she even stopped sewing, and the rest of the time she slept. She kept the shutters closed, the way I do now, and she slept . . . I'll never forget how proud we were when we first bought this place. She made it look so pretty: we painted the walls, planted window boxes . . . Life was good. I thought nothing would ever change. But a house isn't the same as a home, and this became her tomb . . . Now it's my turn, although they call it house arrest, and the lawyer says they'll let me serve out my sentence here. I lie here every night, unable to sleep, smelling my wife's blood below my head.'

Amaia looked intently at the sofa. The cover didn't go with the rest of the décor.

'I had it recovered because of the bloodstains, but they'd stopped making the original fabric so they used this one instead. Otherwise everything's the same. When I lie here, I can smell her blood beneath the upholstery.'

'The house is cold,' said Amaia, disguising the shiver that ran up her spine.

He shrugged.

'Why don't you light the boiler?'

'It hasn't worked since the night of the storm, when the power went.'

'That was over a month ago. You mean to say you've been without heating all this time?'

Yáñez didn't reply.

'What about the people from social services?'

'I only open the door to the fellow who brings the trays. I told them on day one that if they come round here, I'll be waiting for them with an axe.'

'You have plenty of wood. Why not make a fire? There's no virtue in being cold.'

'It's what I deserve.'

Amaia got up and went out to the shed, returning with a basket of logs and some old newspapers. Kneeling in front of the hearth, she stirred the cold ashes to make space for the wood. She took a box of matches from the mantelpiece and lit the fire. Then she sat down again. Yáñez stared into the flames.

'You've also kept your son's room just as it was. I find it hard to imagine a man like him sleeping there.'

'He didn't. Occasionally he stopped for lunch, and sometimes supper, but he never spent the night. He would leave, then come back early the next day. He told me he preferred a hotel.'

Amaia didn't believe it; they had found no evidence of Berasategui staying at any of the hotels, hostels or bed and breakfast places in the valley.

'Are you sure?'

'I think so, but I can't be a hundred per cent sure – as I told the police, my memory is worse than I let on to social services. I forget things.'

Amaia plucked her buzzing phone from her pocket. The display showed several missed calls but she ignored them, scanning through her photos until she found the right image, then touching the screen to enlarge it. Averting her eyes from the photo, she showed it to Yáñez.

'Did your son ever come here with this woman?'

'Your mother.'

'You know her? Did you see her that night?'

'No, but I've known your mother for years. She's aged, but I recognise her.'

'Think again, you just told me your memory isn't so good.'

'Sometimes I forget to have supper, or I have supper twice because I forget I've already had it, but I remember who comes to my house. Your mother has never set foot in here.'

She slipped the phone back into her coat pocket, replaced the dining chair, pulled the shutters to and left. As soon as she was in the car, she reached for her phone and, ignoring the insistent buzzing, dialled a number from her contacts list. After a couple of rings, a man answered.

'Could you please send someone to fix a boiler that broke down on the night of the storm,' she said, and gave him Yáñez's address.

# 3

By the time Amaia parked in the square next to the Lamia fountain, the drizzle had turned to a downpour. She pulled up the hood of her coat and hurried through the arch into Calle Pedro Axular, following the sound of raised voices. The anguish and urgency of those missed calls was reflected in Inspector Iriarte's face as he struggled to contain a group of people intent upon approaching the patrol car. In the rear passenger seat, a weary-looking individual was sitting with his head propped against the rain-beaded window. Two uniformed officers were unsuccessfully attempting to cordon off the area surrounding a rucksack, which lay on the ground in the middle of a puddle. Amaia took out her phone and called for back-up as she hurried over to assist them. Just then, two more patrol cars advanced across the Giltxaurdi Bridge, distracting the angry mob, whose shouts were momentarily drowned out by the wailing sirens.

Iriarte was soaked to the bone, and as he spoke to Amaia, he kept wiping his brow to stop the water going in his eyes. Deputy Inspector Etxaide appeared out of nowhere with a large umbrella, which he handed to them, then went to help the other officers pacify the crowd.

'Well, Inspector?'

'The suspect in the car is Valentín Esparza. His four-month-old daughter died last night while sleeping over at her maternal grandmother's house. The doctor registered the cause as Sudden Infant Death Syndrome. So far, a tragedy. Except that yesterday, the grandmother, Inés Ballarena, paid a visit to the police station. Apparently, the baby was staying the night with her for the first time because it was the parents' wedding anniversary, and they were going out to dinner. She was looking forward to it, and had even prepared a room for her. She fed the baby and put her down for the night, then fell asleep in front of the television in the sitting room next door, although she swears the baby monitor was on. She was woken by a noise, and went to look in on the baby – who from the doorway appeared sound asleep. Then she heard the crunch of tyres on gravel outside. She looked through the window in time to see a large, grey car driving away. Although she didn't see the number plate, she assumed it was her son-in-law, as he has one just like it,' said Iriarte, with a shrug. 'She claims she checked the time and it was just gone two in the morning. She thought the couple must have driven by on their way home to see if any lights were on. This didn't strike her as odd because they live nearby. She thought no more about it, and went back to sleep on the sofa. When she woke up, she was surprised not to hear the baby crying to be fed, so she went into the bedroom where she found the child dead. She was upset, she blamed herself, but when the doctor gave the estimated time of death as between two and three in the morning, she remembered waking up and seeing the car in the driveway. She now believes she was woken by an earlier noise inside the house. When Inés asked her daughter about this, she told her they had arrived home at around one thirty; she doesn't drink usually, so a glass of wine and a liqueur after the meal had knocked her out. However, when Inés questioned the son-in-law, he became agitated, refused to answer, flew into a rage. He told her it was probably a couple

13

of lovebirds looking for a secluded spot; it wouldn't have been the first time. But then Inés remembered something else: she keeps her two dogs outside and they bark like crazy whenever a stranger comes near the house, but they didn't make a sound last night.'

'What did you do next?' asked Amaia.

Whether it was because they were intimidated by the police presence or simply wanted to get out of the rain, the crowd had retreated to the covered entrance of the funeral parlour. A woman at the centre of the huddle was embracing another, who was screaming and sobbing hysterically. It was impossible to make out what she was saying.

'The woman screaming is the mother, the one with her arms around her is the little girl's grandmother,' Iriarte explained, following Amaia's gaze. 'Anyway, as I was saying, the grandmother was in a terrible state. She couldn't stop crying while she was telling me her story. To begin with, I thought she was probably just trying to find an explanation for something that was difficult to accept. This was the first time they let her babysit, her first grandchild, she was distraught . . .'

'But?'

'But, even so, I called the paediatrician. He was adamant: Sudden Infant Death Syndrome. The baby was premature, her lungs weren't properly formed, and she'd spent half of her short life in the hospital. Although they'd discharged her, this past week the mother had brought her to the surgery with a cold – only a sniffle, but in a premature, underweight baby, the doctor had no doubt about the cause of death. An hour ago, Inés turned up at the station again, insisting the girl had a mark on her forehead – round, like a button – which wasn't there earlier. She said that when she pointed it out to her son-in-law, he snapped at her and insisted they close the coffin. So I decided to take a look for myself. As we entered the funeral parlour, we bumped into the father, Valentín Esparza, on his way out. He was carrying that rucksack' – Iriarte pointed to the wet bundle sitting in a puddle – 'and something about the way he was holding it struck me as odd. Not that I carry a rucksack myself, but it didn't seem right.' He clasped his hands to his chest to imitate the posture. 'The minute he saw me, he turned pale and started to run. I caught up with him next to his car, and that was when he started to yell, telling us to leave him alone, saying he had to finish this.'

'To take his own life?'

'That's what I thought. It occurred to me he might have a weapon in there . . .'

Iriarte crouched down beside the rucksack, giving up the shelter of the umbrella, which he placed on the ground as a screen. He opened the flap, pulling the toggle to loosen the drawstring. The little girl's dark, wispy hair revealed the soft spot on her head; her skin had that tell-tale pallor, although her mouth, slightly open, retained a hint of colour, giving a false impression of life, which held them transfixed until Dr San Martín leaned in, breaking the spell.

While the pathologist removed the sterile wrapping from a swab, Iriarte gave him a summary of what he had told Amaia. Then San Martín crouched next to the child's body and gently used the swab to remove the make-up that had been hastily applied to the bridge of the baby's nose.

'She's so tiny.' The sorrow in the usually imperturbable pathologist's voice made Iriarte and Amaia look at him in surprise. Conscious of their eyes on him, he immediately busied himself examining the mark on the child's skin. 'An extremely crude attempt to cover up a pressure mark. It probably occurred at the precise moment when she stopped breathing, and is only visible to the naked eye now that lividity has set in. Give me a hand, will you?' he said.

'What are you going to do?'

'I have to see all of her,' he replied, with an impatient gesture.

'Not here, please,' said Iriarte. He indicated the crowd

outside the funeral parlour. 'You see those people? They're the baby's relatives, including her mother and grandmother. We've had enough difficulty controlling them as it is. If they see her dead body lying on the ground, they'll go crazy.'

'Inspector Iriarte is right,' said Amaia, glancing towards the crowd then looking back at San Martín.

'Very well, but until I have her on my slab I can't tell you if there are any other signs of violence. Make sure you are thorough when you process the crime scene; I remember working on a similar case, where a mark on a baby's cheek turned out to be made by a button on a pillowcase. Although I can give you one piece of information that might help.' San Martín produced a small digital device from his Gladstone bag, holding it up proudly. 'A digital calliper,' he explained, pulling apart the two metal prongs, and adjusting them to measure the diameter of the mark on the baby's forehead. 'There you are,' he said, showing them the screen. 'The object you're looking for is 13.85 millimetres in diameter.'

They stood up, leaving the forensic technicians to place the rucksack inside a body bag. Amaia turned to see Judge Markina standing a few metres away, watching in silence. No doubt San Martín had notified him. Beneath his black umbrella, and in the dim light seeping through the leaden clouds, his face looked sombre; even so, she registered the sparkle in his eye, the intensity of his gaze when he greeted her. Although the gesture was fleeting, she looked nervously at San Martín then at Iriarte to see if they had noticed. San Martín was busy giving orders to his technicians and outlining the facts to the legal secretary beside him, while Iriarte was keeping a close watch on the relatives. The rumour had spread among them, and they began angrily to demand answers even as the mother's howls of grief grew louder and louder.

'We need to get this guy out of here now,' declared Iriarte, motioning to one of the officers.

'Take him directly to Pamplona,' ordered Markina.

'I'll get a police van to move him there by this afternoon at the very latest, your honour. In the meantime, we'll take him to the local police station. We'll meet there,' Iriarte said to Amaia.

She nodded at Markina by way of a goodbye, then started towards her car.

'Inspector . . . Do you have a moment?'

She stopped in her tracks, wheeling round only to find him standing beside her, sheltering her with his umbrella.

'Why didn't you call me?' This wasn't exactly a reproach, or even a question; it had the seductive tone of an invitation, the playfulness of flirtation. The grey coat he wore over a matching grey suit, his impeccable white shirt and dark tie – unusual for him – gave him a solemn, graceful air, moderated by the lock of hair tumbling over his brow and the light covering of designer stubble. Beneath the canopy of the umbrella she felt herself being drawn into a moment of intimacy, conscious of the expensive cologne emanating from his warm skin, his intense gaze, the warmth of his smile . . .

Suddenly, Jonan Etxaide appeared out of nowhere.

'Boss, the cars are all full. Could you give me a lift to the police station?'

'Of course, Jonan,' she replied, startled back to reality. 'If you'll excuse us, your honour.'

Having taken her leave, she made her way towards the car without a backward glance. Etxaide, however, turned once to contemplate Markina, who was standing where they had left him. The magistrate responded with a wave.

# 4

The warmth of the police station hadn't succeeded in bringing the colour back to Iriarte's cheeks, but at least he'd managed to change out of his wet clothes by the time Amaia arrived.

'What did he say?' she asked. 'Why was he taking her body?'

'He hasn't said a word. He's sitting curled up in a ball in the corner of his cell, refusing to move or speak.'

She made to leave, but when she got to the door she turned to face the inspector.

'Do you think Esparza's behaviour was motivated by grief, or do you believe he is involved in his daughter's death?'

'I honestly don't know,' said Iriarte. 'This could be a reaction to losing his daughter, but I can't rule out the possibility he was trying to prevent a second autopsy, fearing it would confirm his mother-in-law's suspicions.' He fell silent, then sighed. 'I can't imagine anything more monstrous than harming your own child.'

The clear image of her mother's face suddenly flashed into Amaia's mind. She managed to thrust it aside only for it to be replaced by another, that of the midwife, Fina Hidalgo, breaking off newly sprouted shoots with a dirty fingernail, stained green: *The families mostly did it themselves; I only helped occasionally when they couldn't bring themselves to destroy the fruit of their womb, or some such nonsense.'*

'Was the girl normal, Inspector? I mean, did she suffer from brain damage or any other disabilities.'

Iriarte shook his head. 'Besides being premature, the doctor assured me she was a normal, healthy child.'

The holding cells at the new police station in Elizondo had no bars; instead, a wall of toughened glass separated them from the reception area, allowing each compartment to be viewed from outside, and making it possible for the occupants to be filmed round the clock. Amaia and Iriarte walked along the corridor outside the cells, all of them empty save for one. As they approached the glass, they could see a man crouched on the floor at the back of the cell between the sink and the toilet. His arms were looped around his knees, his head lowered. Iriarte switched on the intercom.

'Valentín Esparza.'

The man looked up.

'Inspector Salazar would like to ask you a few questions.'

He lowered his face again.

'Valentín,' Iriarte called out, more firmly this time, 'we're coming in. No need to get agitated, just stay calm.'

Amaia leaned towards Iriarte. 'I'll go in alone, I'm in plain clothes, I'm a woman, it's less intimidating . . .'

Iriarte withdrew to the adjacent room, which was set up so that he could see and hear everything that went on.

Amaia entered the cell and stood facing Esparza. After a few seconds, she asked: 'May I sit down?'

He looked at her, thrown by the question.

'What?'

'Do you mind if I sit down?' she repeated, pointing to a wooden bench along the wall that doubled as a bed. Asking permission was a sign of respect; she wasn't treating him as a prisoner, or a suspect.

He waved a hand.

'Thank you,' she said, sitting down. 'At this time of day, I'm already exhausted. I have a baby too – a little boy. He's five months old. I know that you lost your baby girl yesterday.' The man raised his pale face and looked straight at her. 'How old was she?'

'Four months,' he said in a hoarse voice.

'I'm sorry for your loss.'

He swallowed hard, eyes downcast.

'Today was supposed to be my day off, you know. And when I arrived I found this mess. Why don't you tell me what happened?'

He sat up, motioning with his chin towards the camera behind the glass, and the spotlight illuminating the cell. His face looked serious, in pain, but not mistrustful.

'Haven't your colleagues told you?'

'I'd like to hear it from you. I'm more interested in your version.'

He took his time. A less experienced interrogator might have assumed he had clammed up, but Amaia simply waited.

'I was taking my daughter's body away.'

Amaia noted the use of the word body; he was acknowledging that he had been carrying a corpse, not a child.

'Where to?'

'Where to?' he asked, bewildered. 'Nowhere, I just . . . I just wanted to have her a bit longer.'

'You said you were taking her away, that you were taking her body away, and they arrested you next to your car. Where were you going?'

He remained silent.

She tried a different tack.

'It's amazing how much having a baby changes your life. There's so much to do, so many demands on you. My boy gets colic every night after his last feed; sometimes he cries for as long as two or three hours. All I can do is walk round the house trying to calm him. I understand how that can drive some people crazy.'

Esparza appeared to nod sympathetically.

'Is that what happened?'

'What?'

'Your mother-in-law claims you went to her house early in the morning.'

He started to shake his head.

'And that she saw your car drive away . . .'

'My mother-in-law is mistaken.' His hostility was palpable. 'She can't tell one car from another. It was probably a couple of kids who pulled into the driveway hoping to find a quiet place to . . . you know.'

'Yes, except that her dogs didn't bark, so it must have been someone they knew. What's more, your mother-in-law told my colleague about a mark on the girl's forehead, which wasn't there when she put her to bed. She also said she was woken up by a noise, and when she looked out of the window she saw your car driving off.'

'That bitch would say anything to get me into trouble. She's never liked me. You can ask my wife, she'll tell you: we went out to dinner and afterwards we went straight home.'

'My colleagues have spoken to her, but she couldn't help much. She didn't contradict your story, she simply doesn't remember anything.'

'I know, she had too much to drink. She isn't used to it, what with the pregnancy . . .'

'It must have been difficult for you this last year.' He looked at her, puzzled. 'I mean, the risky pregnancy, forced rest, no sex; then the baby is born premature, two months in hospital, no sex; at last she comes home, more worries, caring for the baby, and still no sex . . .'

He gave a faint smile.

'I know from experience,' she went on. 'And on the day of your anniversary, you leave the baby with your mother-in-law, you go out to a nice restaurant, and after a few glasses of wine your wife is legless. You take her home, put her to bed, and . . . no sex. The night is young. You drive over to your mother-in-law's house to check that everything's all right. You arrive to find her asleep on the sofa, and that irritates you. Entering the girl's room, you suddenly realise the child is a burden, she is ruining your life, things were much better before she came along . . . and you make a decision.'

He sat perfectly still, hanging on her every word.

'So, you do what you have to do, only your mother-in-law wakes up and sees you driving away.'

'Like I told you: my mother-in-law is a fucking bitch.'

'I know how you feel – mine is too. But yours is also very astute. She noticed the mark on the girl's forehead. Yesterday, it was barely visible, but today the pathologist is in no doubt that the mark was made by an object having been pressed into her skin.'

He heaved a deep sigh.

'You noticed it too, that's why you tried to cover it with make-up. And to ensure no one else would see it, you ordered the coffin to be sealed. But your bitch of a mother-in-law is like a dog with a bone, isn't she? So you decided to take the body to prevent anyone asking questions. Your wife, perhaps? Someone saw you two quarrelling in the funeral parlour.'

'You've got it all wrong. That was because she insisted on cremating the girl.'

'And you were against it? You wanted a burial? Is that why you took her?'

Something appeared to dawn on him.

'What will happen to the body now?'

Amaia was intrigued by Esparza's choice of words; relatives didn't usually refer to their loved one as a body or corpse, but rather as the girl, the baby, or . . . She realised she didn't know his child's name.

'The pathologist will perform a second autopsy, after which the body will be released to the family.'

'They mustn't cremate her.'

'That's something you need to decide among yourselves.'

'They mustn't cremate her. I haven't finished.'

Amaia recalled what Iriarte had told her.

'What haven't you finished?'

'If I don't finish, this will all have been in vain.'

Amaia's curiosity deepened:

'What exactly do you mean?'

Suddenly, Esparza seemed to realise where he was, and that he'd said too much. He immediately clammed up.

'Did you kill your daughter?'

'No,' he replied.

'Do you know who did?'

Silence.

'Perhaps your wife killed her . . .'

Esparza smiled, shaking his head, as if he found the mere thought laughable.

'Not her.'

'Who, then? Who did you take to your mother-in-law's house?'

'No one.'

'No, I don't believe you did, because it was you. You killed your daughter.'

'No!' he yelled suddenly. '. . . I gave her up.'

'Gave her up? Who to? What for?'

He grinned smugly.

'I gave her up to . . .' He lowered his voice to a muffled whisper: '. . . like all the others . . .' he said. He murmured a few more words, then buried his head in his arms.

Amaia remained in the cell for a while, even though she realised that the interview was over, that she would get no more out of him. She buzzed for them to open the door from outside. As she was leaving, he spoke again:

'Can you do something for me?'

'That depends.'

'Tell them not to cremate her.'


Deputy Inspectors Etxaide and Zabalza were waiting with Iriarte in the adjoining room.

'Could you hear what he was saying?'

'Only the part about giving her up to someone, but I didn't hear a name. It's on tape; you can see his lips move, but it's inaudible. He was probably talking gibberish.'

'Zabalza, see if you can do anything with the audio and video, jack up the volume as high as it'll go. I expect you're right, he's messing with us, but let's be on the safe side. Jonan, Montes and Iriarte, you come with me. By the way, where is Montes?'

'He's just finished taking the relatives' statements.'

Amaia opened her field kit on the table to make sure she had everything she needed.

'We'll need to stop somewhere to buy a digital calliper.' She smiled, as she noticed Iriarte frown. 'Is something wrong?'

'Today is your day off . . .'

'Not any more, right?' she grinned, picking up the case and following Jonan outside to where Montes was waiting for them in the car with the engine running.

# 5

She felt a kind of sympathy bordering on pity for Valentín Esparza when she entered the room his mother-in-law had decorated for the little girl. Confronted with the profusion of pink ribbons, lace and embroidery, the sensation of déjà vu was overwhelming. This little girl's *amatxi* had chosen nymphs and fairies instead of the ridiculous pink lambs her own mother-in-law had chosen for Ibai, but other than that, the room might have been decorated by the same woman. Hanging on the walls were half a dozen or so framed photographs of the girl being cradled by her mother, grandmother and an older woman, possibly an aunt. Valentín Esparza didn't appear in any of them.

The radiators upstairs were on full, doubtless for the baby's benefit. Muffled voices reached them from the kitchen below, friends and neighbours who had come round to comfort the two women. The mother seemed to have stopped crying now; even so, Amaia closed the door at the top of the stairs. She stood watching as Montes and Etxaide processed the scene, cursing her phone, which had been vibrating in her pocket since they left the station. The number of missed calls was piling up. She checked her coverage: as she had suspected, because of the thick walls it was much weaker inside the farmhouse. Descending the stairs, she tiptoed past the kitchen, registering the sound of hushed voices typical at wakes. She felt a sense of relief as she stepped outside. The rain had stopped briefly, as the wind swept away the black storm clouds, but the absence of any clear patches of sky meant that once the wind fell the rain would start again. She moved a few metres away from the house and checked her log of missed calls. One from Dr San Martín, one from Lieutenant Padua of the *Guardia Civil*, one from James, and six from Ros. First she rang James, who was upset to hear that she wouldn't be home for lunch.

'But, Amaia, it's your day off—'

'I'll be home as soon as I can, I promise, and I'll make it up to you.'

He seemed unconvinced.

'But we have a dinner reservation . . .'

'I'll be home in an hour at the most.'

Padua picked up straight away.

'Inspector, how are you?'

'I'm fine. I saw your call, and—' She could barely contain her anxiety.

'No news, Inspector. I just rang to say I've spoken to Naval Command in San Sebastián and La Rochelle. All the patrol boats in the Bay of Biscay are on the alert and they know what to look for.'

Padua must have heard her sigh. He added in a reassuring tone:

'Inspector, the coastguards are of the opinion, and I agree, that one month is long enough for your mother's body to have washed up somewhere along the shore. It could have been swept up the Cantabrian coast, though the ascending current is more likely to have carried it to France. Alternatively, it could have become snagged on the riverbed, or the torrential rains could have taken it miles out to sea, into one of the deep trenches in the Bay of Biscay. Bodies washed out to sea are

26

rarely found, and given how long it's been since your mother disappeared, I think we have to consider that possibility. A month is a long time.'

'Thank you, Lieutenant,' she said, trying hard not to show her disappointment. 'If you hear anything . . .'

'Rest assured, I'll let you know.'

She hung up, thrusting her phone deep into her pocket, as she digested what Padua had said. A month in the sea is a long time for a dead body. But didn't the sea always give up its dead?

While talking to Padua, she had started to circle the house to escape the tiresome crunch of gravel outside the entrance. As she followed the line in the ground traced by rainwater dripping from the roof, she reached the corner at the back of the building where the eaves met. Sensing a movement behind her, she turned. The older woman from the photographs in the little girl's bedroom was standing beside a tree in the garden, apparently talking to herself. As she gently tapped the tree trunk, she chanted a series of barely audible words that seemed to be addressed to some invisible presence. Amaia watched the old woman for a few seconds, until she looked up and saw her.

'In the old days, we'd have buried her here,' she said.

Amaia lowered her gaze to the trodden earth and the clear line traced by water falling from the eaves. She was unable to speak, assailed by images of her own family graveyard, the remains of a cot blanket poking out from the dark soil.

'Kinder than leaving her all alone in a cemetery, or cremating her, which is what my granddaughter wants to do . . . The modern ways aren't always the best. In the old days, we women weren't told how we should do things; we may have done some things wrong, but we did others much better.' The woman spoke to her in Spanish, although from the way she pronounced her 'r's, Amaia inferred that she usually spoke Basque. An old Baztán *etxeko andrea*, one of a generation of invincible women

27

who had seen a whole century, and who still had the strength to get up every morning, scrape her hair into a bun, cook, and feed the animals; Amaia noticed the powdery traces of the millet the woman had been carrying in the pockets of her black apron, in the old tradition. 'You do what has to be done.'

As the woman shuffled towards her in her green wellingtons, Amaia resisted the urge to go to her aid, sensing this might embarrass her. Instead she waited until the woman drew level, then extended her hand.

'Who were you speaking to?' she said, gesturing towards the open meadow.

'To the bees.'

Amaia looked at her, puzzled.

*Erliak, elriak*
*Gaur il da etxeko nausiya*
*Erliak, elriak*
*Eta bear da elizan argia*[1]

Amaia recalled her aunt telling her that in Baztán, when someone died, the mistress of the house would go to where the hives were kept in the meadow and ask the bees to make more wax for the extra candles needed to illuminate the deceased during the wake and funeral. According to her aunt, the incantation would increase the bees' production three-fold.

Touched by the woman's gesture, Amaia imagined she could hear her Aunt Engrasi saying, 'When all else fails, we return to the old traditions.'

'I'm sorry for your loss,' she said.

Ignoring Amaia's hand, the woman embraced her with surprising strength. After releasing her, she lowered her eyes

[1] Bees, bees / The master died today / Bees, bees / We need candles for the church

to the ground, wiping her tears away with the pocket of the apron in which she had carried the chicken feed. Amaia – moved by the woman's dignified courage, which had rekindled the lifelong admiration she'd felt towards that generation – maintained a respectful silence.

'He didn't do it,' the woman said suddenly.

Trained to know when someone was about to unburden themselves, Amaia didn't reply.

'No one takes any notice of me because I'm an old woman, but I know who killed our little girl, and it wasn't that foolish father of hers. All he cares about is cars, motorbikes and showing off. He loves money the way pigs love apples. I should know, I courted men like that in my youth. They would come to pick me up on motorbikes, or in cars, but I wasn't taken in by all that nonsense. I wanted a real man . . .'

The old woman's mind was starting to wander. Amaia steered her back to the present:

'Do you know who killed her?'

'Yes, I told them,' she said, waving a hand towards the house. 'But no one listens to me because I'm an old woman.'

'I'm listening to you. Tell me who did this.'

'It was Inguma – Inguma killed her,' she declared emphatically.

'Who is Inguma?'

The old woman's grief was palpable as she gazed at Amaia.

'That poor girl! Inguma is the demon that steals children's souls while they sleep. Inguma slipped through the cracks, sat on her chest and took her soul.'

Amaia opened her mouth, confused, then closed it again, unsure what to say.

'You think I'm spouting old wives' tales,' the woman said accusingly.

'Not at all . . .'

'In the annals of Baztán it says that Inguma awoke once and took away hundreds of children. The doctors called it whooping cough, but it was Inguma who came to rob their breath while they slept.'

Inés Ballarena appeared from around the side of the house.

'*Ama*, what are you doing here? I told you I'd fed the chickens this morning.' She clasped the old lady by the arm, addressing Amaia: 'You must excuse my mother, she's very old; what happened has upset her terribly.'

'Of course,' murmured Amaia. To her relief, at that moment a call came through on her mobile. She excused herself and moved away to a discreet distance to take the call.

'Dr San Martín, have you finished already?' she said, glancing at her watch.

'Actually, we've only just started.' He cleared his throat. 'I've asked a colleague to help me on this occasion,' he said, unable to disguise the catch in his voice, 'but, I thought I'd let you know what we've found so far. The victim was suffocated with a soft object, such as a pillow or cushion. You saw the mark above the bridge of the nose; when you conduct your search, keep in mind the measurement I gave you. Forensics are currently examining a few soft, white fibres we found in the folds of the mouth, so that'll give you some idea of the colour. We also found traces of saliva on her face, mostly belonging to the girl, but there is at least one other donor. It might have been left by a relative kissing her cheek . . .'

'When will you be able to tell me more?'

'In a few hours.'

Amaia ended the call and hurried after the two women. She caught up with them at the front door.

'Inés, did you bathe your granddaughter before you put her to bed?'

'Yes, the evening bath relaxed her, it made her sleepy,' she said, stifling a sob.

Amaia thanked her, then ran up the stairs. 'We're looking for something soft and white,' she said, bursting into the bedroom.

30

Montes lifted an evidence bag to show her.

'Snow white,' he declared, holding aloft the captive bear.

'How did you . . .?'

'From the smell,' explained Jonan. 'Then we noticed that the fur looked flattened . . .'

'It smells?' Amaia frowned; a dirty toy seemed incongruous in that room where everything had been carefully thought out down to the last detail.

'It doesn't just smell, it stinks,' said Montes.

# 6

By the time she left the house, Amaia's mobile showed three more missed calls from Ros. She'd resisted the temptation to return them, sensing that her sister's unusual persistence might herald an awkward conversation, which she didn't want her colleagues to witness. Only once she was in the privacy of her car did she make the call. Ros answered on the first ring, as if she'd been waiting with the phone in her hand.

'Oh, Amaia, could you come over?'

'Of course, what's the matter, Ros?'

'You'd better come and see for yourself.'

Amaia parked outside Mantecadas Salazar and made her way through the bakery, exchanging greetings with the employees she passed en route to the office at the back. Ros was standing in the doorway with her back to Amaia, blocking her view of the interior.

'Ros, are you going to tell me what's going on?'

Ros spun round, ashen-faced. Amaia instantly understood why.

'Well, well. The cavalry has arrived!' Flora said by way of greeting.

Concealing her surprise, Amaia approached her eldest sister after giving Ros a peck on the cheek.

'We weren't expecting you, Flora. How are you?'

'As well as anyone could be, under the circumstances . . .'

Amaia looked at her, puzzled.

'Our mother met a horrible death a month ago – or am I the only one who cares?' she said sarcastically.

Amaia flashed a grin at Ros. 'Of course, Flora, the whole world knows how much more sensitive you are than everyone else,' she retorted.

Flora responded to the jibe with a grimace, then planted herself behind the desk. Motionless in the doorway, arms hanging by her sides, Ros was the image of helplessness, save for her pursed lips and a glint of repressed rage in her eye.

'Are you planning to stay long, Flora?' asked Amaia. 'I don't suppose you have much free time with all your TV work.'

Flora adjusted the height of the chair then sat down behind the desk.

'Yes, I'm extremely busy, but I thought I'd take a few days off,' she said, rearranging a pile of papers on the desk.

Ros pressed her lips together even more tightly. Observing this, Flora added nonchalantly, 'Actually, given the way things are, I may decide to stay on.' She pushed the wastepaper basket towards the desk with her foot then swept up the brightly coloured post-it notes and ballpoint pens with tasselled toppers that clearly belonged to Ros and tossed them in.

'Great,' said Amaia. 'I'm sure Auntie will be delighted to see you when you stop by later. But, Flora, in future, if you want to drop in at the bakery, let Ros know beforehand. She's a busy woman now that she's signed a contract with that big French supermarket chain – that deal you were forever chasing, remember? – so she hasn't time to tidy up the mess you leave behind.' She leaned over the wastepaper basket to retrieve Ros's belongings and replace them on the desk.

'The Martiniés,' Flora hissed under her breath.

'*Oui*,' replied Amaia with a mischievous grin. She could tell from Flora's expression that her barb had hit the mark.

'I set the whole thing up,' Flora huffed. 'I did the research, I spent over a year making the necessary contacts.'

'Yes, but Ros clinched the deal on their first meeting,' replied Amaia gaily.

Flora stared at Ros, who avoided her gaze, walking over to the coffee machine and setting out some cups.

'Do you want coffee?' she said, almost in a whisper.

'Yes, please,' replied Amaia, eyes fixed on Flora.

'No, thanks,' said Flora. 'I wouldn't want to take up any more of your precious time,' she added, rising from her seat. 'I just wanted to tell you that I came here to arrange *Ama*'s funeral service.'

The remark took Amaia by surprise. The notion of a service had never entered her head.

'But—' she started to protest.

'Yes, I know, it isn't official, and we'd all like to believe that somehow she managed to scramble out of the river and is still alive, but the fact is, she probably didn't,' she said, staring straight at Amaia. 'I've spoken to the magistrate in Pamplona in charge of the case, and he agrees that it's a good idea to hold a service.'

'You called Judge Markina?'

'Actually, he called me. A charming man, incidentally.'

'Yes, but . . .'

'But, what?' demanded Flora.

'Well . . .' Amaia swallowed hard, her voice cracking as she spoke: 'Until we find her body, we can't be sure she's dead.'

'For God's sake, Amaia! You saw the clothes they dragged out of the river. How could an old, crippled woman have survived that?'

'I don't know . . . In any case, she isn't officially dead.'

'I think it's a good idea,' Ros broke in.

Amaia looked at her, astonished.

'Yes, Amaia, I think we should turn the page. Holding a funeral for *Ama*'s soul will close this chapter once and for all.'

'I can't. I don't believe she's dead.'

'For God's sake, Amaia!' cried Flora. 'Where is she, then? Where the hell is she? She couldn't possibly have escaped into the forest in the dead of night!' She lowered her voice: 'They dragged the river, Amaia. Our mother drowned, she's dead.'

Amaia squeezed her eyes shut.

'Flora, if you need any help with the arrangements, call me,' said Ros calmly.

Without replying, Flora picked up her bag and strode to the door.

'I'll tell you the time and venue as soon as I've arranged everything.'

With Flora gone, the two sisters settled down to drink their coffee. The atmosphere in the office was like the aftermath of an electrical storm, both women waiting for the charged energy in the air to subside and for calm to be restored before speaking.

'She's dead, Amaia,' Ros said at last.

'I don't know . . .'

'You don't know, or you haven't accepted it yet?'

Amaia looked at her.

'You've been running from Rosario all your life, you've become accustomed to living with that threat, with the knowledge that she is out there, that she is still out to harm you. But it's over now, Amaia. It's over. *Ama* is finally dead, and – God forgive me for saying so – but I'm not sorry. I know how much she made you suffer, what she almost did to Ibai, but I saw her coat with my own eyes: it was sodden with water. No one could have climbed out of that river alive in the middle of the night. Trust me, Amaia: she's dead.'

Amaia parked her car opposite Aunt Engrasi's house and sat for a while, enjoying the golden glow illuminating the windows from inside, as though at its heart a tiny sun or fire were perpetually burning. She gazed up at the overcast sky; night was falling, and although the lights had been on all day, it was only now that they shone in all their glory. She recalled how, as a child, she'd look forward to the occasions when her aunt would ask her to take the rubbish out because it meant she could steal away to the low wall down by the river. She'd sit there, entranced by the sight of the house all lit up, until her aunt began calling for her. Only then would she go inside, her hands and face burning with cold. The sensation of returning home was so intensely pleasurable that she turned it into a custom, a way of drawing out the joy of re-entering the house. She thought of it as a kind of Taoist ritual, one that she'd carried into adulthood, only abandoning the habit when she became a mother. She so longed to see Ibai that no sooner did she reach the door than she would rush inside, eager to touch her son, to kiss him. Tonight, rediscovering this secret, magical game, she reflected on the way she clung, to the point of obsession, to those rituals that had kept her sane through her traumatic childhood. Perhaps it was time for her to leave the past behind.

She climbed out of the car and made her way into the house. Without stopping to take off her coat, she entered the sitting room, where her aunt was clearing up after her game of cards with the Golden Girls. James was holding a book, distractedly, watching Ibai who was in his baby hammock on the sofa. Amaia sat down next to her husband and took his hand in hers.

'I'm so sorry, things got complicated. I couldn't get away.'

'That's okay,' he said, without conviction, and leaned over to kiss her.

She slipped out of her coat and draped it over the back of the sofa, then gathered Ibai into her arms.

'*Ama*'s been gone all day, and she missed you, did you miss me?' she whispered, cradling the boy in her arms. He grabbed a strand of her hair, tugging it painfully. 'I suppose you heard about what happened at the funeral parlour this morning,' she said, looking up at her aunt.

'Yes, the girls told us. It's a terrible tragedy. I've known the family for years, they're good people. Losing a young baby like that . . .' Engrasi broke off to go to Ibai and tenderly stroke his head. 'I can't bear to think about it.'

'No wonder the father went mad with grief. I can't imagine what I'd do,' said James.

'The investigation is ongoing, so I can't comment – but that isn't the only reason why I'm late. Clearly, she hasn't been here, otherwise you'd have told me already.'

James and Engrasi looked at her, puzzled.

'Flora is here in Elizondo. Ros was in a real state when she called me – apparently, the first thing Flora did was stop off at the bakery, just to wind her up. Then, when I arrived, she announced that she'd come to arrange a funeral service for Rosario.'

Engrasi stopped ferrying glasses back and forth, and looked at Amaia, concerned.

'Well, I've never had much time for Flora, as you know, but I think it's a great idea,' said James.

'How can you say that, James! We don't even know for sure that she's dead. To hold a funeral would be utterly absurd!' exclaimed Engrasi.

'I disagree. It's been over a month since the river took Rosario—'

'We don't know that,' Amaia broke in. 'The fact that her coat was in the water doesn't mean a thing. She could have thrown it in there to put us off the scent.'

'To do what? Listen to yourself, Amaia. You're talking about an old lady, wading across a flooded river in the dark during a storm. You've got to admit, that's highly unlikely.'

Engrasi was standing between the poker table and the kitchen door, lips compressed, listening to them argue.

'Highly unlikely? You didn't see her, James. She walked out of that clinic, came to this house, stood where I am now and took our baby boy. She trudged for miles through the woods

37

to get to the cave where she intended to offer him up as a sacrifice. That was no feeble old woman – she was determined and able. I know, I was there.'

'It's true, I wasn't there,' he replied tersely. 'But if she's still alive, where has she been all this time? Why hasn't she turned up? Scores of people spent hours searching for her, they fished her coat out of the river – she must have drowned, Amaia. The *Guardia Civil* thinks so, the local police force thinks so, I spoke to Iriarte and he thinks so. Even your friend the magistrate agrees,' he added pointedly. 'The river swept her away.'

Ignoring his insinuations, Amaia shook her head and carried on rocking Ibai, who, disturbed by their raised voices, had started to cry.

'I don't care. I don't believe it,' she muttered.

'That's the problem, Amaia,' snapped James. 'This is all about you and what you believe. Have you ever stopped to think what your sisters might be feeling? Has it occurred to you that they could be suffering too, that they might need to walk away from this episode once and for all, and that what you believe or don't believe isn't the only thing that counts?'

Ros, who had just come in, was standing in the doorway looking alarmed.

'Everyone knows you've suffered a lot, Amaia,' James went on, 'but this isn't just about you. Stop for a moment and think about what other people need. I see nothing wrong with what your sister Flora is trying to do. In fact it might prove beneficial to everyone's mental health, including mine, which is why I'll be going to the funeral, and I hope you'll come with me, this time.'

There was a note of reproach in his voice, and Amaia felt hurt, but above all shocked that James should bring up a subject she thought they'd resolved; it wasn't like him. By now, Ibai was screaming at the top of his lungs, wriggling in her arms, upset by the tension in her body, her quickened

38

breathing. She held him close, trying to calm him. Without saying a word, she went upstairs, ignoring Ros, who stood motionless in the doorway.

'Amaia . . .' Ros whispered to her sister as she brushed past.

James watched her leave the room then looked uneasily from Ros to Engrasi.

'James—' Engrasi started to say.

'Please don't, Auntie. Please, I beg you, don't feed Amaia's fears, or encourage her doubts. If anyone can help her turn the page, it's you. I've never asked anything of you before, but I'm asking you now – because I'm losing her, I'm losing my wife,' he said dejectedly, slumping back in his seat.

Amaia kept rocking Ibai until he stopped crying, then she lay down on the bed, placing him beside her so that she could enjoy her son's bright eyes, his clumsy little hands touching her eyes, nose and mouth until gradually he fell asleep. Just as his mother's tension had overwhelmed him earlier, she felt infected now by his placid calm.

Amaia realised how important the show at the Guggenheim had been for James; she understood why he was disappointed that she hadn't gone with him. But they'd talked about this. If she *had*, Ibai would probably be dead. She knew that James understood, but understanding wasn't the same as accepting. She heaved a sigh, and Ibai sighed too, as though echoing her. Touched, she leaned over to kiss him.

'My darling boy,' she whispered, marvelling at his perfect little features, enveloped by a mysterious calm she only experienced when she was with him, bewitching her with his scent of butter and biscuits, relaxing her muscles, drawing her gently into a deep sleep.

She realised she was dreaming, and that her fantasies were inspired by Ibai's scent. She was at the bakery, long before it became the setting for her nightmares; her father, dressed in his white jacket, was flattening out puff pastry with a steel rolling pin, before it became a weapon. The squares of white dough gave off a creamy, buttery smell. Music drifted through the bakery from a small transistor radio her father kept on the top shelf. She didn't recognise the song, yet, in her dream, the little girl who was her was mouthing some of the lyrics. She liked to be alone with her father, she liked to watch him work, while she danced about the marble counter, breathing in the odour she now realised was Ibai's, but which back then came from the butter biscuits. She felt happy – in that way unique to little girls who are the apple of their father's eye. She had almost forgotten how much he loved her, and remembering, even in a dream, made her feel happy once more. Round and round she spun, performing elegant pirouettes, her feet floating above the ground. But when she turned to smile at him, he had vanished. The kneading table was empty, no light penetrated the high windows. She must hurry, she must go home at once, or else her mother would become suspicious. 'What are *you* doing here?' All at once, the world became very small and dark, curving at the edges, until her dream landscape turned into a tunnel down which she was forced to walk; the short distance between her and the bakery door was transformed into a long, winding passageway at the end of which shone a small, bright light. Afterwards, there was nothing, the benign darkness blinded her, the blood drained from her head. 'Bleeding doesn't hurt, bleeding is peaceful and sweet, like turning into oil and trickling away,' Dupree had told her. 'And the more you bleed the less you care.' It's true, I don't care, the little girl thought. Amaia felt sad, because little girls shouldn't accept death, but she also understood, and so, although it pained her, she left her alone. First she heard the panting, the quick gasps of eager anticipation. Then, without opening her eyes, she could sense her mother approaching, slowly, inexorably, hungry for her blood, her breath. Her little girl's chest that scarcely contained enough oxygen to sustain the thread of consciousness that bound her to life. The presence, like a weight on her abdomen, crushed her lungs, which emptied like a pair of wheezing bellows, letting the air escape through her mouth, as the cruel, ravenous lips, covered her mouth, sucking out her last breath.

James entered the room, closing the door behind him. He sat down beside her on the bed, contemplating her for a moment, experiencing the pleasure of seeing someone who is truly exhausted sleep. He reached for the blanket lying at the foot of the bed, and drew it up to her waist. As he leaned over to kiss her, she opened startled unseeing eyes; when she saw it was him, she instantly relaxed, resting her head back on the pillow.

'It's okay, I was dreaming,' she whispered, repeating the words, which, like an incantation, she had recited practically every night since she was a child. James sat down again. He watched Amaia in silence, until she gave a faint smile, then embraced her.

'Do you think they might still serve us at that restaurant?'

'I cancelled; you're too tired. We'll go there another time . . .'

'How about tomorrow? I have to drive to Pamplona, but I promise I'll spend the afternoon with you and Ibai. In which case, you have to invite me out to dinner in the evening,' she added, chuckling.

'Come downstairs and have something to eat,' he said.

'I'm not hungry.'

But James stood up and held out his hand, smiling, and she followed him.

# 7

Dr Berasategui had lost none of the composure or authority one might expect from a renowned psychiatrist, and his appearance was as neat and meticulous as ever; when he clasped his hands on the table, Amaia noticed that his nails were manicured. His face remained unsmiling as he greeted her with a polite 'good morning' and waited for her to speak.

'Dr Berasategui, I confess I'm surprised that you agreed to see me. I imagine prison life must be tedious for a man like you.'

'I don't know what you mean.' His reply seemed sincere.

'You needn't pretend with me, Doctor. During the past month I've been reading your correspondence, I've visited your apartment on several occasions, and, as you know, I've had the opportunity to familiarise myself with your culinary taste . . .' His lips curled slightly at her last words. 'For that reason alone, I imagine you find life in here intolerably vulgar and dull. Not to mention what it must mean to be deprived of your favourite pastime.'

'Don't underestimate me, Inspector. Adaptability is one of my many talents. Actually, this prison isn't so different from a reformatory school in Switzerland. That's an experience which prepares you for anything.'

Amaia studied him in silence for a few seconds, then went on:

'I have no doubt that you're clever. Clever, confident and capable; you had to be, to succeed in making those poor wretches perpetrate your crimes for you.'

He smiled openly for the first time.

'You're mistaken, Inspector; my intention was never for them to sign my work, but rather to perform it. I see myself as a sort of stage director,' he explained.

'Yes, with an ego the size of Pamplona . . . Which is why, to my mind, something doesn't add up. Perhaps you can explain: why would a man like you, a man with a powerful, brilliant mind, end up obeying the orders of a senile old woman?'

'That isn't what happened.'

'Isn't it? I've seen the CCTV images from the clinic. You looked quite submissive to me.'

She had used the word 'submissive' on purpose, knowing he would see it as the worst sort of insult. Berasategui placed his fingers over his pursed lips as if to prevent himself rising to the bait.

'So, a mentally ill old woman convinces an eminent psychiatrist from a prestigious clinic, a brilliant – what did you refer to yourself as? – ah yes, stage director, to be her accomplice in a botched escape attempt, which ends in her being swept away by the river, while he's arrested and imprisoned. You must admit – not exactly your finest moment.'

'You couldn't be more mistaken,' he scoffed. 'Everything turned out exactly as planned.'

'Everything?'

'Except for the surprise of the child's gender; but I played no part in that. Otherwise I would have known.'

Berasategui appeared to have regained his habitual composure. Amaia smiled.

'I visited your father yesterday.'

43

Berasategui filled his lungs then exhaled slowly. Clearly this bothered him.

'Aren't you going to ask me about him? Aren't you interested to know how he is? No, of course you aren't. He's just an old man whom you used to locate the *mairus* in my family's burial plot.'

Berasategui remained impassive.

'Some of the bones left in the church were more recent. That oaf Garrido would never have been able to find them; only someone who had contact with Rosario could have known, because she alone had that information. Where are the remains of that body, Dr Berasategui? Where is that grave?'

He cocked his head to one side, adopting a faintly smug expression, as though amused at all this.

It vanished when Amaia continued:

'Your father was much more talkative than you. He told me you never spent the night with him, he said you went to a hotel, but we've checked, and we know that isn't true. I'm going to tell you what I think. I think you have another house in Baztán, a safe house, a place where you keep the things no one must see, the things you can't give up. The place where you took my mother that night, where she changed her clothes and no doubt where she returned when she ran off leaving you in the cave.'

'I don't know what you're talking about.'

'I'm referring to the fact that Rosario didn't change at your father's house, or in your car. The fact that there's a period of time unaccounted for between you leaving the hospital and stopping off at my aunt's house. While we were busy rooting around among the souvenirs in your apartment, you stopped off somewhere else. Do you expect me to believe that a man like you wouldn't have covered such a contingency? Don't insult my intelligence by pretending to make me believe you acted like a blundering fool . . .'

This time Berasategui covered his mouth with both hands to stifle the urge to respond.

'Where's the house? Where did you take Rosario? She's alive, isn't she?'

'What do you think?' he blurted unexpectedly.

'I believe you devised an escape plan, and that she followed it.'

'I like you, Inspector. You're an intelligent woman – you have to be, to appreciate other people's intelligence. And you're right, there *are* things I miss in here – for example, holding an interesting conversation with someone who has an IQ above 85,' he said, gesturing disdainfully towards the guards at the door. 'And for that reason alone, I'm going to make you a gift.' He leaned forward to whisper in her ear. Amaia remained calm, although she was surprised when the guards made no effort to restrain him. 'Listen carefully, Inspector, because this is a message from your mother.'

This time she recoiled, but it was too late, she could already smell Berasategui's shaving lotion. He gripped her tightly about the throat as she felt his lips brush her ear: 'Sleep with one eye open, little bitch, because sooner or later *Ama* is coming to eat you.' Amaia grabbed his wrist, forcing him to release her, then stumbled backwards, knocking over her chair. Berasategui leaned back, rubbing his wrist.

'Don't kill the messenger, Inspector,' he said with a grin.

She continued to back away until she reached the door, looking with alarm at the guards, who remained impassive.

'Open the door!'

The two men stood staring at her in silence.

'Are you deaf? Open the door. The prisoner has assaulted me!'

Seized with panic, she approached the man nearest to her, spitting her words so close to his face that her saliva landed on his cheek:

'Open the door, you sonofabitch! Open the door, or I

45

swear I'll . . .' The guard ignored her, looking towards Berasategui, who with a condescending nod gave his permission. The guards opened the door, smiling at Amaia as she went out.

# 8

She hurried along the corridor, fighting the impulse to break
into a run, acknowledged the guard manning the next security
gate, and continued to the main entrance, where she had
recognised one of the guards when she arrived. Still, she waited
to retrieve her bag and gun before asking to see the prison
governor.

'He's not here. He's in Barcelona, at a conference on prison
security, but you can speak to his deputy if you want,' said
the man, reaching for the phone.

Amaia reflected for an instant.

'No, don't bother. It's not important.'

She climbed into her car and took out her mobile, glancing
suspiciously at the CCTV cameras dotted about the prison.
She put the phone down and drove off, found a parking space
several streets away, then dialled a number she had never used
before.

Judge Markina's calm voice answered at the other end of
the line.

'Inspector, this is the first time you've ever called me on
this—'

'This is official business, your honour. I've just left the prison
in Pamplona after interviewing Berasategui . . .' Conscious of

the tremor in her voice, she broke off and took a deep breath to compose herself.

'Berasategui? Why didn't you tell me you were going to see him?'

'I'm sorry, your honour, this was an informal visit, I wanted to ask him about . . . Rosario.'

She heard him click his tongue in disapproval.

'All the information we have points to him and Rosario stopping off somewhere that night, at a safe house where she was able to change her clothes, somewhere they could hide in case things didn't go according to plan . . . I refuse to believe that a man as organised as Berasategui wouldn't have factored in a contingency like that.'

Markina was silent at the other end of the line.

'But that isn't why I called. The interview went well, until I asked him if Rosario was still alive . . . Then he gave me a message from her.'

'What! Amaia, the man's playing with you, he's an arch manipulator!' he burst out, abandoning his usual restraint. 'He hasn't any message from your mother – you gave him an opening, he recognised your weakness, and he pounced.'

She heaved a sigh, starting to regret having mentioned it to him.

'What exactly did he say?'

'That's not important, it's what happened next that worries me. While he was passing on the so-called message, he grabbed me by the throat.'

'Did he hurt you?' Markina broke in, alarmed.

'The two guards who were in the room with us didn't move a muscle,' she went on. 'No, he didn't hurt me, I freed myself and retreated to the door, but the guards wouldn't budge, even when I yelled at them to open the door. They waited until Berasategui authorised them to do so.'

'Are you sure you're okay?' If he hurt you—'

'I'm fine,' she interrupted. 'The point is, they acted like a pair of trained monkeys. He even joked about how stupid they were, and they remained completely submissive.'

'Where are you? I want to see you. Tell me where you are, I'll come straight away.'

She glanced about, disoriented.

'The prison governor is at a conference, and I don't know his deputy, but we need to act now. Who knows how many other guards he has under his thumb.'

'I'll see to it. I have the director's mobile number right here. I'll call to recommend Berasategui be moved to a maximum-security unit and placed in an isolation cell. The problem will be solved in ten minutes. But right now I need to see you. I need to know you're okay.'

Amaia leaned her head against the steering wheel, trying to order her thoughts. Markina's response had unnerved her; he appeared genuinely concerned, and she found his reaction to the possibility of any harm coming to her at once infuriating and flattering.

'Have you received the pathologist's report about the Esparza case?'

'No. I want to see you now.'

'My sister told me you'd called her.'

'Yes. She left a message with my secretary, and I returned her call out of politeness. She wanted to know whether I considered it appropriate to hold a funeral service for your mother. I told her I saw no objection. And now, can I see you?'

She smiled at his insistence; she should have known Flora's version would be somewhat doctored.

'I'm fine, honestly. Anyway, I need to go back to the police station to see the pathologist's report, which should be arriving any minute.'

'So, when?'

'When what?'

'When can I see you?'

'I have another call,' she lied. 'I need to hang up.'

'All right, but promise me: no more visits to Berasategui on your own. If anything happened to you . . .'

She ended the call, staring at the blank screen for a while without moving.

# 9

The leaden skies that had inspired Pamplona's inhabitants to rename it *Mordor*, gave way in Baztán to a hazier, more luminous atmosphere – a shimmering mist that dazzled the eye, shrouding the landscape in an eerie light and blurring the horizon. The police station at Elizondo seemed strangely calm compared to yesterday, and getting out of the car, Amaia noticed that this silence had descended like a blanket over the entire valley, so that even from up there she could hear the murmur of the River Txokoto, barely visible behind the old stone edifices. She turned her gaze back to the office: half a dozen photographs of the cot, the white bear, the corpse in the rucksack, the empty coffin from which Valentín Esparza had snatched his daughter's body, and finally the pathologist's report, open on top of her desk. San Martín had confirmed asphyxia as the cause of death. The shape and size of the bear's nose perfectly matched the pressure mark on the baby's forehead, and the white fibres found in the folds of her mouth came from the toy. The saliva traces on her face and on the toy belonged to the child and to Valentín Esparza; the foul odour coming from the toy was related to a third saliva trace, the source of which hadn't yet been verified.

'This proves nothing,' remarked Montes. 'The father could have kissed the baby goodbye when he left her at his mother-in-law's house.'

'Except that when San Martín confirmed there were saliva traces, I asked the grandmother if she'd bathed the girl before putting her to bed, and she said she had. So, any traces of saliva from the parents would have been washed away,' explained Amaia.

'A lawyer could argue that at some point he kissed the toy with which the baby was suffocated, thus transferring his saliva to her skin,' said Iriarte.

Zabalza arched an eyebrow sceptically.

'That's perfectly feasible,' protested Iriarte, looking to Amaia for support. 'When my kids were small, they often asked me to kiss their toys.'

'This girl was only four months old – I doubt she asked her father to kiss the bear. Besides, Esparza isn't the type to do that kind of thing. And the grandmother claims he stayed in the kitchen that day, drinking a beer, while his wife went up to see to the baby,' said Amaia, picking out one of the photographs to examine it more closely.

'I have something,' said Zabalza. 'I did a bit of work on the recordings from Esparza's cell. I couldn't make out the words, even with the volume on full. But since the image is quite clear, it occurred to me to send it to a friend who works with the deaf and can lip-read. He was absolutely certain that Esparza was saying: "I gave her up her to Inguma, like all the other sacrifices." I ran a check on Inguma and couldn't find anyone with that name or nickname.'

'Inguma? Are you sure?' Amaia asked, surprised.

'That's what my friend said: "Inguma".'

'How strange, because the baby's great-grandmother insisted that Inguma was responsible for the girl's death. According to her, Inguma is a demon, a creature that enters people's bedrooms at night, sits on their chests while they're asleep, and robs them of their breath,' she said, looking to Jonan for confirmation, who held a combined degree in anthropology and archaeology.

'That's right.' Deputy Inspector Etxaide took over. 'Inguma is one of the oldest, most sinister creatures in traditional folklore, an evil genie that enters victims' houses at night and suffocates them. Inguma is thought to be responsible for terrible nightmares and what we now call sleep apnoea, where the sleeper stops breathing for no apparent reason. In extreme cases, death can occur. The majority of sufferers are people who smoke or are overweight. Interestingly, sleeping with the windows open was thought to be dangerous, because Inguma could enter more easily; people suffering from respiratory problems kept their windows closed at night, blocking every possible opening, as it was believed the genie could slip through the tiniest crack. Naturally, cot deaths were also blamed on Inguma, and before putting their children to bed people would recite a magic formula to ward off the demon. As when addressing witches, it was essential to begin by stating that you believed in them, but didn't fear them. It went something like this:

*Inguma, I do not fear you.*
*I call upon God and the Virgin Mary to protect me.*
*Until you have counted every star in the sky,*
*Every blade of grass upon the earth,*
*Every grain of sand upon the beach,*
*You will not come to me.*

'It's a wonderful spell, commanding the demon to perform a task that will take an eternity. Very similar to the *eguz-kilore* used against witches, who must count all the thorns on a thistle before entering a house. As this takes all night, by the time dawn comes they have to run and hide. What's interesting about Inguma is that, although it's one of the least-studied night demons, it has identical equivalents in other cultures.'

'I'd like to see Esparza explaining to Judge Markina that his daughter was killed by a night demon,' said Montes.

'He hasn't confessed to killing her, but he hasn't denied it either. He insists that he gave her up,' explained Iriarte.

'"Like all the other sacrifices",' added Zabalza. 'What does he mean? Do you suppose this isn't the first time he's done this?'

'Well, he's going to have a hard time blaming it on a demon,' said Montes. 'I questioned some of his neighbours this morning and was lucky enough to find a woman who'd been watching television late that night. She "happened" to look out of her window, and saw the couple arrive home after their evening out. Twenty minutes later, she was surprised to hear the car leave again. She said she was worried the baby might be unwell, so she listened out. Twenty minutes later, she heard the car return. This time, she peeped through the spyhole in her front door, just to make sure the baby was all right, and saw Esparza go into the house alone.'

Iriarte shrugged.

'Then we've got him.'

Amaia agreed.

'Yes, everything points to the husband, but three things need clearing up: the smell and saliva traces on the bear; Esparza's obsession with his daughter's body not being cremated; and what he meant by "Like all the other sacrifices." Incidentally,' she said, holding up the photograph she had been examining, 'is it a trick of the camera, or is there something in the coffin?'

'Yes,' admitted Iriarte. 'Initially, we mistook it for quilting, but the funeral director alerted us. It seems Esparza placed three bags of sugar wrapped in a white towel in the coffin. Clearly, so that the bearers wouldn't notice it was empty.'

'Right,' said Amaia, putting the photograph down next to the others. 'We'll wait and see if the tests on the third trace open up another line of inquiry; he may have picked up someone on the way. Good work,' she added, signalling that the meeting was over. Jonan lagged behind.

'Is everything okay, boss?'

She looked at him, attempting to disguise her unease. Who was she trying to fool? Jonan knew her almost as well as she knew herself, but she was aware that she couldn't always tell him everything. She put him off the scent by mentioning something else that was bothering her.

'My sister Flora is in Elizondo, insisting we hold a funeral service for our mother; just thinking about it makes me feel sick, and as if that weren't enough, the rest of my family is siding with her, including James. I've tried to explain my reasons for thinking she's still alive, but I've only succeeded in making them angry with me for preventing them from closing this chapter in their lives.'

'If it's any consolation, I don't believe she fell in that river either.'

Amaia gave a sigh, looking straight at him.

'Of course it is, Jonan, very much so . . . You're a good cop, and I trust your instinct. It's a great relief to have you on my side.'

Jonan nodded without much conviction, as he went round the table gathering up the photographs.

'Do you need me to go somewhere with you, boss?'

'I'm off home, Jonan,' she replied.

He smiled wistfully at her on his way out, leaving her with the familiar feeling of having been unable to pull the wool over his eyes.

As she drove towards the Txokoto River, she passed *Juanitaenea*, the house that had belonged to her grandmother. James had planned to restore it so that they could live there; the building materials he'd ordered were sitting on pallets outside the house, but there was no sign of any activity.

She was tempted to stop off at the bakery on her way, but decided against it: she had too much going on in her head to become embroiled in another discussion with Ros over the funeral. Instead, she crossed the Giltxaurdi Bridge and parked near the old market. She knew the house she was looking for was close by, but all the houses on that street looked the same and she couldn't remember which one it was. In the end she took a guess, smiling with relief when Elena Ochoa opened the door.

'Can we talk?' Amaia asked her.

The woman responded by seizing her arm and pulling her into the house, then she leaned out to look up and down the street. As on her previous visit, Amaia followed Elena through to the kitchen. Not a word was exchanged as Elena made coffee for them both, placing two cups on a plastic tray covered with kitchen roll. Amaia was grateful for the silence; every instant the woman spent on her precise coffee-making ritual gave Amaia time to order the instincts – for she could scarcely call them thoughts or ideas – that had brought her there. They clattered in her head like the echo from a blow, as the stream of images in her mind amalgamated with others engraved on her memory. She had gone there searching for answers, yet she wasn't sure she had the questions. Aunt Engrasi always used to tell her: 'You'll only find the answers if you know which questions to ask.' But all she had to go on in this case was a small, white coffin, weighted with bags of sugar, and the word 'sacrifice'. It was an ominous combination.

She noticed that the woman was trying to steady her hands as she spooned sugar into two cups. She began to stir the brew, but the chink of the spoon on the china seemed to exasperate her to the point where she hurled the spoon on to the tray.

'Forgive me, my nerves are bad. Tell me what you want, and let's be done.'

This was Baztán hospitality. Elena Ochoa had no desire to speak to her, in fact she couldn't wait for her to leave the house and would heave a sigh of relief when she saw her walk through the door, yet she wouldn't renege on the sacred ritual of offering a visitor something to drink or eat. She was one of those women who did what had to be done. Reassured by that thought, Amaia cupped her hands round the coffee she wouldn't have time to drink, and spoke.

'When I came here last, I asked you whether the sect had ever carried out a human sacrifice . . . '

At this, Elena began to shake uncontrollably.

'Please . . . You must leave, I have nothing to say.'

'Elena, you've got to help me. My mother is still out there. I need you to tell me where that house is, I know that's where I'll find answers.'

'I can't – they'll kill me.'

'Who?'

She shook her head, terrified.

'We'll give you protection,' said Amaia, casting a sidelong glance at the little effigy of the virgin with a flickering candle in front of it, and a worn string of rosary beads draped at the base; beside it stood a couple of postcards bearing images of Christ.

'You can't protect me from them.'

'Do you think they carried out a sacrifice?'

Elena stood up, emptying the remains of her coffee into the sink, her back to Amaia as she washed up her cup.

'No. The proof is that you're still alive; at the time, the only pregnant woman in the group was Rosario. I've thanked God a thousand times for keeping you safe. Perhaps in the end they were trying to impress us, to cow us into submission by making themselves seem more dangerous and powerful . . .'

Amaia took in the array of talismans with which Elena had surrounded herself: the poor woman was desperately trying to convince herself that she was in control, and yet her body language betrayed her.

'Elena, look at me,' she commanded.

Elena turned off the tap, dropped the sponge and swung round to look at her.

'I had a twin sister who died at birth. The official cause was registered as cot death.'

Pale with fear, the woman raised her hands, placed them over her distraught face, moist with tears, and asked: 'Where is she buried? Where is she buried?'

Amaia shook her head, watching the woman flinch as she went on to explain:

'We don't know. I found her tomb, but the coffin was empty.'

Elena gave a terrible, visceral howl, and lunged at Amaia, who leapt to her feet, startled.

'Leave my house! Leave my house and never come back!' she screamed, corralling Amaia to force her to walk on.

Before opening the front door, Amaia turned once more to plead with the woman.

'At least tell me where the house is.'

After the door slammed shut, she could still hear the woman's muffled sobs coming from inside.

Instinctively, she reached into her pocket for her phone and dialled Special Agent Aloisius Dupree. She pressed it tightly to her ear as she walked back to her car, listening hard for the faintest sound at the other end of the line. She was about to hang up, when she heard a crackle. She knew he was there, the FBI agent who had been her mentor during her time in New Orleans, and who remained an important part of her life, despite the distances. The sound that reached her through the earpiece a moment later made a shiver run up her spine: the repetitive drone of a funeral chant, the echo of voices suggesting a large space, possibly a cathedral. There was something bleak and sinister about the way three words were repeated over and over again in a monotone. But it was the shrill, anguished death cry that made her stomach turn. The tortured death throes continued for a few seconds, then at last the pitiful sound faded, she assumed because Dupree was moving away.

When at last he spoke, his voice betrayed the same anguish she herself felt.

'Don't call me again, I'll call you.' Then he hung up, leaving Amaia feeling so small and far away from him that it made her want to scream.

She was still holding her phone when it rang. She looked at the screen with a mixture of hope and panic. She recognised the FBI's ID number and heard Agent Johnson's friendly voice greeting her from Virginia. He announced that the seminars at Quantico had been given the green light, and they were hoping she might contribute to the area of studies concerned with criminal behaviour. They were currently in the process of requesting permission from her superior.

Up to that point, their conversation didn't differ from any of the previous conversations she'd had with FBI officials, but the fact that she'd received the call moments after speaking to Dupree didn't escape her notice, and what Agent Johnson said next instantly confirmed to her that they were monitoring her calls.

'Inspector, have you had any type of contact with Special Agent Dupree?'

Amaia bit her lip, hesitating, as she recalled the conversation she'd had with Agent Johnson a month or so ago, when he'd advised her not to use official telephone lines for anything relating to Agent Dupree, and had given her a special number to call. On the rare occasions when she had managed to get in touch with Dupree, his voice always sounded far away, plagued with echoes; invariably, they got cut off, and on one occasion his number had vanished from her phone as if the call had never taken place. Then there had been the mysterious emails she'd asked Jonan to look into; he'd succeeded in tracking the source to an IP address in Baton Rouge, Louisiana – at which point the FBI stepped in and ordered him to desist with the search. Johnson had asked her about Dupree as if he'd forgotten what she'd told him during their last conversation, namely that Dupree always answered her calls. In any event, Johnson was calling her now because he knew she had just spoken to Dupree. Informing her that she had been accepted on to the course was simply a pretext.

'Not very often. I occasionally call to say hello, the same way I do with you,' she said, nonchalantly.

'Have you spoken to Agent Dupree about the case he is currently working on?'

Johnson sounded as if he were ticking boxes on an internal questionnaire sheet.

'No, I didn't even know he was working on a new case.'

'If Agent Dupree gets in touch with you again, will you inform us?'

'You're freaking me out, Agent Johnson, is something wrong?'

'Only that in the last few days we've had trouble contacting Agent Dupree. I expect the situation has gotten a little complicated, and for reasons of security he's decided to lie low. There's no need for you to be alarmed, Inspector. However, if Dupree does get in touch with you, we'd be grateful if you'd let us know immediately.'

'I'll do that, Agent Johnson.'

'Thank you, Inspector, we look forward to seeing you here very soon.'

She hung up, then sat in her car for ten minutes waiting for the phone to ring again. When it did, she recognised Johnson's private number on the screen.

'What was that all about?'

'I told you, Dupree has his own way of doing things. He's been incommunicado for some time, which, as you know, is normal when you're working undercover. Finding the right moment can be difficult. However, that, together with Agent Dupree's somewhat irreverent attitude, is causing them to question the security of his identity.'

'You mean they think his cover might have been blown?'

'That's the official version. The truth is, they think he may have been taken hostage.'

'What do you think?' she said, warily, wondering how far she could trust Johnson. How could she be sure this second call wasn't also being recorded?

'I think Dupree knows what he's doing.'

'So do I,' she declared, with all the conviction she could muster, as the grotesque cries she had heard when Dupree answered his phone resounded once more in her head.

# 10

They had spent the afternoon at the shopping centre on Carretera de Francia on the pretext of buying clothes for Ibai, and to escape the cold brought by the fog that was thickening as night fell; by the time they left for dinner in the evening, they could scarcely see beyond the far bank of the river. The Santxotena restaurant was relatively lively, the murmur of laughter and voices reaching them as soon as they crossed the threshold. They were in the habit of reserving a table by the kitchen that opened on to the spacious dining room, so that they could watch the orderly bustle of three generations of women, clad in starched white aprons over black uniforms, moving about the kitchen as if it were a formal dance they'd rehearsed a thousand times.

After choosing from the wine list, James and Amaia were content to enjoy the atmosphere in the restaurant for a while. They hadn't touched on the subject of the funeral, and had avoided bringing to a head the palpable tension that had arisen between them that afternoon. They knew they needed to talk, but had made a tacit agreement to wait until they were alone.

'How's the investigation going?' James asked.

She looked at him, debating how to answer. Since she joined the police force, she had been meticulous about never discussing her work with her family, and they knew not to ask. She had no desire to talk to James about the more disturbing aspects of her job, in the same way she felt there were scenes from her past it was best not to mention, even though he already knew about them. She found it difficult to talk about her childhood, and for years she'd buried the truth beneath a false veneer of normality. When the barriers holding back all that horror had burst open, driving her to the edge of sanity, confiding in James had been the chink in the wall of fear that allowed light to flood in, creating a place for them to come together – a place that had delivered her back to a world where, if she was vigilant, the old ghosts could not touch her.

And yet, she'd always known that fear never goes away completely, it merely shrinks back to a dark, dank place, where it waits, reduced to a tiny red light you can still see even if you don't want to, even if you refuse to acknowledge its existence, because it prevents you from living. She also knew that fear is a private thing, that no amount of talking about it, or naming it, will make it go away; that the old cliché 'a burden shared is a burden halved' didn't apply where fear was concerned. She had always believed that love would triumph over everything, that opening the door and revealing herself to James with all the baggage of her past would suffice.

Now, sitting opposite him, she still saw the handsome young man she had fallen in love with. The self-assured, optimistic artist no one had ever tried to kill, with his simple, almost childlike way of looking at things that enabled him to follow a steady path, safe from life's cruelties. It allowed him to believe that turning the page, burying the past, or talking to a psychiatrist for months about your mother's desire to eat you, would help her to overcome her fears, to live in a world of green meadows and blue skies sustained by simply willing it to be so. This belief that happiness was a choice struck her as so naïve as to be almost insulting. She knew James didn't really want to know how her work was going, and that when he asked he wasn't expecting her to explain that she had questioned a psychopath about where her mother or her vanished sister's body were.

She smiled at him, because she loved him, because his way of seeing the world still intrigued her, and because she knew that part of love was making the effort to love someone.

'Quite well. I'm hoping to wrap up the case in a couple of days,' she replied.

'I spoke to my father today,' he said. 'He hasn't been feeling well lately. My mother insisted he have a check-up and they've found a lesion in his heart.'

'Oh, James! Is it serious?'

'No, even my mother is relaxed. Apparently he has a small blockage in one of his coronary arteries due to early stage arteriosclerosis. He needs a bypass to prevent future heart attacks. However, he'll have to stop working. My mother has been pressuring him to hand over the day-to-day management of the company, but he likes to keep busy, so while his health held out he was content to carry on indefinitely. She seems almost happy about it, and is already talking about the trips they'll make when he gets over the surgery.'

'I hope it all goes well, James, and I'm glad you're taking it this way. When's the operation?'

'Next Monday. That's why I asked how your work was going. I was hoping the three of us could fly over there together. My parents haven't seen Ibai since the baptism.'

'Hm . . .'

'We could leave after the funeral. Flora stopped by this morning to tell us she thinks it'll be on Friday. She's going to confirm tomorrow. We'd only stay for a few days. I doubt you'll have a problem taking vacation at this time of year.'

Too many loose ends, too much that needed sorting out. Yes, the investigation would be officially closed in a few days, but there was that other business; she had yet to receive confirmation from the commissioner's office about whether she'd be attending the seminars at Quantico, and she hadn't even mentioned that to James.

'I don't know, James . . . I'll have to think about it.'

The smile froze on his face.

'Amaia, this is really important to me,' he said solemnly.

She instantly grasped the implication. He had given her a glimpse yesterday. He had his own needs, his own plans, he wanted a place in her life. The image of the stalled works at *Juanitaenea* flashed into her mind, together with Yáñez's words: 'a house isn't the same as a home'.

She reached across the table to clasp his hand.

'Of course, it's important for me too,' she said, forcing a smile. 'First thing tomorrow, I'll put in a request. As you say, I doubt they'll object, no one goes on holiday at this time of year.'

'Excellent,' he replied cheerily. 'I've been looking at flights. As soon as you've got permission, I'll book our tickets.'

James spent the rest of the dinner planning their trip, excited at the idea of taking Ibai to the States for the first time. She listened, saying nothing.

# 11

She was aware of his hot breath on her skin, of becoming intensely aroused as she sensed his closeness. He murmured something she couldn't hear, but she didn't care, something about his voice mesmerised her. It evoked the contours of his mouth, his moist lips, the smile she had always found so troubling. Inhaling the warmth of his skin stirred her desire; she longed for him, eyes closed, holding her breath, as her senses yielded to pleasure. She felt his lips on her neck, descending in a slow, unstoppable advance, like lava flowing from a volcano. Every nerve in her body was engaged in a furious struggle between pleasure and pain, pleading for more, wanting more, the hairs on the back of her neck prickling, her nipples contracting, a burning sensation between her thighs. She opened her eyes, glancing about, confused. The little light she always left on at night permitted her to recognise the familiar shape of their bedroom in Engrasi's house. Her body tensed, alarmed. James whispered in her ear as he went on kissing her.

It was daylight, and Ibai was already awake. She could hear him moving, gurgling softly as he kicked his legs in the air, pushing off the duvet, which would end up at the foot of his cot. She didn't open her eyes immediately; it had taken her ages to fall asleep again after they made love, and, eyelids still heavy, she relished the idea of lazing in bed for another five minutes. She heard James get up, gather Ibai in his arms and whisper to him:

'Are you hungry? We'll let *Ama* snooze.'

She heard them leave the room, as she lay there, trying in vain to relax into a peaceful, dreamless sleep. All of a sudden, the dream about Markina came flooding back. She knew better than anyone that we aren't responsible for our dreams, that the most pleasurable fantasies and the sickest nightmares come from a mysterious, unreachable place beyond our control. Still, she felt guilty. Wide-awake now, irritated at having had to renounce those five extra minutes of peace, she analysed her feelings. She realised the sense of guilt came not from having dreamt about Markina, but rather because she had made love with her husband stimulated by the desire she felt for the judge.

As James entered the room, bringing her a cup of coffee, the mobile on her bedside table made an unpleasant buzzing noise.

'Good morning, Iriarte.'

'Good morning, Inspector. We've just had a call from the prison in Pamplona. Berasategui has been found dead in his cell.'

She hung up, leapt to her feet, dressing between sips of coffee. She hated drinking it like that; she'd got into the habit of drinking her morning coffee in bed back when she was a student and it remained her preferred way to start the morning. Rushing to get ready was something she detested; it always augured a bad day.

The prison governor was waiting for them at the entrance, pacing up and down like a caged animal. He extended his hand courteously, then invited them to follow him to his office. Amaia refused, requesting to see the body immediately.

A guard escorted them through the various security gates until they reached the isolation cells. They could tell which one was Berasategui's from the guard posted outside the metal door.

'The doctor found no signs of violence on the body,' explained the director. 'He was placed in isolation yesterday at Judge Markina's request, and hadn't spoken to anyone since.' He signalled to the guard to unlock the door, then ushered them in.

'But someone must have come in here,' said Inspector Montes, 'if only to confirm that he was dead.'

'One of the guards noticed he wasn't moving and raised the alarm. The only people to have entered the cell are the prison doctor, who confirmed that he was dead, and myself. We called you immediately. It appears he died of natural causes.'

The cell, which contained no personal effects, was clean and tidy, the bedclothes smoothed out, military fashion. Dr Berasategui lay face up on his bunk, fully dressed down to his shoes, face relaxed, eyes closed. The scent of his cologne filled the cell, yet the perfect neatness of his clothes, his hands clasped on his chest, gave the impression of an embalmed corpse.

'Natural causes, you say?' Amaia frowned. 'This was a thirty-six-year-old man who kept himself in good shape; he even had a gym in his apartment. Not only that, he was a doctor, so he'd have been the first to know if he was unwell, don't you think?'

'I must admit, this is the best-looking corpse I've ever seen!' Montes joked, nudging Zabalza, who was searching the perimeter of the cell with a flashlight.

Amaia pulled on the gloves Inspector Etxaide handed to her and approached the bunk. She studied the body in silence for a few minutes, until she became aware of Dr San Martín standing behind her.

'What have we here, Inspector? The prison doctor tells me

there are no signs of violence, and suggests death by natural causes.'

'There are no objects in here with which he could have harmed himself,' said Montes, 'and whatever the cause of death, you can see from looking at him that he didn't suffer.'

'Well, if you've finished here, I'll take him away. The results of the autopsy should be ready later today.'

'Berasategui didn't die of natural causes,' Amaia broke in. The others said nothing, and she thought she heard Zabalza sigh. 'Look at the way he's arranged, right in the centre of the bed. Clothes smoothed out, shoes polished. Hands placed exactly as he'd want us to see them when we walked in here. This guy was a proud, vain narcissist, who would never have let us discover him in an embarrassing or humiliating attitude.'

'Suicide doesn't fit the profile of a narcissistic personality,' Jonan ventured.

'Yes, I know, that's what threw me when we walked in. On the one hand, it fits; on the other, it doesn't. Suicide may not be typical of someone with his personality, but if Berasategui were going to take his own life, this is exactly how I imagine he'd go about it.'

'But the body shows no signs of suicide,' protested Zabalza.

His curiosity piqued, San Martín approached Berasategui's corpse, felt his throat, lifted his eyelids and looked down his throat.

'All the hallmarks of a heart attack, but it's true he was relatively young and in good shape. On the other hand, there are no lesions, no defensive wounds, or other signs of injury. Anyone would think,' said the doctor, looking round at the company, 'that he simply lay down and died.'

'Quite right, Doctor. That's exactly what he did: he lay down and died. But to do that, he needed help. How long had he been in isolation?' she said, addressing the director.

'Since approximately eleven o'clock yesterday morning,

69

shortly after Judge Markina called me. I was away, but my deputy informed me fifteen minutes after he'd been moved.'

'Are there any cameras in these cells?' asked Montes, shining a flashlight into the corners of the room.

'No, they aren't necessary. Guards monitor prisoners in isolation through the windows in the cell doors. But we have CCTV out in the corridors. I assumed you'd want to see the tape, so I've prepared a copy.'

'What about the two men who were guarding him yesterday?'

'They've been suspended, pending an investigation of that other incident,' replied the director, looking uncomfortable.

Montes and Etxaide, having no idea what this 'other incident' might be, turned to look at her, demanding answers. Ignoring them, Amaia approached the bunk once more and said:

'Dr Berasategui had no wish to die, but his personality prevented him from permitting another to take his life for him.'

'He didn't want to die, yet he killed himself . . .?'

She leaned over the body, illuminating his face with her flashlight. Berasategui's bronzed skin revealed a whitish residue confined to the wrinkles around his eyes.

'Tears,' announced San Martín.

'Yes, sir,' she agreed. 'True to his nature as a narcissist, Berasategui lay down here, out of self-pity, wept over his own death. Copiously,' she said, feeling a patch of fabric visibly darker than the rest. 'He cried so much he soaked the pillow with his tears.'

# 12

Montes felt satisfied. The CCTV footage revealed a guard approaching Berasategui's cell, and slipping something through the window, which, although it wasn't visible on camera could easily have been something he used to kill himself. The guard had finished his shift and made himself scarce by the time they sent a patrol car to his house. He was probably in France or Portugal by now. Even so, knowing that bastard Berasategui was dead had made Montes's day.

As he leaned forward to turn on the radio, the car swerved slightly, the front tyre touching the white line at the side of the road.

'Careful!' cried Zabalza from the passenger seat. He'd been subdued throughout the journey and Montes assumed he was sulking because he'd refused to let him drive. What the hell! No brat was going to take the wheel while Montes was in the car. He glanced sidelong at him, grinning.

'Calm down, you're as a tense as a teenage boy's scrotum,' he said, laughing at his own joke, until he saw that Zabalza was still irritated.

'What's the matter with you?'

'She drives me crazy . . .'

'Who?'

'Who do you think? The fucking star cop.'

'Watch your mouth, lad!' warned Montes.

'Didn't you see that mystical act she puts on? The way she stood looking at Berasategui's body, as if she felt sorry for him, waiting for the room to go quiet before she spoke, as if she was about to pass judgement. As for that bullshit about him crying – for fuck's sake! Everyone knows that corpses cry, piss themselves, leak fluid from every orifice.'

'Berasategui certainly didn't piss himself . . . I imagine he was careful not to drink anything, because he wanted to be immaculate when we found him. Besides, the pillow was sodden. I think the guy really did weep over his own death.'

'Rubbish,' scoffed Zabalza.

'No, it isn't rubbish. You should be watching, not criticising, you might learn something.'

'Who from? That clown?'

The two men were thrown forward slightly, as Montes stepped on the brakes, pulling over into a lay-by.

'Why did you do that?' Zabalza cried, startled.

'Because I don't want to hear you talk about Inspector Salazar like that again. Not only is she your superior, she's an outstanding police officer and a loyal colleague.'

'For fuck's sake, Fermín!' Zabalza laughed. 'Don't get so upset. You're the one who coined the phrase "star cop" remember.'

Montes looked straight at him as he started the car again.

'You're right, and I was wrong. They say hindsight is twenty-twenty, don't they? If you have any problems, you can always come to me, but I warn you, I won't hear any more of this kind of talk,' he said, joining the motorway again.

'I don't have any problems,' muttered Zabalza.

As she left the cell, Amaia noticed the prison governor standing further along the corridor talking to Judge Markina, whose hushed voice brought back vivid recollections of her dream the night before. She concentrated on the brief summary she would give him before making her escape, but it was too late, the murmur of his voice had drawn her in, even though she was too far away to hear what he was saying. She stood watching his gesticulations, his habit of touching his face when he spoke, the way his jeans narrowed at the waist, how the blue of his shirt gave him a youthful air. She found herself speculating about how old he was, thinking it odd that she didn't know. She waited for Dr San Martín to arrive and then joined them. She did her best to avoid Markina's gaze while she gave a brief report, but without making it too obvious.

'Will you attend the autopsy, Inspector?' asked San Martín, with a sweeping gesture that included Deputy Inspector Etxaide.

'Start without me, Doctor, I'll join you later. Perhaps you'd like to go, Jonan, there's something I have to do first,' she added evasively.

'Going home again today, boss?' he teased.

She smiled, admiring his astuteness.

'All right, Deputy Inspector, would you like to come with me?'

# 13

The receptionist at the University Hospital hadn't forgotten Amaia, judging by the way the woman's face froze the instant she saw her. Even so, the inspector fished out her badge, prodding Jonan to do likewise. Both detectives placed their badges squarely on the counter.

'We'd like to see Dr Sarasola, please.'

'I don't know if he's here,' the woman replied, picking up the receiver. She gave their names, listened to the reply then, with a sour expression, motioned towards the lift doors. 'Fourth floor, they'll show you the way.' There was a tone of caution in the woman's voice as she said these last words. Amaia grinned at her and winked, then started towards the lift.

Sarasola received them in his office, behind a desk heaped with papers, which he pushed aside. He stood up, accompanying them to the chairs over by the window.

'I imagine you're here about Dr Berasategui's death,' he said, as they shook hands.

Few things happened in Pamplona without Sarasola's knowledge; even so, Amaia and Deputy Inspector Etxaide were somewhat taken aback. Noticing their expressions, he added:

'The prison governor has family ties with Opus Dei.'

Amaia nodded.

'So, how may I help you?'

'Did you visit Dr Berasategui in prison?'

They knew that Sarasola had visited him. She'd asked the question to see whether he'd admit it.

'On three separate occasions – in a purely professional capacity, I might add. As you know, I have a special interest in cases of abnormal behaviour that possess the nuance of evil.'

'Did Dr Berasategui mention anything to you about Rosario's escape, or what happened that night?' asked Etxaide.

'I'm afraid our conversations were rather technical and abstract – although fascinating, needless to say. Berasategui was an excellent clinician, which made discussing his own behaviour and actions a daunting task. He thwarted all my attempts to analyse him so that in the end I limited myself to offering him spiritual solace. In any event, nothing he might have said about Rosario or what happened that night would be of any use. One thing I *do* know is that you should never listen to people who have embraced evil, because they only tell lies.'

Amaia stifled a sigh, which Jonan recognised as a sign that she was becoming impatient.

'So did you talk about Rosario, or have you lost interest in the matter?'

'Of course, but he immediately changed the subject. Knowing what you do now, Inspector, I trust that you no longer hold me responsible for Rosario's escape.'

'I don't. However, I am beginning to suspect that this is all part of a far more intricate plan, starting with Rosario's transfer from Santa María de las Nieves and culminating in the events of that night – which weren't your fault, either.'

Sarasola leaned forward in his chair and looked straight at Amaia.

'I'm glad you're beginning to understand,' he said.

'Oh, I understand, but I still find it difficult to believe that a man like you didn't notice that something untoward was going on in this clinic.'

'This isn't my—'

'I know, I know, it's not your clinic, but you know perfectly well what I mean,' she snapped.

'And I apologised for that,' he protested. 'You're right, once I became involved in the case I should have kept a closer eye on Berasategui, but in this instance I, too, am a victim.'

She always found it distasteful when someone who wasn't dead or in hospital referred to themselves as a victim. Amaia knew only too well what it meant to be a victim, and Sarasola wasn't one.

'In any event, Berasategui's suicide doesn't add up. I visited him in prison too, and I'd have said he was more of an escape risk than a suicide risk.'

'Suicide is a form of escape,' Jonan broke in, 'although it doesn't fit his profile.'

'I agree with Inspector Salazar,' replied Sarasola, 'and allow me to tell you something about behaviour profiles. They may work, even for individuals suffering from mental illness. But they are far from reliable when dealing with someone who is the embodiment of evil.'

'That's exactly what I mean when I talk about a premeditated plan. What would drive a man like that to take his own life?' declared Amaia.

'The same thing that drove him to carry out those other acts: to achieve some unknown end.'

'Bearing that in mind, do you believe Rosario is dead, or that somehow she got away?'

'I know no more than you. Everything points to the river having—'

'Dr Sarasola, I was hoping we had got beyond that stage in our relationship. Why not help me instead of telling me what you think I want to hear?' she said.

'I believe that, besides inciting those men to commit murder, Berasategui devised a way of drawing you into the investigation by leaving your ancestors' bones in the church at Arizkun, that for months he was working towards Rosario's transfer from Santa María de las Nieves, and her subsequent escape from this clinic. The plan was meticulously carried out, which makes me think that he took every possible contingency into account. Rosario may be an elderly woman, but after seeing the images of her leaving the clinic with Berasategui, I . . .'

'You what?'

'I believe she's out there, somewhere,' he admitted.

'But why involve me, why this provocation?'

'I can only think that it's connected with your mother.'

Amaia took a photograph out of her bag and passed it to him.

'This is the inside of the cave where Berasategui and my mother were preparing to kill my son, Ibai.'

Sarasola studied the image, looked at Amaia for a few seconds, then at the photograph again.

'Doctor, I suspect that the *tarttalo* killings are the grisly tip of an iceberg aimed at drawing our attention away from a far more horrible crime. Something connected to these sacrileges that would explain the clear symbolic use of bones belonging to children in my family, why they wanted to kill my son and didn't, and, I believe, the Church's response to a desecration, which on the face of it wasn't all that shocking.'

Sarasola looked at them in silence, then examined the photograph once more. Amaia leaned forward, touching the priest's forearm.

'I need your help, please. Tell me what you see in this picture.'

'Inspector Salazar, you're aware that you share the name of an illustrious inquisitor. When the witch hunts reached their apogee, your ancestor, Salazar y Frías opened an investigation into the presence of evil in the Baztán Valley, which spread across the border to France. After dwelling among the population for over a year, he concluded that the practice of witchcraft was much more deeply rooted in the local culture than Christianity itself, which although firmly established, had been bastardised by the old beliefs that held sway in the area prior to the foundation of the Catholic Church. Salazar y Frías was an open-minded man, a scientist and investigator, who employed methods of inquiry and analysis similar to those you use today. Of course, many of the people questioned were undoubtedly driven to confess to such practices to avoid being tortured by the Inquisition, the mere mention of which sent them into a panic. I admire Salazar y Frías's decision to put a stop to that insanity, but among the numerous crimes he investigated, many remained unsolved, in particular those involving the deaths of children, infants and young girls, whose bodies subsequently disappeared. Such stories appear in several statements; however, once the cruel methods of the Inquisition were abolished, all the statements taken at that time were deemed unreliable.

'What I see in this photograph is the scene of a sacrifice, a human sacrifice, the victim of which was to be your son. Human sacrifice is a heinous practice used in witchcraft and devil worship. It was the appearance of children's bones in the desecrations at Arizkun that raised the alarm; it is common in devil worship to use human remains, especially those of children. However, the sacrifice of a living child is considered the highest offering.'

'I know about Salazar y Frías. I understand what you're saying, but are you suggesting a connection between the practice of witchcraft in the seventeenth century and the desecrations in Arizkun, or what nearly happened to Ibai?'

Sarasola nodded slowly.

'How much do you know about witches, Inspector? And I

don't mean witch doctors or faith healers, but rather the ones described by the Brothers Grimm in their fairy tales.'

Jonan leaned forward, interested.

'I know that they're covered in warts and dwell deep in the forest,' said Amaia.

'Do you know what they eat?'

'They eat children,' replied Jonan.

Amaia laughed.

The priest turned to her, irritated by her sarcasm.

'Inspector,' he cautioned, 'stop playing games with me. Ever since you walked in here, I've had the impression that you know more than you're willing to let on. This is no laughing matter; stories that become folklore after being passed down through generations usually contain a grain of truth. Perhaps witches don't literally eat children, but they feed off the lives of innocents offered in sacrifice.'

Sarasola was shrewd enough to have figured out that, as a homicide detective, she had more reasons for asking him about this subject than those she was prepared to admit.

'All right, so what do they get in exchange for these sacrifices?'

'Health, life, riches . . .'

'And people actually believe that? I mean now, as opposed to in the seventeenth century. They believe that by performing human sacrifices they will obtain some of these benefits?'

Sarasola sighed despairingly.

'Inspector, if you wish to understand anything about how this works, then you must stop thinking about whether it's logical or not, whether it corresponds to your computerised world, your profiling techniques. Stop thinking in terms of what you think a modern person would believe.'

'I find that impossible.'

'That's where you are mistaken as are all those fools who base their idea of the world on what they see as logical, scientifically proven fact. Believe me, the men who condemned

Galileo for suggesting that the Earth revolved around the Sun did exactly the same thing: based on their centuries-old understanding of the cosmos, they argued that the Earth was the centre of the universe. Think about this before you reply: do we know, or do we believe we know because that's what we've been told? Have we ourselves tested each of the absolute laws which we accept unquestioningly because people have been repeating them to us over the centuries?'

'The same argument could apply to the belief in the existence of God or the Devil, which the Church has upheld for centuries—'

'Indeed, and you are right to question that, though perhaps not for the reasons you think. Find out for yourself, search for God, search for the Devil, then draw your own conclusions, but don't judge other people's beliefs. Millions live lives based on faith: faith in God, a spaceship that will take them to Orion, the belief that by blowing themselves to bits they will enter paradise, where honey flows from fountains and virgins attend their every need. What difference does it make? If you want to understand, you must stop thinking about whether it's logical, and start accepting that faith is real, it has consequences in the real world, people are prepared to kill for their beliefs. Now consider the question again.'

'Okay, why children, and what is done to them?'

'Children under two are used in ritual sacrifices. Often they are bled to death. In some cases they are dismembered, and the body parts used. Skulls are highly prized, as are the longer bones, like the *mairu-beso* used in the desecrations at Arizkun. Other rituals make use of teeth, nails, hair and powdered bone made by crushing up the smaller bones. Of all the liturgical objects used in witchcraft, the bodies of small children are the most highly valued.'

'Why children under two?'

'Because they are in a transitional phase,' Jonan broke in. 'Many cultures believe that, prior to reaching that age, children move between two worlds, enabling them to see and hear what happens in both. This makes them the perfect vehicle for communicating with the spirit world, or obtaining favours.'

'That's correct. Children develop instinctual learning up to the age of two: standing, walking, holding objects, and other imitative behaviour. After that, they start to develop language, they cross a barrier, and their relationship with their surroundings changes. They cease to make such good vehicles, although similarly, youths of pre-pubescent age are also prized by those practising witchcraft.'

'If someone stole a corpse for such purposes, where might they take it?'

'Well, as a detective I imagine you've already worked that out: to a remote place, where they can perform their rituals without fear of being discovered. Although, I think I see where you're going with this. You're imagining temples, churches or other holy places. And you'd be quite right if we were talking about Satanism, whose aim is not only to worship the Devil, but also to offend God. However, witchcraft is a far more wide-ranging branch of evil than Satanism, and the two aren't as closely related as you might think. Many creeds use human remains as vehicles for obtaining favours; for example, Voodoo, Santería, Palo and Candomblé, which summon deities as well as dead spirits. They perform their rituals in holy places as a way of desecrating them. And, of course, Arizkun is situated in the Baztán Valley, which has a long tradition of witchcraft, and of summoning Aker, the devil.'

Amaia remained silent for a few seconds, looking out of the window at the gloomy Pamplona sky to avoid the priest's probing gaze. The two men said nothing, aware that behind Amaia's calm appearance her brain was working hard. When she turned once more to Sarasola, her sarcasm had given way to resolve.

'Dr Sarasola, do you know what Inguma is?'

'Mau Mau, or Inguma. Not what, but who. In Sumerian demonology, he is known as Lamashtu, an evil spirit as old as time, one of the most terrible, cruel demons, surpassed only by Pazazu – the Sumerian name for Lucifer. Lamashtu would tear babies from their mother's breast to feed on their flesh and drink their blood, or cause babies to die suddenly during sleep. Demons that killed babies while they slept existed in ancient cultures too: in Turkey they were known as "crushing demons", while in Africa the name translates literally as "demon that rides on your back". Among the Hmong people he is known as the "torturing demon", and in the Philippines the phenomenon is known as *bangungut*, and the perpetrator is an old woman called Batibat. In Japan, Sudden Infant Death Syndrome is known as *pokkuri*. Henry Fuseli's famous painting *The Nightmare* portrays a young woman asleep on a chaise longue while a hideous demon crouches on her chest. Oblivious to his presence, the woman appears to be trapped in a nightmare. The demon has many different names, but his method is always the same: he creeps into the rooms of sleeping victims at night and sits on their chests, sometimes clutching their throats, producing a terrifying feeling of suffocation. During this nightmare, they may be conscious, but unable to move or wake up. At other times Inguma places his mouth over that of the sleeper, sucking out their breath until they expire.'

'Do you believe . . .?'

'I'm a priest, Inspector, and you're still thinking about this in the wrong way. Naturally, I'm a believer, but what matters is the power of these myths. In Rome, every morning at dawn, an Exorcism Prayer is performed. Various priests pray for the liberation of possessed souls, and afterwards they attend to people who come to them asking for help. Many are psychiatric cases, but by no means all.'

'And yet exorcism has been shown to have a placebo effect on people who believe themselves to be possessed.'

'Inspector, have you heard of the Hmong? They are an ethnic group that live in the mountainous regions of China, Vietnam, Laos and Thailand, and who collaborated with the Americans during the Vietnam War. When the conflict ended, their fellow countrymen condemned them, and many fled to the United States. In 1980, the Center for Disease Control in Atlanta recorded an extraordinary rise in the number of sudden deaths during sleep: two hundred and thirty Hmong men died of asphyxia in their sleep in the US, but many more were affected; survivors claimed to see an old witch crouched over them, squeezing their throats tight. Alerted to what was happening, parents began sleeping next to their sons to rouse them from these nightmares. When the attacks took place, they would shake them awake, or drag them out of bed. The most terrifying part was that, trapped in their waking dream, the boys could see the sinister old woman, feel her crooked fingers on their throats. This didn't happen in a remote region of Thailand, but in places like New York, Boston, Chicago, Los Angeles . . . All over the country, every night, Hmong men suffered such attacks. Those who didn't succumb were kept under strict surveillance in hospital, where the invisible attacks, in which the victims seemed to be strangled by some invisible creature, were witnessed and videoed. Doctors were at a loss to diagnose a specific illness. The Hmong's own shamans concluded that the demon was targeting this particular gener-ation of Hmong because they had become distanced from their centuries-old traditions and protections. Requests to perform purification rites around the victims were mostly refused, because they involved animal sacrifice, even though in cases where permission was granted, the attacks ceased.

'In 1917, seven hundred and twenty-two people died in their sleep in the Philippines, suffocated by *Batibat*, which translates literally as "the fat old woman". And in 1959 in Japan, five hundred healthy young men died at the hands of *pokkuri*. It is believed that when Inguma awakens, he goes on a murderous rampage until his thirst is quenched, or until he is stopped by some other means. In the case of the Hmong people, the phenomenon that claimed the lives of two hundred and thirty healthy boys remains unsolved to this day.' His eyes fixed on Amaia. 'Even science could offer no explanation: autopsies were carried out, but the cause of death could not be determined.'

# 14

In accordance with Amaia's orders, Dr San Martín had started the autopsy without them. When she and Etxaide approached the steel table, at the centre of a room filled with medical students, the pathologist had his back to them, and was busy weighing the internal organs on a scale. He turned, smiling when he saw them.

'Just in time, we're almost done. The toxicology tests show high levels of an extremely powerful sedative. We've identified the active ingredient, but I won't hazard a guess as to the name of the drug. As a doctor, Berasategui would have known which one to use and how much to take. Most are injectable, but the small abrasions on the sides of the tongue suggest he took it orally.'

Amaia leaned over to examine through the magnifying glass the row of tiny blisters either side of the tongue, which San Martín was holding up for her with a pair of forceps.

'I can smell a sweet, acidic odour,' she remarked.

'Yes, it's more noticeable now. Perhaps the cologne Berasategui doused himself in masked it. A vain fellow indeed.'

Amaia examined the body as she listened to San Martín. The 'Y' incision started at the shoulders, travelling down the chest to the pelvis, laying bare the glistening insides, whose vivid colours had always fascinated her. On this occasion, San Martín and his team had forced open the ribcage to extract and weigh the internal organs, doubtless interested to see the effects of a powerful sedative on a healthy young male. The startlingly white ribs pointed up towards the ceiling. The denuded bones had a surreal look, like the frame of a boat, or a dead whale's skeleton, or the long, eerie fingers of some inner creature trying to climb out of his dead body. No other surgical procedure quite resembled an autopsy; the only word that came close to describing it was wondrous. She understood the fascination it held for Ripper-type murderers, many of whom were skilled at making precise incisions at exactly the right depth to enable them to extract the organs in a particular order without damaging them.

Amaia observed the assistants and medical students, listening attentively to San Martín, as he pointed to the different sections of the liver, explaining how it had stopped functioning. By then, Berasategui was almost certainly unconscious. He had sought a dignified, painless death, but even he couldn't avoid the procedure, which, he knew would inevitably follow. Berasategui hadn't wanted to die, he had certainly never considered taking his own life. A narcissist like him would only have accepted suicide if he were forced to relinquish the control he exercised over others. And yet she had seen for herself how he had surmounted that obstacle in prison. He'd done what he did, against his own will, and that constituted a discrepancy, an abnormal element, which Amaia couldn't ignore. Berasategui had wept over his own suicide like a condemned man forced to walk a green mile from which there was no return.

Turning to share her thoughts with Jonan, she saw that he was standing back, behind the students gathered around San Martín. Arms folded, he was gazing at the nightmarish vision of the wet, naked corpse splayed open on a table, ribs exposed to the air.

'Come closer, Deputy Inspector Etxaide, I've been saving the stomach until last . . . I thought you'd be interested to see the contents, although there's no doubt he swallowed the sedative.'

One of the assistants placed a strainer over a beaker, and then, tilting the stomach, which San Martín had clamped at one end, she emptied the viscid, yellow contents into the receptacle. The stench of vomit mixed with the tranquiliser was nauseating. Amaia looked on as Jonan retched, and the students exchanged knowing looks.

'Here we see traces of sedative,' said San Martín, 'indicating that he reduced his food and liquid intake in order to absorb the drug more rapidly. The contact of the drug with the mucous membrane stimulated the production of stomach acid. It would be interesting to dissect the intestine, trachea and oesophagus to see how it affected those organs.'

The suggestion was greeted with general enthusiasm except by Amaia.

'We'd love to stay, Doctor, but have to get back to Elizondo. If you'd be so kind as to give us the name of the sedative as soon as possible; we already know one of the guards supplied him with it, and probably also removed the empty phial. Having the name would help us find out how he got hold of it and whether he acted alone.'

Jonan was visibly relieved at the news. After saying goodbye to San Martín, he walked ahead of her towards the exit, trying not to touch anything. Amaia followed, amused at his behaviour.

'Hold on a moment.' San Martín handed over the reins to one of his assistants, and, tossing his gloves into a waste bin, plucked an envelope from his pigeonhole. 'The test results of the decaying matter on the toy bear.'

Amaia's interest quickened.

'I thought they'd take much longer . . .'

'Yes, the process was problematic because of the singular

87

nature of the sample. Doubtless a copy will be waiting for you in Elizondo, but since you're here . . .'

'What's so special about the sample? Isn't it saliva?'

'Possibly. In fact, everything suggests that it is indeed saliva. The singularity resides in the vast quantity of bacteria present in the fluid, hence the ghastly stench. And, of course, the fact that it isn't human.'

'It *is* saliva, but it *isn't* human? Where is it from then, an animal?'

'The fluid resembles saliva, and it could come from an animal, although, judging from those levels of bacteria, I'd say a dead one. I'm no expert in zoology, but the only animal I can think of is a Komodo dragon.'

Amaia's eyes opened wide with surprise.

'I know,' declared San Martín. 'It sounds absurd, and, needless to say we have no sample of Komodo dragon saliva with which to compare it. But that's what came to mind when I saw the amount of bacteria it contained. Enough to cause septicaemia in anyone who touched it.'

'I know a zoologist who might be able to help us. Has a sample been kept?'

He shook his head. 'It was relatively fresh when the toy bear arrived at the lab, but I'm afraid it degraded too quickly to be of use.'

Amaia always let Jonan drive when she needed to think. Berasategui's suicide had taken them by surprise, but it was the conversation with Sarasola that was occupying her mind. The murder of Valentín Esparza's little girl, his attempt to make off with her body, a body he insisted shouldn't be cremated. But more than anything, it was the coffin weighted with bags of sugar that had brought back the painful image of another white coffin resting in her family vault in San Sebastián; only a month ago she had prised it open to discover that someone had replaced the body with bags of gravel.

She needed to question Valentín Esparza again. He had read out his statement before the magistrate, adding nothing new. He admitted to taking his daughter's dead body because he wanted to be with her for a while. But it was his remark about giving up his daughter to Inguma, the demon that robbed children's breath, 'like all the other sacrifices', that continued to echo in her head. He had smothered his daughter. Traces of his skin and saliva had been found on the toy; besides the mystery of the unknown bacteria, the method was painfully familiar.

She called ahead to Elizondo to convene a meeting as soon as they arrived, but otherwise she hardly spoke during the journey. It wasn't raining that afternoon, although it was so damp and cold that Jonan decided to park in the garage. As she was reaching to open the car door, she turned to him.

'Jonan, could you collect some data on the frequency of Sudden Infant Death Syndrome in the valley in the last five years, say?'

'Of course, I'll get on to it right away,' he said with a smile.

'And you can wipe that grin off your face. I don't believe for a moment that a demon is responsible for the Esparza girl's death. However, I have a witness who says that a sect was set up in a farmhouse here in the valley in the seventies, a sort of hippy commune. They started to dabble in the occult, and went as far as carrying out ritual animal sacrifices. The witness claims there was some talk about sacrificing humans, specifically newborn babies. When the witness stopped attending the meetings, she was harassed by some of the other sect members. She can't remember exactly how long the gatherings continued, but in all likelihood the group eventually dispersed. As I say, it was clearly the father not a demon who killed that child. But in light of Esparza's attempt to abduct the body, together with what Sarasola told us, and the proliferation of sects and other cults known to European police forces, I think it's worth checking for any statistical anomalies in infant death rates here in the valley compared to other regions and countries.'

'Do you think your sister's body may have suffered the same fate?'

'I don't know, Jonan, but the feeling of déjà vu when I saw the photographs of that empty coffin convinced me we're looking at the same modus operandi. This isn't evidence, it's just a hunch, which may lead nowhere. Let's compare your data with that of our colleagues, and then we'll see.'

She was about to enter the house when her phone rang. The screen showed an unknown number.

'Inspector Salazar,' she said, answering.

'Is it nighttime already in Baztán, Inspector?'

She recognised instantly the gravelly voice on the other end of the phone, even though he was speaking in a whisper.

'Aloisius! But, what is this number . . .?'

'It's a safe number, but you mustn't call me on it. I'll call you when you need me.'

She didn't bother to ask how he would know when she needed him. Somehow their relationship had always been like that. She moved away from the house and spent the next few minutes explaining to Dupree everything she knew about the case: her belief that her mother was alive, the dead girl that had to be given up, Elena Ochoa's behaviour, Berasategui's message from her mother, and his staged suicide. The unusual saliva sample resembling that of an ancient reptile which only existed on the far away island of Komodo . . .'

He listened to her in silence, and, when she had finished, he asked:

'You're faced with a complex puzzle, but that's not why you called . . . What did you want to ask me about?'

'The dead girl's great grandmother claimed that a demon by the name of Inguma entered through a crack, sat on the girl's chest, and sucked the air from her lungs; she says that this demon has appeared on other occasions, and taken many children's lives. Father Sarasola explained to me that Inguma exists in other cultures: Sumerian, African, and Hmong, as well as in the old, dark folktales of the Baztán Valley.'

She heard a deep sigh on the other end of the phone. Then nothing. Silence.

'Aloisius, are you there?'

'I can't talk any more. I'll try to send you something in the next few days . . . I have to hang up now.'

The disconnection tone reached her through the earpiece.

# 15

Ros Salazar had smoked from the age of seventeen up until the moment when she decided she wanted to become a mother. But apparently that wasn't to be. Since separating from Freddy, her relations with men had amounted to a few half-hearted flirtations in bars; Elizondo didn't offer too many other options when it came to finding a partner, so the chances of meeting someone new were minimal. And yet she still found herself increasingly obsessed about her prospects of becoming a mother, even though in her case that would probably mean going it alone. With that in mind, she had refrained from taking up smoking again, although occasionally, late at night, after her aunt went to bed, she would roll a joint. Afterwards, on the pretext of getting some fresh air, she would walk to the bakery. There she would sit in her office, peacefully smoking, enjoying the solitude of remaining behind in her place of business after everyone else had gone home.

She was surprised to see that the lights were still on, her immediate assumption being that Ernesto had forgotten to switch them off before locking up. As she opened the door, she noticed that her office light was also on. She reached for her phone, punched in the number for the emergency services, her finger poised over the call button, then shouted:

'Who's there? The police are on their way.'

She heard a sudden noise of things being moved, a thud followed by a rustle.

Just as she pressed the button, Flora's voice rang out:

'Ros, it's only me . . .'

'Flora?' she said, ending the call and approaching the office. 'What are you doing here? I thought we were being burgled.'

'I . . .' Flora faltered. 'I thought . . . I was sure I'd forgotten something, and I came to see if I'd left it here.'

'What?'

Flora glanced about nervously.

'My bag,' she lied.

'Your bag?' repeated Ros. 'Well, it's not here.'

'I can see that, and I was just leaving,' she said, pushing past her sister towards the exit.

A moment later, Ros heard the heavy door of the bakery slam shut. She scanned the office, scrutinising each object. She had surprised Flora doing something suspicious, that much was clear, something that had caused her to make up that ridiculous excuse about her bag. But what could have prompted her to sneak into the bakery in the middle of the night?

Ros moved the swivel chair out from behind the desk and placed it in the centre of the room. She sat down, felt in her pocket for the joint she had brought with her, and lit it. She took a long draw, which made her feel dizzy. She exhaled, leaning back in the chair and turning in a slow circle, letting each object in the room tell its story. One hour and several turns later, her eye alighted on the wall where her favourite painting of the covered market hung. She would often contemplate the scene, because of the calm it radiated, but that wasn't what drew her attention now. The painting had spoken. She rose to make sure she had interpreted its message correctly, smiling when she saw the heel marks left by Flora's shoes on the sofa below. She stood on the same spot, and lifted the frame, which was heavier than she'd expected.

She wasn't surprised to see the safe, she knew it was there; Flora had installed it years ago, to keep the cash with which to pay their suppliers. Nowadays, she paid them by bank transfer, so, to all intents and purposes, the safe should have been empty. Resting the painting on the sofa, Ros ran her fingers over the wheel lock, although she realised there was no point in trying the combination. She returned to the chair, gazing at that box buried in the wall, musing over many things until the small hours of the morning.

It had started to rain before dawn. Amaia had been aware of the rhythmical pitter-patter against the bedroom shutters during the many micro-awakenings that plagued her sleep, and which she found particularly irksome now that Ibai had started to sleep through. Although the rain had stopped by the time she got up, the wet streets were uninviting, and it came as a relief to enter the warm, dry police station.

As she made her way in, she greeted Montes, Zabalza and Iriarte, gathered as usual around the coffee machine.

'Do you fancy a coffee, boss?' Montes asked.

Amaia paused, noting with amusement Zabalza's sulky expression.

'Thanks, Inspector, but there's no pleasure in drinking coffee out of a plastic cup. I'll make myself a proper one later, in a mug.'

Deputy Inspector Etxaide was waiting for her in her office.

'Boss, I've dug up some interesting facts about SIDS.'

She hung up her coat, switched on her computer and sat down at her desk.

'I'm listening.'

'Sudden Infant Death Syndrome, or SIDS, is the name given to unexplained deaths among babies younger than one, but sometimes as old as two. Death occurs during sleep and is apparently painless. Two out of every thousand babies in Europe die of SIDS, ninety per cent within the first six months. Statistically, SIDS is the most widespread cause of death among healthy babies over one month old, although that is largely because if no other cause is discovered during autopsy, death is attributed to SIDS.'

He placed a printout on the desk in front of her. 'I've made a list of the various risk factors, and how to minimise them, although they're fairly wide-ranging; from prenatal care, breastfeeding and passive smoking, through to how the baby is positioned during sleep. Interestingly, most deaths occur in winter. The average number of deaths in Spain from SIDS is the same as in the rest of Europe. Seventeen children died from SIDS in Navarre in the last five years, four of them in Baztán – numbers which are also well within the norm.'

Amaia looked at him, considering the information.

'In all cases, an autopsy was performed and the cause of death was registered as SIDS. However, in two of them, the pathologist recommended that social services investigate the family,' he said, handing her a sheaf of stapled pages. 'There's no additional information, but it seems both cases were closed without any further action being taken.'

After knocking gently, Montes poked his head round the door.

'I hope I'm not interrupting. Etxaide, are you coming for a coffee?'

Clearly surprised by the invitation, Jonan glanced at Amaia, arching his eyebrows.

'Go ahead, it'll give me time to read through all this,' she said, holding up the report.

After Jonan had gone out, Montes poked his head round the door again, and winked.

'Get out of here!' she said, grinning.

As Montes left, Iriarte entered.

'A woman has been found dead,' he announced. 'Her daughter drove all the way from Pamplona to check up on her because she wasn't answering the phone. Apparently, when she got there the mother had vomited huge amounts of blood. She rang the emergency services, but paramedics couldn't save the woman. The doctor who examined the body suspects that something isn't right, so he called us . . .'

Driving across the bridge, she could see in the distance various vehicles belonging to the emergency services. It was only when they reached the end of the street that Amaia saw which house they were attending. In that instant, all the air seemed to be sucked out of the car, leaving her gasping for breath.

'Do you know the dead woman's name?'

'Ochoa,' said Iriarte. 'I can't remember her first name.'

'Elena Ochoa.'

She needed no confirmation from Iriarte. A pale, distraught woman, looking like a younger version of her mother, stood smoking a cigarette outside the front door. Next to her, a man, presumably her partner, had his arm around her, practically holding her up.

She passed by without speaking to them, walked along the narrow corridor, and was guided to the bedroom by a paramedic. The heat in the room had intensified the pungent smell of blood and urine emanating from the pool surrounding Elena's body. She was on her knees, jammed between the bed and a chest of drawers, arms clasped about her midriff, body leaning forward so that her face was resting in a patch of bloody bile. Amaia was relieved that Elena's eyes were closed. Whereas her posture betrayed what must have been the agony of her final moments, her face appeared relaxed, as if the precise instant of death had been a great release.

Amaia turned towards the doctor, who stood waiting behind her.

'Inspector Iriarte told me you'd found some anomaly . . .'

'Yes, at first I thought she must have suffered a massive internal haemorrhage that filled her stomach with blood, causing her lungs to collapse. But when I looked closer, I could see that her vomit was made up of what appear to be tiny splinters.'

Amaia leaned over the pool of bloody vomit and saw that it did indeed contain hundreds of wood shavings.

Crouching down beside her, the doctor showed her a plastic container.

'I took a sample, and this is what was left after washing off the blood.'

'But, surely those are—'

'Walnut shells, cut into razor-thin slices . . . I can't begin to think how she swallowed them, but ingesting this amount would certainly perforate her stomach, duodenum, and trachea. Worst of all, when she vomited them up again, they must have torn her insides to shreds. She seems to have been prescribed anti-depressants. They're on top of the microwave oven in the kitchen. Of course, she may not have been taking them. I can't think of a more horrible way to kill oneself.'

Elena Ochoa's daughter had inherited her mother's appearance, her name and her hospitality towards guests. She insisted on making coffee for everyone in the house. Amaia had tried to protest, but the boyfriend intervened.

'It will take her mind off things,' he said.

From the same chair she had occupied during her most recent visit, Amaia watched the young woman moving about the kitchen. As before, she waited until the cups had been set out and the coffee poured before speaking.

'I knew your mother.'

'She never mentioned you,' said the daughter, surprised.

'I didn't know her well. I came here a couple of times to ask her about my mother, Rosario; they were friends in their youth,' she explained. 'During my last visit, she seemed agitated.

Had you noticed anything strange about your mother's behaviour in the last few days?'

'My mother has always suffered with her nerves. She became depressed after my father passed away. She never really got over it. I was seven at the time. She had good days and bad, but she was always fragile. It's true that, in the last month or so, she was beginning to show signs of paranoia. On the other occasions when that happened, the doctor advised me to be firm, not to feed her fears. But this time I could tell she was genuinely terrified.'

'You know her better than anyone. Do you think your mother was capable of taking her own life?'

'You mean, did she kill herself? Never, not in a million years. She was a practising Catholic. Surely you don't think . . . My mother died of internal bleeding. She complained of stomach pains when I spoke to her on the phone yesterday. She said she'd taken an antacid and some painkillers, and was going to try drinking camomile tea. I offered to drive up and see her after work. I've been living in Pamplona with Luis for a year,' she said, indicating the young man. 'We come up most weekends and stay the night. Anyway, she told me not to bother, that it was just a bit of heartburn. Last night, I called her again at bedtime and she told me the camomile tea had helped. But when I called early this morning she didn't answer . . .'

'Elena, the doctor found shards of walnut shell in her vomit – too many for her to have swallowed them accidentally. He also suggests that the internal bleeding was caused by her vomiting them up.'

'But that's impossible,' the young woman replied. 'My mother hated walnuts, the very sight of them sent her into a panic. She refused to have them in the house – I know, because I did all her shopping. She would rather have dropped dead than touch one. When I was little, a woman came up to me in the street once and gave me a handful of walnuts. When I got home, my mother acted like I'd brought poison into the house. She made me throw them outside, and searched my things to make sure I hadn't kept any. Then she scrubbed me from head to foot and incinerated my clothes while I cried my eyes out, terrified. She made me swear never to accept walnuts from anyone – obviously, after that, I didn't. Although, oddly enough, the same woman offered me walnuts several times over the following years. So, you see, my mother would never have eaten them knowingly. There must be some other explanation.'

'I've seen many suicides like this,' said Dr San Martín, 'often among the prison population. They're always gruesome. Remember Quiralte, the fellow who swallowed rat poison? And I've seen cases of people ingesting crushed glass, ammoniac, metal shavings . . . It's the serene deaths like Dr Berasategui's that are exceptional, not the horrific ones.'

'Doctor, could she have swallowed the walnut shavings accidentally, perhaps mixed into food?' asked Iriarte.

'I'll be able to tell you more when I've examined the stomach contents, though, judging from the quantity of shavings present in her vomit, I'd say that's unlikely, if not impossible.' He turned to Markina: 'If you have no further questions, your honour, I'd like to get the autopsy under way as soon as possible.'

Markina nodded his approval and the pathologist turned to Amaia. 'Will you be attending the autopsy, Inspector Salazar?'

'I'll be going,' broke in Iriarte. 'The victim was known to the inspector's family.'

Dr San Martín murmured his condolences and set off briskly towards his car. A moment later, Amaia hurried after him, tapped on the window, and leaned in to speak to him.

'Doctor, about the little Esparza girl: we've been looking

at recent cases of cot death in the area and there were a couple that caught our attention. In both cases, the pathologist recommended that social services look into the victim's family.'

'How long ago was this?'

'About five years.'

'Then it must have been Maite Hernández – she was the other resident pathologist at the time. I try to avoid carrying out autopsies on small children, so she must have handled the cases you're talking about.' Amaia recalled San Martín's sorrow as he contemplated the little Esparza girl's body; how he had looked away, as if shamed by his natural feeling of revulsion. If anything, that display of humanity had made him go up in her estimation, though she'd always admired his professionalism and his ability to juggle work and, his great passion, teaching.

'Dr Hernández was awarded a post at Universidad del País Vasco,' he went on. 'I'll call her when I get back to my office. I'm sure she won't object to speaking to you.'

Amaia thanked him and stood watching as he drove off. The street was now empty of vehicles; and the neighbours had returned to their houses for lunch, driven inside by the rain. As she gazed along the row of houses, Amaia glimpsed shadows moving behind the shutters, even the odd window cracked open despite the increasingly heavy downpour: clearly the neighbours were keeping an eye on proceedings.

Markina put up his umbrella, holding it over her.

'I've been to your village more times in the past few days than in my entire life. Not that I mind.' He grinned at her. 'In fact, I've been thinking of coming here, though I'd hoped for different reasons.'

Eager to get away from the indiscreet windows overlooking Calle Giltxaurdi, she didn't reply but set off down the street, confident that he would follow.

'You never called me back, and yet you knew I was worried

about you. Why won't you tell me how you are? So much has been going on these past few days.'

Omitting any mention of her visit with Sarasola, she briefed him on her conclusions about Berasategui's death, how they thought he'd obtained the drug he'd used to end his life.

'We've looked into the missing prison guard. He wasn't one of the two who were present during my interview with Berasategui; they had already been suspended. He lives with his parents, who didn't object to showing us his room. In it, we found a plastic bag from a chemist's on the other side of town. When we showed the pharmacist a photograph of the guard, he remembered him instantly, because he wasn't often asked to supply that particular sedative in liquid form. He checked the prescription, as well as Berasategui's name – which hadn't been struck off the medical register. And since everything appeared to be in order, he had no choice but to dispense the drug. CCTV footage from the prison clearly shows the guard outside the cell, doubtless waiting for Berasategui to take the drug so that he could retrieve the empty vial. We've put out a search warrant on him, and have checked that he isn't with any of his relatives. No news on that front for the moment.'

They had reached the old covered market. All at once, Markina stopped dead in his tracks, obliging her to do the same in order to remain under the shelter of his umbrella. He moved forward a couple of steps and then stopped again, grinning. She couldn't decide if he was teasing her or incredibly happy to see her; he gazed at her in silence for a few seconds, until, finally overwhelmed, she lowered her eyes, only long enough to collect herself, and said:

'What is it?'

'When I complained just now that you hadn't been in touch, I wasn't referring to how the investigation was going.'

She lowered her gaze once more, smiling this time. When she looked up again she was back in control.

'Well, that's all the news you'll get from me,' she retorted.

His smile faded. 'Do you remember what I told you when we left Berasategui's apartment that night?'

Amaia didn't reply.

'My feelings haven't changed, and they aren't going to.'

He was standing very close. His nearness aroused her; his voice, merging with the vivid memory of her dream the night before, instantly evoked the warmth of his lips, his mouth, his embrace . . .

When a large cultural foundation chose to sponsor an artist's work, their decision was based on advice from their art and finance consultants, who would take into account the artist's talent and the quality of their work, as well as their likely future success, and the long-term cost effectiveness of the investment. Thanks to glowing reviews of James's exhibition at the Guggenheim in the prestigious journals *Art News* and *Art in America*, the prices his work could command had risen. Now he was on his way to a meeting in Pamplona with representatives of the Banque National de Paris Foundation, hopeful that the outcome would be a major commission.

Adjusting the rear-view mirror, James grinned at his reflection in the glass. Heading for the motorway, his route took him through Txokoto towards Giltxaurdi Bridge. As he drove down the street near the old market, he saw Amaia sheltering under an umbrella held aloft by a man, the two of them in conversation. Slowing down, he lowered the window to call out to her. But something at once imperceptible and obvious made his voice freeze on his lips. The man was leaning in towards her as he spoke, oblivious to everything around him, while she listened, eyes lowered. It was raining and they were huddled beneath the umbrella, inches apart, and yet it wasn't their proximity that troubled him, but rather the expression in her eyes when she looked up: they were shining with defiance, the challenge of a contest. James knew that was the one thing Amaia couldn't resist, because she was a warrior governed by the goddess Palas: Amaia Salazar never surrendered without a fight.

James closed the car window, and drove on without stopping. The smile had vanished from his face.

# 16

She swallowed a mouthful of cold coffee, screwing up her face in disgust as she banished the cup to the edge of her desk. She had eaten nothing since breakfast; the vision of Elena Ochoa, slumped over in a pool of her own blood, had taken away her appetite, as well as something else: the slim hope that Elena might have eventually overcome her fears and talked. If only she had told her where the sect's house was located . . . She sensed it played a vital role.

Elena's death, coming on the heels of Berasategui's, had confounded her. She felt that events were slipping through her fingers, as if she were trying to hold back the River Baztán. In front of her on the desk was a pile of papers: Deputy Inspector Etxaide's report on cot deaths in the area; a transcript of her conversation with Valentín Esparza in his cell; Berasategui's autopsy report; a few sheets of A4 filled with her scribbled notes. Unfortunately, after digesting the contents she was left with the impression that nothing stacked up: she was at an impasse, rudderless. She skimmed through the sheets of paper, frustrated.

She checked the time on her watch: coming up to four o'clock. San Martín had called her an hour earlier to give her the number of the pathologist who had carried out the autopsies on the babies mentioned in Jonan's report. He had briefed the woman and arranged that Amaia would call her at four o'clock. She picked up the telephone, waiting until the last second before dialling the number.

If the doctor was surprised by her punctuality, she didn't mention it.

'Dr San Martín told me you are interested in two particular cases. I remember them well, but I've dug out my notes, to be on the safe side. Two healthy female babies, with nothing in their autopsies to suggest they died from anything other than natural causes – if we consider death from SIDS to be a natural cause. Both the doctors who signed the respective death certificates entered SIDS as the cause. One of the babies was sleeping on her front, the other on her back. In both cases, my misgivings were caused by the parents' behaviour.'

'Their behaviour?'

'I met with one couple at the request of the father. He became threatening, told me that he'd read about pathologists holding on to people's organs, and that his daughter had better be intact after the autopsy. I tried to reassure him that organs were only removed in cases where the family had given their consent, or if a person left their body to research. But what shocked me most was when he declared that he knew how much a dead child's organs could fetch on the black market. I told him that if he meant donor organs then he was mistaken; they would need to be removed under strict medical conditions immediately post-mortem. He insisted he wasn't referring to the black market in donor organs, but in dead bodies. His wife tried to shut him up, she kept apologising to me, and blaming his outburst on the trauma they were going through. But I believed he was serious; despite being an ignorant oaf, he knew what he was talking about. The reason why I contacted social services was primarily because I felt sorry for their other child, the baby's older brother, sitting in the waiting room, listening to his father mouth off like that. I didn't think it would do any harm if they took a look at the family.

'The other couple's behaviour was also shocking, but in a completely different way. When I walked into the waiting room at the Institute of Forensic Medicine to tell them we would soon be releasing their daughter's body, far from grieving they looked positively euphoric. I've seen many responses in my time, ranging from sorrow through to utter indifference, but when I left that room and heard the husband assure his wife that from then on their fortunes would improve, I confess I was shocked. I thought they might be words of reassurance, but when I turned to look at them, they were smiling. Not in a forced way, as if they were trying to be strong, but because they were happy.' The doctor paused as she remembered. 'I've seen deeply religious people respond to the death of their loved ones in a similar way, because they believe they are going to heaven, but in those cases, the dominant emotion is resignation. This couple weren't resigned, they were joyous.

'I alerted social services because they had two other young children, aged two and three, and the family were living in a relative's basement apartment with no central heating. The husband had been on benefits his whole life. According to the social worker, despite the hardships they clearly suffered, the surviving children were well looked after, as was the brother of the other deceased baby. So, no further action was taken.'

Amaia was about to speak when the pathologist added: 'When Dr San Martín called me today, I remembered a third case, back in March 1997, towards the end of the Easter holidays. The date stuck in my mind because a train derailed in Huarte Arakil killing eighteen people, so we were inundated, and then a case of cot death came in. On this occasion too, the parents asked to see me, refusing to leave until they had spoken to me. It was pitiful. The wife was dying of cancer. They begged me to speed up the process so that they could take the body. Again, they appeared less grief-stricken than one would expect under the circumstances. Indeed, the contrast between that couple and the distraught relatives of the train-crash victims couldn't have been starker. They might as well have been waiting to pick up their car from the garage. I checked at the time, and they had no other children so there was no cause for social services to be involved.

'Give me an address, and I'll send you my notes, together with the number of the social worker who dealt with the other two cases, in case you want to speak to her.'

'One other thing, Doctor,' Amaia said.

'Of course.'

'The last case you mentioned – was that a baby girl, too?'

There was a pause while the doctor checked her notes.

'Yes, a baby girl.'

Within an hour, the social worker had dug out the files and returned Amaia's call. Both cases had been closed with no further action taken. One family had received financial assistance, which they'd elected to discontinue. That was all the information she had.

Amaia called Jonan. To her surprise, he seemed to have switched off his mobile. Crossing the corridor, she knocked gently on the open door of the room where Zabalza and Montes were working.

'Inspector Montes, could we have a word in my office?'

He did as she asked, closing the door behind him.

'Deputy Inspector Etxaide has put together a report on all the families in Baztán who have lost children to SIDS. At first glance, nothing stands out, but the pathologist referred two couples to social services. During our conversation, she referred to a third case in which the parents also behaved strangely. One of the couples, she said, seemed positively elated. Another received state benefits for a while, but then signed off. I'd like you to pay both families a visit this morning; invent whatever pretext you want, but avoid any mention of babies.'

Montes sighed. 'That's a hard one for me, boss,' he said, flicking through the reports. 'Nothing makes me more angry than parents who can't look after their kids.'

'Be honest, Montes, everything makes you angry,' she retorted. He flashed her a grin. 'Take Zabalza with you, it will do him good to get out of the office – besides, he's more tactful than you. Incidentally, have you any idea where Jonan is?'

'It's his afternoon off, he told me he had things to do . . .'

Amaia was busy jotting down what the pathologist and the social worker had told her; for a moment, she didn't notice that Montes was still hovering by the door.

'Fermín, was there anything else?'

He stood looking at her for a few seconds, then shook his head.

'No, nothing.'

He opened the door and went out into the corridor, leaving Amaia with the sensation that she was missing something important.

Preoccupied, she had to admit that she was getting nowhere. She put away the documents, and, glancing at her watch, remembered James's big meeting in Pamplona. She called his mobile and waited. He didn't pick up. Then she switched off her computer, grabbed her coat and headed home.

Recently, Aunt Engrasi and the Golden Girls appeared to have relinquished their regular card game in favour of a joyous ritual that consisted of passing Ibai from one lap to the next and making googly eyes at him as they clucked merrily. She managed with some effort to prise away the child, who was infected by the old ladies' laughter.

'You're spoiling him,' she chided jokingly. 'He's having too much fun, he won't go to sleep,' she added, whisking the baby upstairs amid their angry protests.

She placed Ibai in his cot while she prepared his bath, slipping out of her warm jumper, and placing her holstered gun on top of the wardrobe. She'd have to find a safer place for it, she reflected. Three-year-olds were like monkeys and could climb anything. Back in Pamplona, she kept it locked in the safe, and they were planning to install a safe at *Juanitaenea*. Her thoughts drifted to the pallets outside the house and the stalled building work. Picking up her phone, she tried James's mobile again; two rings only, as if he'd refused her call.

She took her time bathing Ibai; he loved being in the water, and she loved seeing her child so happy and relaxed. And yet she had to admit that James's silence was starting to affect her ability to enjoy even this special time with their son. Once Ibai was dry and in his pyjamas, she dialled James's number again, only to be cut off a second time. She sent a text: James. I'm worried, call me. A minute later he texted back: I'm busy.

Ibai fell asleep as soon as he had finished his bottle. She plugged in the baby monitor, then went down to sit with Ros and her aunt, who were watching television. She couldn't concentrate on anything that wasn't the sound of tyres on the cobblestones outside. Hearing James's car pull up, she slipped on her coat and went outside to greet him. He was sitting motionless in the car the engine switched off and the lights out. She climbed into the passenger seat.

'For heaven's sake, James! I was worried.'

'I'm here, aren't I?' he replied coolly.

'You could have called—'

'So could you,' he interrupted.

Stunned by his response, she went on the defensive.

'I called several times, but you didn't pick up.'

'Yeah, at six in the evening. Why didn't you call during the day?'

She accepted his reproach, then felt a flash of anger.

'So you saw my call but didn't pick up. What's going on, James?'

'You tell me, Amaia.'

109

'I've no idea what you're talking about.'

He shrugged.

'You don't know what I'm talking about? Fine, then there's no problem,' he said, making to get out of the car.

'James,' she restrained him with a gesture. 'Why are you doing this to me? I don't understand what's going on. All I know is that you had a meeting today with representatives of the Banque National de Paris. You haven't even told me how it went.'

'Do you care?'

She studied his profile as he stared straight ahead, jaw clenched in anger. Her handsome boy was getting frustrated, and she knew she was to blame. Softly, her voice laced with affection, she protested: 'How can you even ask me that? Of course I care, James – you mean more to me than anything in the world.'

He looked at her, struggling to keep a stern face as the expression in his eyes melted. He smiled weakly.

'It went okay,' he conceded.

'Oh, come on! Just okay, or really well?'

He beamed. 'It went well, incredibly well.'

She flung her arms around him, kneeling on her seat so that she could hold him tight. They kissed. Just then, her phone rang. James pulled a face as she fumbled for it in her pocket.

'I have to take this, it's the police station,' she said, freeing herself from the embrace.

'Inspector Salazar, Elena Ochoa's daughter just called. I wouldn't have bothered you, but she insisted, she says it's urgent . . . I've texted you her number.'

'I need to make a quick call,' she told James, clambering out of the car. Moving out of earshot, she dialled the number. Marilena Ochoa answered immediately.

'Inspector, I'm in Elizondo. After everything that's happened, we decided to stay the night. When I went to bed just now, I found a letter from my mother under the pillow.' The young woman's voice, which had sounded strong, buoyed by a sense of urgency, gave way as she started to cry. 'I can't believe it, but it seems you're right and she *did* take her own life . . . she left a note,' she said, overcome with grief. 'I did everything I could to help her, I did what the doctors said, I played down her paranoia, her fears . . . And she left a note. But not for me, for you.' The young woman broke down. Realising she would get no more sense out of her, Amaia waited until the person she could hear in the background trying to console Marilena came on the phone.

'Inspector, this is Luis, Marilena's boyfriend. Please come and get the letter.'

James had stepped out of the car. She walked over and stood looking up at him.

'James, it's within walking distance, I need to pick up a document here in Elizondo. I can walk there,' she added, as if to prove that she wouldn't be long.

He leaned forward to kiss her, and without saying a word entered the house.

# 17

Winter had returned with a vengeance after a lull of a few hours. She regretted not picking up her scarf and gloves on her way out as she felt the cold north wind blow through the empty streets of Elizondo. Turning up the collar of her coat, she clasped it about her neck and set off at a brisk pace towards Elena Ochoa's house. She rang the doorbell and waited, shivering in the wind. The boyfriend opened the door, but refrained from asking her in.

'She's exhausted,' he explained. 'She took a sleeping pill, and it's knocked her out.'

'I understand,' said Amaia. 'This is a terrible blow . . .'

He handed her a long white envelope, which she could see was unopened. Her name was written on the front. She slipped it into her pocket, noticing the look of relief on the young man's face as he watched it disappear.

'I'll keep you informed.'

'If that letter is what we think it is, please don't bother – she's suffered enough.'

Amaia followed the bend in the river, drawn by the orange lights in the square, which gave a false impression of warmth on that cold, dark night. She walked past the Lamia fountain, which only gushed water when it rained, and carried on walking until she came to the town hall, where she paused to run the fingers of one hand over the smooth surface of the *botil harri*. Her other hand was still clutching the envelope in her pocket; it gave off an unpleasant heat, as though contained within were the last flicker of the author's life.

The wind swept through the square in great gusts, making it impossible for her to stop and read the letter. She headed down Calle Jaime Urrutia, hesitating beneath each streetlamp looking for a sheltered spot. She didn't want to read it at home. Finding nowhere, she crossed the bridge, where the wind's roar vied with the noise of the weir. Reaching Hostal Trinkete, she turned right and made her way towards the only place where she knew she would enjoy complete solitude. She felt in her pocket for the silky cord her father had fastened to the key all those years ago. When she inserted it in the lock, the key turned halfway but would go no further. She tried again, even though she realised Ros had changed the lock on the bakery door. Surprised and pleased at her sister's initiative, she slipped the now useless key back in her pocket, her fingers brushing the envelope as she did so. It seemed to be calling to her, like a living creature. Walking into the wind, she set off at a brisk pace towards her aunt's house, but instead of going in, she climbed into her car and switched on the overhead light.

*I told you they would find out, and they did. I've always been careful, but I was right: there's no protection from them. Somehow they've put it inside me, I can feel it tearing at my guts. Like a fool, I thought it was heartburn, but as the hours go by I realise what's happening, it is devouring me, killing me, so I may as well tell you.*

*It's a rundown old farmhouse, with brown walls and a dark roof. I haven't been there for years, but they used to keep the shutters closed. You'll find it on the road to Orabidea, in the middle of a huge meadow, the only one*

113

*of its kind in the area. There are no trees, nothing grows there, and you can only see it from the bend in the road.*

*It's a black house, I don't mean the colour, but what's inside. I won't bother warning you not to go poking around there, because if you are who you claim to be, if you survived the fate they had in store for you, they'll find you anyway.*

*May God protect you,*
*Elena Ochoa*

The incongruous ring of her phone in the enclosed space of the car made her jump. She dropped Elena Ochoa's letter, which fell between the pedals. Nervous and confused, she answered the call, leaning forward to try to reach the piece of paper.

She could sense the weariness in Inspector Iriarte's voice at the end of what for him had been an arduous day. Amaia glanced at her watch, as she realised that she'd completely forgotten about Iriarte. It was gone eleven.

'They've just finished doing Elena Ochoa's post-mortem. I swear, I've never seen anything like it in my life, Inspector.' Amaia heard him take a deep breath, then exhale slowly. 'San Martín has recorded the cause of death as suicide by ingestion of sharp objects – talk about an understatement! But what else could he put? In all his years as a professional, he'd never seen the like either,' he said, giving a nervous laugh.

She felt the beginnings of a migraine and she started to shiver, vaguely aware that these physical sensations were related to Elena's letter, and to Inspector Iriarte's seeming inability to explain himself.

'Take me through it, Inspector,' she ordered.

'You saw the amount of walnut shavings she spewed up. Well, there were traces in the stomach too, but the intestines were full—'

'I understand.'

'No, you don't, Inspector. When I say "full", I mean literally filled to bursting, like an over-stuffed sausage. In some places, the shavings had perforated the intestinal wall, even reaching the surrounding organs.'

The migraine had suddenly taken hold; her head felt like a steel helmet being hammered from outside.

Iriarte took a deep breath and went on:

'Seven metres of small intestine and another metre and a half of large intestine, crammed with walnut shavings until they were twice the normal size. The doctor couldn't believe that the gut wall hadn't exploded. And do you know what the strangest thing was? He couldn't find a single piece of nut, only the shells.'

'What else did San Martín say? Could she have been force-fed?'

Iriarte sighed.

'Not while she was still alive. The intestine is highly sensitive; the pain would probably have killed her. I have photographs. San Martín is busy preparing the autopsy report. I expect we'll have it by tomorrow morning. I'm going home now, though I doubt I'll be able to sleep,' he added.

Convinced she wouldn't either, Amaia took a couple of sedatives. Then she slipped into bed alongside James and Ibai, letting the rhythmical breathing of her loved ones bring her the peace she so desperately needed. She spent the next few hours trying to read, gazing every now and then at the dark recess of the window, at the shutters open a crack so that from her side of the bed she could glimpse the first light of dawn.

Amaia wasn't aware of having fallen asleep, although she knew she had been sleeping when the intruder came in. She didn't hear her enter, she couldn't hear her footsteps or her breathing. She could smell her: the scent of her skin, her hair, her breath was engraved on Amaia's memory. A scent that rang alarm bells; the scent of her enemy, her executioner.

She felt a desperate panic, even as she cursed herself for having let down her guard, for having allowed her to come this close, for if Amaia could smell her, then she was too close.

The little girl inside her prayed to the god of all victims to take pity on them, alternating her prayer with the command that must never be disobeyed: *don't open your eyes*, *don't open your eyes*, *don't open your eyes*, *don't open your eyes*, *don't open your eyes*. She let out a scream of rage not of fear, a scream that came from the woman not the little girl: *You can't hurt me, you can't hurt me now*. Then she opened her eyes. Rosario was stooping over her bed, inches from her face, so close she was a blur; her eyes, nose and mouth blotting out the room, the cold still clinging to her garments, making Amaia shiver.

Rosario's grinning mouth became a slit in her face, her feverish eyes studying Amaia, amused at her fear. Amaia tried to scream, but the warm air she pushed out of her lungs with all her might died in her mouth. She realised with horror that she couldn't move. Her limbs felt leaden, immobilised under their own weight on the soft mattress. Seeing her prey paralysed, Rosario's smile widened, hardening as she drew closer, until her hair brushed Amaia's face. Closing her eyes, Amaia screamed as loud as she could and this time she managed to expel the air trapped inside her. Although the scream that rang out in her dream failed to emerge from the woman asleep on the bed, she managed to whisper the word 'no'. That was enough to wake her up.

Drenched in sweat, Amaia sat up in bed, snatching at the scarf draped over the lampshade to dim the light. She looked first at James and Ibai to make sure they were sleeping, then at the top of the wardrobe, where her gun still lay, as it did every night. She knew the instant she woke up that no one else was in the room, and yet she couldn't shake off the vivid sensations she'd experienced in her dream: her pulse was racing, her limbs felt heavy, her body ached from her attempts to free herself. And Rosario's smell . . .

She waited for her breathing to return to normal, before scrambling out of bed. Then she retrieved her gun, gathered some clean clothes and went to take a shower, hoping to wash the hateful imprint of that smell from her skin.

# 18

She began her search for the black house at dawn. Breakfast consisted of a cup of coffee, which she drank standing up, leaning against the kitchen table, gazing out of the window, where the Baztán sky showed no signs of a fresh dawn.

She drove along the main road from Elizondo to Oronoz-Mugaire, turning off at Orabidea. It was one of the most remote areas of the valley, a place where time seemed to have stood still, preserving intact the fields, farmhouses, all the natural charm and power of a place that was as harsh as it was beautiful. Several kilometres separated the farms, some of which were still without electricity. In the spring of last year, James had convinced her to visit *Infernuko Errota*, or Hell's Mill, one of the most magical, unique spots in Baztán. Fifteen kilometres further along that same road, a track led from Etxebertzeko Borda to the eponymous mill, hidden amid the vegetation. It was only accessible on foot, or on the back of a donkey, which is how those who made their way to the mill under cover of night must have travelled. Hell's Mill, built during the Carlist Wars, was vital to the survival of the soldiers who fled to the hills during the conflicts. It was a modern structure erected on top of three tree trunks that spanned the river. The inhabitants of Baztán would go there, mules loaded with sacks of grain, which they milled under cover of darkness to provide flour for their families. Navigating the rustic beauty of that slippery path in the thick Baztán night, guiding their animals along that perilous trail by the river, must have felt like a veritable descent into hell. Hence the name. The people of Baztán always found a way to do what needed to be done.

The only other place she knew along that road was the shooting range on the outskirts of Bagordi. She switched off the satnav, which kept recalculating her position every few seconds as the signal dropped out. She drove up the hill, stopping now and again to study the ordnance survey map, open on the passenger seat. Elena's vague directions hadn't specified whether the house was on a plateau or in a valley, only that it was surrounded by a vast meadow, the only one of its kind in the area. She decided to check all the farmhouses, even those that didn't fit the description, including the tiny shepherd's huts, which in recent years had been converted into dwellings but still didn't feature on the map. She waved at a few farmers who came out to meet her down the end of impassable tracks, pretending she was lost or had left the main road by accident, ignoring their wry smiles, and the persistent bark of sheepdogs frantically chasing the wheels of her car.

At about ten in the morning, she stopped to stretch her legs, crossing off on the map all the places she had ruled out. She had brought some coffee in an old thermos flask of Engrasi's, which she remembered from when she was a child. She cupped the lid, which served as a drinking vessel, taking small sips as she leaned against the car boot admiring the landscape. She shuddered as the hot, sweet brew brought back the memory of her dream. Night terrors, or a clear warning which she should ignore at her peril? What would Agent Dupree have said about it? Was it information that the brain processed differently, and which came to her in dreams, or was she simply having a nightmare, reliving the naked fear she'd experienced as a child? Instinctively, she took out her phone, despite knowing full well that she and Dupree only ever spoke late at night. She glanced at the screen, saw that there was no signal, and put the phone back in her pocket, reflecting that she'd received no calls all morning.

'Nature is our protector,' she whispered, admiring the splendour of the trees soaring on either side of the road, forming a natural barrier against the light. Suddenly aware of the sheer power of the forest, Amaia reflected that, rather than cutting through the trees, the road was like a channel through which the energy of the hills flowed like an invisible river.

She didn't need to speak to Dupree to know what he would have said. She was a police officer, a trained detective; she knew that when an alarm went off, you didn't cover your ears. Recently she had started to understand that the rational and the irrational, modern policing methods and the old traditions, detailed analysis and simple intuition were part of the same world, and that a combination of both approaches to reality was essential for the investigator. Her sister could arrange all the funeral masses she wanted; Amaia knew, although she couldn't prove it, that her mother's soul lived on in her body, and that the threat hanging over her since she was child was as real as ever. Berasategui's message had confirmed that. She felt it in her guts, her skin, her heart and her mind, which continued to transmit those terrifying messages to her in her sleep.

She remembered how the impression of the dream had stayed with her for several minutes. The ache in her limbs when she awoke was real, as was the anxiety of having lain there unable to move; even Rosario's scent on her skin, which she'd had to scrub off with soap and hot water. She took another sip of coffee, retching as the bitterness evoked her mother's smell. She tossed the remainder into the bushes, wondering, as she recalled Sarasola's account of the Inguma, whether nightmares could actually kill you. Whether the demons that inhabit them were powerful enough to break through the fragile barrier between the two worlds and hunt down their quarry. What would have happened if she hadn't woken up? Her sensations during those nightmares were so vivid they felt real; like the Hmong, she was conscious of being asleep, of the moment when her mother appeared, and when she opened her eyes she could see her, smell her, she even felt her hair brushing her face. How much more could she perceive? Would she have felt Rosario's touch? Her dry lips, her moist tongue licking her face, eager for her blood? Would she have felt her mother's mouth closing over her lips to steal her breath? Could the Rosario of her nightmares have sucked the life out of her, like the legendary Inguma?

Out of the corner of her eye, she glimpsed a movement to her left, amid the dense undergrowth. Glancing up at the stillness of the treetops, she decided it couldn't have been the wind, yet straining her eyes she could make nothing out beneath the dark canopy of the trees. As she opened the boot to put away the thermos flask, she saw it again. Whatever it was, it was tall enough to rustle branches at chest level. Closing the boot again, she walked towards the edge of the forest. She stopped dead as she glimpsed an elongated shadow concealed behind the trunk of a large beech tree. Presumably, this was what had rustled the tiny shoots doomed to perish in the shade of the towering tree.

She remained perfectly still, aware of the trembling that started in her legs then spread to her entire body. Her hand instinctively reached for the gun at her waist, even as she reminded herself not to draw it. The watcher remained hidden behind the tree. Hoping to lure it out, she stepped backwards, lowering her head and staring at the ground.

The effect was instantaneous. She felt the watcher's eyes alight on her: a cruel, fierce, soulless gaze that pierced her like a shot through the heart. Startled by the hostile presence, she stepped backwards and nearly fell over. She collected herself, scanning the undergrowth in time to see her watcher slip out of sight. She thrust her hand inside her Puffa jacket and ran her fingers over the reassuring bulk of her Glock, then immediately reproached herself. She took a deep breath, reminding herself to stay calm. She needed to see it again, she had yearned for its presence so intensely it made her heart ache; and, sensing its closeness yet knowing it was so far away felt deeply frustrating, because she couldn't express her need, or even recapture the feeling of security it gave her, which she so craved. She walked to within touching distance of the trees along the roadside. Suddenly, she became aware of a stillness enveloping the forest. The chirps and flutters, even the whisper of the trees fell silent, as if Nature herself were waiting with bated breath. Taking another step forward, she saw the shadow slowly begin to emerge from its hiding place. She felt a mounting terror, as she heard the high-pitched whistle of the guardian of the forest ring out behind her, on the other side of the road: the *basajaun*, the protector whose presence she had longed for, was alerting her to danger. As Amaia drew her gun, the shadow she had mistaken for her guardian slipped away into the darkness.

She ran back to her car and started the engine, the loose gravel at the side of the road spraying up as she drove away at high speed. As soon as she reached the next farmsteads, she stopped the car. Her hands were still trembling. 'It was a wild boar. Yes, a wild boar, and the whistling in the forest was simply a shepherd calling his dog.' She adjusted the rear-view mirror to look at herself; the eyes of the woman staring back at her didn't look at all convinced by those explanations.

She spent the rest of the morning investigating roads, lanes and paths. It was shortly after midday when, driving past a house she had already ruled out, she saw the meadow. A vast expanse of bright green grass, extending from the sides and back of a house that couldn't have been more than ten years old. The house had a red gable roof, with big picture windows at the front, wooden decking with a table large enough to seat ten, and a modern-looking barbecue. Seeing it from the bend in the road, she realised why she hadn't noticed it until now. Although the house stood in a meadow, the whole of the front part was hidden behind a wall overgrown with vegetation. Hidden among the foliage in the middle of the wall she made out a green metal mailbox. She drove back down the road, pulled over, and saw that the wall and the fence behind were attached to the property. She walked along the wall until she reached the mailbox, where she read the name: Martínez-Bayón. She continued along the wall then turned left. There she discovered a fence covered in creepers, and behind it a modern gateway with a roofed structure, a video intercom system, and the plaque of a security company gleaming incongruously from a horizontal rafter, on to which the name Argi Beltz was neatly carved. A few yards ahead she saw a garage.

'Argi Beltz,' she whispered. Black light. *It's a black house*, Elena Ochoa's words echoed in her head. She walked up to the entrance, stood in front of the camera and rang the bell. She waited, then pressed it again, and then a third time, before giving up; just as she was about to walk away, she was sure she heard a faint crackle coming from the intercom, although there was no light to indicate that the receiver had been picked up. She had the feeling she was being watched, which irritated rather than disturbed her. She walked back to her car then drove up the hill to the bend in the road from where she could see the property. This had to be the place; according to Elena, it was the only house in the area surrounded by a big meadow, and yet the building itself bore no resemblance to the description she had given. Thirty years had gone by since Elena had seen it last. A new buyer could have rebuilt on the site of the old house, or, gone the whole hog and had the terrain evened out, in which case this wasn't the place she was looking for.

She drove slowly, taking in every detail, until, about a half a mile on, a dip in the landscape and the unmistakable outline of two neat hayricks indicated the next farmhouse. A carved wooden plaque bore the name Lau Haizeta ('Four Winds'). Amaia drove towards it, stopping to look at the huge stone cross at the entrance. She wasn't surprised by it: many of the houses and farms in Baztán had stone crosses outside to protect them, some as large as, or even larger than a person. In Arizkun, virtually every house, stable, chicken coop, had one next to the *eguzkilore,* or silver thistle, which also guarded the farmhouses. What surprised her was that she counted as many as six as she drove up to the front door, four dogs trotting silently beside the car. She instantly understood why. The owner of the house, a dour-looking woman, was standing in a doorway on the ground floor. She waited for Amaia to climb out of the car before approaching, presumably to get a better look at her.

'Good afternoon,' she said in Spanish.

'*Egun on, andrea,*' Amaia greeted her in Basque, noticing how the woman's face instantly relaxed when she heard her Baztán accent. 'I wonder if you could help me?'

'Of course, do you need directions?'

'Well, actually, I'm looking for a house. I think it's the next farmhouse along, except that it doesn't fit the description I was given. The place I'm looking for is old, and that house is relatively new, so I must be mistaken.'

As the woman listened, her expression hardened.

'I know nothing about any house, please leave,' she hissed.

Amaia was taken aback by the woman's sudden change of attitude; seconds earlier, she had been eager to help, but now, at the very mention of that house, she was ordering her off the property. She always tried to avoid identifying herself as a police officer when she was on a fact-gathering mission; some people went on the defensive when they saw a badge, even those who had nothing to hide. In this case, she felt she had no choice. Rummaging in the pocket of her Puffa jacket, she pulled out her ID.

The effect was instantaneous: the woman relaxed, nodded approvingly, and said:

'Are you investigating those people?'

Amaia reflected. Was she investigating them? Yes, damn it, she was. If they were in any way connected to her mother, then she would investigate them to hell and back.

'Yes,' she replied.

'Would you like a coffee?' the woman asked, ushering Amaia into the kitchen. 'It's freshly ground,' she added, unscrewing a small, Italian percolator.

She placed a tray of biscuits in front of Amaia, leaving her alone in the kitchen while she went upstairs. She returned minutes later, bringing with her an old cocoa tin, which she set down on the table. After pouring the coffee, she opened the tin, which contained photographs. She rifled through them until she found the one she was looking for.

'This was taken fifty years ago, when my parents rebuilt the chimney, which was struck by lightning. It was taken from the roof. In the background, you can see the house you mentioned. Of course, it looks different now, but I assure you it's the same house.'

The woman handed Amaia the black-and-white photograph. In the foreground, a man dressed in overalls and a beret posed on the roof beside an enormous chimneystack. Behind him stood an old farmhouse, with what could have been brown walls and a dark roof in the middle of a meadow, just as Elena Ochoa had described.

'I think this might be it.'

'I *know* it is,' the woman said.

'What makes you so sure?'

'Because nothing good has ever entered that house, only strange people, wicked people. But they don't frighten me. This is my land, I'm protected here.' Amaia remembered the big stone cross, like a sentinel guarding the entrance. 'Mark my words, evil things have gone on in that house. I never knew the original owners. It had been empty for years by the time I was born, but my *amatxi* told me it belonged to two brothers and a sister. Their mother died young, and their father went insane with grief. It was the custom then to confine relatives like that to the attic. The brothers were coarse brutes, who treated their sister like a slave and refused to let her marry. Apparently, she met a man, a horse trader, and they fell in love. The day the man called round at the house to take her away, he was greeted by one of the brothers. "There she is," he grinned, pointing to a barrel. When the man opened the lid he found his beloved's body hacked to pieces. The two brothers set upon him, but the horse trader knew how to defend himself; he stabbed one of them, then fled. My *amatxi* told me that by the time the *Guardia Civil* arrived, one brother had bled to death and the other had hanged himself from a rafter. Imagine the scene: the sister hacked to bits, one brother in a pool of blood and the other purple-faced and bloated, swinging from a rafter. But the worst was yet to come. They found the father's mummified corpse chained to a bed in the attic. The authorities shut up the farmhouse, and it stood abandoned for seventy years. People around here used to say that the ghosts of the former occupants haunted it,' she said with a shudder.

Amaia made a mental note of the dates so that she could check them afterwards.

'And then in the seventies, the hippies moved in. Well, they weren't exactly hippies, but they all lived together, girls and boys, as many as twenty, not including the visitors who came and went, some of whom seemed a lot older. They organised cultural encounters, spiritual gatherings, that kind of thing. Occasionally, I'd pass them on the road and they'd invite me along. I always refused. In those days I was a young mother with four children. I didn't have time for all that nonsense.

The house looked nothing like it does now,' she said, pointing at the photograph. 'Although it was built to last, standing empty all those years had taken its toll. The place was run down. They had a vegetable garden, where they grew a few things, a couple of hens, some sheep and pigs, which roamed free, rolling in their own muck.

'It must have been around that time when the couple who live there now arrived. I won't call them husband and wife, because I don't think they're married. They weren't Christians, and they never attended Mass. They had a little girl. I never knew her name. She died of a brain haemorrhage when she was about a year old. At the time, I remember asking the priest when the funeral was, and he told me she hadn't been baptised. I realise that anyone can suffer a brain haemorrhage can happen to anyone, but I tell you, that child was neglected. One day – she was barely a toddler – she turned up here. She'd crawled all the way across that field on her own, presumably attracted by my children's voices as they played outside. My eldest daughter saw her, picked her up and washed her face and hands, which were covered in mud. Her nappy was soiled and her clothes were filthy. I'd made doughnuts for the children's tea, and my daughter decided to give her a piece. I've brought up four children, Inspector, and that girl wasn't just hungry, she was ravenous. She wolfed it down so fast I was afraid she might choke, so we softened the doughnut in some milk. My daughter tried to feed it to her, but she kept plunging her hands in the bowl, cramming the pieces into her mouth. I've never seen a child eat like that – it was shocking.

'I went down the road to tell her parents that she was safe with us, only to find them frantically searching for her. A perfectly normal reaction for any parent, except that their concern was at odds with their evident neglect of the child. Back in those days, there was no such thing as social services, people were left to their own devices, but sometimes I wish I had done more for that child. From my upstairs balcony, I can see one side of their house and the open field. I used to watch her outside, playing alone in the muck, dressed in rags. I gathered up some of my children's cast-offs, set aside my disgust for that rabble, and took them round. The father opened the door. There were lots of people inside holding some kind of celebration. He didn't invite me in, and I didn't want him to. He told me the girl had died.' The woman's eyes filled with tears. 'I went back home and cried for three days. I didn't even know her name, but it still breaks my heart to think of her. A poor, neglected creature, despised and ill-treated from birth. They didn't even hold a funeral service for her.'

'And that same couple still lives there?'

'Yes. Not long after that, the group broke up, but they stayed behind. I imagine they must have bought the place. They seem to have done well for themselves; the house has been completely refurbished, they've built a garden at the front, and a wall around the property. I've no idea what they do for a living, but they own a fleet of luxury cars – BMWs, Mercedes . . . They have a lot of visitors, who also own fancy cars; I've seen them parked out on the road. I don't know who they are, but they certainly have money, which seems incredible when you think that they looked like a pair of penniless tramps when they first came here.'

'Are the people who visit them from around here? How do they get on with the locals?'

'Their visitors aren't from around here, and they don't mix with the locals.'

'Do you know if they are at home now? I called by, but no one answered the door.'

'I don't, but it's easy to find out. When they're in, the shutters are closed; when they're out, they are open.'

Amaia raised her eyebrows, puzzled.

'Yes, ma'am, the opposite to everyone else. I told you they were strange. Come with me,' she said, getting to her feet and ushering Amaia towards the staircase. They walked through one of the bedrooms and out on to an enormous balcony running the entire length of the house.

'Well I'm damned!' she exclaimed, pointing towards the shutters, which were open on the ground floor, and closed on the top floor. 'I've never seen that before.'

The walls of the house had been whitewashed, and the original windows enlarged, the tiny screens replaced by hardwood shutters. From the balcony, Amaia had a good view over the property, which, surrounded by the garden, didn't bear much resemblance to the old photograph.

As she thanked the woman and prepared to leave, she showed her a couple of photographs on her mobile: one of Dr Berasategui's car, the other of her mother, Rosario.

'I've seen that car parked out on the road a few times. I remember it because of the doctor's badge on the windscreen. I don't recognise the woman.'

Amaia had just pulled up next to the wall of the house again when a four-wheel-drive BMW sailed by, turning into the concealed driveway behind the fence. Leaping out of her car, she ran after the vehicle, catching up with it outside the automatic gates, which were slowly opening. She pulled out her badge, holding it up so that the man and woman in the car could see it, her free hand instinctively going to the Glock at her waist. The driver lowered the window, with a look of alarm.

'Is something wrong, Officer?'

'Nothing's wrong. Switch off the engine and step out of the vehicle, please. I want to ask you some questions.'

The man did as she asked, and the woman walked round the car until they were both standing in front of her. They must have been in their sixties, but had a youthful appearance. The woman was elegantly dressed, and looked as if she'd come straight from the hairdresser; the man was wearing smart trousers and a shirt open at the collar. His watch was a Rolex, which Amaia had no reason to doubt was genuine.

'How can we help you?' the woman asked amiably.

'Do you own this house?'

'Yes.'

'I'm afraid I bring bad news. Your friend Dr Berasategui is dead.' She scrutinised their faces. Clearly they weren't surprised; there was a swift exchange of glances, as though unsure whether to admit they knew him. The man spoke first, raising a hand to silence the woman. He looked straight at Amaia, gauging how emphatic his response should be, as he decided not to deny it.

'Oh, how dreadful! What happened? Was he involved in an accident, Officer?'

'Inspector. Inspector Salazar, Homicide. The cause of death hasn't yet been established,' she lied. 'The investigation is ongoing. What was the nature of your relationship with the deceased?'

The man's initial restraint had vanished. He stepped forward and said:

'Forgive me, Inspector, you've just informed us of the death of our friend. We're terribly upset and need time to assimilate the news,' he added, smiling weakly to make it clear exactly how upset he was. 'Our relationship with Dr Berasategui is subject to professional confidentiality. I suggest you contact my lawyer if you have any further questions.' He handed her a card, which the woman had fished out of her wallet.

'I understand. You have my heartfelt condolences,' retorted Amaia, taking the card. 'In any case, I didn't come here to ask you about Dr Berasategui, but rather about this woman,' she said, raising her phone level with the man's eyes. 'Have you ever seen her with him?'

The man glanced at the screen, while the woman leaned in, donning a pair of spectacles.

'No,' they replied in unison.

'We've never seen her before,' said the man.

'Thank you, you've been most helpful,' said Amaia. She put away her phone, making as if to turn around, but instead moved closer to their car, where she had a better view of the house. 'I don't suppose you're aware that in recent years there have been a lot of cot deaths in the area. We're looking into all the cases in the valley. I realise this was a long time ago now, but I understand that your little girl passed away very young. I don't suppose the cause of death was Sudden Infant Death Syndrome, by any chance?'

The woman gave a start, crying out as she clasped her partner's arm. When at last the man spoke, his face was ashen.

'Our daughter died of a brain haemorrhage aged fourteen months,' he said curtly.

'What was her name?'

'Her name was Ainara.'

'Where is she buried?'

'Our daughter died during a trip to the UK, Inspector. We didn't have much money in those days and couldn't afford travel insurance. We buried her there. This is an extremely painful subject for my wife, so please don't insist.'

'Very well,' said Amaia. 'One other thing: before you arrived, I rang the bell. No one answered, but I had the impression that someone was in the house.'

'There's no one in the house!' the woman screamed.

'Are you sure?'

'Get back in the car!' the man commanded the trembling woman. 'As for you, leave us in peace. I told you, if you have any questions, speak to our lawyer.'

# 19

Although the couples they were looking for had moved house in the past few years, they weren't difficult to find: two had stayed in the same villages – one in Lekaroz, one in Arraioz – and the third had moved to Pamplona from Elbete. The wind that had been battering Elizondo all night would keep the rain away from the valley that day, while in Pamplona it was raining so hard that, even this city, which was better prepared than most to deal with torrential downpours, seemed incapable that morning of absorbing another drop. Great pools formed around the cavernous drains clogged by the deluge, the heavy raindrops dancing off them so it looked like it was raining backwards, the water sprouting from the ground, soaking the shoes and trouser legs of passers-by. Montes and Zabalza made a dash from the car, sheltering as best they could beneath the narrow awning outside a café. They closed their umbrellas, already sopping wet, and Montes cursed the rain as they entered the café.

He approached the counter and ordered two coffees, feigning interest in a sports newspaper while he watched Zabalza, who had flopped onto a chair and was staring at the TV screen. The guy was in a bad way, probably had been for some time, but Montes was so immersed in his own problems, he hadn't noticed until now. He recognised the same traits in himself: constantly angry with everyone and everything, convinced the world owed him something, and smarting at the injustice of never getting it. He felt sorry for Zabalza. It was like crossing a desert, and the worst thing was, if no one came to your rescue, you were doomed to die alone and mad . . . With your manhood intact, granted. For men like Zabalza, brains and brawn were practically synonymous, and often in such cases, the courage needed to evolve was overtaken by hollow pride, which engulfed you with its amalgam of hatred and self-pity. Montes knew from experience, he had been poisoned by it, to the point of preferring to take his own life rather than admit he was mistaken.

He placed a cup in front of Zabalza, stirring sugar into his own.

'Here, drink this, it might put some colour back in your cheeks, then you can tell me what's on your mind.'

Zabalza slid his eyes away from the screen. 'What makes you think there's anything to tell?'

'For fuck's sake, Zabalza, I've been listening to the cogs in your brain spin round all morning.'

Zabalza cocked his head to one side, in a gesture of defeat.

'Marisa and I fixed a date for the wedding yesterday.'

Montes's eyes opened wide.

'Sonofabitch! You're getting married and you weren't going to tell me?'

'I'm telling you now, aren't I?' protested Zabalza.

Montes rose to shake his hand, pulling Zabalza to his feet to give him a firm embrace.

'Congratulations, my boy, that's more like it!'

A few of the other patrons turned around and stared at them. Montes sat down again, beaming.

'So that's what this was all about! Fuck, I thought it was something serious . . .'

'Well . . . I don't know . . .'

Montes looked at him, still smiling.

'I know what you're going through – because the same thing happened to me: it's that feeling of imminence. Once you've fixed a date, there's no turning back, you know you're going to be a married man, and for some men those weeks or months feel like a walk to the gallows. Take it from me, it's normal to be plagued with doubt. Right now, all your reasons for taking this step have faded into the background, and you can only think about why you shouldn't, especially if you've been through some rough patches with your partner,' Montes's voice had softened to a murmur, and Zabalza noticed him staring into the bottom of his cup, 'or even a trial separation, because of some problem that seemed insuperable at the time. But you tell yourself, nobody's perfect, especially not you, and you have to give the relationship a chance.'

'Well!' said Zabalza. 'I wasn't expecting that kind of talk coming from you.'

'Why? Because I'm divorced? Maybe you assume my experience has turned me against marriage. I won't deny that it did, for a while, but it also taught me that, of the many rights we possess, the most important is the right to make a mistake, to admit that, to value it, instead of turning it into a life sentence.'

'The right to make a mistake . . .' echoed Zabalza. 'But what if our mistakes hurt others?'

'That's the way of the world, lad. You make your own choices, your own mistakes, and you leave others to make theirs.'

Zabalza contemplated him for a few seconds, mulling over his words.

'That's a sound piece of advice,' he said.

Montes nodded, standing up to pay for their coffees at the bar. Glancing round at Zabalza, he thought he looked as morose as before, if not more so.

The days were starting to get longer. As the sun went down, a mysterious golden glow prolonged the afternoons, making the river sparkle and casting a silvery light on the new buds, which Amaia had only just noticed on the trees outside the police station. She turned to face the room, where her team were gathered for the meeting she had called.

Inspector Iriarte had been unusually quiet while they waited for everyone to arrive. He was sitting stiffly in his chair, staring at the autopsy report on Elena Ochoa. During the year or more they had been working together, Amaia had come to appreciate Iriarte. He was a good man, an excellent detective, exceptionally responsible and conscientious; a cop who went by the rule book, perhaps a little too much so to make a truly brilliant detective, but in all the time she'd known him she had never seen him lose his cool.

It occurred to her that in some ways Iriarte resembled her husband. Like James, he knew about and accepted the dark side of humanity, the awful, wretched lives some people led, and, like James, he chose to live within the margins of what he could understand and control. James's artistic side allowed him to go along with Engrasi's fortune-telling, or the benign powers of the goddess Mari, much as a child thrilled by a magic show in which a human agent is behind the façade. Possibly Iriarte had taken things a step further, and his decision to join the police force arose from a simplistic understanding of the world, of family values, of what constituted goodness, and his determination to protect them at all costs. What upset him wasn't in the autopsy report lying on the table in front of him – San Martín's verdict that Elena Ochoa's cause of death was suicide by ingestion of sharp objects – but rather what he'd seen on the slab at the Navarre Institute of Forensic Medicine.

While they were taking their seats, Montes commenced in a cheerful voice.

'Well, boss, we have a few little surprises for you. This morning we visited the two couples mentioned in Jonan's report, and the one added by the pathologist. All three couples have since moved house, although two of them remained in the same village. We started with the couple in Lekaroz – who insinuated that pathologists were involved in organ trafficking. I don't know where they lived back then, but they own a big mansion now. We told them we were investigating a spate of burglaries in the area and they invited us in. They even showed us round their garage. I could retire on the proceeds from just one of their cars. Apparently, they're in the pharmaceutical business. The couple in Arraioz also seem to be doing very well financially. The caretaker told us they were away on holiday, but we were able to see the house from the outside, and the newly built stables. It seems they own a gas prospecting company in South America, so it's no wonder they elected to stop receiving benefits. The third couple are also rolling in money, which isn't surprising as they've always been lawyers. This is the case where the mother had cancer and the girl who died was an only child. They used to live in Elbete, but moved to Pamplona. We haven't seen the house, but their chambers are impressive: two hundred square metres in the posh part of town. What's amazing is that the wife, who was terminally ill in 1987, isn't just alive, she's as fresh as a daisy.'

'Are you sure it's the same woman? Perhaps the husband remarried.'

'It's definitely her. Her name is on the plaque outside: Lejarreta & Andía. Besides, we spoke to her in person. She's alive and well, and still quite attractive,' he added, nudging Zabalza, who lowered his gaze, embarrassed.

'Lejarreta & Andía. Never heard of them,' said Iriarte.

'That's probably because they're commercial not criminal lawyers, import–export, that sort of thing.'

'The name rings a bell,' said Amaia, getting up to fish out of her coat pocket the elegant business card Martínez-Bayón had given her outside his house: *Lejarreta & Andía. Lawyers*.

She placed the card on the table for everyone to see, pausing for a few seconds to collect her thoughts.

'I think you're all aware that Elena Ochoa, the woman who died yesterday, was a family friend – a friend of my mother, to be precise. You also know that since the night we arrested Berasategui and Rosario disappeared, I've had my doubts about their movements after leaving the clinic and before arriving at my aunt's house. I've always thought they must have gone somewhere else, to a safe house, where Rosario changed her clothes. We know they didn't go to his father's house, and that brings us back to Elena Ochoa. She told me that in the late seventies, early eighties she joined a sect – a kind of hippy commune that was operating out of a farmhouse in Orabidea. To begin with, they organised cultural encounters and spiritual gatherings, but soon they started to dabble in the occult. They sacrificed small animals, and there was talk of carrying out a human sacrifice, which was when Elena decided to leave. Apparently, the sect remained active for some years. Groups like that sprung up everywhere in those days, no doubt influenced by pseudo-Satanist groups like the Manson Family, who gained notoriety after their infamous killing spree. Lots of young people, disillusioned with Christianity and the conservative values of the time, experimented with free love, drugs and occultism – a heady cocktail, which enhanced the sex appeal of cult leaders. The majority of cults disbanded when the LSD ran out.

'Following Elena Ochoa's directions, I found the farmhouse this morning. In fact, it's been completely modernised and is now protected by a high wall and CCTV cameras. The owners are a respectable, wealthy couple in their sixties; they were the founding members of the sect. A neighbour of theirs gave me a positive ID on Berasategui's car, and when questioned the couple admitted they knew him. However, when I pressed them about the nature of their dealings with him, they handed me this card: Lejarreta & Andía. Lawyers . . .'

'It could be a coincidence, they must have a lot of clients,' said Iriarte.

'Yes, it could be,' she conceded, 'but the neighbour also told me they had a baby girl who died, and when I mentioned this, they became hysterical. That could also be a coincidence, but I'm starting to see too many dead babies.'

'Are you suggesting these couples killed their children? The autopsies gave the cause of death as SIDS.'

Amaia evaded the question.

'What we need is to find out whether one or more of these couples are linked to the two lawyers, to Berasategui, or to the Martínez-Bayóns. I'd also like to get hold of a copy of the girl's death certificate. Her name was Ainara Martínez-Bayón. She died of a brain haemorrhage aged fourteen months, apparently during a trip to the UK, where she was also buried. Jonan, could you look into that? Don't you have a friend who works at the Spanish Embassy in London?' she said, rising to signal the end of the meeting. She walked over to the door, where she waited for everyone to file out, intercepting Montes before he had a chance to leave. 'Montes, one moment.' She called him back, closed the door, then turned towards him.

Inspector Montes was one of those people who look you straight in the eye when they have something to say to you; she put it down to his impulsive, sincere nature. On at least two occasions in the past few days Amaia had been convinced he was about to open up, but in the end he hadn't.

She went straight to the point.

'Fermín, I think there's something you've been wanting to tell me for a few days now.'

He nodded, feeling both relief at facing the inevitable and anguish at being unable to avoid it, but he said nothing. Amaia realised that speaking to him as his superior in her office might not be the ideal place for him to open up; Fermín Montes was the kind of guy who preferred to talk over a drink.

'Do you have time for a beer and a chat after work?'

'Of course, boss,' he replied, breathing a sigh. 'But first, come and have a coffee – I'm inviting everyone. We're celebrating: Zabalza's getting married.'

She let Montes go on ahead, taking a few seconds to wipe the look of consternation off her face, as she heard the sounds of jubilation with which the others greeted the news.

After three beers and a plate of deep-fried squid at the Casino Bar, Montes seemed relaxed enough to talk. She laughed at the joke he'd just told, then said:

'Okay, Fermín, are you going to tell me now, or are you waiting until I'm totally pissed?'

He lowered his eyes and pushed his glass towards the middle of the bar.

'Do you fancy a stroll?'

She left a banknote on the bar then followed him outside.

In the past hour, the temperature had dropped several degrees, and the icy gusts of wind had sent everyone fleeing indoors. They crossed the square in silence, and then walked down the main street. Finally, Fermín came to a halt outside the doors to the church, and looked her straight in the eye. Whatever it was he wanted to say, he was clearly finding it very difficult.

'I don't know how to tell you this, but here goes. A few days ago, Flora and I got back together.'

Amaia opened her mouth, incredulous, barely whispering:

'What do you mean, you got back together?'

He avoided her probing gaze for an instant, as though searching among the shadows surrounding the church for the words to explain something he himself found inexplicable.

'I was on my way to the police station a few days ago, when I saw her in her car. She called me over . . . We talked, and now we're back together.'

'For fuck's sake, Fermín! Have you gone mad? Have you

forgotten what she did to you? What you were about to do to yourself?'

He looked away again, chewing his lip as he gazed up at the clear, cold night sky above Baztán.

'She's wicked, Fermín. Flora is wicked, she'll destroy you, she'll finish you off, she's a fucking devil, can't you see that?'

Montes exploded, seizing her by the shoulders and shaking her, as he drew his face close to hers:

'Of course I can! I know what she's capable of, but what can I do? I fell madly in love with her the first day I met her. I've tried to convince myself otherwise, but the fact is I haven't stopped loving her during all this time, and somehow I know that Flora is my last chance.'

He was so close she could see the torment in his eyes, feel his suffering. She raised her hand, placing it gently on his cheek as she shook her head.

'For fuck's sake, Fermín . . .' she said despairingly.

'I know . . .'

They stepped away from each other, and as if by tacit consent, started to walk in silence towards Calle Santiago. When they reached the bridge, she came to a halt.

'Fermín, you must never, under any circumstances, tell Flora anything – and I mean anything – about what happens or is said inside or outside the police station regarding any of these cases. Never.' He nodded. 'Never,' she repeated. 'Say it.'

'Never, I give you my word. I've learned my lesson.'

'I hope so, Inspector Montes, because if you give me any cause to suspect otherwise, it won't matter how much respect I have for you, I'll make sure not only that you're taken off this case, but that you're dismissed from the police force, for good.'

For the first time in her life, Amaia crossed the bridge without noticing the sound of water in the weir. Fuelled by a mounting anger that made her oblivious to the cold, she approached her aunt's house at a brisk pace. At the last moment she decided to walk off her rage before going in. Then she noticed Flora's car parked outside the arched entrance. She stopped in her tracks, gazing at the vehicle as if it had been left there by some extra-terrestrial being. She marched into the house without taking off her coat and put her head round the sitting room door. They were all gathered around Flora, listening politely as she told them how well she had organised Rosario's funeral service. Flora was holding a saucer in one hand and a cup in the other, taking small sips from it as she spoke.

Amaia was vaguely aware of her family's voices greeting her and Flora's no doubt sarcastic contribution. As if from a long way off she heard her own voice, angry and sharp, addressing her sister.

'Get your coat and come outside with me.'

Her words and manner brooked no argument.

Flora's smile faded. 'Is anything the matter, Amaia?'

Amaia didn't reply, she grabbed her sister's coat from the stand in the entrance and threw it at her feet. Ignoring the pleas and protests of the others, she waited silently by the front door until Flora brushed past her. She followed her outside, closing the door behind them.

'What's all the fuss about?'

'Stop pretending, Flora! Stop pretending that you're a normal person and tell me what the hell you're up to.'

'I've no idea what you're talking about.'

'I'm talking about Fermín Montes, the man whose life you nearly destroyed, the police officer who was suspended from duty for the best part of a year because of you.'

Flora collected herself, adopting her habitual air of barely contained irritation.

'I don't see why I owe you an explanation. Fermín is a man and I'm a woman, we're both grown-ups.'

'That's where you are wrong, Sister. Don't forget, I was

141

there the night Víctor died. I know what really happened. I know what your interest in Montes was then; what I don't understand is what you want from him now. Just leave the poor guy alone.'

Flora laughed.

'Well, little sister, I didn't know you had such strong feelings for Fermín.' Her face twisted into a sneer. 'You can't prove what happened the night Víctor died – you haven't a clue. I admit I wasn't altogether honest with Fermín when we first met, but I was still a married woman then, and he knew that. Things are different now. My interest in him is sincere.'

'Sincere, my eye! Although I believe the interest part – *interest* being the word that defines all your relationships. I'm sure the same applies to Fermín, only your interest has nothing to do with him being a man, because if I'm not mistaken what interests you, Flora, comes in a different package: young, blonde and very pretty.'

Flora's customary disdain gave way to a rage as intense as Amaia's, uniting the two sisters perhaps for the first time ever. Choked with anger and grief, her voice cracked as she spoke.

'You know nothing about my relationship with Anne! I forbid you to mention her name.'

Amaia gazed at her sister in astonishment. Flora, back arched, as if she were supporting a terrible weight. All the life seemed to drain from her, her face darkening in front of Amaia's eyes, like someone gravely ill. This wasn't the first time Amaia had seen her sister like this. Whenever she mentioned Anne Arbizu, her response seemed so dramatic, so genuine, that Amaia was still more convinced that her sister's passion for Anne couldn't compare to anything she had felt for a man, a passion so devastating that it continued to consume her, and had even driven her to kill.

She contemplated her sister in silence. There wasn't much

more she could say to a person who was stooping to pick up her shattered dignity. Flora pulled her coat tightly about her, flashing her sister a final look of contempt as she climbed into her car. Amaia removed her phone from her pocket and took several photographs of the front of the vehicle.

# 20

Ibai would wake up early, sometimes just before dawn. Later, towards nine thirty or ten in the morning, he would go to sleep until midday, but during those first hours, he was jolly and communicative, gurgling incessantly. Amaia took the boy in her arms, closing the bedroom door behind her so that James could go on sleeping. She spent the next couple of hours walking around the house with her son, pointing out each cherished object, gazing through the window at the River Baztán flowing past the house, serene in that cold morning glow. She sang made up songs about how beautiful he was and how much she loved him. He gazed at everything, wide-eyed, beaming at her, pressing his moist lips to her cheek in what seemed like kisses. She received them with joy, planting hundreds more on his little blond head, breathing in his sweet aroma of butter and biscuits.

The previous evening had been less agreeable. James and her aunt had made their disapproval of her treatment of Flora clear throughout the meal. Only Ros had tried, unsuccessfully, to make conversation. Then, on their way to bed, even though Amaia had explained to them that her argument with Flora had nothing to do with the funeral, James had said:

'Just before you barged in, Flora had confirmed that the

service will take place in the Santiago parish church the day after tomorrow. Regardless of your quarrel with your sister, I hope you do as I asked and accompany me to the church.'

She made a pot of coffee with one hand, loath to let go of Ibai even for a second, as she reflected about how well James knew her. It didn't matter how many promises he forced out of her, he knew she was stubborn, and that she never gave up without a fight. She understood his reasons for wanting her to accept, even if only for the duration of the service, that Rosario was dead. On the other hand, she found it intolerable that, loving her as he did, he was capable of asking her to go against her own nature.

As she saw him enter the kitchen with his dazzling smile, a pair of pyjama bottoms and a snug, Denver Broncos T-shirt that showed off his six-pack, she remembered why she adored him.

'You've pinched my dressing gown,' he whispered, kissing her as he stroked Ibai's head.

'Here, you can have it back, I'm late,' she said.

Handing him their son, she slipped out of the roomy gown, beneath which she was naked except for her knickers. James purposefully mispronounced an expletive, making her chuckle, as she recalled him telling her how, when he'd first arrived there, and, like all foreigners, he had learned to swear in Spanish, and had created a personal repertory of nonsense swear words, for his own amusement.

As she closed her bedroom door behind her, Amaia heard her aunt go downstairs. She climbed into the shower and stood beneath the stream of hot water waiting until she heard James enter the bathroom and disrobe. She smiled because it felt good that some things were so predictable, so wonderfully predictable.

Detective Inspector Etxaide was waiting for Amaia in her office. She could tell the moment she entered that he had made a discovery. He was grinning like a child unable to contain his excitement, shifting his weight from one foot to the other and drumming his fingers on the file he was clutching.

'Good morning, Jonan, have you got something for me?'

'Morning, boss. I'm not sure which is more significant: what I've found or what I haven't found.'

As she sat down, he opened the file and took out some documents to show her.

'This is Ainara Martínez-Bayón's birth certificate. She was born in Elizondo on 12 March 1979, but it was a home birth, so that could be inaccurate. There's the name of the house "Argi Beltz", Orabidea, signed by Dr Hidalgo. Now for the part I don't have: the death certificate – most likely because there isn't one. And this is where they may have shot themselves in the foot. If they'd said they were travelling in India, for example, we probably couldn't do much, but in England thirty years ago, they were already computerising data. There's no record of Ainara's death that year in any British hospital, or indeed that of any Spanish child. Also, if, as they claim, she suffered a brain haemorrhage, an autopsy would have been carried out, and there's no evidence of that either. What's more, according to my contact, when a Spanish citizen dies abroad, the embassy is informed immediately, and if the family doesn't have the means to repatriate the body, then the state pays. If they had decided to bury her in the UK, there'd be a record of it. One other thing: in those days, when taking a minor abroad, a couple would have had to present a Family Book to prove the child belonged to them, and the child's name would be included on one of their passports. I'm in the process of checking that with the passport office, but it could take a while as not all of their files have been computerised. I also went to the registry office to compare the address on the birth certificate with that in the Family Book, and there's no mention of the girl's death there either.'

'When might we have the information on the passports?'

'I'm not sure, boss. The person looking into it has my number, and has promised to call as soon as they find anything.'

She thought for a moment, then stood up with a sigh grabbing her Puffa jacket from the peg.

'Good, then they can reach you anywhere. Come with Iriarte and me, we're going to talk to Esparza's wife.'

As they passed the office where Montes and Zabalza worked, she poked her head round the door. 'Good morning. Any progress since yesterday?'

'Yes, boss,' said Montes. 'Zabalza has found a link between the two couples in Arraioz and Lekaroz and the lawyers, Lejarreta & Andía, which isn't surprising, as both have businesses that operate abroad. But so far we've found no connection between them and Berasategui, and I doubt we will, because, as you know, that type of relationship is confidential. You're more likely to find something out from your friend the priest.'

'Maybe I'll ask him,' she replied, 'but not today.'

The same gravel that had betrayed Esparza's presence on that ill-fated night crunched beneath their tyres as they parked outside the farmhouse.

Inés Ballarena was standing in the doorway waiting for them; she had on a knitted hat and a thick overcoat against the cold, and although she was unable to smile, she politely ushered them in. Amaia motioned to Iriarte and Etxaide to follow her, making her excuses and heading around the side of the house, to where she had seen the old *amatxi*. Greeting her as she approached, Amaia saw the woman smile, a knowing look on her face.

'I see you've come back for more. Perhaps you've begun to understand, perhaps you've begun to realise that this old woman might be right.'

'I've always believed you were right,' declared Amaia.

'Then stop looking for killers made of flesh and blood.'

'Should I be looking for Inguma?'

'You needn't look for Inguma, Inguma will find you, probably already has . . .'

Amaia shuddered at the memory of Rosario leaning over her bed, of her mouth drawing closer.

'Who are you?' she asked, smiling.

'Just an ignorant old woman.'


The young mother's appearance made a shocking impression. Dressed from head to toe in black, she was clutching a paper napkin like a wilted flower in her lap. Her eyes were red and her pale face, devoid of make-up, was covered in blotches, tiny burst blood vessels, from all her weeping. Her grief having entered a calm phase, she seemed to float amid whispered words and delicate gestures.

'We're very grateful to you for agreeing to talk to us today. We realise that it's your daughter's funeral this afternoon,' said Iriarte.

If the young woman heard him, she didn't show it. She continued to stare into space with a mournful expression of silent grief.

'Sonia, my dear,' her mother said softly.

The young woman looked up.

Amaia had joined them and sat facing her.

'In order to understand what happened, there are things we need to know, things only you can help us with, because you know your husband better than anyone.' Sonia nodded. 'Valentín seems like a man interested in money and appearances. You own a beautiful house, which is beyond your means – your mother tells us she helps you with the mortgage – and yet it seems Valentín was planning to buy a luxury car. During our search of the property, we found several catalogues, and the local showroom has confirmed this.'

'He's always been very ambitious; he always wants more, he's never satisfied. I've quarrelled with my mother and *amatxi* over it in the past.'

'A year ago,' Inés broke in, 'he tried to persuade us to remortgage our farm to lend him the money for a new house. Naturally, I refused. I've nothing against people wishing to better themselves, but not at any price, like Valentín. It's not good enough, and I told him so.'

Amaia addressed the young woman again.

'Sonia, I want you to think carefully. Have you noticed any changes in Valentín's behaviour recently?'

'Yes, lots, but nothing bad, in fact, even *Ama* and *Amatxi* started to see him in a better light. It all began when I got pregnant. I was told I had a high risk of miscarrying and needed complete bed rest. During all that time, Valentín was patient with me in a way I would never have expected. He read books about pregnancy, became interested in everything traditional, everything to do with Baztán, our roots, the region. He talked about the importance of being aware of the power of this earth, and became obsessed with eating food grown organically in the valley, he even suggested a home birth. I wasn't keen on the idea, I was afraid of the pain, but he insisted . . . On one occasion, he brought a local midwife here.'

Amaia gave a start.

'Do you remember her name?'

'Josefina, Rufina – something like that.'

'Fina?'

'Yes, that's right, Fina Hidalgo, an attractive older woman. She told me she'd attended hundreds of deliveries, and explained the procedure for a home birth. I felt reassured. But, well, in the end I went into labour in the seventh month, and my baby was born prematurely, in hospital, of course.'

'We understand you quarrelled with your husband at the funeral parlour. He says it was because he wanted your daughter to have a traditional burial, whereas you insisted on cremation.'

She shook her head.

'That wasn't the reason. Yes, to begin with, but look, in the end we're burying her, because that's what *Amatxi* wants. The argument in the mortuary started over that. He was so insistent, it seemed so important to him that I was on the verge of giving in, when he said something . . . something terrible, which I'll never forgive him for, because only a man who didn't love his child could say such a thing, a cruel, heartless person who replaces people like they were objects . . .'

She started to weep, as if a floodgate had opened in that dark, humid place of tears and despair.

Inés embraced the girl, who buried her face in her mother's neck. After a minute or two, the girl sat up straight and looked at them, the red patches on her pale face angrier than before.

'He said not to worry, he'd make me pregnant again, and in nine months I'd have another child to replace my baby girl. I screamed at him, I said I didn't want another child, that my little girl was irreplaceable! How could he say such a terrible thing? I couldn't possibly think about having another child, least of all to fill the space left by my little girl.' She looked straight at Amaia. 'You have a child yourself, you know what I'm talking about. Perhaps I will be a mother again one day, but what he was suggesting was so abhorrent to me, the way he treated our daughter like an object, the very thought of having another child disgusted me. And as he spoke, I realised that if I *did* have another child to substitute the one I lost, I wouldn't be able to love it, not in the same way, I might even grow to hate it.'

'Just one more question. Have you or Valentín ever had dealings with a psychiatrist at the University Hospital by the name of Berasategui, or with a legal firm in Pamplona called Lejarreta & Andía?'

150

'This is the first time I've heard those names.'

They took their leave, and Inés Ballarena walked them out to the car. As they drove off, Amaia glimpsed her in the rear-view mirror standing motionless on the same spot.

Jonan looked puzzled.

'I haven't seen a woman that young dressed in black for a long time.'

'You need to get out more on a Saturday night,' quipped Iriarte.

'I don't mean wearing black clothes. I think there's a big difference, but maybe for most people it's too subtle to notice. I can always tell when someone's wearing black or someone's dressed in mourning,' explained Etxaide.

'She's suffered a great deal,' said Amaia, 'and I think she'll suffer a lot more. What her husband said to her was dreadful. Jonan, when we get back, call the prison and arrange a meeting for me with Esparza. I want to talk to him again, as soon as possible.'

'The case is closed,' said Iriarte. 'We know Esparza killed his daughter.'

'I think there's a lot more to this case than meets the eye.'

'We have the culprit. It isn't our job to understand why he did what he did.'

'Not why, but to what ends, Inspector. Esparza told us that he gave her up, he gave up his daughter's life. I want to know to what ends.'

Iriarte shook his head sceptically as he joined the main road.

'To the police station, then?'

'Not yet. I hope your phones have good cameras: we're going to Irurita to take some pictures,' she replied.

With its long balcony, picture windows and Victorian green-house, Fina Hidalgo's stone house was a splendid sight. A flagstone path led from the main door to the heavy iron gate, painted black and left temptingly ajar, not so much to invite visitors to enter as to allow passers-by to gaze with envy at her beautiful borders. Amaia rang the bell and waited, watching with amusement the delight on her colleagues' faces as they contemplated the pretty garden.

Nurse Fina Hidalgo emerged from the greenhouse where she had received Amaia on her last visit. She wore a pair of close-fitting jeans, a loose shirt of the same material, and her hair was swept back with a hairband; she had on gardening gloves and was holding a small pair of secateurs in one hand. Her expression hardened when she saw them.

'Who gave you permission to come on to my property?'

'Navarre police,' said Amaia, flashing her badge, even though she knew perfectly well that Fina had recognised her. 'The gate was open, and we tried the doorbell.'

'What do you want?' Fina demanded, keeping her distance.

'We'd like to ask you a few questions.'

'Ask away,' she replied boldly.

'We're investigating the death of a baby girl in the valley about thirty years ago. We know that you and your brother attended the delivery, because he signed the birth certificate. We'd be obliged if you could tell us whether he also signed the death certificate.'

'Well, to me that sounds more like a request than a question. Was there something else?'

'Yes, as a matter of fact. I'd like to ask you about your relationship with Valentín Esparza. Also, I have a list of couples whose babies died soon after they were born, and I'm wondering whether you were the midwife who assisted those families post-partum,' Amaia said, edging back towards the gate. As she'd hoped, this prompted the woman to follow her.

'You'll have to get a search warrant for the certificate,' Fina declared, emboldened, as she pursued Amaia down the path. 'As for the other questions, you can get in touch with my lawyers. I have no intention of talking to you.'

Amaia had reached the pavement.

'Your lawyers . . . let me guess: Lejarreta & Andía, am I right?'

The woman smiled, showing her gums, as she strode forward.

'Yes, and you can be sure that by the time they've finished with you, you'll be laughing on the other side of your face.'

'Now,' Amaia commanded, as Etxaide and Iriarte took several photographs of the woman.

'It's illegal to take pictures of me on my own property!' she shouted.

'Technically, you aren't on your own property,' Amaia grinned, pointing down at the woman's feet, which were touching the pavement.

'You fucking bitch! I'll make you pay for this, you'll be sorry,' she screamed, retreating towards the house.

Still with a grin on her face, Amaia motioned towards the vehicle parked opposite.

'One more question: is that your car? Etxaide, take some photographs, will you – it's parked on a public road.'

The woman's screams were broken off by the door slamming behind her.

# 21

As she manoeuvred her car round the hairpin bends on the Orabidea road, Amaia was feeling more optimistic than she had in days. At long last, she had the sense she was getting somewhere.

After their visit to Fina Hidalgo, she had sent Etxaide and Iriarte back to the station. She wanted to pay another visit to the farmhouse next door to Argi Beltz, and preferred to go alone. The woman had been so helpful, she didn't want to risk changing the nature of the relationship she had established with her by showing up with two fellow officers in tow.

As she drove up a steep hill, she glanced with irritation at her phone, which kept losing coverage. She'd received three calls, but each time she answered, the line went dead. She drove at speed to the highest point, looked for a place where she could pull over, and dialled Etxaide's number.

'Boss, you're not going to believe this: a few hours ago, Esparza was stabbed by another inmate. They've rushed him to hospital, but they don't think he's going to make it.'

The familiar reek of disinfectant, the green lines on the floor, and the inexplicably draughty corridors greeted them as they

154

entered the ICU. They had been allocated a room so that one of the consultants could give them a medical report. Inside were the prison governor, two uniformed guards, two young doctors, possibly interns, two nurses and finally Dr Martínez-Larrea. With the addition of her and Jonan, the room felt ridiculously cramped.

Dr Martínez-Larrea and Amaia were old acquaintances. He was an arrogant chauvinist, who seemed to think that male doctors belonged to a superior species that had jumped up a rung on the evolutionary ladder. They had clashed about a year ago when she was working on the *basajaun* case. She shot him a fierce look as she walked in, secretly pleased to see him lower his eyes. From then on, he addressed his comments to her, catching her eye only fleetingly.

'The patient, Valentín Esparza, was admitted to this hospital at twelve forty-five this afternoon having sustained a dozen serious wounds to the stomach caused by a long, sharp object. The skin was broken in several places, rupturing some of his internal organs and main arteries. He was taken straight into surgery, where we attempted to staunch the internal bleeding, but his injuries proved fatal. Valentín Esparza was pronounced dead at ten past one.' He folded the sheet of paper from which he had been reading, muttered an apology, then left the room, followed by his entourage of medical staff.

'I'd like a word with you,' Amaia told the prison governor, ignoring his pale, harried expression.

'Perhaps later,' he suggested. 'I need to inform his relatives, the magistrate—'

'Now,' she insisted, then turned to the others: 'Gentlemen, if you wouldn't mind leaving us for a moment.'

As soon as they were alone, the governor slumped in a chair, visibly intimidated. She stood directly in front of him.

'Explain to me what the hell is going on in your prison. How is it possible that in the last month three inmates have died on your watch, all of whom were involved in cases I'm working on – two in the last week alone?' He didn't reply, burying his face in his hands. 'The suicides – Dr Berasategui and Garrido – I can understand, to a degree; if someone is determined to kill themselves, it must be difficult to stop them. But what I find inexplicable – and I'm sure any layperson would agree with me – is that you could allow a suspected child-killer to mix with other inmates. You sentenced him to death, and I'm going to make sure you're held responsible.'

The man appeared to react; he lowered his hands from his face, clasping them in front of her imploringly.

'Of course he wasn't allowed to mix with the other inmates – I'm not that stupid. We put in place the strictest security protocols as soon as he arrived. He was on suicide watch in a separate cell, with twenty-four-hour surveillance. We gave him a cellmate, a mild-mannered fellow, who was in for embezzlement – he had one month left to serve.'

'So, how did this happen? Who had access to him? Who killed him?'

'I swear to you, I don't understand . . . It was him, the reliable cellmate – he stabbed Esparza with a sharpened toothbrush handle.'

Amaia sat down in the chair facing him, silently contemplating the governor, who appeared genuinely distraught. She wondered how everything could be going to shit, about the now glaringly obvious 'coincidence' that all the people involved in this 'non-case' – for it could hardly be considered a proper investigation – kept ending up dead. After a few minutes, she stood up and walked out, tired of watching the governor's snivelling.

It was cold in Pamplona, and the ground was still wet where it had rained earlier. The skies were clear now, although the sun hadn't come out, only a bright light that dazzled the eyes. As they walked to the car, Amaia explained to Jonan how

Esparza had died, her breath forming into wisps about her face. If the temperature continued to plummet and the rain stayed away, the ground might freeze overnight. Jonan's phone rang. He took the call, raising his free hand as if to silence her while he listened to what the person at the other end of the line was saying.

'That was the call we were waiting for,' he told her when he'd finished. 'From the passport office. It seems they did travel to the UK on those dates . . .'

She gave a frown.

'. . . But no child was included on either of their passports, and my contact assures me they couldn't possibly have taken her out of the country without the correct paperwork.'

'It was so long ago they could blame it on an administrative error, and we'd have no way of proving it.'

'There's something else; they spent a weekend there; I don't see how the girl could have died of a brain haemorrhage, been given an autopsy and buried, all within forty-eight hours.'

'What do you think, Jonan?'

'I think they travelled to the UK without the girl, simply to give themselves an alibi, a convincing explanation they could use if anyone asked about her. I don't think she ever made it to London.'

Amaia stood motionless, staring silently at Deputy Inspector Etxaide as she considered his theory.

'What do we do now?' he asked.

'You go home, I'm going to talk to Judge Markina.'

It was too early to have dinner, so on this occasion Markina had suggested they meet in a quiet taverna decorated with paraphernalia from a nineteenth-century apothecary, soft lighting, plenty of comfy chairs and music that didn't require you to shout. Amaia felt grateful for the inviting warmth of the place as she slipped off her coat.

Markina was sitting alone at the far end of the room,

staring into space, pensive. He was dressed formally in a dark suit, waistcoat and tie. Amaia walked slowly from the bar to the table; she didn't often get the chance to observe him without having to confront his gaze. His languorous demeanour gave him the air of an English romantic, elegant even in repose, with a sensuality she found irresistibly attractive. She sighed, and, in a private act of contrition, resolved to focus solely on putting across her case, on winning his support, for without it she would be incapable of advancing further into that labyrinth where every step she took, every new trail she followed was being silenced by the most persuasive of arguments. Death.

He smiled when he saw her, rising to pull out a chair for her.

'Don't do that,' she said.

'When are you going to start using the informal *tu* with me?'

'I'm here about work.'

He smiled. 'As you wish, Inspector Salazar.'

A waiter brought over two glasses of wine and placed them on the table.

'I imagine it must be something important if you asked to see me.'

'You heard about Esparza's death . . .'

'Yes, of course. I received a call from the courthouse. I spoke to the governor on the phone, and he explained everything to me. It's unfortunate, but these things happen. Child killers have a hard time in prison.'

'Yes, except that his assailant had no previous convictions for violence and was about to be released.'

'As I'm sure you know, the rules that operate in a prison are very different from those on the outside. In my experience, the kind of behaviour and responses that appear rational to us don't apply in there. The fact that his assailant wasn't a murderer doesn't mean much. The pressure exerted on a prisoner by fellow inmates can make him behave in ways he would never have contemplated in the outside world.'

She heard him out in silence.

'However, I don't suppose you came here to talk about a dead prisoner, did you, Inspector Salazar?'

'Not only because he's dead, but because of what he told me when he was alive, as well as a few other things we've dug up in the course of our inquiries. Esparza was obsessed with money, to the point of nearly falling out with his wife's family. There's no question that he killed his daughter, but when I asked him about it, he said something very strange. He insisted he had given her up, "like all the other sacrifices". He told me that he took her body because he needed to finish something. I believe that Esparza was convinced he had to carry out some sort of ritual involving his daughter's body, an important ritual. He told his wife they could have another child to replace the dead girl, and that their fortunes would improve from now on. Yesterday, I requested an interview with him. And today he is dead.'

Markina gestured for her to continue.

'And then there's Dr Berasategui. The reason I visited him in prison was to ask where he and Rosario went between leaving the clinic and attacking my aunt and kidnapping my son. You remember the storm that night. I'm convinced they took shelter somewhere; we've established that he didn't go to his father's house, so maybe to a farmhouse, or a shepherd's hut . . . But now Berasategui is dead too, so he can't answer any more questions either.'

Markina nodded again, listening intently.

'Rosario was a member of a sect, established in Baztán in the late seventies, early eighties. A pseudo-Satanist group that performed animal sacrifices, and even went as far as to propose human sacrifices of newborns or young infants. Apparently, these cults believe that children under the age of two are in transit between two worlds, and therefore better suited to their aims. That brings us to Elena Ochoa, the woman who died the day before yesterday in Elizondo. Elena was an old friend of my mother, Rosario. They attended meetings together, until Elena could no longer tolerate the savagery of their rituals, and she left. Elena told me where the farmhouse was, and I went to see it out of curiosity. The owners are founding members of the original sect, and they live in the house, which has been improved beyond recognition. They also had a daughter, Ainara, who died aged fourteen months, according to them, during a trip to the UK. We've checked their story, and have found no trace of any death certificate, no record of any admission to hospital, no proof the child ever travelled there: she wasn't included on either of the parents' passports, even though it was obligatory at the time when taking a child out of the country. We also have a witness who has positively identified Berasategui's car as having been parked outside the property on more than one occasion. The couple admitted knowing him, but when I asked about the nature of their relationship, they referred me to their lawyers, a wealthy couple with a practice in Pamplona.

'At the same time, we've been looking into all cases of infants under the age of two who have died of SIDS in the last five years in this region. After ruling out male children, we found three cases of interest. What caught our attention wasn't the cause of death – which seemed straightforward – but the parents' behaviour. This was every bit as suspicious as my mother's behaviour, and indeed social services were called in to monitor the couples who had other children. All three couples, along with my mother, are linked to that house, that cult, and one of them happens to have a law practice in Pamplona.'

'Well, Berasategui had no children,' protested Markina.

'No,' she conceded.

'Did social services highlight any cause for concern in their reports?'

'No,' she replied, irritated.

'Have you established a direct link between all these families?'

'Possibly a retired nurse, a midwife who may have assisted at all the births.'

'Retired? How long for? The Esparza girl was born four months ago in Virgen del Camino Hospital. Was she working there then?'

'No, she's a freelance midwife. Her name is Fina Hidalgo. Her brother was Dr Hidalgo, GP to my family and many others in the valley. She was his assistant for years. As was the custom in those days, my sisters and I were born at home. She told me herself that after her brother died she worked in various hospitals, and that although she's retired she still practices independently as a midwife. The Esparzas didn't meet her at the hospital. Valentín brought her to their house to try to convince his wife to have a home birth.'

Markina gave a sceptical look, indicating the flimsiness of her argument. She redoubled her efforts.

'There are several reasons to suspect Fina Hidalgo's involvement: she attended my mother on the day I was born and my twin sister died; her brother signed my sister's death certificate; she tried to assist at the birth of Esparza's little girl, and I suspect that she delivered those other babies.'

'You suspect – so you aren't certain?'

'No,' she confessed. 'To be certain, I'd need to search Dr Hidalgo's private files for the children's death certificates.'

'You're suggesting that Fina Hidalgo is an angel of death.'

Amaia reflected. Angels of death are characterised by the belief that they are carrying out an important humanitarian role by murdering their fellow men. They often work in the medical profession, or in old people's homes, caring for the sick and the elderly, or those with mental or physical disabilities. They are frequently women. Because they choose victims who are physically frail, and whose deaths arouse little suspicion, they are difficult to detect. They rarely stop killing, because they are convinced of the legitimacy of their actions, and there is no end to their potential victims. They claim to be motivated purely by compassion, and are often extremely kind and thoughtful towards people who are suffering.

'During a conversation I had with her, she admitted that sometimes when a baby was born sick or deformed, it was necessary to help the parents rid themselves of the burden of bringing up such a child.'

'Was anyone else present during that conversation?'

'No.'

'She will doubtless deny it, as will the couples concerned.'

'Those were her words.'

Markina remained thoughtful for a few seconds. He wrote something down in his diary and looked once more at Amaia.

'Besides a search warrant, what else do you need?'

'If we find the death certificates among Dr Hidalgo's papers, we'll need an exhumation order.'

Markina sat up in his chair, frowning at her.

'Whatever for? The Esparza girl was buried today.'

'To exhume the bodies of those little girls whose parents appeared to rejoice over their deaths, the daughters of the couples I just mentioned to you.'

'I'll give you the warrant to search Dr Hidalgo's private files, but you must understand the seriousness of what you are asking. You'll need to show me irrefutable proof that those little girls were murdered if I'm to let you disturb their graves. Exhumations are complicated affairs because of the distress and pain they cause the relatives. Any magistrate would think long and hard about authorising an exhumation, especially that of a child, and you're asking me to dig up three. We'd be under intense pressure from the media, and unless we were absolutely certain of what we were going to find, we'd risk upsetting an awful lot of people.'

'If we have good reason to suspect that a single one of

those children was murdered, any action is justified,' she retorted.

Markina looked at her, impressed by her vehemence, and yet he remained firm. She made to protest, but he held up a hand.

'For the moment, there's nothing to back us up. You say that social services found no evidence of abuse, and that the autopsy reports suggest death by natural causes. The behaviour of the midwife strikes me as suspicious, but there's no direct link between all these people. The fact that some of them are acquainted, or connected with a particular law firm, is like saying that there are six degrees of separation between us and the president of the United States. You need to bring me something more solid. However, I should warn you that ordering the exhumation of babies is deeply repugnant to me, and I'll do everything in my power to avoid it.' Markina seemed visibly affected. His habitually relaxed expression betrayed a mixture of anger and concern that gave his face new depths, a hint of maturity and engagement she hadn't seen until now, and which, without detracting from his charm, made him appear stronger and more masculine. He rose to his feet, picking up his coat. 'I think we should take a stroll.'

Amaia followed him outside, at once surprised and intrigued by his attitude.

'Sudden Infant Death Syndrome is one of nature's most terrible inventions. A mother puts her child to bed, and when she goes to check on him, he is dead. I'm sure as a mother it isn't difficult for you to imagine the horror that such a random, incomprehensible event can unleash on a family. The fear of having done something wrong, of being somehow to blame, plunges them into a waking nightmare of guilt, grief and mistrust. The suddenness with which such deaths occur produces responses that may not always appear rational; those affected suffer a form of temporary insanity, where any reaction, however incongruous, could be considered normal . . .'

163

He paused for a moment, as though reflecting on the horrific implications of what he was saying.

Amaia didn't have to be a behavioural expert to realise how deeply affected Markina was by the subject: it was obvious that the knowledge and subtlety of his observations about the suffering caused by this kind of loss came from first-hand experience.

They walked for a while in silence, crossing the road to the Baluarte Congress Centre, where they strolled along the promenade. A torrent of questions jostled for position in Amaia's head, and yet her training as an interrogator told her that if she waited, the answers would come by themselves, that asking would only make him clam up. Markina was intelligent, cultured and educated, obliged by his profession as a magistrate to give the impression of reliability, self-control and infallibility. He was probably debating with himself that very instant over whether to continue being candid or retreat to the secure vantage point of his position. Amaia noticed he had slackened his pace, just enough to avoid her gaze, each step a perfect pretext not to look her in the eye as he spoke.

'When I was twelve years old, my mother got pregnant. As my parents were no longer in the flush of youth, I imagine it was unplanned. Even so, they were delighted, I don't think I had ever seen them so happy as when my brother was born. He was three weeks old when it happened. My mother gave him his morning feed, changed his nappy and put him back in his cot. Around midday, we heard her screaming. I remember my father and I running upstairs to find her leaning over my brother's cot, giving him the kiss of life, when even I could see that he was dead. I remember my father prising her away from his body, trying to persuade her that it was no good, while I looked on in horror, not knowing what to do.

'Sometimes I think I can still hear her screams, the terrible howls rising from her throat, like the cries of a wounded animal . . . This went on for hours. Then the silence came, and that was even worse. She stopped speaking, except to ask where her baby was. We no longer existed for her, she never spoke to me or to my father again, she never touched me. A healthy baby's death from natural causes is impossible to bear. She convinced herself that she was to blame, that she'd been a bad mother. She tried to take her own life, and was admitted to a mental hospital. Her grief, her feelings of guilt and the incomprehensible nature of her child's death drove her insane. She forgot she had a husband, she forgot she had another son, and she shut herself away with her grief.'

Amaia came to a halt. He walked on a few paces then stopped. She drew level, turning to look at him. She saw his eyes, brimming with tears, as for the first time he looked away, allowing her to study him up close. She liked seeing him like this. Seeing the man behind that mask of perfect masculinity. She had an instinctive dislike of perfection, and now she realised that was what bothered her about him: his beauty, elegance and polished exterior. She could appreciate those qualities individually in any person, but the perfect phrase and the perfect smile always made her suspicious. She realised now that, like her, Markina had made sure he was in complete control of his life in an effort to banish the pain and humiliation of having been rejected by the person who was supposed to love you, abandoned by the one person who was supposed to protect you. It pleased her to know that, beneath that perfect physique raged a furnace with which Markina had forged his ideal life, a life in which nothing escaped his control. Amaia derived an intense satisfaction from discovering the strict codes of conduct people like Markina applied to their lives, but above all to themselves. She may have agreed more or less with his views, but when you had to fight side by side with someone, it helped to know that they were honourable, that they wouldn't betray you.

He gave her an apologetic look.

'I wouldn't be shocked by any response in someone who loses a child like that,' he resumed. 'Describe to me the most insane behaviour of a couple in the throes of grief, and I'll believe you. I refuse to open graves only to unleash a torrent of suffering. Unless you bring me a witness who actually saw someone kill their child, or a statement from the pathologist who carried out these autopsies, retracting their original findings and presenting fresh evidence, I refuse to authorise any exhumation of a child's body.'

Amaia nodded. She was no longer able to contain her curiosity.

'What happened to your mother?'

He looked away, towards the row of orange lights standing like sentinels along the avenue.

'She died two years later, in the asylum. A month after that, my father also died.'

She stretched out her gloved hand until it was touching his. Later on, she would ask herself why she had done that. Touching someone opens a path that can be navigated in both directions. She felt the heat of his hand through her leather glove, like an electric current shooting through her. He slid his gaze from the lights back to her, as he clasped her hand tightly, guiding it to his lips. He held it there long enough to plant a tender kiss on her fingertips that penetrated her glove, her skin, her bones, spreading like a shockwave through her nervous system. When he let go, it was she who resumed walking unsettled, confused, determined not to look at him, the imprint of his lips still burning on her hand as if she'd been kissed by a devil. Or an angel.

Deputy Inspector Etxaide had changed his overcoat for a grey Puffa jacket with a hood, which he was glad of as he paced up and down the street until he saw them leave the bar. He maintained a discreet distance as he followed them through the city centre. Things got complicated when they crossed over the road to the Congress Centre, because the esplanade offered no cover, and even wearing a jacket she'd never seen him in, she might still recognise him and he couldn't take that risk. A group of youths heading in the same direction offered the perfect solution. Without losing sight of Amaia and Markina, he shadowed the kids, pretending to be part of the group, until they reached the stairs to the building, where, oblivious to the cold, they sat down to chat. Etxaide mounted the steps, feigning interest in the notices announcing forthcoming conferences and exhibitions. The couple had turned towards the avenue. They were walking very close together. He could hear them talking, but not what they were saying, and he noticed their hands touch briefly. Their body language betrayed an intimacy between them that excluded everything else, which was perhaps why they didn't see him there, watching their every move.

Her car was parked three blocks away. Amaia walked in silence, aware of Markina's presence beside her, but lacking the courage to turn and look at him. Although she regretted the boldness that had compelled her to touch him, at the same time she felt secretly joined to him by the most anomalous part of her life: both had been rejected by their mothers. She had become the focus of Rosario's hatred, while in Markina's case, a grieving mother had selfishly abandoned her living son in favour of her dead son. She thought of Ibai, and felt strangely close to that woman, for if anything ever happened to him, the world would end. Would her love for James, Ros, or Aunt Engrasi be enough to keep her going? What if Ibai were her eldest child and she lost another? Could she love another child more than she loved Ibai? Could a mother love one child more than another? The answer was yes. It was a well-known fact among behaviourists, and although for centuries people kept up the deception, the fact was that parents loved each child in a different way, they brought each child up in a different way, with different rules. But was it possible to hate one child among others, single him or her out for that dubious honour? Was it possible to hate one of your children to the point of killing them while caring for and protecting the others? Even the most deranged killers followed a pattern, which often only made sense to them; an abnormal pattern, whose twisted logic the investigator must try to comprehend. Amaia was sure that her mother's behaviour wasn't controlled by evil voices in her head, or the result of some abnormality in the structure of her brain, but rather an obscure yet powerful motive that dictated her behaviour towards Amaia and her twin sister, while sparing Flora and Ros.

She wondered how Markina had coped, if indeed he had, and to what extent he had been scarred by losing his entire family in such a short space of time, being plunged from a happy, almost idyllic setting into the most unmitigated personal tragedy. Afterwards, his fortunes had improved; at least he'd been able to concentrate on his studies, a career . . . Although she didn't know how old he was, she'd heard he was the youngest magistrate on the circuit.

Spotting her car, she turned to tell him they'd arrived, only to find him smiling.

'What's so funny?' she asked.

'I feel better, having confided in you. I've never told that to anyone.'

'Have you no other relatives?'

'Both my parents were only children.' He shrugged. 'On the bright side, I'm a wealthy man,' he joked.

She opened the car door, took off her coat and threw it on the passenger seat. Then she hurriedly got in and switched on the ignition, as she tried to think of a businesslike way of saying goodbye.

'So, can I count on getting a warrant to look through Dr Hidalgo's files?'

Markina leaned inside the car, looked at her and smiled.

'I'm going to kiss you, Inspector Salazar.'

She froze, scarcely able to control her nerves, hands clasped together as he drew near. She closed her eyes as she felt his lips, concentrating on the kiss in her dream, a kiss she'd been yearning for ever since she met him, desiring, coveting almost, his soft, sensual mouth, and yet hoping beyond hope to feel the dreary disappointment that often follows when you get what you want. The reality behind the fantasy.

The kiss he planted with exquisite delicacy on the corner of her mouth was short and sweet, lingering just enough to break down her defences. Her lips parted. Then, he properly kissed her.

When he drew away, he was smiling in that inimical way.

'You shouldn't . . .'

'You shouldn't have done that,' he finished her sentence. 'Maybe not, but I thought I should. Thanks for listening.'

'How did you manage to get over it?' she asked, genuinely intrigued. 'How did you get on with your life without letting it affect you?'

'By accepting that she was ill, that she lost her mind and wasn't responsible for her own actions, that she suffered more than anyone because of them. If you're asking whether I always saw things that way, then the answer is no, of course not, but one day I decided to forgive her, to forgive my father, and my baby brother, to forgive myself. You should try it.'

She gave a forced smile.

'Can I count on the search warrant?'

'You won't give up, will you? If I refuse to give you an exhumation order you'll search people's files, and if you find nothing there, you'll look somewhere else, but you'll never give up. You're a true detective.'

She accepted his criticism, gripping the steering wheel as she sat up straight in her seat. Her face radiated determination.

'You're right, I'll never give up. I respect your reasons for refusing the exhumation order at this point, but I'll bring you what you want. I doubt I'll be able to persuade the pathologist to admit she made a mistake in her autopsy reports; I can't expect someone to commit professional suicide without any hard evidence, evidence which in this case happens to be six feet underground. However, if my witnesses stop dying on me, I may be able to obtain a statement from one of the parents; it's unlikely all the couples were equally committed. I interviewed Esparza's wife today, and although she didn't see him kill the girl, her testimony was damning. I'll get those statements, I'll bring you what you want, and you'll have no choice but to give me that order.' His expression clouded. Realising her tone had hardened, she grinned, and said laughingly: 'Now, move aside, your honour, I'm closing the door.'

Easing the door closed, he stepped back on to the pavement. He stood for a long time watching after she had merged with the traffic.

# 22

While she drove, she ran through her plans for the following day, trying hard to rid herself of the warm impression of Markina's kiss, etched perfectly on her lips. She would pay Fina Hidalgo an early visit, drag that witch out of bed if necessary, force her to watch as she examined every birth certificate, every death certificate. Obtaining the warrant was only a partial victory, but she had to start somewhere, and the doctor's files were a good enough place. She might not find enough evidence to convince Markina, but if she could establish the connection she was certain must exist between Fina Hidalgo and those families, it would be a step in the right direction. She would interview them separately, find the weakest link and put the screws on until she got a confession.

Then she remembered something, an idea she couldn't quite define, which had come to her while she was bargaining with Markina. Something that seemed important enough at the time to make her think she mustn't forget it. And yet she had, and the feeling that it could be crucial grew stronger every minute, as she tried desperately to remember precisely when in the conversation it had occurred. The lightning bolt, as Dupree referred to it, a spectacular electrical discharge whose depth of insight could fry your brain, a spark originating somewhere in the nervous system, capable of illuminating in a millisecond the dark areas, a spark brimming with information that might hold the key to a case, if you paid attention.

It was close to midnight when she arrived in Elizondo. Driving down the deserted Calle Santiago, she crossed the bridge, turned right then left after Hostal Trinkete and stopped off at *Juanitaenea*. The vegetable garden, abandoned after Yáñez's arrest, was starting to show signs of neglect. She noticed that some of the plant poles had fallen over, and in the dim light from the streetlamp she could see that the area nearest the road was overgrown with weeds. Illuminated only by a crescent moon, the house itself had a vaguely sinister quality, added to by the cement bricks, piled untidily on pallets outside the entrance.

Engrasi was sitting by the fire watching television. Amaia went over to her, rubbing her cold hands together.

'Hello, Auntie, where is everyone?'

'Hello, my dear. Goodness, you're freezing!' she said, clasping Amaia's hands as she leaned over to kiss her. 'Sit down and warm yourself. Your sister has gone to bed, and James took Ibai up a while ago, and he hasn't come down again so I suppose he must have fallen asleep . . .'

'I'll go up and see them, I'll only be a minute,' she said, 'I'm starving.'

'Haven't you had supper?' I'll rustle something up.'

'No, please don't, Auntie. I can make myself a snack when I come back down,' she said as she started up the stairs, although she could already see Engrasi heading into the kitchen.

Engrasi was right. James had fallen asleep next to Ibai. Seeing them together like that, she felt a pang of remorse about Judge

172

Markina's kiss. 'It means nothing,' she told herself, pushing it from her thoughts.

James opened his eyes and smiled, as if he'd sensed her presence.

'And what time of night is this to be arriving home, missy?'

'You sound like Aunt Engrasi,' she replied, stooping to kiss Ibai first, then James.

'Get into bed with us,' James pleaded.

'First I need to eat something. I won't be long.'

As she was leaving the room, she turned to look at him.

'James, I just drove past *Juanitaenea*, and the building work seems to be at a standstill . . .'

'I don't have the energy to oversee the project right now, Amaia,' he said, looking pointedly at her. 'I have too many other things to worry about. Maybe when we get back from the States. Have you booked your leave yet?'

She hadn't. No way was she going to take time off work; her instincts told her she was close to finding an important lead, and this wasn't the right time to break off the investigation. But she also knew that she was taking a gamble; James was an exceptionally patient man, and thus far in the relationship she had always got her own way, but recently he had started to hint that this might change.

'Yes,' she lied. 'But they haven't got back to me yet – you know how it is . . .'

James took off his trousers and climbed back into bed without looking at her.

'Don't be long.'

Amaia closed the door behind her, unsure whether he was referring to her coming to bed or getting time off work to make the trip.

A steaming bowl of fish soup was waiting for her on the table. As an accompaniment, Engrasi had put out a chunk of bread and a glass of red wine. Amaia ate her soup in silence; only when her spoon was scraping the bowl did she realise how fast she had eaten it. She looked up at her aunt, who hadn't taken her eyes off her.

'You really *were* hungry. Do you want anything else?'

'Only to talk to you. There's something I have to tell you . . .'

Engrasi pushed the bowl aside, stretching her hands across the table in a gesture they had shared since she was a child, and which she claimed eased communication and openness. Amaia seized her aunt's hands, conscious of how incredibly small and soft they were.

'I'm still in touch with Dupree.'

'I knew it,' Engrasi hissed, snatching her hands away.

Amaia gave a mocking laugh.

'Don't fib. How could you possibly have known?'

'Watch your tongue, young lady; there's nothing your aunt doesn't know.'

'Auntie, you need to understand that Dupree is important to me. His advice and guidance have helped me in my investigations. I'm not stupid, Auntie, I can tell the good guys from the bad guys, and Dupree is a good guy. He's my friend, but I also love you. I need you both. I'm going to keep calling him, and I don't want to have to lie to you about it unless you give me a very good reason to do so.'

Engrasi looked at her for what seemed like an eternity. Then she stood up, went over to the sideboard and came back carrying the small black silk bundle containing her tarot cards.

'Oh no, Auntie!' Amaia protested.

'We each have our methods. If you accept his, then you must accept also mine.'

With nimble fingers, she removed the wrapping to reveal the brightly coloured cards, which gave off a musky aroma. She shuffled the pack and placed it on the table for Amaia to cut. Then, carefully, she made Amaia choose twelve cards, which she turned over, arranging them in a circle. She contemplated them for a while; the connecting lines which only she could see. Then she said:

'I'm not sure I can do this any more.'

Amaia gave a start. This was the first time she'd heard her aunt admit that she couldn't do something. She looked as healthy and full of life as ever, but the fact that she would say that about something she'd been doing all her life, something she had an innate talent for, alarmed Amai.

'Auntie, are you feeling all right? Do you want to leave this for another time? It's not important. If you're tired we could—'

'Tired, my eye! I don't mean I'm losing my faculties. I'm not that old! Only that I find it increasingly difficult to read your cards because of my personal involvement. There are things I can't see, because I don't want to see them.'

'Tell me what you see,' said Amaia.

'What I can see, I would prefer not to see either,' replied Engrasi, pointing a bony finger at one of the cards. 'You and James have a serious problem; you and Flora also have a problem. Then there's the problem between Flora and Ros, which involves you. And as if that weren't enough, you still have an evil threat hanging over you.'

Amaia never ceased to be amazed at her aunt's ability to put her finger on things, although she suspected this had more to do with her aunt's love for her, how well she knew her, than her fortune-telling skills.

'You should be careful of Dupree—'

'Why, Auntie? Tell me why. Dupree is possibly one of the finest people I know.'

'I'm not denying that. In fact, I'm sure he is, but he makes you open doors that should be kept closed.'

Amaia moved the cards around on the table, shuffling them together, a look of dejection on her face.

'You know that what you're asking goes against my nature.

I don't believe in closed doors, in walls, in burying things. Buried secrets are like zombies, the living dead that come back to haunt you for the rest of your life. Have you never stopped to wonder why I'm a police officer, Auntie? Do you think people choose this job like any other? I have to open doors. I will knock down walls, I will dig deep until I unearth the truth, and if Dupree can help me to do that, then I welcome his help, as I do yours.'

Engrasi stretched her arms across the table once more, seizing Amaia's hands, then went about shuffling the cards.

'You assume that behind those closed doors lie truth and light. What if they open on to chaos and darkness?'

'I'll gather the chaos into a big heap, and set fire to it to illuminate the darkness,' she said with a chuckle.

Engrasi's face grew serious, belying the tenderness in her voice.

'This is no joking matter, and if you don't believe me you can ask Dupree when he calls, which should be any minute now.'

Amaia followed her aunt upstairs. As she was kissing her goodnight, she felt her mobile vibrate in her pocket.

'That'll be him,' declared her aunt. 'Go downstairs, or you'll wake everyone up. And don't forget to ask him about what I said.'

Amaia ran downstairs, hurriedly closing the sitting room and kitchen doors before answering the call.

'Good evening, Aloisius,' she replied, feeling her heart race as she waited to hear him speak. At last Agent Dupree's voice reached her, a hoarse, distant whisper, as if he were inside an echo chamber.

'Is it nighttime already in Baztán, Inspector Salazar? How are you?'

'Dupree,' she sighed, 'I'm worried. I've forgotten something important. I had it for a second, and then it was gone.'

'If you had it, you can be sure it's still there. Stop thinking about it, and it will come back.'

'I've obtained a warrant to search the files in the house of the midwife who assisted Rosario at my birth, and who probably also delivered all the baby girls who died in their sleep. Possibly, I'll know more tomorrow.'

'Possibly . . .'

'Aloisius?'

He didn't reply.

'I've spoken to Agent Johnson a few times. I think he genuinely admires you and is worried about you. He asked if we were still in touch . . . He says it's a while since you contacted your superiors.'

Silence.

'I didn't tell him anything; I was waiting to talk to you. He thinks you are in danger . . . Are you? Are you in danger?'

Dupree didn't reply.

'I imagine you have your reasons.'

'Come on, Inspector, you know as well as I that the system is riddled with bureaucracy. If we followed the rules, we'd never get anywhere. I'm working on an extremely complex case, one of those cases . . . Do you tell your superiors everything you do? Do you tell them how you get your great results? Do you think they'd approve of your methods? Could you even begin to explain to them what they are?'

'I want to help you,' she replied. Again, silence. 'My aunt says that if you're my friend, you'll never ask for my help, but I know that you're my friend, and you don't even have to ask.'

'Not yet, I'm the one who still has to help you.'

'Is that what my aunt meant?'

'Your aunt is a very clever woman.'

'She says I should stay away from you.'

'Your aunt's advice is sound.'

'Do you think so?'

'At least it comes from the heart, and she's right to advise you to be careful. You're surrounded by people who aren't what they seem.'

The call was cut off. Thirty seconds later, Amaia was still staring at her phone, wondering what it all meant.

# 23

She had set her alarm clock for six in the morning, and by seven a.m. she was in the car park at the police station waiting to leave for Irurita. She took out her phone and reread the message which had been sent with the search warrant attached, feeling in her pocket for the printed version she would show to Fina Hidalgo. She waited until her team were all in their cars, then climbed into hers, so that she was driving behind the small convoy. The sky appeared white on that cold morning, a light breeze buoyed the high clouds, preventing the sun from breaking through, but also keeping the rain away. There was no sign of activity at Dr Hidalgo's beautiful stone house. Amaia felt almost smug about her evil plan to drag Fina Hidalgo out of bed, give her the surprise of her life. However, no sooner had they rung the bell than the woman opened the door as if she'd been waiting for them to arrive. She was dressed in a pair of beige slacks and a brown roll-neck sweater, her hair in a loose bun fastened with Japanese hair sticks. She smiled when she saw them. Deputy Inspector Zabalza presented her with the warrant and explained how the search would be carried out. She stood aside to let them pass, pointing towards the back of the house where the office was located.

Amaia knew something was wrong as soon as Fina Hidalgo

opened the door; she didn't look the faintest bit surprised. She'd been expecting them. Knowing this, and yet being unable to prove it, infuriated her. She pushed past the officers walking ahead of her along the corridor and entered the masculine study, which Dr Hidalgo's sister had preserved exactly as it was when her brother was alive. The cardboard boxes stood on the desk, each bearing a date written in marker pen. It was obvious they were empty; the lids had been hastily thrown on the floor. Fina Hidalgo walked in behind Amaia, pretending to read through the search warrant.

'What bad luck! Those files have been gathering dust for years. I imagine my brother had a sentimental attachment to them . . . And, well, I suppose I hung on to them as a sort of souvenir. Actually, I'd forgotten they existed until someone reminded me of them recently,' she said, giving Amaia a significant look. 'I've never been one for housework, but I decided to give the study a thorough spring-clean yesterday, starting with those boxes.'

Amaia pounced on her. 'Where are they, what have you done with them?'

'Why, the only thing one *can* do with a pile of old papers: I burned them,' she replied, gesturing towards the window.

They rushed over as one to see the smoking remains of a bonfire in the back garden.

Amaia stood motionless at the window. She was so incensed she couldn't move, and Fina Hidalgo hovering behind her didn't help. Etxaide and Zabalza hurried outside to where the remains of the fire lay smouldering. She watched them stamp on the embers, presumably to extinguish the last flames. Looking up at the heavy curtains, she casually tore one of them from its rail, then opened the window.

'Come here, boss, I think we might be able to salvage a few fragments,' said Etxaide. 'Maybe forensics can do something with them.'

Burnt paper required special handling. It had to be collected

180

layer by layer, each piece protected in a separate plastic pouch. The process could take several hours.

Amaia entered the house once more and found Fina Hidalgo sitting at the table in her splendid kitchen, where she'd laid out hot coffee, buttered toast, various jams and a bowl of walnuts.

'Would you like some coffee?'

Amaia didn't answer, although judging from the expressions on her colleagues' faces, they would have gladly accepted. She restrained them with a gesture.

The old nurse smiled genially.

'Did you know that breakfast is the most important meal? A complete breakfast sets you up for the day: bread, coffee and a few walnuts,' she said, offering a handful to Amaia. 'They are from my own garden. Don't be afraid – take them, won't you?'

Amaia's colleagues watched the scene, aware that they were witnessing a battle of wits between the two women.

Amaia ignored her and turned towards the door.

'Let's go,' she said, addressing her team. 'No one must eat anything this woman offers them.'

Out in the street, Iriarte and Montes caught up with her.

'Can someone explain what the hell happened in there?'

Amaia didn't answer. She climbed into her car and drove half a mile, at the head of the convoy this time, until she came to a clearing used for cattle auctions. She parked and got out, motioning to the others to do the same, and when all the men were gathered in a group, she went over to them.

'She was expecting us. She knew we were coming. I obtained the warrant late last night, but the actual authorisation only arrived first thing this morning. I want a list of everyone who knew about the search; I want you to check all outgoing calls from the police station, and I want the mobile numbers of anyone unconnected with the case, so that we can rule them out.'

'Are you implying that one of us warned her about the

search? Do you realise the seriousness of what you're saying?' said Iriarte.

'Yes, I do, but I sent each of you a text telling you the search was on for this morning, and that bitch even had time to make us breakfast. If it makes you feel any better, I don't believe this was premeditated, but I do think there's been a leak.'

'But, boss, that information wasn't classified. I talked about it myself at the police station this morning, when some of the officers on night shift asked why they were there so early,' admitted Deputy Inspector Etxaide.

'Who did you tell?' she demanded, glaring at him.

'I don't remember, it was in the canteen . . .'

'Don't be annoyed, boss, but I talked about it too,' confessed Fermín. 'We've never had to keep hush-hush about work-related matters in the past . . . For fuck's sake, we were sequestering a GP's files, not raiding a cocaine plantation.'

She looked away.

'You're right,' she said. 'But that doesn't change the fact that the information was leaked. Unless one of you mentioned it to someone on the outside.'

They shook their heads as one.

'Go back to the police station. I have a visit to make. But when I return, I want the name of the person responsible.'

# 24

The woman at Lau Haizeta greeted Amaia with the same hospitality as before. Amaia stayed outside, stroking the dogs. At the end of winter, with spring just round the corner, their coats had formed into long, thick tufts, like the fleeces of the sheep they watched over.

'If you pet them too much, they'll follow you everywhere,' the woman warned, sticking her head round the door to tell her that the coffee was ready. But Amaia lingered for a while, laughing as the dogs jumped up, vying for her attention, their antics finally dispersing, like a welcome breeze, the anger and irritation she had brought with her. Fina Hidalgo's smug expression as she sat in her kitchen, like a proud queen holding court, seemed like a clear admission of guilt. The way she had offered Amaia the walnuts, looking her straight in the eye as she held them out, knowing that she knew, was also a silent confession. Much as she sympathised with Iriarte's indignation, with Jonan's reasoning and Montes's justifications, it was obvious to her that the information must have been leaked from the police station. In her estimation, Zabalza was still the unknown quantity; something about the guy wasn't right. Perhaps what jarred were his efforts to appear 'normal', to fit in, while remaining true to himself.

She knew he disliked her, but he didn't have to like her to be a good cop, and there were times when she thought he might have the makings of one; and yet she didn't trust him. For all that, there was no evidence of any connection between Zabalza and Fina Hidalgo, and she didn't think he disliked her enough to jeopardise an investigation simply to make her look bad.

Amaia sipped her coffee while the woman regaled her with stories about her dogs, what good companions and guard dogs they made. After an hour had passed, she glanced at her watch again. She realised she was killing time, because she didn't know what to do next, because her options had run out. She fished out her phone, and showed the woman the photographs of Fina Hidalgo and her car, taken outside the midwife's house. The woman recognised her instantly.

'That's Fina Hidalgo, the doctor's sister. I've known her for years.'

'Have you ever seen her visit Argi Beltz?'

'Many times, she's one of their most frequent visitors, even now.'

Before she put her phone away, Amaia searched for the photograph of her sister Flora to show to the woman.

'I recognise her too, I've seen her on television. Doesn't she do that baking programme? I heard she's originally from here in the valley.'

'Have you ever seen her go to the house? Take a look at the car.'

'Very fancy, but no, I haven't seen it.'

Amaia said goodbye to the owner of Lau Haizeta with a mixture of optimism and disappointment. What good was the woman's testimony confirming that all those people had visited Argi Beltz, if she couldn't establish any other link between them that wasn't purely social? She drove to the top of the hill, stopping the car in the place with the best view of

184

the house; afterwards, on a whim, she drove down the hill again, parked outside the property and sat staring at the fence that concealed the main entrance and garage doors. Then, she glimpsed a movement in her rear-view mirror. Startled, she turned and saw a woman, who had climbed the grassy knoll opposite the property and was taking photographs over the fence with what looked to Amaia like a zoom lens. She climbed out of the car and made her way up the slope, the long slippery grass hindering her ascent. The woman was about forty, well built, wearing designer sports clothes, that were clearly too small for her, and which her exertions had caused to ride up, revealing thick folds of flab about her midriff. She was so absorbed by what she was doing that she remained oblivious to Amaia's presence until she was only a couple of metres away. Seeing her, she screamed:

'This is a public place! I can take photos if I want.'

'Calm down,' Amaia tried to reassure the woman.

'Stay away from me,' she cried, slipping backwards, and landing on the grass. Still screaming, the woman scrambled to her feet. 'Leave me alone, I have every right to be here.'

Amaia pulled out her badge.

'Calm down, it's all right, I'm a police officer.'

The woman looked at her suspiciously. 'Why aren't you in uniform?'

Amaia smiled, showing her the badge. 'Detective Inspector Amaia Salazar.'

The woman looked her up and down.

'You're very young. I don't know, when I think of an inspector, I imagine someone much older.'

Amaia shrugged apologetically. 'I'd like to have a word with you, if that's all right?'

The woman mopped her sweaty brow with her hand, brushing aside her fringe, which remained plastered to her temple. She nodded.

'I think we'd better go down, don't you?' suggested Amaia.

The woman began a slow, lumbering descent, slipping several times on the long grass, though without falling over this time. Amaia offered the woman her hand, which she accepted, and together they went down to the car.

'Did *they* call you?' the woman asked when they reached the road.

'You mean the owners of the house?' said Amaia, pointing towards the property. 'No, I happened to be driving by, when I saw you taking photographs.'

The woman took off her top and used the sleeves to tie it around her bulky hips. The underarms of her T-shirt were drenched with sweat.

'This wouldn't be the first time they've "asked" me to leave. But I'm not breaking the law.'

'I'm not suggesting you are, I'd simply like to know why you're so interested in that house. Are you planning to buy it?' Amaia said, drawing the woman out.

'Buy it? I'd rather live on a rubbish dump. I'm not interested in the house, only in what those murderers are doing in there.'

Amaia felt her body tense, then, collecting herself, she asked:

'What makes you think they are murderers?'

'I don't think – I know. They killed my children, and now they refuse to give me their bodies, so I have nowhere to go to mourn them.'

The indictment couldn't have been clearer. Not only was the woman accusing the couple of having murdered her children, but of having stolen their bodies. Amaia was about to suggest they go somewhere else to continue the conversation when she realised there was something missing.

'Where's your car? How did you get here?'

'I walked . . . Well, my father drops me off at a nearby shepherd's hut, then picks me up at lunchtime. Since I've been ill, the doctors say it's good for me to walk every day,' she added. 'I'm not allowed to drive because of the medication I'm on.'

186

'May I invite you for a coffee? I'd like to talk to you, but not here,' she said.

The woman glanced suspiciously at Amaia's car and then at the house, trying to make up her mind.

'I can't drink coffee, because of my nerves, but I'll accompany you. You're right about not wanting to talk here; God knows what those murderers are capable of.'

On the way to Etxebertzeko Borda, Amaia cast sidelong glances at the woman, who was perspiring heavily and reeked of stale sweat. Her hair was gathered untidily into a ponytail, from which a few lank strands hung loose. Even so, the cut of her fringe and highlights suggested she went to a professional hairdresser. The camera slung about her neck also looked expensive, as did the jewellery she wore. Her longish nails were manicured, and her rings dug unattractively into her puffy fingers. Amaia imagined that the woman had gained weight rapidly. Some people had difficulty admitting they need a larger size, or in her case two.

She parked near the restaurant, and they walked in silence towards the entrance, passing the outside tables where she and James sat in the summer, and from where you could hear the murmur of the river. As they walked through the door, a waiter emerged from the kitchen to greet them. While Amaia ordered their drinks, the woman picked out a table as far as possible from the bar area, although, after bringing their order, the waiter returned to the kitchen where they heard him join in with the chatter of female voices within.

'What makes you think those people killed your children? Do you realise the seriousness of what you're saying? Do you have proof? Are you aware that if you don't, they could sue you for libel?'

The woman stared at her blankly for a few seconds without speaking. She looked puzzled, as if she hadn't understood. Amaia was wondering what kind of medication the woman was on, when she responded vehemently:

'When I say those people murdered my sons, I mean they are responsible for their deaths. And, yes, I realise the seriousness of what I'm saying, and of course I have proof. I didn't see them kill my children, if that's what you're asking, but my husband took part in their evil rituals and gave up my babies to them. And as if that weren't enough, they stole their bodies leaving me with an empty grave.' The woman took out her phone to show Amaia a photograph of two babies barely three months old dressed in blue pyjamas.

'What did they die of?'

The woman started to cry.

'Cot death.'

'Both of your children died of Sudden Infant Death Syndrome?'

The woman nodded, still crying.

'Yes – the same night.'

Amaia ran through Jonan's list in her head. She couldn't recall a case of twins dying at the same time, and they couldn't possibly have overlooked such a shocking coincidence.

'Are you sure the cause of death recorded by the doctor wasn't something else? Respiratory failure perhaps, or asphyxiation, or they might have choked on their own vomit? Those causes can sometimes be confused with cot death.'

'My children didn't suffocate, they didn't choke to death, they died in their sleep.'

Despite the cool temperature in the restaurant, she was still perspiring, and her acrid breath, expelled in nervous gasps, reached Amaia from across the table. She was clearly unwell – her reference to taking medication that prevented her from driving, and not being able to drink caffeine, suggested a serious nervous disorder. Amaia lowered her eyes, recognising that she'd allowed herself to be drawn in by a woman with mental problems. It was odd that the focus of her obsession should be precisely that house and those people, but her account seemed to contradict the findings of Amaia's inquiry. For a start, she'd lost two male children, when all the other victims had been female. And there had been no mention in the official records of twin brothers dying simultaneously.

'I never wanted kids, you know? It was my husband who was keen on the idea. I suppose I was quite a selfish person; I'm an only child, you see. I liked travelling, skiing, enjoying life. Besides, I was getting on for thirty-six when we met. He was a bit younger, a very handsome Frenchman. Lots of people said that he'd married me for my money, but when he insisted we have kids, I really believed he wanted to start a family, so I got pregnant, and then everything changed. I never imagined I could feel such love for another human being; after all that had happened, I thought I'd be incapable of looking after them, or of loving them even. But Mother Nature is wise and she makes us love all our babies. I adored them the instant I saw them, and I took good care of them. I was a good mother from the day they were born.'

She looked at Amaia, taking her silence for scepticism. 'You might find it hard to believe, seeing the way I am now, but I wasn't always like this. I don't mind admitting that when my sons died I went crazy – there's nothing strange about that. The pain of losing them and seeing how my husband reacted was too much for me to bear.'

'How did he react?' Amaia broke in, immediately cursing herself for having interrupted.

'He told me that from then on things would look up, our fortunes would improve. We built a splendid tomb, which my ex-husband smothers in flowers, but it's as empty as his heart, because on the day of their funeral, he spirited my sons away.'

'You said ex-husband; are you divorced?'

The woman gave a mocking laugh.

'I couldn't rise to the occasion. As he'd predicted, his fortunes improved after that – not that we needed more money; my

189

family is extremely wealthy, we own mines in Almandoz. But he wanted money of his own, and a wife receiving psychiatric treatment, who had gained forty kilos, and went round telling everyone her babies' graves had been robbed didn't fit in with his plans. He left me, married his French whore, and now they're expecting a baby . . . My sons would be three years old now.'

'Your ex-husband lives in France?'

'Yes, in our old house in Ainhoa. I couldn't stay there after what happened, but he doesn't care; he lives there with his new wife and his soon-to-be new baby.'

'So, your sons died in France?' said Amaia.

'Yes, and that's where they're supposed to be buried, in the beautiful cemetery in Ainhoa – except they aren't there.'

Amaia stared intently at the woman, who seemed oblivious as she fingered her fringe, wet with perspiration, in an effort to neaten it.

'Would you be prepared to make a statement at the police station about what you've just told me?'

'Of course,' she replied. 'I'm fed up with being ignored. I don't know where else to turn.'

'I should warn you that unless we can verify your claims, your statement will be worthless. I want you to write down everything you've just told me, including dates and any details that might help corroborate your testimony. Anything you can remember, no matter how trivial it might seem. I'll need a telephone number I can reach you on.'

The woman looked at her blankly, then replied: 'Have you got a pen?'

The conference room on the first floor was too big for a meeting of five people. She would normally have called the team into her office to go over the morning's tasks, instead of standing in front of them like a New York police sergeant assigning them their daily duties. However, after the debacle of the search at Fina Hidalgo's house, she felt she needed to explain to them about leadership, loyalty and commitment. Having also summoned the twenty-two officers who were working on the relevant shift, she began with a brief summary of events leading up to them obtaining the search warrant, and what had transpired between then and the abortive search. She made clear her suspicions that Fina Hidalgo had been expecting them, and asked everyone present to commit to ridding the force of attitudes that could jeopardise investigations.

This was the first time she had summoned them to a meeting in the conference room; that was usually Iriarte's job. He was sitting, head down, in the front row, no doubt annoyed at having been demoted. She scrupulously avoided singling out any member of her team or even looking at them, but despite her attempts to include everyone who'd been on duty during the relevant period, it was obvious her message was directed at them in particular. When the meeting was over, she asked them to remain behind.

'A new witness has come forward.'

They all looked at her, intrigued.

'A woman who claims her two babies died of SIDS at the same time. She also says that, after they died, her ex-husband – they had since divorced – who visited the Martínez-Bayón couple at their home in Orabidea, assured her their fortunes would improve. Does that sound familiar? She's agreed to come in and make a statement this afternoon. I'd like you all to be present, and to ask questions you think might be pertinent.'

They nodded.

'I ought to warn you. She's a bit . . . odd.' She thought about how to describe the witness without undermining her credibility. 'The loss of her sons left her traumatised, and she is on prescribed medication, which makes her seem confused. When we spoke, she came across as quite competent: she was able to supply dates, and her account of events seemed clear. However, we need to check the facts, because based on her mental state a lawyer would have no difficulty pulling our case apart. She should be arriving any minute.'

Yolanda Berrueta was wearing a maroon dress with a matching jacket, which she carried over her arm, and thick tights. Her hair, clean and recently combed, was secured with a large clip. She seemed nervous, and was clutching a cardboard folder, which bore the imprint of her sweaty fingers. Amaia accompanied her to an office on the first floor and offered to take the file, but the woman held it to her chest in a defensive manner. She introduced Yolanda to her colleagues and informed her that the interview would be taped.

'I'd like you to tell my colleagues what you told me this morning, adding any fresh details you may have remembered and which you think might be relevant.'

'I met Marcel Tremond, my ex-husband during a ski trip in Huesca; we got engaged and then married. I didn't want children: I liked the good life, also I considered myself too old to be a mother. But Marcel was younger than me, and he convinced me. Finally, I got pregnant, and after I gave birth, I devoted myself to looking after my babies. The poor little things were underweight, but we looked after them. One evening, when they were about two months old, I went to check on them while they were asleep, and saw that they'd stopped breathing.'

Her voice was a dull monotone, but her face was beaded with sweat, as if she'd been caught in a rain shower.

'We rushed them to the hospital, but they couldn't save them. My babies died.' She started to cry softly. Iriarte passed her a box of tissues. Yolanda took a handful, applying them to her damp face in layers, like an Egyptian death mask. 'I'm sorry,' she murmured through spread fingers.

'Don't worry, carry on when you're ready.'

She peeled the tissues off her face, rolling them into a moist ball in her hand.

'There was a wake, then the funeral, but I wasn't allowed to see my children. Marcel said it would be better for me to remember them as they were, and he asked for the coffins to be sealed. Why did they treat me like that? Did they think I was too fragile to see my boys? Didn't they realise how terrible it is for a mother not to see her dead children? Why wouldn't they let me see them?'

Sitting behind her, Inspector Montes looked searchingly at Amaia as Yolanda continued her story.

'I know why. Because they weren't inside their coffins – my boys had been stolen.'

Iriarte broke in. 'You believe someone kidnapped your children? Do you think they might still be alive?'

'If only they were! No, when we left for the hospital, they were already in cardiac arrest; their little faces had turned blue, and their fingers too. They died that night.'

'So, you claim that their bodies were stolen.'

'I don't claim anything: I know. I saw it with my own eyes. I was so weak, they thought I couldn't walk, but mothers have hidden reserves of strength. I went into the room where the metal casket was and I opened it; inside were some bags of sugar wrapped in a towel. But my babies weren't there.'

'Did you mention this to anyone?' asked Amaia.

'I told Marcel, but he insisted I'd gone into the wrong room. At the time I thought he must be right, they had dosed me with sedatives, and I had got confused. But, tell me, why would anyone put bags of sugar inside a casket?'

'Did you tell anyone else about it?' asked Iriarte.

'No, no, I burst into tears, so they gave me another injection. When I woke up, it was all over and they'd taken the coffins.'

'What makes you think your husband was involved?'

'He changed. He started to act differently. He was so attentive

193

while I was pregnant, but after the children died, he lost all interest in me; he abandoned me when I most needed him.'

'Some people react badly to grief,' said Amaia, looking straight at her. 'What other changes did you notice?'

'He was never at home – because of work, he said, his business was doing well. But I didn't believe him. He couldn't be working all the time. So I started to follow him.'

Amaia noticed Zabalza glancing at Montes, and Montes's expression when he looked back.

'You followed your husband?' she asked.

'Yes, and this morning, after you said to write everything down, I remembered something.'

She opened the folder, which she had kept close to her throughout the interview, and placed on the table high-quality images printed on A4 paper. They showed a car parked by a wall, which Amaia recognised as the one surrounding the Martínez-Bayóns' house; in one of them, the mailbox was visible.

'That's Marcel's car, and that's the house he was visiting. These are the only photos I could find, but I'm sure there are more on my memory sticks. I took loads – until they saw me, and started parking inside the gates.'

Some of the photographs showed other cars parked on the narrow road.

'You told Inspector Salazar that your husband is a businessman,' Iriarte said. 'Did you know that the owners of that house are also in business? Did you consider the possibility that their meetings may have been work-related?'

'No, I didn't,' she stammered.

'Are you aware of your husband having had any dealings with the legal firm Lejarreta & Andía?' asked Inspector Montes.

'I've never heard of them.'

'Where did you give birth?' asked Amaia.

'At a French hospital called Notre Dame de Montagne.'

'Did you at any point consider having a home birth?'

'My husband suggested it when I first got pregnant, but once we found out I was expecting twins the subject never came up again. Besides, if I'm honest, the idea gives me the creeps; why have a home birth when you can be in a hospital? The thought of lying there with the whole family watching seems primitive to me.'

'Do you know a midwife called Fina Hidalgo?'

'No.'

Zabalza, who was taking notes, asked: 'Is the hospital where you gave birth the same one your babies died in?'

'Yes, they were treated there from birth.'

'Could you tell us the name of your doctor, so we can ask for a copy of the autopsy?'

'There was no autopsy.'

'Are you sure?' said Amaia, surprised. 'It's routine procedure when someone dies in hospital.'

'There *was* no autopsy,' the woman insisted, brushing aside her fringe, now wet with perspiration and plastered to her brow in a way that looked comical. Then she raised her arms to unstick her hair from the back of her neck. Montes watched as several beads of sweat trickled down her neck to join the damp circles under her arms.

'Would you like a glass of water?' he asked.

'No, I'm fine . . .'

She radiated heat like someone with a fever, and her body odour filled the room. Montes signalled to Etxaide to open the window, but Amaia restrained him with a gesture.

The woman took five more sheets of paper filled with tiny, cramped handwriting out of the file. As she passed them over the table, Amaia received a waft of stale sweat.

'I've written down everything I can remember. It's all true, but sometimes I get confused about what happened when . . . It's because of the medication, but those are the facts – you can check them for yourselves.'

195

'Thank you, Yolanda,' said Amaia, extending her hand, only to discover that the other woman was still clutching the wet ball of tissues. Yolanda hurriedly changed it over to her other hand, and Amaia felt her feverish heat as she shook her hand firmly. 'You've been a great help. We'll be in touch over the next few days. If you remember anything else, don't hesitate to call us. Deputy Inspector Zabalza will show you out. Do you need a lift home?'

'No thank you, my parents are waiting for me outside.'

They held off opening the window until they were sure she was out of earshot.

'Fuck! I thought I was going to suffocate,' said Montes, leaning out and breathing in a lungful of fresh air.

'So, what conclusions can we take from this?' asked Amaia.

'That she stinks like a pig and sweats like a bull.'

'That's unkind, Montes,' said Amaia reprovingly. 'Yolanda is on medication, one of the side effects of which is bromhidrosis, or body odour. Don't you know about stress-related perspiration? Have some respect.'

'I have respect, what I don't have is a nose of steel. The woman stinks of piss!'

'That's because when the sweat reaches the pores it produces ammonia and fatty acids. I'm sure you've encountered far worse smells during your days on the beat. Right, so, do any of you have observations that aren't related to this poor woman's body odour?'

'I knew her a long time ago,' said Iriarte. 'She obviously didn't recognise me. Her father is Benigno Berrueta, who owns the Almandoz mines; her mother is from Oieregi, where they used to live. She was eighteen then, and forty kilos lighter. She was a spoilt little rich kid, and extremely pretty. Even at that age she drove a sports car. It's pitiful to see how life has treated her.'

'Well, they're still loaded. The father was waiting for her

outside in a BMW that must have cost at least eighty grand,' Zabalza broke in.

'That's not what I meant: divorced, two dead babies and a mental breakdown. I wouldn't swap places with her for all the money in the world.'

'So,' Montes summed up, 'we have a middle-aged rich kid – who we mustn't forget is undergoing psychiatric treatment – accusing her ex-husband – who, let's not forget this either, has remarried and is expecting another child – of stealing their sons' bodies. What can I say? I feel sorry for her too, but a magistrate is going to see a crazy, embittered woman wreaking revenge on her ex-husband.'

'I warned you that she was odd, and that we had to tread carefully. I realise how the situation would appear to a magistrate, but I think she's telling the truth – or at least, I think she believes what she's saying. We only have to check her story, and right now, this woman, with her glaring faults, is all we have. And of course that detail about bags of sugar in the casket is extremely significant.'

They nodded as one.

'Montes and Zabalza, find out if Marcel Tremond or any of his companies have dealings with Lejarreta & Andía. We'll request the autopsy reports from the hospital where the babies died; if they don't have them, we'll contact the relevant pathologist's office. Let's see if Yolanda is right and no autopsies were carried out. And remember your manners, we have no jurisdiction in France, and no warrant. Iriarte, I'd like you to accompany Etxaide and me to Ainhoa, on a day's outing, to take a look around and see what the locals have to say. For the time being, we will limit ourselves to checking Yolanda's statement word for word without involving any third parties . . .'

# 25

In Amaia's opinion, Ainhoa was the prettiest village in southern France. The first community you came to after crossing the Dantxarinea border, it was located in Nouvelle-Aquitaine, in the French Basque commune of Laburt. Its position, on the road to Santiago de Compostela, suggested it had probably been a stopping-off place for pilgrims, much like Elizondo. After parking next to the traditional pelota court, they strolled down the broad avenue, admiring the thirteenth-century architecture, reminiscent of the Txokoto neighbourhood in Elizondo, except for the dark wooden beams, which in Ainhoa were painted bright green, red, yellow and blue. They also observed the stone plaques and coats of arms with strange, Frenchified, Basque names.

The Tremond family house stood at the end of the avenue where the road curved gently, opening on to a landscape of hills dotted with quaint-looking dwellings. They walked past, admiring the patio, which they could see through the open gate. Round stones set in the ground formed a perfect circle in what had once been the coach yard.

What made Ainhoa special, what for Amaia gave the town all its character, was the cemetery surrounding the church. Juan Pérez de Baztán, squire of Jaureguizar and Ainhoa, had dedicated his church to Our Lady of the Assumption; through the ages, the original building had undergone so many changes and alterations that it was difficult to pin down the style. Burials in the environs of the church began in the sixteenth century, as the population grew, and also to accommodate the many pilgrims who died before reaching their destination. It was a cemetery where family tombs were arranged in rows and packed so close together that one had to clamber over some to get to others. The many circular headstones were decorated with geometric symbols, Basque crosses and above all sun engravings; some symbols revealed the deceased person's profession, others were elaborately decorated telling the story of the occupant's life from cradle to grave. Perched on a grassy knoll at the centre of the village, the cemetery could be seen from streets, houses, shops and cafés all over the village; with no boundary wall to separate them, the living and the dead mingled in a casual, benign manner, which outsiders found unnerving.

The church was dark, cold and silent. Empty apart from a man and woman sitting in the front pew. After circling the churchyard once, they found the Tremond family tomb. Just as Yolanda Berrueta had told them, it was festooned with flowers, mostly white – the traditional colour for a child's grave. As they approached the blackened stone structure, Amaia noticed Iriarte's reluctance to step on the neighbouring graves, proverbially a mark of disrespect.

'Don't worry,' she said. 'It must be the custom here, other-wise most of these tombs would be unreachable.'

Deputy Inspector Etxaide moved aside some of bouquets so he could read the inscriptions on the slab. The children's names were missing.

He replaced the flowers, stepping backwards on to another tomb, pulling a face as he did so.

'Boss, from where I'm standing, the slab seems to be tilting slightly,' he said, stepping forward again, and running his fingers over the gap where the slab joined the sides of the tomb. 'No, actually, someone has tried to prise open the tomb, and the sandstone has crumbled.'

Feeling the place Jonan had indicated, she found the gap where the slab had been forced.

An old lady who could have been ninety was watching them from the path. Jonan went over to her, smiling. After a brief exchange, he kissed her on both cheeks, then returned to Amaia and the sullen Iriarte, who seemed affected by the melancholy of the place.

'Madame Marie tells me the priest won't be here until midday.'

Amaia glanced at her watch: they had half an hour to kill.

'Why don't we get a coffee, it's freezing out here,' she suggested, grinning at Iriarte's sombre expression as they made their way towards the steps down to the main street.

There was a café on the corner, but on the way, Amaia paused to look at the souvenirs in the window of a shop facing the churchyard.

'Jonan, come over here. What does that say?' she asked.

Etxaide read the French then translated.

'*Our neighbours opposite may be at peace, but we have a better life. We aren't planning to move in the near future.*'

Amaia grinned. 'Gallows humour, Inspector Iriarte; it comes from living with the dead,' she said, attempting to raise a laugh. Since the abortive search at Fina Hidalgo's house the previous day, she'd found him more morose than usual.

'Imagine living here,' he murmured, gesturing towards the balconies on the first and second floors. 'The first thing you'd see every day is a graveyard. I don't think that's healthy.'

'There used to be a graveyard outside the old church in Elizondo. After the river washed it away, they moved it out to Camino de los Alduides.'

'I would never buy a house where I was forced to look

at funerals and exhumations,' he said, appalled at the thought.

They entered the shop. Amaia browsed for a while, looking through the embossed leather bookmarks with scenes from Ainhoa.

The shopkeeper greeted them with a friendly smile. 'Are you here sightseeing?'

'Yes, but our main reason for stopping off is because we have acquaintances here. They live down the road in the house with red shutters – the Tremond family.'

The man nodded enthusiastically. 'Yes, I know them.'

'We just visited the tomb where their sons are buried. What a terrible tragedy!'

The shopkeeper nodded, wistfully this time. Amaia knew from experience how some people loved to talk about the misfortunes of others.

'Oh, yes, indeed, a tragedy. The mother's grief drove her insane; she's tried several times to force open the tomb during her fits of mania.' He lowered his voice as though confiding a secret. 'She's a very nice woman, and I'm extremely fond of her, but more than once I've been obliged to call the police. I could see her from here, trying to lift up the slab with a crowbar. I didn't like to get her into trouble, but what she was doing was too awful for words.'

'You did the right thing,' Amaia reassured him. 'You're a good neighbour, and I'm sure the family is grateful to you.'

The man smiled with the satisfaction of having done his duty and been commended for it. As they emerged from the store, they saw the priest dressed in a cassock and dog collar striding across the graveyard. Giving up the idea of coffee, they followed him into the church.

'I am acquainted with the family and their terrible ordeal,' the priest told them. 'The ex-wife has lost her mind. Every week she comes here to try to convince me that her children aren't inside the tomb, that someone stole their bodies, that as a mother she knows instinctively that her sons aren't in there. I have the greatest respect for a mother's instinct; it's one of the most powerful forces of nature – our Mother Mary's love for her son is a cornerstone of our religion. The grief of a mother who loses a child is like no other on earth, which is why I understand Yolanda's suffering, but I cannot condone her behaviour. Her sons died and were buried here in this churchyard. I myself officiated at the funeral, I witnessed their coffins being lowered into the tomb.'

'A local man told us that Yolanda has tried to break into the tomb. Is that true?'

'I'm afraid it is,' the priest said sadly. 'On more than one occasion. This is a small village, and everyone knows about it, so if anyone sees her they either call me or they call the police. You must understand, Yolanda isn't dangerous or violent, she's simply obsessed . . .'

'One other question: why aren't the children's names inscribed on the tombstone?'

'Oh, I'm afraid the graves are so old, and the sandstone so eroded, that most people place a loose plaque on the tomb with the names and dates of the deceased. That's what they did for the children, but Yolanda smashed them to pieces out on the road, claiming the plaques were false, that her sons weren't in there.'

When they got back to the police station, Iriarte ended his pained silence with a request:

'Inspector, could I speak to you in my office?'

Amaia went in, closing the door behind her, as Iriarte walked slowly over to his chair.

'Take a seat, Inspector,' he said. 'I've been thinking this over since yesterday . . .'

He didn't need to tell her. At the start of the *tarttalo* investigation a year ago, she had seen how deeply affected Iriarte was by the appearance of the babies' arm bones. Finding the

Esparza girl's body stuffed in a bag hadn't exactly helped brighten his vision of the world, and the Kafkaesque deaths of Elena Ochoa, Berasategui and Esparza had made him even more sullen and introverted. He had barely said a word since the debacle at Fina Hidalgo's house.

'Salazar, the moment I met you on the *basajaun* case, I knew I was in the presence of a brilliant detective. Since then I've taken part in investigations at a level I could never have dreamed of, and having you here at the police station is a luxury we all appreciate.' He moistened his lips, revealing his awkwardness at what he was about to say: 'You aren't the easiest person to work with – and why should you be? We are what we are, and your complexity is no doubt part of what makes you so good at your job. Our profession is a difficult one, we all have differences of opinion, and I'm no exception. More than once during this past year, I've had serious doubts about some of the decisions you've made, but I've always either given you my support or kept quiet . . .'

Amaia nodded, recalling the rainy day Iriarte had accompanied her as she spread the dark Baztán earth over her ancestors' bones in the family *itxusuria*.

'But . . .' she said.

He smiled, acknowledging that there was a but.

'I won't bring into question the integrity of our entire team; I won't hang those officers out to dry. I admit that Fina Hidalgo burning those files ahead of our visit was more than mere coincidence, and I understand your frustration and suspicions, but I refuse to lay the blame on members of our team without a scrap of evidence. As superintendent of this station, I've opened an internal investigation into whether any information has been leaked from here. But there's something you must understand: I've lived in Baztán all my life, and I've been at this police station for many years, and unless a piece of information is labelled confidential, people will talk. Someone could have mentioned it in all innocence to a relative, or blurted it out in a public place . . . However, I can vouch for the integrity of my officers; none of them called Fina Hidalgo, and I think it was a mistake to ask them to hand over their mobile phones.'

Amaia heard him out in silence, appreciating how difficult it was for Iriarte to confront her on this matter. And as she listened, her mood changed, her initial irritation gave way to deep regret. Watching him search for the right words to tell her she was mistaken, avoiding her gaze for more than three seconds at a time, speaking calmly and deliberately to remove any trace of hostility from his voice . . .

'You're right,' she conceded. 'I was frustrated after the fiasco at Hidalgo's, and I doubt that any of those men is capable of sabotaging an investigation out of personal resentment. But the fact is, whether the leak was accidental or not, Fina Hidalgo destroyed evidence because someone tipped her off, and that has jeopardised this investigation. I want you to get to the bottom of it. This is a police station, not a school playground. These officers ought to understand what it means to wear this uniform.' Amaia softened her tone: 'I appreciate your loyalty and your honesty, and I return the compliment. I overstepped myself and I apologise; my intention wasn't to undermine your authority. I just wanted everyone to understand the seriousness of what had happened.'

'Rest assured, we do.'

As Amaia stood up to leave, Iriarte added: 'There's one other thing, Inspector Salazar. Your invitation to take part in the FBI seminars has arrived, along with authorisation papers from Pamplona. They're on your desk, awaiting your signature.'

Inspector Montes took his seat with a smile.

'Well, that was easy. Marcel Tremond has several businesses registered in Navarre, Aragon and La Rioja, most of them to do with wind-farm technology, turbine engines, that sort of thing. Lejarreta & Andía are named as legal representatives in every case. So there's a definite link.'

'I wasn't so lucky,' Jonan broke in. 'The test results of the paper samples lifted from the bonfire at Fina Hidalgo's came in: it turns out there was too much damage for them to be able to make out any writing,' he said, placing a printed sheet on the table. 'Apart from that, I've spent the day firing off emails and talking on the phone to a French pathologist and the hospital where Yolanda's boys died. She's right: there was no autopsy. The paediatrician who treated them from birth signed the death certificate, and deemed it unnecessary. The funeral was organised by a local undertaker, who transported the bodies from the funeral parlour to the cemetery. Marcel Tremond asked to be left alone with his boys to say a last farewell, but that's nothing unusual. No one else was left alone with the coffins, which they clearly remember the father requesting remain sealed.'

Amaia gazed pensively at her two officers as she absorbed this information. She had been certain their inquiries would bear fruit, and now that she'd been proved right it was like a weight being lifted from her shoulders. She gave a sigh, aware that with this fresh information, added to what she already knew, the case was beginning to gain momentum – just when she was starting to doubt her ability to see it through to the end.

'My witness, a neighbour of the Martínez-Bayóns, has identified Tremond's car as one of those she has seen parked outside Argi Beltz. Unfortunately, I suspect she's beginning to understand the ramifications of all this, because she informed me today that she wouldn't be able to swear to it in court as she didn't write down the number plate. She's in no doubt about those of Fina Hidalgo and Valentín Esparza, and Berasategui's car had a special badge. She has seen all three entering and leaving the property on several occasions. She isn't sure about Marcel Tremond, but she has seen Yolanda taking photographs of the house.'

Iriarte nodded.

'Argi Beltz appears to be the link between all those people and Berasategui. Even if we can't prove they met each other there, we know they've all visited the house. Bearing in mind our psychiatrist friend's penchant for the bones of dead babies, I'm sure any magistrate would see reasonable and sufficient grounds for ordering an exhumation.'

'Possibly, but Markina isn't just any magistrate,' she declared.

'Inspector, Judge Markina has no jurisdiction in France,' said Iriarte, looking straight at her, waiting for his meaning to sink in. 'I'm acquainted with Judge De Gouvenain. A couple of years ago we collaborated with French police on a drug-trafficking case where one of the suspects turned up dead in Navarre after a settling of scores. She's a pragmatist, used to dealing with the ugly side of life, but with great compassion. She won't balk at authorising an exhumation order, especially if the aim is to alleviate a mother's pain. I think if you explain to her that Yolanda Berrueta's grief has made her unbalanced, and that this could have been avoided if she'd been able to see from the beginning that her sons' bodies were indeed inside the tomb, Judge De Gouvenain is sure to give her permission.'

'It's too risky. I can't do it like that. What if their bodies aren't in the tomb? What if, as I suspect, Marcel Tremond took his dead sons to the same place where Esparza planned to take his daughter, and where my mother possibly took my twin sister? If the bodies are missing, how will I explain to Judge De Gouvenain why I failed to mention these other aspects of the investigation?'

'In that case,' said Iriarte, 'let the French police deal with it. Tell them what we've got so far, and let them request the exhumation order. But leave out any reference to your mother and sister. If De Gouvenain thinks you are personally involved, she may refuse to sign the order; but aside from that, I see no problem. The case has got as far as Esparza's death, and then we established a link between him and Berasategui. The *tarttalo*'s sensational crimes reached beyond our borders; in fact, I received several emails and calls from our French colleagues, which means De Gouvenain must have heard about it. Present it as a vague suspicion. I'm sure that a possible crime with links to the *tarttalo* committed in her territory will be far too tempting for an ambitious woman like Judge De Gouvenain to resist.' Iriarte looked at his watch. 'The Chief of Border Police works late, and I have his number.'

'Okay,' said Amaia as she scribbled her signature on the authorisation papers for the seminars at Quantico. 'Go ahead and make the call.'

# 26

In the past few hours, after a brief respite, the rain had returned. As if to compensate, the clouds had formed a protective layer, raising the temperature and dispelling the cold breeze. They were accompanied by the Chief of Border Police and two patrolmen, whose job it was to ensure that Judge Loraine de Gouvenain's orders were carried out to the letter: they would remove the slab and they would descend into the crypt to verify that the children's bodies were inside their coffins. No permission was given for them to be lifted to the surface, or disturbed in any way. The order stated that Yolanda Berrueta was permitted to look inside to make sure that her children's bodies were where they were supposed to be.

They waited with the French police patrol and the cemetery workers, sheltering from the rain beneath the tiny portico at the entrance to the church. The priest had his arm around Yolanda, who rested her head on his shoulder, emotional yet serene, as he whispered words of encouragement to her.

The rain soaking into the porous sandstone had turned the tombs a darker shade, showing up the shiny moss and lichen climbing up the sides. Fortunately, the rain seemed to have deterred onlookers; and so far as any passersby were concerned, a group of people huddled in the entrance to Our Lady of the

Assumption wasn't so out of the ordinary, even if there were a couple of uniformed police officers among them. In the car park, next to the entrance to the churchyard, a dark blue official-looking car rolled to a halt. Moments later, the chief's mobile rang.

'Come with me, please,' he said. 'Judge De Gouvenain has arrived.'

Amaia pulled up the hood of her Puffa jacket and followed him into the rain.

The car window glided down and Judge De Gouvenain peered outside, looking none too happy at the sight of the rain pouring down. Amaia had expected someone quite different, perhaps because of Iriarte's description of her as a tough woman, accustomed to dealing with the ugly side of life. Loraine De Gouvenain's hair was scraped into a bun, and she wore a coral dress and lightweight coat, defying the last days of winter. The chief leaned in to speak to her, and Amaia did the same. A smell of spearmint wafted out from inside the car, coming from a tin of lozenges the judge was holding, and to which she seemed partial.

'Chief, Inspector,' she greeted them, 'I imagine it will take a while to remove the slab. My legal secretary will oversee the procedure. Let me know when it's done; I've no intention of ruining my shoes in this rain.'

As they rejoined the group, Amaia remarked: 'Madame le Juge won't be happy if she has to descend into the crypt.'

'She'll do whatever's necessary. She can't stand rain, but she's one of the best. Her father was head of the Sûretè in Paris, and believe me, it shows. De Gouvenain is that rare beast: a magistrate who actually makes our job easier.'

It turned out Madame le Juge was right: the whole operation took well over an hour. The cemetery workers started by removing the flowers heaped on top of the slab, then exchanged worried looks.

'What's wrong?' asked Amaia.

'The slab is so fragile, they're afraid it will break if they lever it off. So, they're going to have to use a small hydraulic crane to lift it. There's one at the municipal depot close by, but they will need another vehicle to transport it.'

'How long will that take?'

'Another half hour . . .'

The chief went over to inform Judge De Gouvenain of the delay. The priest invited them to wait inside the church, but they all refused.

'How do you spot a lawyer in a cemetery?' Jonan asked. 'He's the only walking corpse,' he added, indicating a group of people coming towards them through the churchyard huddled under one umbrella.

Amaia recognised Marcel Tremond. Alongside him was a man who was undoubtedly his lawyer. On his other side was a heavily pregnant young woman in a red coat, holding his arm for support. Seeing them, Yolanda let out the guttural cry of a frightened animal. Amaia turned to her, leaving the chief to deal with Tremond's lawyer.

'Are you okay, Yolanda?'

Yolanda leaned over and whispered something in her ear. Amaia joined the chief, interrupting the lawyer's protests.

'Yolanda Berrueta claims that your client is under a restraining order which prohibits him from coming within two hundred metres of her. Is this true?'

The chief's expression hardened, as he looked questioningly at the man.

'And who, may I ask, are you?' demanded the lawyer.

'Inspector Salazar, head of the murder squad, Navarre regional police.'

He studied her with renewed interest.

'Ah, so you're Salazar. Well, you have no jurisdiction here.'

'Wrong again,' retorted the chief sarcastically. 'Read the court order. If you can't, I'll translate it for you.'

The lawyer looked daggers at him, then focused his attention on the document. Turning towards the couple waiting beneath the umbrella, he whispered something that prompted angry protests.

'You have twenty seconds to leave the cemetery,' said the chief. Without waiting for a reaction, he turned to the uniformed officers: 'If they resist, arrest them and take them to the police station,' he ordered.

The lawyer escorted his clients out of the cemetery, although from where she stood, Amaia could see that they came to a halt two hundred metres down the street, respecting the restriction.

The rain was pelting down, forming puddles between the tombs. After the crane arrived, it took a further fifteen minutes to secure it on the stony ground. Then they slid a couple of straps beneath the slab and slowly started to raise it.

'Halt!' cried the chief, running towards them, his phone pressed to his ear.

'What's the matter?' asked Amaia, alarmed.

'Put the slab back where it was, Judge De Gouvenain has revoked the order.'

Amaia opened her mouth, incredulous.

'Come with me,' he said. 'She wants a word with you.'

Once again, the swish of the window, and behind it Judge De Gouvenain keeping her distance.

'Inspector Salazar, could you explain to me why I've just received a call from a Spanish magistrate who informs me that he is in charge of this case, and has expressly refused to allow you to dig up any children's graves. Who do you think you are? You've made a fool of me in front of one of my colleagues, to whom I have been forced to apologise – all this because you don't know where to draw the line.'

As Amaia leaned towards the window, the judge looked with visible displeasure at the large raindrops trickling down the sides of her hood and falling on to the upholstery inside the car door.

'Your honour, Judge Markina refused the order for a different case, which in principle is unrelated to this matter. I already explained—'

'That isn't what he told me. By going over his head, you've placed me in a very awkward position, Inspector. I am extremely annoyed and I intend to take this up with your superiors. I hope you never need my help in the future, because I assure you, it won't be forthcoming,' she declared, pressing the button to activate the car window, which slid up making her disappear in her spearmint bubble, as the engine started.

Amaia's face flushed with humiliation and anger. She could feel the chief's eyes boring into her as she took out her phone, which immediately got wet, and dialled Markina's number. She heard one, two, three rings then nothing. Markina had cut her dead, in more ways than one.

# 27

Jonan drove, while Amaia sat in the back, letting Iriarte take the passenger seat. Distancing herself from her silent colleagues, she tried to banish the deep sense of shame gripping her chest, threatening to burst out in a cry of rage against the world. The gravediggers' irritation; Yolanda's sobs as she demanded an explanation; the priest's silent disapproval; the Chief of Border Police's solemn face as he murmured an apology; the wolf-like grin of the lawyer, Lejarreta, as they passed him on their way back to the car . . .

She couldn't face going into the police station. As soon as they arrived, she took the wheel from Jonan, and left without saying a word. She drove slowly, observing the speed limit, concentrating on the hypnotic movement of the windscreen wipers as they swept the raindrops off the glass. Her languid demeanour belied the rage seething within her; a fury so intense it seemed to consume every ounce of energy she possessed.

She left Elizondo, driving through the banks of fog hovering above the motorway like gateways to another world, creating the impression of entering another dimension. As she kept an eye out for the exit that would take her on to the road that followed the river, she caught sight of sheep standing miserably in the fields, water cascading off their winter fleeces. It was hard to tell where the fleece ended and the grass began; making them look like strange creatures that had sprouted from the soil.

When she saw the bridge, she stopped the car, rummaged in the boot for her wellingtons, checked she had her phone, which a hundred yards further on would have no coverage, and her Glock.

The intense cold meant that the snow on the peaks hadn't yet thawed, so despite the rain the river wasn't too swollen. Plumes of fog rose into the air like ghosts where an occasional stone riffled the surface. As she crossed the footbridge, she could see the wreckage from the floodwaters that had swept through only a month previously, on the night her son had come close to dying at the hands of Rosario. On one side, the railing had disappeared, as if it had never been there, while the bars of the other were wreathed with twigs and dead leaves. Could an elderly woman have survived the current of a river that had washed away an eight-metre railing as if it were a dead branch?

She felt her feet sink into the marshy expanse covered with bright green grass that had shot up once the waters of the River Baztán receded. Below the pristine surface, the earth yielded beneath her feet, slowing her advance, as with each step she had to extract her boots from the mire.

When she reached the abandoned farmhouse, she leaned against its solid walls, scraping off the build-up of mud that was weighing down her wellingtons. Then, lowering the hood of her jacket, which restricted her vision, she took out her Glock and entered the forest. She didn't care if it was logical or not, her instinct told her that someone else besides the lord of the forest was watching her, someone who had been about to show themselves . . . Or perhaps that encounter the other day *had* only been a wild boar, and the whistle she'd taken to be a warning had merely been a shepherd summoning his dog . . . She was sure she'd seen someone – or something –

disappear into the shadows, but it could easily have been a wild boar, she told herself.

'All right, girl, but be prepared,' she whispered. 'And if paranoia is what comes with post-traumatic stress, then at least let it be of some use.'

She threaded her way through the trees, following a path made by animals. She glimpsed a deer through the undergrowth, their eyes meeting for an instant before the animal fled. Beneath the thick canopy of trees, the water of the past few hours had traced small, dark rivulets that led her to the clearing where the stream flowed noisily down the hill between moss-covered rocks. She crossed the little stone bridge, passing the spot where a beautiful young woman trailing her feet in the icy water had once announced that the lady was coming. She glanced up at the sky, which continued to bleed that soft drizzle which would go on all day, but which showed no sign of the approaching storm.

She reached the hill, out of breath after making her way through the undergrowth. Looking up, she saw that the stairway in the rock, wet from the rain, was also covered in mud. Calculating the effort it would take, she tucked her gun into her waistband and began her ascent. Once she'd passed the outcrop that formed a natural viewpoint, she pulled up her hood for protection and started to climb a narrow pathway, overgrown with brambles. The thorns scratched at her Puffa jacket, making soft hissing sounds. When she emerged into another clearing, she pushed her hood down and glanced about. A few yards above her loomed the low, dark mouth of the cave, only partially visible. To her left was the precipice, perilously obscured by vegetation; behind her, the path she had walked up, and to her right the table rock, empty of offerings. She could tell from the overgrown path that no one had been up this way since she was last there. Overwhelmed by the solitude, she stooped to pull a jagged stone out of the soft ground, and rubbed it on her clothes to clean off the mud.

215

She stepped forward, placing it on the polished surface of the table rock. And then, nothing.

The effort of climbing had consumed the rage fuelled by her humiliation and shame, leaving only cold, dead embers. Motionless in that place, her face damp from the rain, aware of the round droplets weighing on her eyelids, Amaia Salazar lowered her head. The raindrops falling from her eyelashes unleashed a sea of tears that flowed from her with such force that she stumbled forward, overcome. Falling to her knees, she pressed her face to the rock and covered her eyes with her hands. She was oblivious to the rain trickling down the back of her neck from her sodden hair. Oblivious to the hardness of the surface, to her wet, mud-soaked trousers, to the earthy smell as she attempted to bury her face in the rock, as if it were the lap of the mother she never had.

Then she became aware of the soft, warm hand resting on her head in that ageless gesture of comfort and blessing. She didn't move, or stop crying, but her tears lost their urgency and soon became an expression of gratitude. She held on to that illusion, knowing that if she looked up, no one would be there and it would only confirm that the soothing hand was not real.

She couldn't say how long she remained in that position; a few seconds, perhaps longer. She waited, then raised her head and got to her feet. Once again she pulled up her hood and set off along the bramble-covered track. She turned only once: the stone she had placed on the table rock had vanished. A loud rumble of thunder made the mountain shake.

Amaia didn't return to the police station. Not that she thought anyone would blame her for what had happened, but she felt mentally drained and physically ill. All she wanted was to go home.

She parked outside the archway leading to Engrasi's house. Realising that she still had on her muddy wellingtons, she sat down on one of the stone benches to pull them off. When she stood up, she felt drained. Her clothes were soaked through and covered in mud, her wet hair plastered to her head. Amaia was no stranger to humiliation and disgrace; she was well-schooled in those particular subjects, so much so that by the time she was nine she'd graduated with flying colours. She'd come to realise that, far from making you stronger, these lessons in life prepared you for nothing; constant exposure was merely an unrelenting drill that kept grinding into the rock that is you, seeking out a vein of weakness. If you were lucky, you could hide away for years, but sooner or later the pain would return, making you want to bury yourself in that dark cavern where the human heart resides, renouncing the light that only served to accentuate your misery. She thought about Yáñez, his wife's blood staining the sofa, the shutters closed so he couldn't see, so he couldn't be seen, hiding his shame.

She took off her wet, muddy Puffa jacket and flung it on top of her wellingtons, then went into the house. Dragging her legs, which had become as heavy as alabaster pillars, she felt instantly enveloped by the warm atmosphere of her aunt's home. Her skin pale from the rain and cold in the hills, she entered the sitting room where her family were preparing to have lunch. She had no appetite whatsoever. It was all she could do to find the strength to hug her aunt.

'I'm just tired and wet,' she said, registering Engrasi's look of concern. 'I'll have a shower and a nap, and I'll be good as new.'

She gave James a fleeting kiss. He realised something was wrong, but chose simply to watch her in silence as she focused all her attention on Ibai. He was playing in what looked like an inflatable swimming pool. It took up a sizeable area of the floor space, which explained why the coffee table in front of the sofa had been pushed against the wall.

'For heaven's sake, James, haven't you gone a bit overboard?' she said, grinning at the profusion of colours, shapes and fabrics that made up this monstrosity, big enough for at least four children, although Ibai seemed to love it.

'It wasn't me. Why do you always assume I'm responsible for such follies?'

'Who else?'

'Your sister, Flora,' he replied, grinning.

'Flora?' Thinking about it, Amaia wasn't so surprised; she had seen the way her sister looked at Ibai, how she cradled him in her arms at every opportunity. She even kept a beautiful framed photograph of him on the sideboard of her palatial sitting room in Zarautz.

As she let the hot water wash away the cold and some of her aches and pains, she wished it were as easy to rinse away her remorse and shame, flushing it down the plughole to be carried away by the River Baztán. She felt that this morning's events had undermined her to an extent she would never have thought possible. She'd got it wrong, she'd made a mistake, a serious error of judgement, and in Amaia Salazar's world you paid dearly for such errors. Wrapping her bathrobe around her, she refrained from demisting the glass to look at her reflection, and collapsed on to the clean, inviting bed that smelled of the husband she believed she loved, and the son she knew she loved, and she fell asleep.

She was familiar with this dream. Occasionally she would recognise dream landscapes as if they were real places she had visited, and the reassuring thought that they were merely a projection of her mind gave her the freedom to move about inside these dream spaces, looking for information and details she might have missed the first time. In this one, the waters of the Baztán flowed noiselessly between two strips of dry land covered in circular stones, which shaped the banks of the river until it flowed into the dark region of the forest. She could hear no sound of birds, not even the murmur of the river. Then she saw her, the little girl who she had always assumed was herself aged six or seven, but who she now knew to be her sister, and a product of her imagination, for her sister had perished long before she reached that age. The little girl was wearing a white night-dress with lace edging, and the pink ribbon *Amatxi* Juanita had chosen for her. Oblivious to the cold, she dangled her bare feet in the water, which lapped gently at her ankles, soaking the lace edging. Amaia was glad to see her, and a sincere, childlike joy flowed from her heart, and sprang from her lips. The little girl didn't respond, she was sad, because she was dead. And yet she hadn't surrendered; she looked straight at Amaia, raising her arm to indicate the banks further down the river. 'The dead do what they can,' reflected Amaia, as she followed her sister's gesture to see where she was pointing. On either side of the river, dozens of white flowers had sprouted, as tall as the little girl. Amaia watched their petals unfurl, and as the breeze touched them, a heady perfume of butter and biscuits reached her; she dissolved into ecstasies of tenderness as she recognised Ibai's smell, the scent of her river child. Burning with curiosity, she sought out her sister's gaze, but she had disappeared, replaced by a dozen beautiful young girls. Clad in sheepskins that barely covered their breasts and thighs, they sat combing their long tresses, which touched the surface of the water where their feet were submerged.

'Damned witches,' whispered Amaia.

They smiled, flashing their needle-sharp teeth at her, splashing their webbed feet on the calm surface of the water, which bubbled, as though heated by an underground furnace.

'Cleanse the river,' they said.

'Wash away the crime,' they demanded.

Amaia looked downriver once more, only to see that the flowers had turned into small snow-white coffins that began to quiver, as if the bodies inside were struggling to escape from their eternal resting place. The coffins danced about on the stones by the river, making a sound like rattling bones. Then the lids flew off, emptying the contents on to the dry riverbed: nothing. There was nothing inside them.

The sound of someone entering the room woke her up. Eyes half-open, she made to sit up as James perched on the edge of the bed.

'You should dry your hair, you'll catch cold,' he said, passing her the towel that had fallen close to the bed.

'How long have I been asleep?' she asked, feeling the remnants of her dream dissipate despite her efforts to cling to them.

'Did you sleep? Your aunt asked me to come and tell you that lunch is ready.'

She could feel his eyes on her as she rubbed her hair with the towel.

'What's wrong, Amaia? And don't say nothing. I know you well enough to tell when you aren't okay.'

She paused, putting aside the towel, but remained silent.

'I've been thinking,' he went on, 'if all this torment is about Rosario's funeral, if it's having such a bad effect on you, I'll understand if you don't come.'

She looked at him, surprised.

'This isn't about Rosario, James. The case I'm working on has run into difficulties, to the point where the entire investigation may have been compromised, and I'm to blame. I made a big mistake, and now everything's up in the air.'

'Do you want to tell me about it?'

'No. I'm not even sure what happened. I have a lot of figuring out to do before I can even consider talking about it to anyone.'

He reached out to touch her tousled hair, brushing it from her face with great tenderness.

'I've never known you to give up, Amaia, but sometimes it's better to surrender today, so you can carry on the fight tomorrow. I don't know if this is one of those moments, but no matter what happens, I'll be by your side. I love you more than anyone.'

She laid her head on his shoulder overwhelmed with exhaustion.

'I know you do, James. I've always known that.'

'I think it will do you good to get away for a bit and relax. We'll spend a few days with my family, and in no time at all we'll be home again.'

'That reminds me,' she said. 'I think we'll need to prolong our stay. I've been officially invited to take part in two weeks of intensive FBI seminars; I thought you and Ibai could maybe spend that extra time at your parents' house, then we can all fly back together.'

'That's a great idea,' he said.

She received no calls. That afternoon, she immersed herself in her family's love and protection and the benevolent influence of the house. She ate lunch at home, took an afternoon nap with Ibai, baked a cake, prepared dinner with James as they drank a glass of wine, and listened to the Golden Girls play cards in the other room. Later on, she took Ibai upstairs to give him his evening bath, one of the most rewarding moments of her day.

Perched on the toilet seat, Engrasi watched as the boy, supported from behind by his mother, splashed about, revelling in the water like the river prince he was.

'Auntie, what do you make of Flora's sudden interest in Ibai? She was too busy filming her TV programmes to come and see him when he was born, she missed the baptism, yet now she behaves like a doting aunt. I can't help thinking . . .'

'What?'

'Well, you know what Flora's like. There's always a reason behind anything she does. I've no idea what that might be, but I find her sudden adoration of Ibai suspicious. She must want something. If she thinks she can butter me up that easily, she's got another think coming.'

Aunt Engrasi pondered this for a moment.

'I think you're mistaken, Amaia. I believe she truly loves the child. The fact that she showed little interest to begin with means nothing; she fell in love with him the moment she saw him the way we all did. Flora has a tough exterior, but she's a woman like any other; she wanted children, you know what she went through trying to get pregnant, but in the end it didn't happen. And her interest in Ibai isn't so recent; for months now, she's been asking me about him whenever she calls. What's more, I think he is the main reason why she calls. I swear she never used to phone me this often.'

'She never calls me.'

'That's what I'm saying. Deep down, Flora is one of those people who are afraid of appearing human. When I tell her about his little ways, how he is growing, she seems genuinely delighted.'

Amaia recalled once more her surprise at the beautiful photograph of Ibai presiding over the luxurious sitting room in Zarautz. She scooped the baby out of the bathtub, handing him to her aunt, who wrapped him lovingly in a large towel, and placed him on the bed where Amaia would finish drying him.

'Flora is the way she is, but she loves Ibai, believe me. And who could blame her? He's so very special, our little boy.'

Amaia poured a small amount of almond oil on to her palm and began to massage the baby's feet. He relaxed with her touch, fixing her with his beautiful blue eyes.

'Have you noticed that Ibai doesn't have a single mole?' said her aunt, smiling.

Amaia removed the towel so that she could see his little body. She examined his back, the natural folds of his flesh. Engrasi was right: not a single blemish marked the child's perfect skin. Creamy and golden, it bore no resemblance to

222

the mottled appearance of Anne Arbizu's otherwise unblemished skin as she lay stretched out on the pathologist's slab; the image flashed into her mind as she recalled the popular belief that *belagiles,* or witches, have no moles. She covered him with the towel again so that he wouldn't catch cold while she dressed him in his pyjamas.

'Auntie,' she said pensively. 'There's something I'd like to talk to you about.'

'I'm all ears.'

'But not now,' said Amaia, smiling at how Engrasi made herself instantly available whenever she needed her. 'When we have a moment, I'd like to talk to you about the old religion, about what I saw in the forest, what you've seen too.'

'I think we might be able to persuade your husband to leave us women to talk,' Engrasi replied gamely. 'I'm so pleased you're interested in the subject. I worry sometimes that you're too logical . . .'

Amaia looked at her, frowning at the remark, then laughing as she finished dressing Ibai for bed and held him in her arms.

'You know what I mean,' said Engrasi. 'Keeping an open mind, like when you were a child, helps you to understand life better, to confront the more difficult aspects of your job.'

'Yes, I know. Sometimes I think my past has nothing to do with me, and yet it keeps coming back to haunt me.'

Engrasi looked at her niece with sadness, not wishing to end the conversation on that note.

'When we're alone, Auntie . . .' she said, gesturing towards Ibai.

'When we're alone,' agreed Engrasi.

223

# 28

She was flummoxed – she admitted, eyes fixed on the TV screen, while in her mind she replayed the day's events, conversations, facts . . . Thoughts she had thrust aside during the day, having decided to focus on her family. Now, lying next to her husband on the sofa, pretending to be engrossed in in a film he had insisted they watch, her brain was working overtime. The relentless juggling of facts and events was giving her a headache. She thought about going to fetch an aspirin, but didn't want to disturb the pleasurable sensation of being close to James in that relaxed intimacy unique to people who are truly at ease with one another, and which had been lacking between them the past few days.

Her phone rang shrilly in the pocket of the baggy cardigan she wore around the house. She glanced at the time as she reluctantly disentangled herself from James's embrace. Nearly one in the morning. It was Iriarte.

'Inspector, I've just had a call from Ainhoa. Yolanda Berrueta is seriously injured. It appears she tried to force open her children's tomb using some sort of explosive device. She's lost several fingers and an eye, and has been rushed to hospital. Right now, the French police are at the tomb with bomb-disposal experts.'

'Call Deputy Inspector Etxaide and tell him to pick me up at home in forty minutes.'

Iriarte sighed. 'Inspector, the Chief of Border Police called to inform me as a matter of courtesy, but I have to warn you that after this morning I doubt your presence there will be welcome.'

'I'm counting on it,' she replied, undaunted. 'Do you know which hospital they've taken her to?'

'Saint Collette,' he replied, irritated, then hung up.

She called the hospital, identified herself and asked for an update. The patient's condition was critical and she was currently in the operating theatre. That was all they could tell her. She peered out of the window and noticed that it had stopped raining.

It was two thirty when they arrived, having waited for Etxaide to drive up from Pamplona. Amaia was glad of the delay; the explosion had taken place about half an hour after midnight, so those two hours would have given the bomb disposal team time to secure the area, and any curious bystanders would have gone home. With any luck, all they'd find at the scene would be a police cordon and a patrol car.

She was right about the bomb disposal team and the neighbours, though there were still plenty of forensic technicians at work. Amaia and her colleagues walked over to the Chief of Border Police, who greeted them with a mixture of courtesy and disquiet.

'Good evening. You do realise that Judge De Gouvenain will be furious if she finds out that you're here.'

'Come on, Chief, who's going to tell her? You? We're European citizens, we were passing by, saw the commotion and stopped to ask what had happened.'

He contemplated her in silence for a few seconds, then let out a weary sigh.

'She arrived at the cemetery at around midnight, and parked over there,' he said, gesturing towards a large four-by-four vehicle. 'There's no one about at that hour. Then she planted approximately two hundred grams of high explosive – possibly Goma-2, which is used in the mining industry, but that has yet to be confirmed. Her family are mine owners in Navarre, so we assume that's how she got hold of the stuff.'

'I imagine so,' said Amaia. 'Though it can't have been that easy for her to steal. Since the 2004 terrorist attack in Madrid, explosives are no longer kept at mines. The exact amount to be used in each blasting operation is transported under armed guard by bomb-disposal experts specially contracted by the mining companies. Any left-over explosives are destroyed on the spot.'

'The remains of the packaging we found suggest this could have been decommissioned material, pre-dating the terrorist attack. In any event, Yolanda knew how to use a fuse and manual detonator, but unlike an expert, she didn't notice the loss of plasticity, the signs of "sweating".'

'How did she get hurt?'

'She lit the fuse and waited, and when nothing happened, she became impatient. The ground was wet, so she probably thought the fuse had gone out, or the powder had got damp. She was approaching when it went off.'

Amaia lowered her gaze and sighed.

'Two of her fingers were blown to bits, another two were found on a nearby tomb, and she's probably lost an eye. Not to mention the powder burns and the damage to her eardrums. She was still conscious, you know. Despite her wounds, she managed to drag herself to the side of the tomb, to see if her children were in there.'

'And were they?'

He looked at her with renewed displeasure.

'Go and see for yourself – after all, that's why you came, isn't it?'

Ignoring the chief's reproach, she walked over to the police cordon, which extended up to the church entrance, where a light was on. The priest, who had said nothing that morning, decided to chime in.

'Are you satisfied now?' he asked her as she stooped to pass beneath the cordon.

She walked on a few paces, then paused, striding back towards the priest, who stepped back, alarmed.

'No, I'm not. This is exactly what I was trying to avoid, and if you lot, who claim to be so concerned about Yolanda, had any humanity at all, you'd have opened the tomb long ago to relieve her suffering.'

She drew level with Iriarte and Etxaide, who were standing by the tomb. The neighbouring graves had borne the brunt of the damage: crosses and columns shattered, plant stands and urns blown sky high. The Tremond-Berrueta family tomb was largely intact, except for the slab, which, as the gravediggers feared, had been reduced to rubble, and lay scattered over the surrounding tombs; the largest fragment, measuring less than eighteen inches, had come to rest at the foot of the tomb in a pool of blood mixed with rainwater, which had seeped into the cracked stone.

The exposed tomb had been covered with a blue tarpaulin. Iriarte lifted one corner, and they used their torches to see inside. Two decayed-looking adult coffins had been damaged by falling debris. A small metal casket, probably containing ashes, lay on the floor, the lid half off. Slightly further to the right, two white coffins had suffered the most damage from the blast: one lay crushed beneath a piece of debris, probably the same lump of stone that had damaged the larger coffins. The side had split open, and from it protruded what they could see clearly was a baby's hand. The other coffin had turned over, spilling its contents on the ground. The dead child had been dressed in white for the funeral, although the colour was scarcely visible beneath the layer of mould, also covering the child's face, turning it completely black.

Deputy Inspector Etxaide slipped his camera out from under

his coat, looking to Amaia for consent. She nodded, trying to silence her phone, which rang out incongruously in that place. She handed her torch to Iriarte to illuminate the inside of the grave, and glanced at the screen. It was Markina.

'Your honour . . .' she started to say. 'I've been trying all day to—'

'Nine o'clock tomorrow morning, in my office,' he snapped.

She found herself staring at the screen to check he had hung up on her.

# 29

She hadn't slept a wink. She was so overwhelmed and distraught when she got home that the thought of going to bed didn't even occur to her. She spent the early hours writing out what would be her deposition to Judge Markina, stifling the urge to dial Dupree's number. She told herself that if, as she'd always believed, there was some kind of telepathic communication between the two of them, he would know when she needed him and would call her. But no call was forthcoming, and by the time dawn arrived she was filled with trepidation.

The dark rings under her eyes and her dull complexion betrayed her lack of sleep. Her usual self-assurance dissolved the instant she walked into Markina's office.

Inma Herranz smirked when she saw her.

'Good morning, Inspector, how nice to see you, it's been a while,' she said in her mellifluous voice. 'Judge Markina is waiting for you.'

Accompanying Markina were two men and a woman, who were talking to him in Spanish with a strong French accent. Markina introduced them.

'Inspector, this is Marcel Tremond, Yolanda Berrueta's

ex-husband, whom I think you've already met, and his parents, Lisa and Jean Tremond.'

She was grateful to him at least for introducing her as the inspector in charge of the case.

'Monsieur Tremond and his parents have come here of their own free will to acquaint you with a few aspects of Yolanda Berrueta's behaviour they feel you ought to know about,' explained Markina, after they had sat down. 'Whenever you're ready, Monsieur Tremond.'

'Yolanda was always fragile. Although, when she was young this was less noticeable. Because she was spoilt and capricious, she did whatever she wanted. The partying, the drink and drugs didn't help her behaviour, which her parents attributed to her rebellious nature. When we got married, Yolanda had no interest in having children, but I was keen to start a family, and in the end I persuaded her. Her pregnancy with the twins was complicated. She continued to drink and smoke, and even took sedatives; she was obsessed with trying not to gain weight and was on slimming pills. In the end, the twins were prema-ture, underweight and suffered from respiratory problems. And then a miracle occurred. Yolanda changed, she seemed genu-inely remorseful, all she did was cry and talk about what she'd done. She devoted herself to them wholeheartedly, and at last, when they were two months old, we were able to bring them home. After that, we had to hospitalise them twice because of respiratory problems, until that night . . .' He swallowed hard before continuing, under his parents' compassionate gaze, as they listened, obviously distraught. 'She watched over them constantly, she hardly slept, and then she noticed that some-thing strange was happening. We didn't wait for the ambulance, we took them to hospital ourselves, but they never regained consciousness . . . they died the same way they were born, within sixteen minutes of each other. From that moment on, things fell apart. Yolanda suffered a breakdown, she refused to listen to reason, she stopped sleeping and eating. She started to slip out of the house at night, and I would find her in the cemetery, lying prostrate on our children's grave.'

At this point his mother interrupted.

'You can't imagine the torment my son has been through, losing his sons and his wife within such a short space of time. We persuaded him to have her sectioned after her second suicide attempt.'

Amaia had been listening dejectedly to the ex-husband's tale of woe, hardly daring to look at Markina, though she could feel his eyes on her. She couldn't help seeing the similarities between this and Markina's own story.

'Inspector,' he said, addressing her. 'Lisa Tremond is also head paediatrician at the hospital where the children died. If you have any questions, now is the time.'

She hadn't expected this. Markina was inviting her to interrogate the babies' doctor, the person who had signed their death certificates, having elected not to perform the obligatory autopsy. She'd had no idea that this person was also the babies' paternal grandmother. If Markina thought that would put her off, he was mistaken.

'Why was no autopsy carried out on the bodies, as I believe is the usual practice in cases of Sudden Infant Death Syndrome?'

Amaia noticed the woman exchange a quick glance with her son.

'As head of paediatrics, I treated the children from birth. I was with them when they died in hospital, and the cause of death wasn't SIDS but pulmonary insufficiency, which they presented with from birth. However, that wasn't the reason why there was no autopsy; it was to protect whatever remained of Yolanda's sanity. "Don't let them cut open my babies," she begged me. "Don't add to their suffering." I'm aware that I was breaking the rules by not performing an autopsy, but you must understand that I was also their grandmother. I take full responsibility for my actions, whilst insisting I made the right decision.'

231

'Yolanda claims that the boys died of SIDS.'

'The woman is confused,' Marcel Tremond's father cut in angrily. 'She gets things mixed up because of the medication she's on. She can't be sure if something happened today or yesterday – that's what we're trying to explain.' His wife placed a hand on his shoulder in a restraining gesture.

Amaia sighed, which earned her a disapproving look from Markina. Sensing that he was about to end the interview, she hurriedly posed another question:

'What is the nature of your relationship with the legal firm Lejarreta & Andía?' she asked, addressing Marcel Tremond once more.

'They specialise in commercial law and are based in Pamplona. They advise me on my various businesses, and we're also good friends.'

Amaia was taken by surprise; it was one thing for him to admit to knowing them and using their services, but she hadn't expected him to own up to being their friend. She carefully considered how to phrase the next question.

'Am I to assume that they introduced you to the Martínez-Bayóns?'

'Yes, that's correct,' he replied, his manner cagey now.

She had hoped he would deny it so that she could confront him with the evidence of his car parked outside their property.

'So, there's nothing unusual about you visiting their house in Baztán,' she went on. He nodded, undermining her strategy. 'I understand that the couple hold meetings, which were attended by Dr Berasategui, an eminent psychiatrist, now deceased, who has been accused of serious crimes. A witness has placed you at the house on several occasions when Dr Berasategui was there. Given the accusations against him, you'll understand our interest in knowing the nature of those meetings.'

'First let me say that we were shocked to discover the charges against Dr Berasategui. But, as you yourself said, he was a distinguished psychiatrist who led various support groups. And that was how we came to know him: he led our parents' bereavement support group.'

Amaia fidgeted in her seat; she hadn't seen this coming either.

'Perhaps you're unaware that my lawyers also lost a baby girl, as did the Martínez-Bayóns, and all the others who attend those meetings. The truth is, it never occurred to me to join such a group until after Yolanda was admitted to hospital. I realised that, while devoting myself body and soul to looking after her, I had failed to deal with my own grief. This group allowed me to work through the different stages, to look with renewed hope towards the future. I don't know what would have become of me without Dr Berasategui's help. Notwithstanding his double life, I can assure you that, where the group was concerned, his behaviour was exemplary and his support invaluable.'

Markina rose to his feet, extending his hand to signal that the meeting was at an end. He saw them out, and, finally, closing the door behind him, turned to look at Amaia.

'Your honour . . .' she hesitated, unsure what to say. She was determined to stick to her guns, to try to convince him that her suspicions weren't groundless. But she knew she'd made a mistake, and she should admit it.

'Be quiet, Inspector, and listen for once.' He paused for what seemed like an eternity, and she realised that even behind closed doors he was addressing her formally again. 'Since I took up this post, I've respected the way you work, your unorthodox approach. I've put up with your methods for the same reason as the commissioner, the prison governor, the pathologist and his assistants: results. You solve cases – strange, bizarre cases –using methods that show scant regard for rules and regulations, and although that jars with us, we respect you because you're exceptional. However, this time you've overstepped the mark, Inspector Salazar,' She lowered her gaze, deflated. 'I backed you up, yet you went over my head, you made me look ridiculous in front of one of my French colleagues. I'd recently authorised a warrant for you to search Dr Hidalgo's files, and the next thing I know, you are in France opening up a grave.'

'Your honour, it's under a different jurisdiction, it's a different country . . .'

'I'm perfectly aware of that, but why didn't you tell me?'

'You made your attitude towards exhumations very clear. I knew you wouldn't give me permission.'

'And in view of what happened, would I have been right?' Amaia bit her lip, reluctant to admit it. 'Would I?' he insisted. She nodded. 'Have you any idea how much suffering your irresponsible actions have caused this family, forcing them to relive the horror of losing those children? Not to mention that poor wretched woman. For God's sake, she's lost several fingers and the sight in one eye. I warned you about how grief and pain can affect bereaved mothers, I explained in detail,' he said, lowering his voice, 'from my own experience,' he added, sitting down on the chair facing her so that she was forced to look him in the eye. 'I spoke to you about my family, Amaia,' he said, addressing her informally once more, simply, she was sure, to make his reprimand more stinging. 'I spoke to you about my life, but instead of listening, instead of accepting that my experience gave me a deeper understanding of the matter, you thought it undermined my ability to take decisions, you thought it weakened me—'

'My decision to go to Judge De Gouvenain without telling you was a mistake, but I didn't do it because I thought that your experiences in any way weakened you. I hoped to open up a different line of inquiry, to bring you the substantial evidence you asked me for. I admit that I was hasty, and I made a mistake. But those two children dying at the same time, and no autopsy being performed on them; the father linked to Berasategui, to that house, those same lawyers, and his wife telling a story identical to others I know about—'

'Amaia, the woman is crazy,' he snapped. 'I tried to tell you what happens, I tried to explain that they see what they want to see, they will do anything to square the circle.'

She studied him in silence for a few seconds.

'So, am I Amaia again?' she asked in a conciliatory tone.

'I don't know, I don't know. I keep asking myself, why didn't you come to me, damn it, I give you what you need, I give you everything you ask for . . . Incidentally, how did the search at Fina Hidalgo's go?'

'Badly, very badly. By the time we got there, she'd made a bonfire out of the files. I suspect someone tipped her off. All that remained were ashes. She said she was having a clean out, starting with the files – just the files.'

'Do you suspect someone at the police station?'

She hesitated, then said, 'Yes.'

'In that case, Inspector, think again. If you're as convinced as you were about that other matter, you're liable to accuse someone unfairly,' he said, rising from his seat to open the door.

Jonan was sitting waiting for her in a chair opposite Inma Herranz's desk. It was clear from their faces that they had overheard some of her conversation with Markina, and, of course, his parting shot.

Etxaide stood up to open the outer door for her, murmured a goodbye to Inma Herranz, who hadn't stopped smirking and staring at Amaia since she left Markina's office. He saw his boss look daggers at the other woman, who responded with a sneer. On any other occasion, Amaia would have confronted her. This time, she simply ignored her as she left the office.

Jonan drove in silence. Every now and then, he cast a sidelong glance at Inspector Salazar, as though waiting for the opportunity to give vent to something pent up inside him. But Amaia didn't seem willing, hiding behind dark glasses, leaning back in her seat, pensive, with an expression on her face he didn't like. Jonan had seen his boss in many different situations, more or less afraid, more or less confused, and yet there always seemed to be a hidden purpose, an invisible light guiding her along the rocky paths of an investigation. But now she looked lost. Or what was worse, defeated.

'Inspector Iriarte told me that your authorisation to attend the seminars at Quantico has arrived.'

'Yes,' she replied wearily.

'Will you go?'

'They start in a fortnight, I may stay on a bit longer to visit James's parents.'

Jonan shook his head; if she noticed, she said nothing.

'Shall I drop you off at the station or at home?' he asked, as they arrived in Elizondo.

'Drop me at the church. If I hurry, I'll make it in time,' she said, glancing at her watch. 'Today is Rosario's funeral service.'

He parked in the square, outside the cake shop, next to the zebra crossing, where they could see the entrance to the Church of Santiago.

As Amaia made to get out, Jonan asked: 'Seriously?'

'Seriously, what?'

'Are you seriously giving in to this too?'

'What are you talking about, Jonan?'

'About why you're going to the funeral of someone you know is still alive.'

Amaia gave a loud sigh as she turned towards him.

'What do I know? I know nothing, Jonan. I'm probably as wrong about that as I am about everything else.'

'Oh, please! I don't recognise you; it's one thing to make a mistake, to put your foot in it, but it's not like you to quit, and it seems that's what you're doing. Are you calling off the investigation?'

'What do you want me to do? The evidence is overwhelming, Jonan. And I didn't just put my foot in it, I made a *huge* mistake, which could have cost someone their life, and has left them mutilated forever.'

'Yolanda Berrueta is crazy. She was bound to end up doing something like that sooner or later. Judge Markina can't blame you – you've made all the right moves in this investigation. No autopsy was performed on Yolanda's children, her husband had dealings with Lejarreta & Andía, as well as with Berasategui and therefore Esparza; your actions were justified. De Gouvenain thought so, otherwise she wouldn't have authorised the exhumation, even though now she wants to wash her hands of it. If Markina had backed you up, you wouldn't have needed to go to her in the first place.'

'No, Jonan, Markina is right. I went too far.'

He shook his head. 'You're making a mistake.'

She was so stunned, for a few seconds all she could do was stare at him in astonishment.

'What did you say?'

He swallowed hard, rubbing his chin nervously with his hand. Saying this was difficult for him, but he gathered himself and looked her straight in the eye.

'I said, you aren't being objective. Your personal involvement is clouding your judgement.'

Hearing this remark coming, she felt a mixture of astonishment and annoyance, which was instantly replaced by curiosity. She studied him, wondering how much he knew, how much he sensed, aware that in a way he was right.

'Forgive me, boss, but I learned from you that instinct is indispensable for a detective; knowing when to listen to that other language, that other way of processing information. An investigation is all about making mistakes, following a trail, shoring up your discoveries, making more mistakes, opening up a line of inquiry . . . And yet here you are, contradicting everything you taught me, everything you believe in.'

She shook her head wearily.

'I can't think straight, today,' she said, her gaze drifting towards Calle Santiago. 'I'm afraid of making another mistake.'

'And it's better to go with the flow,' he said sarcastically.

She reached for the door handle.

'I don't believe your mother is dead. She left the coat as a decoy, and both the *Guardia Civil* and Markina leapt to conclusions.'

She turned and looked at him in silence.

'As for the screw-up at Fina Hidalgo's house, I think you're right: someone tipped her off,' he added.

'There's no way of knowing who, Jonan. Suspicions aren't enough to—'

'It wasn't necessarily one of ours.'

'What are you insinuating?'

'Markina's secretary hates your guts.'

She shook her head. 'Why would she do something like that?'

'As for Judge Markina—'

'Be careful, Jonan,' she warned him.

'Your personal involvement with him is clouding your judgement.'

Her eyes widened at his audacity, but this time anger got the better of her.

'How dare you!'

'I dare because I care about you.'

She wanted to give a harsh, cutting reply, but she realised that nothing she could say would be as irrefutable as what he had just said. Reining in her anger, she told him:

'I have never allowed my personal life to affect the decisions I make during an investigation, regardless of the implications.'

'Then don't start now.'

She glanced at the church, hesitating, then came to a decision.

'I have to do this, Jonan,' she replied as she stepped out of the car. Even as she said it, she was aware of how absurd it sounded. She shut the door, pulled up the hood of her Puffa jacket and crossed the street. Conscious of Etxaide's eyes on her, she marched across the cobblestones and walked up the steps to the church doors.

As Jonan sat in the car with the window down, watching her through the sleet that had started to fall, she pushed open the door. Although heavy, it yielded softly and silently on its hinges. Immediately she was assailed by the raucous strains of the organ and the smell of musty old bookshops emerging from that place, which for her was a place of funerals.

She stepped back, letting the door close on itself, as she rested her head on the wood rubbed smooth by a thousand hands.

'Damn it,' she murmured.

She retraced her steps, passing Jonan's car. He was looking at her, grinning broadly, with the window still down.

'Get out of here!' she hissed, as she walked past. His smile broadened even more, and as he started the engine, he raised his hand in a gesture of peace.

She hurried across the square and down Calle Jaime Urrutia, the sleet lashing her face, already smarting from the cold. Only when she reached the bridge did she slacken her pace, slowing almost to a halt to look at the weir through the icy raindrops, which solidified the air, making it difficult to see. Beneath the arched entrance to the house, she shook the moisture off her coat before entering. Engrasi was standing at the foot of the stairs; she had on the grey dress she only wore to funerals, and a pearl necklace that gave her the air of an English lady.

'Auntie! What are you doing here? I thought . . . Aren't you . . .?'

'No,' she replied. 'I got up this morning, put on this dress, and these pearls, which make me look like the Queen Mother, and I must admit that I felt quite convinced. But as the time drew near, I began to have my doubts. I said to myself: What are you doing, Engrasi? You can't attend someone's funeral if you believe they are still alive!'

'Oh, Auntie!' said Amaia. She was so relieved she flung herself into Engrasi's arms. 'Thank God!'

Engrasi clasped her niece to her chest for a few seconds, then held her at arm's length and looked into her eyes.

'Even if she were dead, I wouldn't say a prayer for her soul, not after she tried to kill Ibai and almost succeeded in killing me. I'm not that forgiving.'

Amaia smiled; this was precisely the attitude that made her love her aunt so much.

'I've invited Flora to lunch. In fact, they'll all be coming here after the service, so I'd better get changed and start preparing the food.'

'Do you need any help?'

'Yes, but not in the kitchen. Your sisters are going to give us an earful for not attending the funeral, and when they do, I'd like you to remain calm so we don't end up quarrelling. Do you think you can manage that?'

'I can now that I know you feel the same way I do. We can remain calm together. I'm capable of anything with you on my side.'

'I'm always on your side, my dear,' Engrasi said, winking at her.

# 30

The penetrating cold and damp that reigned outside seeped into the sitting room, vying with the intense heat from the fireplace.

Flora held Ibai in her arms, bouncing him up and down gently as she sang to him:

*Sorgina pirulina gainean*
*Ipurdia zikina, kapela buruan,*
*Sorgina sorgina ipurdia zikina*
*Tentela zara tu?*
*Ezetz harrapatu.*[2]

Ibai was laughing aloud, while Amaia looked at Flora, incredulous: her two sisters had always been fascinated by babies, perhaps because neither had been able to have kids, but this was the first time she'd seen Flora clowning and crooning over Ibai. She found it at once intriguing and surprising, because it was so out of character. She remembered what her aunt had said about Flora's fondness for him.

---

[2] The naughty witch is on her broomstick / She has a dirty backside, and a pointy hat / Witch, witch with the dirty backside / Are you a fool? / I bet you can't catch me!

James looked rather solemn as he gave her a peck on the cheek. He poured a glass of wine and handed it to her, then asked:

'Busy morning at work?'

'Yes, I arrived late so I decided to stay here with Auntie.'

'We'll talk later,' he said curtly, and busied himself pouring wine for the others.

Flora insisted on giving Ibai his feed. They exchanged comments about the funeral, the marvellous service, and how many people had attended, but made no allusion to Amaia or Engrasi's absence. Amaia was sure this was down to her aunt's decision not to attend. Engrasi was the head of the family, a woman who had never been shy when it came to voicing her opinions, who had lived her life according to her own rules, and continued to do so; a woman who respected people's freedom to do as they wished, provided they took responsibility for their actions and didn't tell her what to do or think.

Amaia put Ibai to bed then helped her aunt to serve the roast leg of lamb in beer sauce, and everyone sat down to lunch.

'There's something I want to talk about, but I was waiting until we were all here together,' said Flora, looking pointedly at her two sisters, 'to avoid any possible misunderstandings,' she added, glancing at the others. 'I got up early this morning, and went for a walk. I felt like a cup of coffee, so I stopped by the bakery, only to find that I couldn't unlock the door. Do you know anything about this?'

'It's true,' said Amaia. 'The other day, when I tried to get in, I realised—'

'I've changed the lock,' Ros cut in.

'Well, well!' exclaimed Flora. 'And were you planning to let us know?'

'Of course, but, like you, I was waiting until we were all together to avoid any misunderstandings,' she said, staring straight at her sister.

242

Holding Ros's gaze, Flora picked up her glass and said: 'You'll need to give me a copy.'

Ros laid her knife and fork on her plate, still looking at her sister.

'Actually, I won't,' she retorted. At this, everyone around the table seemed to freeze, riveted by this turn of events; even Flora remained perfectly still, glass held aloft. 'I'm in charge of the bakery now. I manage the employees, the schedules, the recipes, the orders, the accounts, the paperwork – everything is organised by me. You're both welcome to drop by and see me, but I see no reason for anyone to go there in my absence. Any interference with my way of working, however small, upsets the whole process, as I'm sure you'll appreciate.'

Amaia glanced at her aunt and at James, then said: 'I think you're right. We carry on as if *Aita* were still alive, coming and going as we please. I respect that it's your place of work, Ros, and I agree that there's no need for us to go to the bakery when you aren't there.'

'Well, I find that utterly unacceptable,' replied Flora. 'It's different for you, Amaia, you've never worked there, but let me remind you that up until a year ago I was the one running the bakery.'

'Yes, but now it's me,' said Ros calmly.

'I still own half the business,' retorted Flora.

'Yes, and that's why I pay you a half share of the profits every month. But now that you're no longer living in Elizondo, or working at the bakery, I don't see why you need open access to a place you scarcely have any connection to.'

Flora raised her head, opening her mouth to speak, but paused for a few seconds while she ate another forkful, smiling as she prepared her assault. She chewed slowly, setting her cutlery on her plate and taking a sip of wine before she spoke:

243

'You always were a stupid child, little sister.' Ros began to shake her head, her lips curving into a faintly menacing smile. 'Yes,' Flora went on. 'You always depended on someone else to do the difficult work for you. I know lots of people like you, always in the shadows, quiet and retiring, until you see an opportunity and then, in a flash, you usurp the throne that doesn't belong to you. Who do you think you are? Don't talk to me about clients, orders, schedules and recipes . . . I built up that client list, so any orders you have are thanks to me. As for recipes, I've written a whole book of them. For God's sake, are you worried I might want to steal yours? It's laughable!'

Amaia broke in.

'Flora, Ros never said that.'

'Be quiet, Amaia,' Ros snapped. 'Keep out of it, this is between Flora and me.' Then she turned to Flora: 'I have double the number of orders you had a year ago. We have new clients, and the old ones are much happier. Our new recipes and the changes we've made to the old ones are a great success. But you must have realised that from the amount of money going into your account every month.'

'I couldn't care less about the money,' Flora said dismissively. 'The fact remains that the bakery is as much mine as it is yours, and I'm considering coming back to live in Elizondo. I've met a man,' she said, giving Amaia a meaningful look, 'and we're in a stable relationship. Besides, now that my programme has been bought by one of the main TV channels, I only need go to the studio one week a month to record all the episodes.'

Ros's expression betrayed her disquiet at her sister's announcement.

Flora continued: 'I could manage the bakery again, but if you disagree, then I can think of only one solution: I buy you out and we dissolve the partnership.'

'Flora, you can't be serious!' cried Engrasi.

'I'm not the one making trouble, Auntie. If Ros doesn't think there's room for both of us, then one of us has to go. If I buy her out, she'll be sitting pretty.'

'Or I could buy you out,' said Ros, with icy calm.

Flora turned to her, feigning surprise.

'You? Don't make me laugh! Either the business is making more money than you claim and you're cooking the books, or you've won the lottery, because as I recall, the house you lived in with Freddy was mortgaged to the hilt, and he went through all your savings, so I can't imagine where you'd get the money from.'

Ros contemplated her sister in silence, holding her gaze with rare defiance. Amaia saw Flora look away and smile, trying to show that she was in control of the situation, though she was clearly disconcerted.

'Well, now that's all cleared up, we'll call in the auditors and get a valuation, and if you can afford to—'

Ros nodded, raising her glass. They finished lunch, James, Engrasi and Amaia making all the conversation. Amaia had anticipated that if anyone tried to pick an argument over lunch, she or Engrasi would be the target; it had never occurred to her that Flora and Ros would end up having words.

Just then, Engrasi looked at her eldest niece with a mischievous glint in her eye, and said:

'So, Flora, who is this gentleman who has succeeded in stealing your heart and making you give up your idyll by the sea?'

'Ask Amaia, it seems she has a soft spot for him herself,' Flora retorted, rising from her seat, and glancing at her watch. 'Speaking of which, I have to go now. We've arranged to meet, and I'm late.'

Amaia waited for her to leave, then shook her head.

'Don't Flora's dramatic exits always give you a feeling of déjà vu? They should study her in Hollywood, revive the lost glamour of Garbo. She's seeing Fermín Montes.'

'You mean Inspector Montes?' said James, surprised.

'Yes, the very same Inspector Montes who nearly blew his brains out because of her. But let's have that conversation another day.'

# 31

The Berrueta family's lawyer had asked if the owner of the Almandoz mines could make a statement at the police station in Elizondo rather than in France. Iriarte had agreed to take care of it; Amaia had received a call from him first thing that morning to tell her she needn't be present; it was Saturday, and besides, she was officially on holiday.

'Is Jonan there yet?'

'No, he isn't due in today.'

'We agreed he'd bring me enlargements of the photos he took yesterday showing the inside of the tomb in Ainhoa . . .'

'Have you checked your emails?'

'Yes, there's nothing. I expect he'll email them to me later or take them in to the station this morning.' She hung up.

She and Engrasi had sent James out to buy sponge cake with Ibai, while they made coffee and settled down for their women's talk.

Amaia filled her cup and sat down opposite Engrasi.

'Auntie,' she said, making sure she had her full attention.

Engrasi switched off the television.

'I first saw him in the forest a year ago, as clearly as I see you now, less than five metres away from me, and on at least three other occasions, two of them quite recently, he has come

247

close enough for me to hear his whistle. That gamekeeper I met last year claimed he had seen him, although he had just been shot, so his perception could have been distorted by the shock. You told me you came across him by chance when you were sixteen, while out gathering kindling in the forest. And then there's the case of Professor Vallejo; I can't think of anyone less likely to have witnessed such an apparition. He has the most logical, scientific mind of anyone I know,' she said, glancing at her aunt, who sat listening quietly. 'But the thing that concerns me right now is not so much *who* has seen him but the number of sightings there have been of late. It was no accident that I saw him, Auntie. He wanted me to see him. And I need to know why.'

'I've been giving this a lot of thought,' said Engrasi. 'I must have read everything that's been written on the myth of the *basajaun*, the folk stories. He is considered the keeper of harmony, the lord of the forest who preserves the balance between life and death. That balance has been disrupted – the unnatural deaths of those girls last year, then the monster who incited men to kill women and leave their remains in our valley, not to mention the fate that almost befell Ibai in that cave – these were deeply disturbing, utterly unnatural crimes and they took place in the domain of the *basajaun*: the mountain and river. I believe he has been forced to show himself in order to try to restore the natural harmony.'

'The river,' murmured Amaia.

'The river,' repeated Engrasi.

*Cleanse the river, wash away the crime*, the voices of the *lamias* echoed in Amaia's head.

'But what does it mean?' she asked. 'What are we to make of the appearance of a mythical creature in the forest? Are we all under the influence of some hallucinogenic plant that grows on the mountain, causing us to see things? Or is there some ancient, enduring power, something that transcends those crimes?'

248

'Oh, Amaia, I understand your need to find out more, but as I keep trying to tell you . . . I'm afraid for you, afraid of the doors you might open, the places where your search may lead you.'

'But what else can I do? These abnormal things keep occurring in the valley, calling out to me, and I can't extricate myself. It isn't just the girls in the river, or the remains in the Arri Zahar cave, or even the bones of the *mairus* in the church . . . Now I'm learning of babies dying, and there's a link to a sinister creature in our folklore.'

'Inguma,' breathed Engrasi.

'The demon that robs people's breath while they sleep.' Amaia gave a wry smile as she thought of Father Sarasola. 'An expert on the subject told me that an identical demon exists in other cultures and religions; the oldest known example appears in Sumerian demonology, but it crops up all over the place – Africa, America, Japan and the Philippines . . . And the nature of the attacks is the same in every case: the victims belong to a particular area, age group or gender, and death occurs during sleep. Even with modern medicine, it seems nothing can be done to prevent it. There are scientifically documented cases, and the Center for Disease Control in Atlanta put out an alert when faced with a spate of inexplicable deaths that seemed to them to constitute a kind of epidemic. What can you tell me about Inguma?'

Engrasi had been nodding emphatically as she listened to her niece; the subject was one she was clearly familiar with.

'Nightmares are a kind of parasomnia,' she said, 'a way of expressing intense pain. I came across one case while I was practising in Paris, and I studied many more. Later, when I found out about your nightmares, I read everything I could on the subject. Nightmares can be part of a severe anxiety disorder, such as Ephialtes Disease, which in Greek literally means "the one that jumps". Sufferers describe all manner of hallucinations, menacing presences leaning over them while they sleep; some speak of shadowy figures, ghostly auras at the foot of the bed or right next to them. In the most disturbing cases, the sufferer can feel the physical presence of the nocturnal visitor. That's as far as the scientific explanation goes, but since ancient times such visitations were attributed to succubae, incubi or daimon – demonic spirits plague human beings with terrible visions or with their presence while they sleep. The most dangerous are those that produce respiratory hallucinations, a feeling of being strangled or asphyxiated.

'In the case I treated in Paris, the victim was convinced that she was being raped each night by a repulsive creature that immobilised her, crushing her beneath its weight, and producing a terrifying sensation of suffocation and fatigue so that she was unable to cry out. I'm familiar with the cases your friend told you about; in the course of my studies, I saw a recording made by the Japanese army. They were concerned about the significant numbers of seemingly healthy soldiers who kept dying in their sleep, trapped in asphyxiating nightmares. The images made my hair stand on end; watching them struggle with an invisible assailant as it choked them and pinned them to the bed was truly horrifying. It's hard to tell yourself these are just nightmares when you're watching footage of young men who actually died.'

Amaia looked at her aunt, brow furrowed.

'My informant also told me that there were valid reasons for the climate of hysteria and paranoia surrounding the phenomenon of witchcraft in the area, the denunciations and confessions of those practices, which were mostly generated by fear of the Inquisition. Following the auto-da-fé in Logroño in 1610, Salazar y Frías settled in Baztán, where he lived among the inhabitants for several months. History remembers him as the "just inquisitor" because he later reported to the Holy Office that he had found no evidence of Satanism in Baztán and was therefore unable to condemn anyone to death.

Even so, he received over three thousand allegations and half that many confessions relating to the practice of witchcraft in one form or another, which he recorded for posterity as something "other" than Satanism.'

'That's true,' said Engrasi. 'A century ago, more people in Baztán believed in witches than in the Holy Trinity.'

'Salazar y Frías alleged that people would perform a number of rituals to ensure protection against witches, but also to obtain their collaboration, or even to control them. Such rituals invariably involved making an offering.'

'I've seen them, and so have you. They would leave all sorts of things – cider, apples, coins – in Mari's cave. Or they'd lay out bread and cheese on a rock, for the *basajaun*. But when people sought a different kind of power the nature of the offerings changed.'

'My expert maintains that among the many papal bulls engendered by tales of witchcraft, some were based on fact: accounts of young girls being kidnapped, virgins sacrificed, and' – she fixed her aunt with a look – 'very young children, who were killed in rituals like the one they were going to perform that night in the cave.'

'There's no denying it. It's been documented by anthropologists who have scoured these valleys and found human remains in places where witches' covens traditionally met. The skull in Zugarramundi being the most famous example.' She paused. 'Do you think something similar could be going on now?'

'What if it were? What if the desecrations and the remains of those murdered women were ritual offerings designed to summon those powers. Auntie, could someone be invoking Inguma to harvest a fresh crop of bodies? What other reason would someone have to steal the body of a dead baby?'

Engrasi covered her mouth with both hands, in a gesture that betrayed her reluctance to speak of such things.

Amaia sighed. 'The use of corpses is common in many occult

religions such as voodoo. The dead are seen as a conduit between the two worlds, and are only ever used to make offerings to the devil.'

'This "other" of which Salazar y Frías spoke, was very real.'

'Was or is?' As she spoke, Amaia checked the messages on her phone; she saw no reply from Jonan, and reflected how he would regret missing out on this conversation when she told him about it.

'Do you realise, my analytical, logical, pragmatic niece, that you're talking about witchcraft in the twenty-first century?'

'"When the new ways don't work, people fall back on the old ones,"' replied Amaia, quoting her aunt.

'I'd like to meet your source,' Engrasi said. 'I find it intriguing that the Old Testament accepts the existence of lesser divinities, otherworldly forces that demanded constant sacrifices in order to survive. Take the story of the god Dagon. Three times his statue was found lying prostrate before the Ark of the Covenant, which had been placed in the temple dedicated to him, the third time with his head and hands severed. This was interpreted as the submission of the lesser divinities to the one God. In his book about the gods and heroes of ancient Greece, Robert Graves writes that when Jesus was born, the lesser divinities went to sleep until the end of time.'

'Or until someone or something roused them . . .'

'If you're right, and someone has invoked Inguma, that would explain why the guardian keeps appearing. It must have taken an offering so astonishing, a crime so monstrous, that I wouldn't be surprised if your Vatican priest were concerned,' she said, fixing Amaia with her gaze, as though hoping to elicit the information that would confirm her suspicions.

Amaia would have been amused by her aunt's perspicacity had she not been assailed by images of the desecrations, her family's violated *itxusuria*, its burial ground, the mound of stones on the table rock, her sister's empty coffin, the Esparza girl's dark, silky hair poking out of the rucksack in the rain, and the words of *Amatxi* Ballarena as she told her how Inguma had awoken in 1440 because someone had wanted to rouse him, and that the demon's quest for lives hadn't stopped until his thirst was quenched.

# 32

She soon regretted her decision to walk to the police station. Despite keeping up a brisk pace, the cold had rapidly seeped into her bones. The Puffa jacket she had worn up the mountain was still damp, and the overcoat she had put on instead was scarcely warm enough, with the pale sky threatening snow. As she entered the building, she bumped into Iriarte and Benigno Berrueta, who stopped in his tracks when he saw her.

'Inspector . . .'

She approached him cautiously; relatives could react unpredictably. Some were driven by grief and despair to search for scapegoats to assuage their own guilt, and the police were an easy target. She'd been on the receiving end a hundred times and had witnessed many more instances. But she relaxed when she saw the man's hands outstretched, his eyes seeking out hers.

'Thank you,' said Berrueta, 'thank you for trying. I heard about the problems you had, and if only they'd let you do your job, this would never have happened. I visited Yolanda in hospital this morning before coming here, and she told me that after the explosion she looked inside the tomb and they were there. My daughter's hand was reduced to a pulp, her eye was hanging out of its socket, and yet she found the strength to shine a torch inside the grave to look for her children. You'll probably think I'm crazy, but I'm glad this happened. It's terrible, but it was the only way. My daughter knew that, and she did what had to be done. Today, for the first time in years, she started to grieve for her children, and I am hoping she has also started on the road to recovery.'

Amaia looked at Iriarte, who was standing next to Berrueta. She extended her hand, which he clasped between his, slipping her his business card . . .

'Thank you again,' he said.

The station was quiet upstairs; on Saturdays most of the officers were on traffic duty, and the crime team hadn't much to do that morning. Amaia stood over her desk, checking her emails on the computer, while she listened to Iriarte.

'It seems they'll be able to save her eye, but she'll be scarred for life. Apart from that, she's out of danger and making a surprisingly speedy recovery. Like her father said, what happened appears to have accelerated the grieving process: acceptance is the hardest part – you can't make any progress until you reach that stage.'

She remained silent for a few seconds while she thought.

'Judge Markina has assured me that De Gouvenain won't be taking this any further.'

Iriarte heaved a sigh of relief. 'At last some good news – it's been thin on the ground lately.'

'Has Etxaide been in?'

'Today's Saturday,' he replied, as if that explained everything.

'Yes,' she said, taking out her phone and checking her emails again. 'But as I told you, we agreed he'd send me the photos he took yesterday at the cemetery in Ainhoa, and he hasn't. It's not like him.'

Iriarte shrugged, and started towards the exit.

She followed, dialling Jonan's number; it rang four times then went to voicemail.

'Call me, Jonan,' she said after the tone.

The cold stung her face as she crossed the threshold, and she accepted gratefully Iriarte's offer of a lift home. As they drove past *Juanitaenea*, he said:

'The refurbishment doesn't seem to be making much headway.'

'No,' she replied, a sudden wave of sorrow overwhelming her. Old Señor Yáñez's words echoed in her head: *A house isn't a home.*

'Well, have a good trip,' said Iriarte, pulling up outside Engrasi's house. 'When are you leaving?'

'Tomorrow at noon,' replied Amaia, climbing out of the car. 'Tomorrow.'

By afternoon, the sky had turned completely white, suggesting it would be snowing soon. At five o'clock, her phone rang, and on the screen she read the words: 'Jonan home'. She wasn't even aware that Jonan had a landline. She heard a woman's voice on the other end of the phone.

'Inspector Salazar? Deputy Inspector Etxaide's mother speaking.' Now she remembered: Jonan had given her their number once when he stayed with them for a few days while he had the decorators in.

'Good afternoon, Señora, how are you?'

'I'm fine, well . . .' Her voice was tremulous. 'Forgive me for calling you, but I can't seem to get hold of Jonan, and . . . I don't like to bother you, I thought perhaps you and he might be working on a case.'

'No, we're not working today. Have you tried his mobile?' she said, instantly feeling foolish; of course she had, she was his mother.

'Yes,' the woman replied. 'I was hoping you might know

where he was. We were expecting him for lunch at one, and . . . well, this might sound foolish, but he always calls if he's going to be late, and he's not picking up.'

'Perhaps he's asleep,' she said, not believing it herself. 'These past few days have been exhausting, we've been working into the early hours, he might not have heard his phone.'

After saying goodbye to Jonan's mother, she dialled his mobile again, and once more the call went to voicemail.

'Jonan, call me as soon as you get this message.'

She rang Montes.

'Fermín, are you in Pamplona?'

'No, I'm in Elizondo. Why?'

'Forget it . . .'

'Boss, what's wrong?'

'Nothing . . . Etxaide didn't show up at the station this morning; we'd arranged for him to bring me some photos, and he hasn't emailed them either. He isn't picking up his phone, and his mother just called me. She's worried because Jonan was supposed to have lunch with them, but he hasn't turned up or called to let them know. She sounded worried. That's the first time she's called me in two years.' After explaining it all, Amaia felt even more anxious.

'Okay,' said Montes. 'I'll call Zabalza. He lives near to Jonan's place. He can easily pop over to check that he's okay. I expect he's fallen asleep with his phone on silent.'

'Good,' she replied. 'Do that.'

James sat among the suitcases open on the bed, crossing things off the list they'd made of essential items, while Amaia rolled up her clothes so that they'd take up the minimum amount of space. She only needed enough for the first week, because everyone attending the Quantico seminars would be kitted out with a uniform when they arrived. This consisted of a track suit, shorts, trainers, four T-shirts, field fatigues, a bulletproof vest, belts, boots, socks and a badge they were obliged to wear at all times, which identified them as a participant in the course. They were also supplied with pens, a notebook, a folder with A4 paper and a cap bearing the letters FBI – the only thing they were permitted to take home with them.

'Is something wrong?' asked James, who had been watching her.

'Why do you ask?' she said, anxiously.

'I've just watched you fold the same T-shirt three times.'

She gazed at the piece of clothing in her hands as if she were seeing it for the first time.

'Yes . . .' she said, tossing it into the suitcase, distractedly.' She was aware of having already experienced this sensation, and she knew what was coming. 'I have to go, James,' she said suddenly.

'Where?'

'Where?' she repeated, pulling off the cardigan she wore around the house, and taking her coat off the hook behind the door. 'I'm not sure yet,' she mused aloud, staring at him.

'Amaia, you're scaring me, what's going on?'

'I don't know,' she said, aware that this was a lie. *Of course you know*, her own voice echoed in her head. She raced down the stairs, James following on her heels, alarmed.

Engrasi, who was keeping an eye on Ibai in his new play area, rose when she saw her.

'What's the matter, Amaia?'

She was about to reply when her phone rang. It was Fermín Montes.

'Boss, Jonan was at home all the time. Zabalza went there and found the door open. Fuck, Amaia! He's been shot.'

Everything around her shattered into a thousand pieces that drifted away towards the ice-cold void of the universe. She had known for hours that something wasn't right, she'd felt the weight in her neck, like something out of an Arab curse that crawls beneath your skin and forces you to carry it around

258

with you for eternity. She found herself trying to remember when she'd first started to feel its menacing presence. She would think about that later, she told herself, she hadn't time now. First she called Iriarte, then the police station in Pamplona, and finally she got in the car, clapping the siren on to the roof. She was fastening her seat belt when Montes leapt into the passenger seat beside her.

'I told you to wait for me.'

She accelerated by way of a reply.

'Aren't we waiting for Iriarte?'

'He's taking his car,' she said, gesturing towards the rear-view mirror. Iriarte's vehicle was right behind them. 'What exactly did Zabalza say?'

'He told me he rang the doorbell, and when Jonan didn't answer, he knocked on the door, which it turned out was open. As soon as he walked in, he saw Jonan lying on the ground. It was obvious he'd been shot.'

'Where?'

'In the chest.'

'But he's alive?'

'Zabalza wasn't sure. He said there was a lot of blood – he called the ambulance and then he called me.'

'What do you mean, he wasn't sure? He's a police officer, for Christ's sake!'

'The pulse can be very weak when someone loses a lot of blood,' explained Montes.

'How many times?' she asked.

'What?'

'How many times was he shot?' she shouted, struggling to make herself heard above the wail of the siren.

'Twice, as far as he could tell.'

'As far as he could tell,' she echoed, speeding up as they reached a straight section of road, cursing every mile that separated them from Pamplona. 'Call him again,' she commanded.

Montes obeyed.

'He isn't picking up.'

'Well keep trying!' she shouted. 'Keep trying, damn it!'

Montes dialled again.

They had reached the first buildings on the outskirts of Pamplona when it began to snow. The flakes fell on to the car with a slowness that, when she thought about it later, seemed as unreal as everything that had happened after Montes's call. And yet those snowflakes, as big as rose petals, would remain etched on her memory until the day she died.

The sky was falling. The sky was dissolving with grief, blanketing the city, and nothing mattered any more.

'Which hospital?' she asked.

Montes didn't reply straight away.

'He's at the house.'

She looked at him uneasily, taking her eyes off the road for too long as it became increasingly treacherous.

'Why?' she asked, her voice that of a desperate little girl demanding answers.

'I don't know,' replied Montes. 'I don't know . . . Maybe they're trying to stabilise him.'

Patrol cars blocked both ends of the street. They flashed their badges, and rather than wait for the cars to move aside, Amaia drove up on to the pavement. Two ambulances were parked outside the entrance to the apartment block, and a dozen uniformed police officers were busy keeping curious neighbours and onlookers away. Leaping out of the car, she ran towards the entrance. Despite the heavy snowfall blinding her and covering every surface, she recognised Dr San Martín's car double-parked outside, and the sight of it triggered in her mind an avalanche of doubt.

'What's he doing here?' she asked Montes, who was right behind her, as they went through the door held open by a police officer. She repeated the question as they hurried past the lift, which was in use, and ran up the stairs:

'What's San Martín doing here?'

She was relieved when Montes didn't reply. The question wasn't aimed at him, it was aimed at the universe; nor did she want him to reply, and yet she couldn't help asking the question. She came to a landing, then continued up the next flight of stairs . . . Was it the fourth or fifth floor? She wasn't sure. Inside her, a ball of fire was growing. She had kept it at bay on the way there, concentrating on the miles burning up beneath her tyres. But the instant she glimpsed San Martín's vehicle, that monstrous portent of grief and misery, it had begun to climb up her throat, like a repulsive creature pushing its way through her mouth. She gulped air as she ran, forcing back the imminent birth of this thing inside her. She wished she could kill it, choke it to death, smother it, prevent it from ever seeing the light. They reached the apartment. She saw Zabalza, pale and distraught, leaning against the wall between Jonan's front door and the lift; overwhelmed, he had slid down on to his haunches. Seeing her, he leapt to his feet – impossibly quickly, she thought, given the state he was in.

Inside Amaia the question clamoured: What's he doing here?

Zabalza intercepted her at the door.

'Don't go in,' he whispered. It was a plea.

'Get out of my way!'

'Don't go in,' he repeated, holding her firmly by the arms.

'Let go of me!' She wriggled free, but Zabalza was determined. The force with which he held her, clasping her to his chest, belied the despair on his face, his thin voice.

'Don't go in, please, don't go in,' he implored, looking searchingly at Montes, who had reached the fourth floor and was shaking his head.

Amaia was aware of Zabalza's cheek against hers, the scent of laundry softener on his jumper, the more acrid smell of sweat underneath. She stopped struggling for a few seconds, and when she felt Zabalza's body slacken, grabbed her gun from its holster, and pressed it into his side. He stiffened as he felt the hard muzzle, raising his arms and gazing at her with infinite sorrow. Amaia entered the apartment. Seeing San Martín crouched over Jonan, she obtained the reply to the question she hadn't wanted to ask, the reply she didn't wish to hear. Jonan Etxaide, Jonan, her closest friend, possibly the finest person she had ever known, lay sprawled on his back, in the middle of a large pool of blood.

He had been shot twice. Once, as Montes had told her, in the chest, just below the sternum. The bullethole was dark and relatively clean, as most of the blood came from the exit wound. The other shot, to the forehead, had left a tiny circular mark, raising the chestnut hair on his crown into a congealed mass. She approached, still clutching her weapon, to the consternation of the other officers inside the sitting room. And at that moment, having tried so carefully not to breathe, she could hold on no longer. She inhaled, giving life to that creature, which rose up her gullet, choking her as she opened her mouth, resigned to letting the horror inside her escape. She felt as if she was suffocating. The pain was so intense her eyes stung as the last breath of air left her lungs, searing her throat. Her head was spinning, and she fell to her knees beside Jonan Etxaide's lifeless body.

Then, the grief that had been gestating inside her was born. And as the tears flowed from her eyes, as her heart imploded with grief, she felt that she loved it, as she did all the fruits of her womb, she embraced it, became one with her sorrow, aware that no other would ever equal it, and yet she would have died rather than feel it. She leaned forward, opened her eyes and amid the tears she saw his pale hands resting in the dark pool of blood, his handsome face wearing the mask of death, his pale mouth open, all colour drained from his lips. A stabbing pain made her clasp

262

her hands to her chest. Only then did she realise she was still holding her gun. She looked down at it, wondering where to put it. Kneeling beside her, Montes carefully prised the gun from her hand, as he looked at San Martín. The Professor, the man who loved to give a running commentary while he worked, was struck dumb; his ashen face wore an expression of despair, his eyes shone with what to Montes seemed like disbelief. His hands were sheathed in gloves as he examined the wounds slowly, with infinite care, running his fingers over Jonan's hair caked with blood, a subtle, unusual gesture, which gave the impression that he was trying to staunch the wound with his fingers, push the shards of bone back into Jonan's skull, the viscous grey matter, the pooled blood staining the floor. A ritual that Montes assumed was new to San Martín, and which he interrupted only to look at Amaia. Free of her gun, she had folded her arms firmly across her chest, in what might have seemed like an attempt to console herself, but which San Martín recognised as a supreme effort to control her urge to touch the body, thereby contaminating the scene. Their eyes met, and he gazed at her, devastated, his lips set in a fold. He didn't speak, he couldn't as he kept running his fingers mechanically through Jonan's hair. Montes and San Martín had never really liked each other; Montes found the doctor's clinical techno-babble irritating, while San Martín considered Montes's policing methods antiquated. But in that instant, as he observed the pathologist's gloved hand resting on Jonan's head, Montes knew that he would be incapable of carrying out the autopsy.

We don't have to experience it in order to recognise it. There's a moment, an event, a word, a gesture, a telephone call that changes everything. And when it occurs, when it erupts, when it is spoken, it breaks the rudder we thought was guiding our lives, confronting us with reality, demolishing all our innocent plans for the future. Everything we thought was solid collapsed, all life's worries seem absurd, because the only absolute is the chaos that forces us to surrender humbly to death's supremacy. She couldn't stop looking at his corpse; otherwise, her brain would go into instant denial, clamouring: no, no, no! And so she forced herself to look, tormenting herself with the sight of his closed eyes, his pale skin, his lips, now dry, the dreadful black holes where death had penetrated, his beloved blood, congealing in a dark, sticky pool. She remained kneeling beside him, motionless, contemplating the face of her best friend, yielding to the sensation that grief was taking her hostage, as she realised she would never recover from Jonan's death, that the pain of losing him would forever be like a thorn in her heart. This knowledge felt like a dead weight, and yet she welcomed the affliction, grateful to have known him for a while, and to regret his passing for eternity.

Feeling a hand on her shoulder, she turned to find Inspector Iriarte beckoning her to follow him. Then she felt huge, burning tears rolling down her cheeks. Amaia dried them with the back of her hand as she stood up, and she and Montes accompanied Iriarte to where Zabalza was waiting in the corridor leading to the kitchen. Iriarte looked deathly pale, he had dark circles under his eyes, which hadn't been there that morning. Once more, he placed his hand on Amaia's shoulder, his bottom lip quivering as he said in a tremulous voice:

'Inspector, I think it's best if you leave us here and someone takes you home.'

'What!' she said, shrugging his hand off her shoulder.

He looked to his colleagues for support, then went on: 'You are obviously deeply traumatised.'

'So are you,' she replied, looking at each of them in turn. 'It would be shocking if you weren't, but no one's going home. I've been in this apartment for at least fifteen minutes, and

I'm still waiting for someone to explain to me what happened,' she said firmly. 'Jonan Etxaide was the finest police officer I've had the good fortune to work with. In the years we spent together, his commitment, good judgment and loyalty were second to none; I consider his loss both a professional and a personal tragedy, but if you imagine for one moment that I'm going to go home and cry, then you don't know me at all. They didn't make me head of homicide for nothing, so let's get to work. We're going to catch the bastard who did this. Zabalza—'

'When I arrived, the door was open, as if someone had left without pulling it shut properly. When I walked in, I saw him lying there,' he said, pointing at the position near the front door, from which you could see the entire sitting room.

'Did you check all the rooms?'

'Yes, there was no one, although the place had obviously been searched and some electronic devices were missing.'

'They didn't take the TV,' said Montes, gesturing towards a flat screen above the hearth.

'I expect they only took what they could carry.'

Amaia shook her head. 'This wasn't a burglary, gentlemen. Where's his mobile?'

'That's missing too.'

'I called him several times, and got his voicemail. If his phone is still on we can put a trace on it,' she said, fishing out her own mobile and dialling Jonan's number again. This time there was no ring tone. It was either switched off, or had no coverage. She switched off her own mobile. When she first entered the apartment, she had recognised Inspector Clemos, from the back-up team of the Pamplona homicide squad. If she wasn't mistaken, they were about to be pushed off the case, and that didn't surprise her; she would have done the same.

'Has anyone questioned the neighbours? Surely they must have heard the shots?'

'No one heard a thing, at least not on this floor. They're carrying out a house-to-house right this minute.'

Amaia turned to look at the door; she could see from the black powder traces left by the forensic team that they'd finished dusting for fingerprints.

'Did they find any prints?'

'Lots, most of them belonging to Jonan, and most of them useless. There's no sign of a forced entry, so it looks like he opened the door to his killer.'

'Someone he knew,' remarked Iriarte.

'Well enough to let them into the apartment. Presumably he didn't see them as a threat, otherwise he would have drawn his weapon. We also found a bullet casing—'

'Let me see,' she asked one of the forensic team. He held up a plastic evidence bag containing the tiny gold casing. Amaia studied it: 'From a nine-millimetre IMI, manufactured in Israel, which explains why the neighbours heard nothing. Subsonic ammunition, used with a silencer. Do you realise what this means?'

'That the murderer came here to kill him,' replied Montes.

'Incidentally, where is Deputy Inspector Etxaide's gun?'

'We haven't found it yet,' said Zabalza.

Amaia stepped forward, leaning into the group and spoke in hushed tones:

'Listen, I want you to photograph everything, on your phones if necessary. Clemos and his team are here for a reason. Any moment now they're going to tell us to go, and I'm sure you'll agree that we can't leave things like this.'

She saw them nod reluctantly, then she brushed past them, heading for the two rooms at the end of the corridor. Iriarte was right, someone had taken a lot of trouble to search the place. She could almost feel the energy of the intruder who had rummaged through Jonan's life with the zeal of a hunter. She'd seen many burglarised homes, the trail of chaos left by the frantic search for valuables. This intruder hadn't made a mess or broken anything; he or she had been content to take Jonan's laptops and cameras, his hard drives along with a clutch of USBs on which he stored copies of case files, as well as photographs. And yet, she knew the intruder had been there, probably standing on the exact same spot, steeped in the aura of the man he or she had just killed. Amaia's eye alighted on a picture of herself and Jonan in dress uniform, on National Police Day, one of three snapshots on a shelf. In one of the others, he stood smiling next to his parents, and in the third he was with another man on the deck of a sailboat. She realised then that, despite being Jonan's friend, she knew next to nothing about his private life. Who was that man? They looked happy in the photograph, but she didn't even know if he had a partner.

Walking back into the sitting room, she saw that they had covered the body with a metallic blanket. She was mesmerised for a few seconds by the light glancing off it, until a noise behind her broke her reverie. The duty magistrate had arrived, accompanied by a legal secretary, and was looking about cautiously. They greeted each other perfunctorily, while Iriarte came over holding out a telephone for her.

'Boss, it's the commissioner. He says he can't get you on your mobile.'

So this was it. It had taken a little longer than she'd expected. She and Clemos exchanged a few awkward glances, and Clemos positioned himself next to the magistrate.

'Yes, my battery's dead,' she lied.

She listened to the commissioner explain that the back-up team would be leading the investigation.

'Sir, I am *head* of homicide,' she protested.

'I'm sorry, Salazar, but I'm not putting you in charge of this investigation. You know I can't, and if the boot were on the other foot, you'd do the same.'

'All right, but I expect to be kept informed.'

'Naturally, and I trust you'll collaborate with the team,

providing any information they might need to help solve this case.'

Before hanging up, the commissioner added:

'Inspector . . . I'm sorry for your loss.'

She murmured her appreciation, then handed the phone back to Iriarte.

# 33

She wished the world would stop. But when someone we love dies, the world keeps turning. She had heard and read the expression often, and that day she wished it were true, in the same way she wished God or true love existed, because if they didn't . . . She had received a first lesson from death when she was very young and had lost her *Amatxi* Juanita, again when she was a teenager and her father died, and also through her own brush with death. When someone we love dies, and also world doesn't grind to a halt, instead it changes shape around us. As if the earth's axis had shifted slightly, in a way that is imperceptible to everyone else, and yet which gives us a clarity of vision, allowing us to perceive aspects of reality we never knew existed. All at once, we are permitted the dubious privilege of seeing behind the scenes of the play, off limits to anyone not taking part. We see the ropes, the pulleys, the scaffolds that move the stage sets, and suddenly we discover that from up close it looks surreal, dusty and grey. The actors' make-up is exaggerated, their over-loud voices are directed by a jaded prompter reciting from a play in which we no longer have a role. When someone we love dies, he or she becomes the lead in a play to which we haven't been invited, the lines of which are unfamiliar to us. For although Jonan Etxaide had been murdered, and would soon be spread out on San Martín's slab, the power of his absence would dominate the days that followed with as much intensity as if he'd been alive and directing the performance.

Her legs, back and head ached. As she sat in the waiting room at the Navarre Institute of Forensic Medicine, she recalled the many times she had observed victims' relatives waiting, as she was now. She glanced around the room, studying the expressions on her colleagues' faces as they sat in a huddle, talking in that hushed tone reserved for funerals and wakes, like the women gathered at Inés Ballarena's farmhouse. She rose from her seat and went over to the window. The big, dry snowflakes had turned the street white, muffling the sounds of the city, which seemed suddenly brought to a standstill. She thought about how pretty Elizondo must look, and she wished she was there. Montes appeared silently by her side, and, with an apologetic gesture, offered her coffee in paper cup. She clasped it in her hands.

'You knew he was dead when you called me.'

Montes paused for a moment then nodded. He could have denied it, but that would have made Zabalza look foolish.

'Yes, Zabalza told me. I take full responsibility.'

Without replying, she turned to face the window, feeling the warm cup of coffee in her ice-cold hands.

Josune had been working as Dr San Martín's assistant for two years. During that time she had grown accustomed to the puzzled look on her friends' faces when she told them what an amusing guy her boss was, how much she loved her job. She couldn't say that about today. She had already prepared everything San Martín might need: his instruments, the cameras, the spotlights. There were no students today, and lying on the slab was the body of that police officer who couldn't stomach autopsies. She drew back the sheet that was

270

draped over him, and looked with sorrow at his face, so young, lips parted, brown hair caked with blood, his skull horribly swollen where the bullet had exited.

He always used to stand back, and never approached the table or touched the bodies. Dr San Martín would poke fun at him after he had left, but she knew he liked Deputy Inspector Etxaide, he appreciated his intelligence, his sensitivity. You could analyse a body without touching it, and his obvious squeamishness towards the dead didn't make him a worse detective. Indeed, when San Martín was playing the professor, she had often noticed his satisfaction with Etxaide's responses.

Yielding to an impulse, she reached out her hand and gently stroked the young man's face. She imagined he had liked her a little too . . . She drew the sheet back over his face and waited for her boss.

Dr San Martín glanced at his watch again as he sat in the office he used primarily as a gallery for his collection of bronzes, which with its oak panelling and heavy furniture took up a disproportionate amount of space on the second floor. He had inherited it from his predecessor, a sophisticated, and apparently ostentatious fellow, who had even installed a mini-bar behind the panelling. In bygone days, this would have been well stocked with expensive liquor, but San Martín kept only a bottle of Macallan's, the seal unbroken. He tore it off and poured some of the peaty liquid into one of the fine cut glass tumblers he had also inherited. He took a small sip, appreciating the liquor, which burned his throat. After draining his glass, he poured himself another generous dose, screwed the top back on, then returned to the comfortable armchair behind the table. He observed that the tremor in his hand had diminished. He had made the correct decision; this wasn't the first time in his career he'd balked at performing an autopsy. It was his custom to avoid newborns

271

and very young children; his hands seemed too big to manipulate their tiny organs; he felt clumsy and brutish, and he couldn't help glimpsing in their tiny faces gestures that haunted him for days. And so, for a while now, he had entrusted such operations to colleagues who didn't share his qualms. Until now, he had never refused to perform an autopsy on an adult, and it was only when he saw Salazar's grief that he realised: there were things a man should do and others he should never do.

The old Bakelite telephone on the table emitted a shrill sound. San Martín lifted the receiver and listened as his assistant announced the arrival of Dr Maite Hernández.

'Good, I'll be right down,' he said.

All the heat she had managed to wrest from the dregs of her coffee evaporated while she spoke on the telephone in the foyer. She had preferred this to being stared at by her colleagues, and the back-up team, who were waiting for San Martín to begin the autopsy.

The snowploughs had done their work, creating white mounds at the sides of the roads, and burying a couple of cars in the process. She descended the steps, listening to James's worried voice on the other end of the phone, aware of the ground crunching beneath her feet and the unnatural silence into which the city had been plunged by the snow, as if night had fallen early.

'Are you all right, Amaia?'

She didn't need to think. 'No, I'm not.'

'I've no idea how long it will take me to get there, I'm not even sure the motorway is open, but I'm leaving right now.'

'No, James, don't come, they've only just started clearing the streets, half the city is shut down.'

'I don't care, I want to be with you.'

'James, I'm fine.' She contradicted herself. 'The place is teeming with police officers, we're still waiting for the autopsy to start, and then we'll have to give statements. This is going to take hours, I won't even be able to be with you . . .'

An uneasy silence descended over the conversation.

'Amaia . . . I realise this isn't the right moment, but there isn't going to be another . . .'

More silence.

'It's about the trip. My father is having surgery on Monday.'

'James,' she started to say, 'right now—'

'I know,' he cut in, 'and I understand, but you do understand that I have to go?'

'Yes,' she sighed.

'I have to be there, Amaia. He's my father and, despite my mother's attempts to play it down, the operation isn't a walk in the park.'

'I said, I understand,' she replied wearily.

'And, well, I'm guessing that if you aren't in charge of the investigation you may be able to join us in a few days' time, after the funeral.'

'After the funeral?' she protested. 'James, I'm head of homicide and Jonan was my colleague and my best friend . . .' As she was speaking, another thought dawned on her. 'Did you say "us"?'

'Amaia, I'm taking Ibai with me, like we planned. You won't be able to look after him, and it's too much of a responsibility for your aunt. In a couple of days we'll all be together.'

A feeling of bewilderment and desolation came over her at the thought of being separated from Ibai. But James was right, she wouldn't be able to look after him, and they should stick to their original plan. She felt a terrible weariness as she reflected once more about how a word had changed the course of her life, demoting her to the rank of spectator in the debacle that was her life. Yes, James was right. And yet, she wanted to protest, to shout 'What?!', to demand, to insist. But she herself didn't know *what*, nor did she have the strength for it.

A taxi pulled up outside, and a middle-aged woman stepped out.

'All right, James, we'll talk about it later. I need to hang up.'

'Amaia.'

'What?' she said, irritated.

'I love you.'

'I know,' she replied, ending the call.

Five minutes later, San Martín came into the waiting room, accompanied by Dr Maite Hernández.

'Inspectors,' he said, addressing the general company. 'For personal reasons, I will not be performing the autopsy on Deputy Inspector Etxaide. My esteemed colleague here, Dr Maite Hernández, will be taking my place. I shall oversee the results,' he added, as they exchanged handshakes.

'Salazar, I believe you two have already met . . .'

Amaia extended her hand, which the woman clasped firmly as she murmured: 'I'm sorry for your loss.'

In response, Amaia heard herself uttering words she had heard from the lips of Johana's mother, as well as one of Lucía Aguirre's daughters, which at the time she hadn't fully appreciated.

'Take care of him in there.' It was a gaffe, an unconscious slip, a prayer from the heart that caused Montes to wince as he emptied his lungs of air, while Zabalza pulled a face, struggling to contain himself.

Clemos and his team followed the pathologist into the autopsy room while Amaia and her colleagues looked on with mournful expressions.

'I thought you might like to wait up in my office,' San Martín suggested, beckoning them towards the stairs.

Amaia would be eternally obliged to San Martín for letting them use his office that day. Stepping into the gloomy, masculine room she had first visited the previous year, she had felt overwhelmed with melancholy. On that occasion, Johana Márquez's mother had told them amid floods of tears about her husband's controlling behaviour towards her daughter, whom he went on to rape and murder. As always, Jonan had been with her, and she recalled how moved he was by the woman's insistence on praying to one of the bronze figurines. Amaia glanced about for the sculpture. The magnificent Pietà, one metre tall, stood in the same place on the conference table; an unusual depiction of the Virgin Mary cradling her dead son in her arms, Christ's face concealed among the folds of her robe like an infant clasped to her bosom. Amaia studied it intently, reflecting that this was the natural gesture, the one demanded by the body, the same urge she'd been forced to suppress when she saw Jonan lying on the floor: to embrace him, clasp him to her heart. Tears pricked her eyes and she swallowed hard, turning away from the sculpture to collect herself.

San Martín gave Amaia his chair behind the heavy table, while Clemos sat across from her, visibly uneasy in her presence. He disliked her. Clemos was one of those macho policemen who resented having a woman for a boss, and took a childish delight in being 'king of the castle'. She gave him a stern look, which he evaded by reading his notes.

'You'll receive a copy of the autopsy report once it's ready,' he began, 'in the meantime . . . Deputy Inspector Etxaide received two shots, one to the chest and a second to the head, after he was on the floor. We recovered one bullet casing – the killer appears to have taken the other – and one bullet which was lodged in the floorboards. Dr Hernández removed a second bullet from the body. The nature of the crime and the type of gun used suggests the work of a hired killer. I have several officers searching Etxaide's house for the murder weapon; they usually get rid of it immediately, either in a rubbish bin or down a drain. We may never find it.'

Clemos glanced up to gauge her reaction to his words, then returned to his notes.

'Everything points to the killer being known to the victim, either that or his appearance posed no threat. We can tell from the position of his body, on the far side of the sitting room, that Etxaide not only opened the door to his killer, but invited him into the apartment. There were no signs of a struggle, and although some computer and photographic equipment was taken, his wallet and other valuable items were untouched, so it appears this wasn't a burglary.'

'What about Jonan's service revolver?' asked Montes.

'Missing. As you know, this is also typical of a hired killer; I wouldn't be surprised if it showed up at some other crime scene in a few years' time. A clean gun is priceless.'

Amaia listened impassively.

'So, we need you to tell us who might have wanted Etxaide dead, who bore a grudge against him, and whether he'd received any threats.'

Montes and Zabalza both shook their heads.

'I can't imagine Jonan falling out with anyone. He wasn't that kind of person,' declared Montes.

'What cases was he working on? Maybe the accused, or the suspects, had it in for him.'

'I've sent you a copy of all the reports,' said Iriarte. 'In the *basajaun* case, the culprit was shot; the main suspect in the *tarttalo* case took his own life in prison; then there was a Colombian who killed his girlfriend and tried to kill himself; a sixty-five-year-old woman who stabbed her husband to death while he was asleep, after suffering years of domestic abuse; and the Dieietzki case – a Russian drug trafficker who arranged the murder of one of his competitors while he was in prison.'

'What about more recent cases?'

'There's the Esparza case,' Iriarte went on. 'A father accused of murdering his four-month-old baby girl. He also committed suicide in prison.'

276

'Yes, I've heard the body count is mounting,' Clemos said, smirking as he exchanged glances with one of his team.

'Watch your mouth, Clemos!' snapped Montes. 'Or I'll—'

'Montes,' Amaia broke in, 'cut the inspector some slack. If we give him enough rope, he might end up hanging himself.'

Clemos glanced at her uneasily, and swallowed hard.

'It was a joke.'

'We aren't in the mood for your jokes,' said Montes, looking daggers at him.

'Well,' Clemos resumed, 'we'll need his computer from the station at Elizondo, as well as access to his desk and personal belongings.'

'Call by whenever it's convenient,' said Iriarte.

Clemos cleared his throat, uneasily. 'And then there are the other elements . . .'

'And what might those be?' asked Amaia.

'Those unrelated to his police work.'

'I don't understand what you're getting at.'

'Could Etxaide have been involved in some shady dealings – drugs, weapons—'

'No. You can rule that out.'

'. . . And we mustn't forget that he was homosexual.'

Amaia cocked her head to one side, narrowing her eyes as she studied Clemos.

'I don't see what part Deputy Inspector Etxaide's sexuality could play in solving this case.'

'Well,' said Clemos, avoiding Amaia's eyes and seeking refuge in those of his colleagues. 'It's well known that sex among the gay community can be somewhat chaotic, and, well . . . they get very worked up over things.' He shrugged.

'Inspector Clemos,' she said, 'before you start speculating you need to clarify your thinking and get your facts straight. Firstly, you've just outlined a series of compelling reasons to suggest the killer was a hitman, and yet now you're saying this could have been a crime of passion. Secondly, there's no evidence that levels of violence are any higher among the gay community than among the heterosexual community. I don't like you, Clemos, and I don't believe you are fit to lead this investigation, but the commissioner has placed you in charge and I have to accept that. However, if I hear you make any further baseless insinuations, I'll have you taken off the case.'

Clemos rose from his seat.

'Very well, if that's the way you want it. I came to talk to you in person out of respect. I could have sent a written report – which is what I'll be doing from now on.'

'Good, I want it on my desk first thing tomorrow morning,' she retorted as he stormed out.

Amaia's team remained at the table, saying nothing but exchanging glances. Amaia closed her eyes and shook her head.

'I know, I went too far . . . But they have no idea who Jonan is . . . who he was. I'm not going to let that jerk get away with making crass remarks.'

'No need to apologise, boss. I came this close to punching his lights out,' said Montes.

'Put yourself in his shoes,' Iriarte broke in. They turned to look at him, irritated. 'These are still the early stages of the investigation, he's obliged to keep an open mind.'

'You've got a point there, Inspector,' Montes rounded on him. 'But all this going by the rule book – doesn't it make you sick sometimes?'

The tension in the air was palpable as the two men locked eyes. Amaia was about to step in when Dr Hernández arrived, accompanied by San Martín.

'Dr San Martín has asked me to answer any questions you might have, so here I am,' she said, taking a seat in the chair vacated by Clemos.

'Tell us what you've found,' said Amaia.

Dr Hernández took out a pen and opened the file she was carrying to display a diagram of a body, which she drew on as she spoke.

'Two shots fired from a nine-millimetre pistol: the first, to the chest, knocked your man down, severing his aorta and causing a massive haemorrhage; the second, to the forehead, was what killed him, although it was superfluous as he would have died of blood loss within seconds. The first bullet became lodged in his neck, and was removed during the autopsy; the second caused an exit wound and was retrieved at the scene of the crime. Judging from the extent of rigor mortis, we estimate time of death at between ten and twelve last night, but we'll have to wait for the test results to confirm that.'

'What do you think happened?'

'He opened the door to his killer, invited him in and offered him a seat.'

'What makes you think that?'

'The trajectory of the first bullet. It travelled upward, as if his assailant were kneeling or sitting down. Look at the diagram and you'll see: the bullet entered just below the collarbone, then became lodged in the neck. If his assailant had been standing, even if he was relatively short, the bullet would have exited through the back or become lodged in the shoulder blade, and yet it was found just below the cranium.'

Amaia studied the diagram.

'Would you both agree that the killer must have been sitting roughly here?' she said, addressing Hernández and San Martín as she pointed to a place on the diagram, then traced a line with her finger.

Amaia addressed her team: 'Let me see the photographs you took of Detective Inspector Etxaide's apartment.'

They all placed their mobiles on the table, showing images of the room from several different angles.

'That doesn't work. His killer couldn't have been facing him while sitting on the sofa. Unless he moved the body.'

'The body lay where it fell,' said San Martín, 'it wasn't moved afterwards.'

'Could he have moved the furniture, then?'

'The furniture wasn't moved either,' said Montes. 'I visited his apartment a few months ago, and that's how it was arranged then.'

'Could his assailant have been very short?' ventured Amaia.

'The same height as an eight- or nine-year-old child? I doubt it.'

'Perhaps there was a struggle, and Jonan pushed the killer over. That might explain why he was shot from lower down,' suggested Zabalza.

'There was no sign of a struggle, no defence wounds or any other marks on his hands, although he could have pushed his assailant towards the door.'

Dr Hernández gazed thoughtfully at the diagram.

'Do you agree with Inspector Clemos that this was the work of a professional killer?' asked Amaia.

Raising her eyes, the pathologist stared off into space.

'Possibly . . . The most obvious elements point in that direction, but there are others that raise questions. For one thing, this shot fired from low down, the strange trajectory, that's not the way hitmen work. And then there's the second bullet. This could have been a coup de grâce, the killer's way of making sure he'd accomplished his mission, but, as I said, the first shot would have been fatal, although his death would have been painful and distressing; a massive haemorrhage would have caused his lungs to collapse, flooding his oesophagus and trachea with blood and leaving him to endure the agony of asphyxia. In which case the second bullet spared him a great deal of suffering. It was almost an act of mercy.'

'You're kidding me!' exclaimed Montes. 'Since when is a bullet to the head an act of mercy?'

'When the intention is to alleviate suffering that is strictly unnecessary.'

'And you think that because the killer shot him twice?' said Montes sceptically.

Dr Hernández extracted a photograph from her file. It was an enlarged image of Jonan's face, taken at the crime scene. As she placed it on the table, she could almost hear the silence spread like a cold wave over the company.

'No. I think that because the killer closed his eyes.'

# 34

The fifty-minute journey to Elizondo took the best part of two hours. Snowploughs and gritters had strewn the road with a mixture of slush and salt, which sprayed up beneath the car tyres like reverse rain. It was no longer snowing, but the cold night air had kept the white mounds at the sides of the road intact, and the sinister darkness of the mountain had been replaced by an orange glow as moonlight reflected off the snow, casting an otherworldly corona over the landscape like the surface of an unknown planet.

Amaia's mobile rang on speakerphone, and she recognised the number on the screen as the one Dupree had last rung her from. She quickly accepted the call, fearing it would be cut off, and searched for a place to pull over. After putting on her warning lights she answered.

'Aloisius?'

'Is it dark already in Baztán, Inspector Salazar?'

'Darker than ever,' she replied.

'I'm so sorry, Amaia.'

'Thanks, Aloisius, how did you hear about it?'

'A murdered cop in Spain is news that spreads fast.'

'But I thought you—'

'Don't believe everything you hear, Inspector. How are you?'

She heaved a deep sigh. 'Lost.'

'You're not lost, you're just frightened. It's normal, you haven't had time to think yet, but you will, inevitably, and then you'll find your way.'

'But I don't know where to begin. Everything around me is falling apart. I don't understand what's going on.'

'Why think about that, Salazar? With all your experience, in life as in your work, surely you don't believe things happen for no reason.'

'I don't know. I can't see any patterns in this chaos. I feel blind,' she sobbed, the tears rolling down her cheeks. 'What happened to Jonan is so . . . I still can't believe it – and you want me to find a reason behind all this?'

'Think.'

'That's all I do, but I find no answers.'

'You'll find them when you ask the right questions.'

'Oh, for God's sake, Aloisius, the last thing I need is advice from the Ninja master . . . Tell me something useful.'

'I already warned you. Someone close to you isn't what they seem.'

'And who is this person?'

'That's for you to tell me.'

'How can I, if I'm blind?'

'You've answered your own question. You can't see, Salazar, but you're only blind because you want to be. Get some perspective. Go back to the beginning. Press reset, Inspector. Remember where this all started. Forget everything you think you know and start from the beginning.'

She sighed wearily. 'Are you going to help me?'

'Don't I always?'

She sat in silence, listening.

'The devil is on your tail, *un mort sur vous*,' he said.

'Aloisius, the case was closed when the father of the girl was killed in prison. The wife made a statement clearly implicating him, but now he's dead there's no case to answer,' she explained, omitting any reference to Yolanda Berrueta's story or the events in Ainhoa.

'Whatever you say, Inspector.'

'Thanks, Aloisius.'

'Try to get some sleep; tomorrow is another day.'


The luggage by the front door upset her in a way she hadn't expected. James and Ibai's suitcases, packed and ready for their departure the following day left her with a terrible sense of loss.

James, Engrasi and Ros had all waited up for her. Their embraces, their hands clasping hers, the genuine sympathy from those who loved her and whose hearts went out to her. She explained nothing, she told them nothing; she had spent the entire afternoon reliving the horror, and now, suddenly, she felt hollowed out. She was conscious of falling into the trap of denial, which she had experienced even as Jonan's lifeless body lay at her feet, as she found herself unable to visualise her dead friend's face, his corpse sprawled on the floor. Her memory was like a haze of blinding light, preventing her from accepting the truth: that he was dead, that Jonan was dead. She could think it, but her brain refused to believe it, and she was too weary to make herself confront that cruel reality, so she let herself fall, or leapt into the trap, which was merciful, and didn't hurt as much.

As she listened to her family talk amongst themselves, she was able for the first time that day to forget her grief and think about something else. Before going to bed, she called the Saint Collette hospital. Yolanda Berrueta was off the critical list, and had been moved on to the ward.


James had been awake for hours, listening to Ibai's soft breathing and watching his exhausted wife sleeping beside him. Even plunged into that sleep she so desperately needed, the grief was still etched on her face. Each time he heard her whimper and start to cry, he stroked her cheek, consoling her from afar, and it occurred to him that things had always been this way with her. Sharing Amaia's life meant accepting that they inhabited parallel worlds: while she slept, he was awake; while he dreamed, she kept watch. It was as if they could never touch; his caresses, his words, his tenderness had to be offered from afar. Though he loved her deeply, he knew that she perceived his love as she might a gentle embrace in a dream. A tear rolled down her cheek. Moved by this, he leaned over and planted a gentle kiss on her lips. She opened her eyes, smiling when she saw him.

'Oh, my love!' She placed her arms about his neck, winning him over once more.

# 35

Amaia and Engrasi had both got up early – Amaia because she was eager to spend every last second with Ibai, and her aunt so as to observe her. She watched her niece stroll about the house cradling the boy and humming fragments of songs Engrasi could barely make out. Even so, she could tell they were filled with sorrow from the way Amaia's arms encircled the child tenderly and her soft, childlike voice as she whispered to him, the fleeting expressions on her pale tear-stained face. Her features seemed frozen beneath a mask of pain so deep it would prevent her from ever smiling again.

When they loaded the luggage into the car at midday, Engrasi stood in the doorway gazing mournfully at them. Amaia took her by the hand and led her into the kitchen.

'What's the matter, Auntie?'

Engrasi shrugged, and this frail gesture filled Amaia with sorrow.

'Tell me.'

'Don't mind me, dear. I suppose I've become accustomed to having you all here, and it breaks my heart to see you go, especially after what's been happening these past few days.'

Amaia embraced her aunt, kissing her snow-white hair.

'I'm afraid, Amaia. I probably shouldn't say this, but I have a bad feeling about you leaving, as if you're never going to come back.'

'Auntie, don't let James hear you say that. He's about to catch a plane, and you know he has faith in your hunches.'

'That isn't what I'm referring to.'

'What then?'

'This is about you, it's all about you.'

Amaia looked at her aunt tenderly; this wasn't the first time she had heard her say these words, and it wouldn't be the last. The same words were spoken by the husbands, wives, mothers and children of police officers the world over . . . But Jonan's death had changed everything.

'I'll be careful, Auntie, I always am. Nothing bad is going to happen to me, I promise. Trust me.'

'Of course,' said Engrasi, pretending to be reassured. 'Go now – they're waiting for you.'

Loading the car, driving to the airport, parking at the terminal and accompanying them to the check-in, all commonplace actions, habits of a lifetime, interrupted as they reached the gate where she smothered Ibai with kisses before passing him to James. They were leaving. She embraced her husband, kissing him with increasing desperation as she realised she couldn't bear him to leave. Without thinking, she blurted:

'Please don't go.'

He looked at her, surprised. 'Darling . . .'

'Please don't go, James, stay here with me.'

He waved the tickets in her face like two inescapable facts.

'I can't, Amaia. Why not come with us?'

She nestled her head against his chest.

'I can't, I can't,' she groaned, pulling away suddenly. 'I'm sorry, I don't know what made me say that. This is just so hard.'

He held her in his arms, and they remained like that for a short while until his flight was announced. Afterwards, she stood watching as they mingled with the other passengers filing towards the security gate, where she lost sight of them.

A chapel of rest had been set up inside the Beloso police station. Local officials, including personnel from the Ministry of the Interior, would stop off there on their way to the cathedral where the funeral would be held. Amaia stood guard in her dress uniform beside the sealed coffin draped with the Navarre flag. Beneath it, the dark wood struck her as ridiculously shiny. From where she was standing, she could see the arrival of Jonan's parents, whom she had only met a couple of times on National Police Day. She watched as they were greeted by officials, her colleagues offering their condolences, while she stood trapped amid an oppressive atmosphere of whispers and muted sounds, which she found intolerable. When someone took over from her, she made her way towards the couple, who were talking to the minister's secretary. Jonan's mother came to greet her, clasping Amaia's hands clad in her black leather uniform gloves. For a few seconds Amaia contemplated her in silence, as she felt her eyes fill with the thick, blinding tears of grief that come unbidden when we encounter a fellow sufferer. Then she drew closer, kissing her on both cheeks.

'We've invited a small group of friends to the house after the funeral. I'd like you to come. Without the uniform,' she added.

'Of course,' Amaia replied. Unable to say more, she pulled her hands free and fled the unnatural atmosphere of the chapel of rest. For the last few minutes, her phone had been vibrating incessantly in her pocket. She read the message and made her way upstairs to the homicide section to look for Clemos.

'Good afternoon,' she said, loud enough so that everyone present was obliged to answer.

'Good afternoon, boss,' said Clemos, rising from his seat. 'Could you come with me,' he said motioning for her to follow him. 'You too, please, Garrues,' he said, addressing one of his officers.

He opened the door on to a small and stuffy room. Waiting inside were two officers from Internal Affairs, both of whom Amaia knew from previous investigations. She greeted them, refusing the invitation to sit down opposite Clemos, who'd installed himself in the desk chair. This was clearly a clumsy attempt to redress the balance after their meeting yesterday; he was trying to show her who was in charge, but he'd miscalculated in giving her the choice, forgetting that choosing where you position yourself in an enclosed space gives you the upper hand.

She stood in silence, staring straight at him.

'We've come across something, and we're hoping you might be able to tell us whether it's significant or not,' he said, gesturing towards the officer he had asked to accompany them. 'Garrues is the IT specialist who has been examining Deputy Inspector Etxaide's police computer. Apparently, Etxaide was something of an expert himself, so I imagine you occasionally went to him for advice.'

'All the time,' she admitted.

She felt her hackles rise as Clemos smiled.

'Have you heard of remote access or VPN?'

'I believe it's a tool or application that allows technicians to access a network without having to be physically present.'

'Did you ever ask Deputy Inspector Etxaide to access your computer in that way, perhaps to solve a problem you were having?'

'No, never. I asked him to set up an email for me once, but I was present at the time. Afterwards, I changed the password, on his advice.'

Garrues nodded, satisfied.

'Boss, we've discovered that Deputy Inspector Etxaide accessed your computer up to twenty times in the past month.'

'That's impossible,' she said.

'We've double-checked: Deputy Inspector Etxaide accessed your emails, as well as various files, some of which he copied, using a remote connection called *team viewer*. What's remarkable is that he must have done this at the station, because for the app to be installed, both computers need to be switched on, and the host computer requires a password before accepting. So the next question is: did Deputy Inspector Etxaide have free access to your work computer?'

'Of course he did, he was my assistant and he often worked in my office, although I never saw him touch my computer.'

The two men from Internal Affairs exchanged glances then gestured for Clemos and Garrues to leave the office. When the door had closed, they invited her to sit down. Again she refused.

'Inspector, we understand that a few days ago an incident occurred during the search of a woman's house, which suggested that she received a tip-off,' one of the men said.

Amaia opened her mouth, but said nothing.

'We also understand that you suspected that someone from the station at Elizondo, or more precisely one of your team, might be responsible for leaking the information.'

'Yes,' she said. 'I admit that, to begin with, I considered that possibility. But after further analysis I ruled it out. I trust my men.'

'Undoubtedly, but the fact is that this warrant,' he said, reaching for a printout, 'referred to a particular file, and that file alone was burned by the woman in question as part of what she described as a "clear out" ahead of your arrival. I don't blame you, Inspector; I would have had my suspicions too.'

'Yes, and I've admitted that I did. But what has this to do with Deputy Inspector Etxaide?'

'He accessed your emails the night before, and first thing next morning.'

She bit her bottom lip, containing herself.

'And yet, the search warrant was no secret,' the officer added.

'Look, I've no idea why Deputy Inspector Etxaide accessed my computer, but I'm sure there's a simple explanation. Could he have done so by accident?'

'The IT specialist just explained that to gain remote access he had to install the app on your computer manually, using a password; that must have been intentional.'

'Perhaps he wanted to send me a photo file that was too big to attach in an email – that happened sometimes,' she suggested as a last resort. 'I was expecting some enlargements he'd made, maybe . . .'

The man from Internal Affairs shook his head.

'Your loyalty towards your men is touching, Inspector Salazar, but I'm afraid the fact is that Deputy Inspector Etxaide accessed your computer remotely up to twenty times in the last month alone, without your permission. Or did you give him permission?'

She shook her head. 'No, I didn't.'

# 36

Jonan Etxaide was cremated with only his family in attendance. Those were his wishes, and his parents respected them. Amaia was relieved not to have to see Jonan's coffin during the interminable funeral service held by the Bishop of Pamplona in front of the city's political and ecclesiastical representatives, who overwhelmed his extraordinarily dignified, serene parents with their attentions. When the service was over and she was finally able to escape the tainted atmosphere inside the cathedral, she heaved a sigh of relief.

'Inspector.' She heard a voice behind her. She knew who it was before turning round; the accent was unmistakable.

'Dr Takchenko, Dr González.' She was genuinely glad to see them. The woman extended her hand, and Amaia felt the strength of her character in the handshake. The man put his arms around her, murmuring his condolences. Amaia freed herself awkwardly from his embrace. Never comfortable with the formulaic responses on such occasions, she made an effort to smile and asked, 'When did you arrive?'

'This afternoon, it wasn't easy because there's still quite a bit of snow on the roads . . .'

Yes,' she said, remembering the weapons courtyard at the

fortress in Aínsa, where the two doctors had their laboratory, and Jonan's fascination with that place.

'I imagine you're spending the night here . . .?'

'Yes, we're staying in the centre of town. Dr González will be heading back tomorrow, but I'm giving a talk here in a few days' time, so we decided to take a short break. This kind of thing makes you think,' she said, sweeping the air with an inclusive gesture.

Amaia looked at them in silence, struck by how absurd conversations seemed now, as if they were all actors, obliged to recite meaningless lines. She had no desire to participate in this charade, to act normally, to pretend that nothing had happened.

'Call me, and we can have lunch together – if you'd like to?'

'I'd like that very much,' said Amaia, forcing a smile.

Dr Takchenko leaned forward. 'I think someone else wants you.'

Amaia turned towards the street, where what looked like an official state car was parked opposite the entrance to the cathedral. The man in the driver's seat was beckoning to her. As she approached, he stepped out of the vehicle and opened the rear passenger door for her. She found Father Sarasola waiting inside. After overcoming her initial surprise, she turned to wave goodbye to the two doctors.

'I'm sorry to be seeing you under these circumstances, Inspector Salazar. This is a terrible loss. Although I only met Deputy Inspector Etxaide briefly, he struck me as a brilliant young man, full of promise.'

'He was,' she replied.

'Would you object to taking a short ride with me?'

She climbed in and the chauffeur immediately started the engine. They sat in silence as the vehicle negotiated the narrow streets of the old quarter, where the funeral-goers mingled with the usual afternoon pub-crawlers.

'Could you tell me about the circumstances surrounding the death of Deputy Inspector Etxaide?'

Sarasola's question threw her; the facts had been reported in the press, and Sarasola was a man who made it his business to keep abreast of everything that went on in the city, so his question must go deeper.

'I could,' she said hesitantly, 'but first I'd like to know why you're asking. The news is in the public domain, and I'm sure you make it your business to know everything that goes on in Pamplona.'

'Naturally, I've read about it in the newspapers,' he said. 'And I have consulted various "friends", but I'd like to know who you think murdered Deputy Inspector Etxaide – and why.'

Sarasola's interest piqued her curiosity, but she was wary of sharing information with him until she had some idea of his motives. She replied evasively:

'Everything happened so fast, the investigation is still wide open and, as I'm sure you also know, another team is in charge of the case.'

He gave a sardonic smile. 'Officially.'

'What do you mean?' she asked.

'What I mean, Inspector, is that I don't believe for one moment that you've withdrawn from the investigation, except for appearances' sake.'

'Then believe me, Father, when I tell you that I haven't a clue where to start.'

The car was heading along one of the tree-lined avenues close to the university. Unlike in the city centre, the snow there looked freshly fallen. Sarasola tapped the chauffeur's window, and the man responded by pulling up a few metres ahead. Then he climbed out of the car, put on his overcoat and lit a cigarette, which he puffed on vigorously as he walked away. Sarasola sat at an angle in his seat so he could look Amaia in the eye.

'Do you think Deputy Inspector Etxaide's death might be connected with the investigation you were working on?'

'You mean the Esparza case? As I'm sure you're aware, the suspect was murdered in prison. We subsequently followed another line of inquiry, but it led nowhere.'

Sarasola nodded. Amaia assumed that news must have reached him about the disastrous events in Ainhoa.

'Inspector, I realise there are things you can't tell me about the investigation, but don't underestimate me. We both know that it wasn't Valentín Esparza but rather his relationship with Dr Berasategui that was significant.'

'As far as we know, their relationship was circumstantial. A witness confirmed that he attended a bereavement therapy group run by Berasategui as part of his voluntary work. There's no reference to Esparza or the group in any of the documents we seized from Berasategui.'

Sarasola sighed, clasping his hands together in an attitude of prayer.

'You don't have all of them.'

She opened her mouth in disbelief. 'Are you saying that you concealed facts and withheld information that could have had a bearing on the investigation?'

'I'm afraid I'm not responsible, Inspector. I answer to a higher authority.'

She stared at him, dumbstruck.

'I will deny we ever had this conversation if you decide to go public, but Deputy Inspector Etxaide's passing has convinced me that there are things you should know.'

'This murder,' she said angrily. 'Deputy Inspector Etxaide didn't pass, he was murdered. And who are you to decide what information we should be privy to when investigating a crime?'

'Calm down, Inspector. You may find it hard to believe, but I'm your friend. I'm here to help you.'

She pressed her lips together, not trusting herself to reply, and waited.

'Dr Berasategui kept files at the clinic which contained details of every case he had ever worked on, including that of Valentín Esparza.'

'Where are they? Do you have them?'

'No, I don't. When Dr Berasategui was arrested, the highest authorities at the Vatican took an interest in the case. As I explained to you when we last met, the practice of psychiatry is often used as a vehicle for discovering cases of interest, which the Catholic Church has been pursuing since its inception.'

'The nuance of evil,' she said.

Arching his eyebrows, he stared straight at her.

'Dr Berasategui had made significant advances in this field, which we subsequently discovered he had kept hidden from us. When the case blew open, the Vatican kept back files of his that were deemed to be of no interest to the criminal investigation, but which contained things of a disturbing nature, things which the general public would have had difficulty coming to terms with. For purposes of security, the papers were taken to Rome.'

'You do realise that they are guilty of stealing evidence?'

He shook his head. 'The authority of the Church is more powerful than that of the police in these matters. Believe me, there's nothing you can do about it. They were taken out of the country in a diplomatic bag.'

'Why are you telling me this now?'

Sarasola let his gaze wander outside for what seemed like a long moment. Amaia waited in silence for him to resume.

'I gave the matter a great deal of thought, and the reason I decided to talk to you is because of the nature of your inquiry when you last came to see me at the clinic.'

'About Inguma?'

'About Inguma, Inspector.' He paused, raising his fingers to his lips, as if still unsure whether to confide in her or keep it to himself. 'Are you aware that in the past few months the

Vatican has appointed eight priests who are authorised to perform exorcisms in Spain? This is no coincidence – nothing the Vatican does ever is. For some time now, the Church has been concerned about the proliferation of groups or sects throughout the country. There are currently sixty-eight of them, divided into four categories. The A groups are relatively benign collectives, which neither physically abuse nor extort money from members. Groups B and C are financially, psychologically and physically abusive; their methods include forced prostitution, the trafficking of drugs, weapons and children, using women as slaves . . . And then there is group D, which combines the worst attributes of groups B and C, but with an added dimension. Group D is made up of Satanists; they commit violence or murder, not for profit but as an offering or sacrifice to the devil. Some of their false prophets came over here as immigrants, bringing with them practices such as voodoo, Santería, and other rituals that are traditional in their own countries; others saw their chance during times of economic and moral crisis to make money out of preying on people's despair and their desire for riches.

'The Church must take some responsibility for having failed to adapt to the needs of its congregation, many of whom have turned away from God; you only need step inside a church in any city on a weekday to see that. Most people nowadays describe themselves as secular, agnostic, or even atheist. And yet nothing could be further from the truth. Since the beginning of time, man has been seeking God, because in doing so he is seeking himself. Man is incapable of renouncing his spiritual nature; much as he professes to the contrary, sooner or later he will follow a dogma, a doctrine, an existential system that will guide his life, provide a formula for happiness, and protection against the emptiness of the universe and the finality of death. Whether they are atheists or practice Santería, whether they are mere consumers or followers of whatever cult or fashion, human beings all want the same thing: to live a perfect, harmonious life. One way or another, they are looking for a kind of purity, protection, a formula to keep them safe from the dangers of the world. Most people go through life without harming anyone, but occasionally their search leads them into the hands of evil. Sects that promise to rid them of incurable illnesses, to give them work, money, business, a home, protection from their enemies – imagined or real – but free from the constraints imposed by the Church. It is good to covet, to envy, to possess at any price, to give rein to greed, anger, revenge; they provide a playground for man's basest instincts.'

Amaia heard him out, but she was becoming impatient.

'I understand what you say, Father, but what has this to do with Deputy Inspector Etxaide's murder?'

'Possibly nothing,' he admitted. 'But a respected psychiatrist, a member of my clinical team, turned out to be the instigator of a series of monstrous crimes. Berasategui planned and carried out his activities over a long period. I understand that the *tarttalo*'s crimes date back to a decade ago. Berasategui must have left university around that time.'

Amaia listened, resisting the urge to prompt or ask questions.

'Is it any wonder that this investigation of yours has me alarmed? First you come to consult me about a demon that kills people in their sleep, then it transpires that Berasategui was connected both to Esparza, who murdered his own daughter, and to your mother, who planned to do the same to your son. And now one of the detectives working on the case has been murdered.'

He fell silent, waiting for her to speak. She thought about her twin's empty coffin, debating whether to tell him about it.

'Father Sarasola,' she said at last. 'Why do I have the impression that, despite everything you've told me, you are holding something back?'

He acknowledged with a nod, then continued: 'As you are aware, Navarre has always been important. A land of saints and a pillar of the Church, but also, and perhaps for those very reasons, the presence of evil has been constant throughout the centuries. I'm not just referring to the work of the Inquisition, to witch doctors and faith healers, but to the monstrous crimes which inspired the myths that have been handed down to us. Witchcraft and satanic practices such as human sacrifice aren't a thing of the past. Three years ago, a man walked into a police station in Madrid accompanied by his lawyer; he said that he could no longer live with his conscience and wished to make a confession. He told the police that in 1979 he had been one of the founding members of a sect based at a farmhouse in the Navarre municipality of Lesaka.'

Amaia pricked up her ears at the mention of that name, recalling her first meeting with Elena Ochoa.

'The sect was run by a leader who described himself as a psychologist or psychiatrist. Although he didn't live at the farmhouse, he would pay regular visits. According to the man's testimony, the sect indulged in traditional witchcraft, invoking ancestral beings. During their ceremonies and covens, as he called them, they sacrificed animals, mostly lambs and cocks, as well as holding orgies and rituals during which they would smear themselves with blood and even drink it. A few months after he joined, one of the couples gave birth to a baby girl. According to the witness's statement, the parents gave up their child to the sect as the highest form of sacrifice. The girl was a few days old when they slaughtered her in a satanic ritual as an offering to the devil. The witness gave a detailed description of how they took the girl's life in a horrific ceremony during which every kind of depravity was perpetrated. Not long afterwards, the sect disbanded, and the members went to live in different parts of the country. Among those involved were lawyers, doctors, even a teacher – many of them parents themselves. A magistrate based in Pamplona is in charge of the case.'

'That's impossible!' she said emphatically. 'I know about every ongoing homicide investigation in this city.'

'As I said, the witness's original statement was taken in Madrid. The case was referred to Pamplona because the alleged crime was committed in Navarre, and the magistrate in charge placed an immediate confidentiality order on the case, due to the delicate nature of the matter, not to mention the possible backlash against those implicated were the details to be made public. Above all, there was concern for the safety of the man who reported the case, who is currently under the protection of both the police and the Church.'

Amaia listened in astonishment. Sarasola made her feel like a complete novice. How could he be aware of a homicide case about which she knew nothing? A stream of images flashed through her mind: a baby girl, barely a toddler, dressed in rags as she crawled across the field between Argi Beltz and Lau Haizeta; her own mother slipping out of the house at night to attend those meetings; her *Amatxi* Juanita weeping as she sang to her; the death certificates destroyed by Fina Hidalgo, and the midwife offering walnuts to her with that twisted grin; her sister's coffin, empty save for a bag of gravel; the dark, silky hair escaping from that rucksack on the ground outside the funeral parlour; Elena Ochoa's body surrounded by a pool of blood, the walnut shells and the scent of death emanating from her still-warm body.

'Did they find the child's body?' she whispered.

'No. The witness doesn't know what happened to it, whether it was buried in the woods or somewhere else. All he can say for sure is that they took it away.'

She tried hard to push aside the images that kept running through her head as though playing on an old projector. She looked straight at Sarasola as she collected her thoughts.

'I know of an almost identical story, which took place at a farmhouse in Baztán. The parents made up the perfect alibi, and the crime was never investigated.'

'Yes,' said the priest. 'At the farmhouse where Berasategui held his bereavement therapy groups; she was a little girl too, and that was in the year . . .'

'In the year I was born,' she finished Sarasola's sentence for him.

# 37

Jonan's parents lived in a tiny attic apartment, which, to compensate for the reduced floor space, boasted a roof terrace extending across the entire building. It overlooked the dark, illuminated city, glowing amid the whiteness, and although the snow had started to melt, it lay pristine on the balcony. Soft music was playing in the background, and a young woman had given Amaia a glass of whisky, which she downed without a word. Jonan's parents stood surrounded by a group of relatives who never once left their side. The father had his arm round his wife's shoulders, and, every now and then she would press her head to his chest in a small, intimate gesture of complete trust. Most of the guests were young. What had she expected? His mother had told her this would be a gathering of friends. They beckoned to her as soon as they saw her and she went over, leaving her glass on a table. Both parents embraced her.

'Thank you for coming, Inspector.'

'Please, call me Amaia,' she replied.

'All right, Amaia,' his mother said, smiling. 'Thank you.'

'Jonan had great admiration and respect for you,' said his father, solemnly.

The words of the man from Internal Affairs came back to her: 'Did you authorise him to access your computer?'

'I admired and respected your son too,' she said, feeling a touch of pettiness, of disloyalty. Someone else came over to greet them and she took the opportunity to escape into the kitchen, where the same young woman was pouring more whisky into glasses. Amaia took one and swigged it back, visualising the smooth, fiery liquid travelling down her throat into her empty stomach. The conversation with Sarasola had left her exhausted. She had gone to their house on Mercaderes, seeking refuge from her fears and insecurities, but had found only the gap left by her absent family, the darkness, the over-sized rooms, her footsteps echoing against the high ceilings, her beloved son's things, James's discreet presence. She had switched on all the lights as she walked round the deserted house, weighed down by what was missing and regretting her decision to go there. Standing in front of the mirror in her bedroom, she had stripped off her clothes, laying her dress uniform out on the bed. She'd gazed wistfully at the red jacket, which they wore during awards ceremonies, but which from that day on, and forever after, would be a funeral costume. She slipped on a pair of jeans, a white shirt and a black jumper, and pulled on some sensible boots so she wouldn't break her neck on the icy pavements. Then, removing the elastic band from her hair, she brushed it, all the while replaying her conversation with Sarasola. Witchcraft, sacrificed babies, empty coffins, the Vatican, Berasategui's sequestered files, the Tremond-Berrueta tomb blown sky high and Jonan's body lying in a pool of blood. Aware of the suspicions of Internal Affairs, she even managed to find some solace in Sarasola's theory that Jonan's murder could be connected with all that. And yet she refused to entertain the possibility that—

She dropped the hairbrush and ran into the bathroom. Holding her hair away from her face, she threw up in the toilet. Once the nausea had passed, she gazed at her distorted reflection in the mirror, her eyes watering from the exertion.

She turned on the tap, washed her face and cleaned her teeth.

'It's impossible,' she said to her image in the glass. And then she had left that house which was threatening to engulf her . . .

As the soothing effect of the second whisky spread through her, she felt relatively normal for the first time in days. When she returned to the sitting room, Montes and Zabalza had arrived and were greeting Etxaide's parents. Iriarte took her to one side.

'What do you think?' She knew he was referring to the theory put forward by the men from Internal Affairs, and she assumed he'd been discussing it with the others.

'I think they're wrong, Iriarte. I want them to be wrong,' she said, lowering her voice.

'I do too,' he said. 'But it makes sense: if he accessed your computer that day, he could have seen the search warrant.'

'Not necessarily, he might have accessed it for a different reason.'

'Without your permission?'

'For God's sake! He knew my every move, he didn't need my permission.'

'Even to look at your personal emails?'

'Enough!' she said, in an over-loud voice, then, glancing about, murmured, 'I'm as confused as you, but we're here as his friends to honour his memory. Let's discuss this tomorrow.'

Iriarte picked up one of the glasses the young woman was passing around, and drifted towards the centre of the room. Montes took his place.

'I don't believe it,' he said. 'Okay, he accessed your computer, we can't deny the facts, but not . . . You know what he was like about computers, he probably wanted to install an anti-virus, or some other gadget,' he said, trying to make light of it.

304

Amaia nodded, unconvinced. 'I don't want to talk about this now.'

'I can understand why, but don't be annoyed with Iriarte – you know how persuasive those guys from Internal Affairs can be when they get the bit between their teeth. He's extremely worried,' said Montes, motioning with his chin towards Iriarte. 'We all are,' he added, gazing at Zabalza, who had sat down and was listening in silence, an untouched drink in his hand, to a group of Jonan's friends, who, with sorrowful faces, were relating what seemed like an amusing anecdote.

'Amaia!' Jonan's mother called her over. Next to her stood a young man whom she recognised instantly from the photograph in Jonan's bedroom. 'I'd like to introduce you to Jonan's partner, Marc.'

She extended her hand, looking into his face and recognising someone in the throes of grief. His red, swollen eyes showed that he'd been crying recently, but there was nothing frail about the way he gripped her hand, as he turned away from Jonan's mother, taking her aside

'Marc,' she apologised, 'I had no idea. I feel terribly embarrassed, but I didn't know Jonan had a partner.'

He grabbed a couple of drinks and gave one of them to her.

'Don't worry. He was a very private person.'

She smiled.

'Shall we go outside?' he suggested, motioning towards the roof terrace. She put on her coat, and they stepped onto the snow, which had started to melt and gave way beneath their feet. They walked over to the handrail, content to contemplate the city lights for a while, sipping their drinks in silence.

'We met in Barcelona a year ago. I was planning to move here next month, you know? We would have been living together by now, but he flatly refused to give up his job, and in the end I applied for a transfer at work; luckily, they have a branch here . . . And now,' he said, spreading his arms in a gesture of despair, 'here I am, but he's gone.'

Amaia felt a mounting rage inside her, the kind that made you want to break into a run, scream, make promises you could never keep.

'Listen, Marc, I swear to you, I'm going to get whoever did this.'

He screwed up his eyes, struggling to hold back the tears.

'What difference does it make? It won't bring him back to me.'

'No,' she said. 'It won't bring him back to us.'

She felt buried beneath the weight of this absolute truth she refused to accept. Huge, round tears rolled down her face, and she let out a sob that caused her whole body to shake. Marc put his arms around her, and the two of them wept unreservedly, in that way that convulses, turns you inside out, leaves your nerves exposed, in that way only grief-stricken people can cry together. They stayed like that, clinging to one another, oblivious to what anyone thought, weeping in each other's arms, joined by an emotion that has the power to unite or isolate human beings like no other.

'We must look like a couple of drunken sailors,' Marc said after a while.

She laughed, wiping her face with her hand and stepping away from him as she realised they were both still holding their drinks. They raised their glasses in silence and drank.

Marc looked out again at the city lights.

'Do you ever get the feeling after something has happened that, while it was going on, you didn't know what it meant, and then afterwards it becomes obvious and you feel like a total idiot? As if you were going through life blindly, irresponsibly, dancing on a minefield.'

She nodded and they exchanged a look of complicity.

'Jonan knew.'

'What did he know?' she asked.

'That he was in danger. Or rather, I'm not sure he *knew* – maybe he just suspected.'

'Did he tell you something?' she asked, her pulse quickening.

'Not exactly. Like I told you, he did and said things that at the time I didn't notice, but which I now realise were significant. I think I would have known if he thought his life was in danger. Besides, his colleagues told me he didn't have his gun when he opened the door, so he can't have felt any imminent threat. But I believe he sensed something might happen to him, because he left a message for you.'

'For me,' she said, surprised.

'Well, not exactly a message. About a fortnight ago he told me he was preparing something for you, and that if he couldn't give it to you, I was to do so.'

Amaia gasped.

'Oh my God! What did he give you?'

Marc shook his head.

'He didn't *give* me anything; that's why I thought nothing of it at the time. He told me to tell you a word.'

'A word?' she repeated, disappointed.

'Yes, he said you'd know how to use it.'

'What word?'

'"Offering".'

'Offering. Is that all?'

'Offering, and his number. Nothing more.'

'Are you sure? Try to remember the context – what were you talking about at the time? Maybe he told you something beforehand?'

'No, that's all he said: that he had something for you, and if he couldn't give it to you, I should remember that word, "offering", and his number.'

She fled, or at least, so it seemed to her. She said goodbye only to Marc and to Jonan's parents. Shivering and exhausted

307

as she was after their crying session on the roof, she felt something close to relief, which she knew would be short-lived. As she left the apartment, she noticed Deputy Inspector Zabalza, still sitting with Jonan's friends, his drink untouched, but now looking unusually relaxed, with a wistful smile on his face. They hadn't exchanged two words since his attempt to stop her from entering Jonan's apartment.

She took the lift down to the ground floor, studying her reflection in the glass, which was garishly lit. Her eyes looked a bit red, that was all; she found herself wishing she had shadows like Iriarte's, or Zabalza's ashen face. She wanted to parade her grief, to break down, to let go for once. She paused in the doorway, buttoning her coat, then looked both ways down the street, trying to get her bearings. She started to walk, frowning at the mounds of dirty snow that were beginning to melt in that slow, watery process that turned the pavements into puddles, and was one thing she hated about that city.

In Elizondo, when it rained or when the snow and ice melted, the water knew where to go. When she was a little girl, she liked going outside after the rain had stopped, to listen to the sound of water dripping from the eaves, running between the cobblestones, sliding over the sodden leaves and down the black tree trunks, returning to the river, which, like a distant, primordial creature beckoned its children to join once more the ancient stream from whence they came. The wet ground would glisten with the light that shone through the parting clouds, making each trickle glow silver as the water found its way back to the river. But here the water had no mother, it didn't know where to go, so it oozed onto the streets like spilled blood.

She saw a huddle of people smoking outside a bar, and thought she recognised someone entering with another group. Then she heard her name, and wheeled round in surprise as she recognised Markina's voice. He was walking towards her from his car, which was parked outside the building she'd just left. She had noticed him among the funeral guests, but he looked different now, younger somehow. He was wearing jeans, and a pea jacket. She came to a halt in the middle of the street and waited for him to draw level with her.

'What are you doing here?' she asked, then instantly regretted it.

'Waiting for you.'

'For me?'

He nodded. 'I wanted to talk to you, and I knew you'd be coming here . . .'

'You could have called.'

'I didn't want to say this over the phone,' he said, walking right up to her, so they were almost touching. 'Amaia, I'm so sorry about Jonan, I know you had a special relationship . . .'

Overcome with emotion, she bit her lip and looked away, towards the distant lights on the avenue.

'Where are you going?' he asked.

'To hail a taxi, I guess.'

'I can drop you off,' he said, gesturing towards his car. 'Where do you want to go?'

She paused, then said, 'For a drink.'

He suggested the bar opposite.

'. . . No, not there,' she said, remembering the group of people that had just gone inside. The last thing she wanted was to have to engage in social chit-chat, or trot out clichéd responses to even more clichéd condolences.

'I know the perfect place,' he said, pressing the remote on his car key.

Her face must have reflected her astonishment as he pulled up outside the Tres Reyes Hotel in the centre of town.

'Don't look so surprised; it has a wonderful English bar where they make the best gin and tonics in town. It also has the advantage of being patronised mostly by people from out of town. I come here when I want a quiet drink and don't care to bump into anyone I know.'

Markina was probably right; in all the years she had lived in Pamplona, she couldn't recall once having set foot inside the hotel lobby.

'You should know, Inspector. Hotel bars are the traditional place for business deals, shady or otherwise, as well as the perfect setting for discreet encounters.'

Eschewing the low tables dotted about the room, she headed for the row of stools by the bar, and sat with her back to the room. The place was sufficiently crowded for them not to stand out, but quiet enough for them to hold a conversation without having to shout. At the far end of the room, a discreet jazz quartet played popular tunes. The barman slid a couple of coasters in front of them and handed them the gin-and-tonic menu, listing a dozen different combinations, which Amaia passed over.

'I think I'll stick with whisky. That's what they were serving at Jonan's parents' house,' she explained. 'I don't even know if there was anything else to drink. A pretty girl passed round a tray of glasses, like at an Irish wake.'

'Two whiskies, then,' Markina said to the bartender.

'Macallan's,' she added.

'Excellent choice, madam,' the man replied politely. 'Did you know that in 2010 a sixty-four-year-old bottle of Macallan's sold at Sotheby's for four hundred thousand six hundred dollars?'

'I hope it wasn't this one,' she joked, as she watched the ceremony with which the bartender decanted the whisky into two glasses. Markina picked them up and handed one to her.

'So, let's continue in the Irish tradition and drink a toast to him.'

She raised her glass and drank, feeling relieved and confused at the same time. She knew that this was partly due to Markina being there with her and having to acknowledge that, aside from the nightmare going on around her, part of her recent sorrow was because he was angry with her. She worried that she had lost the tenuous link that somehow bound them, that she had disappointed him, and would never see that inimical smile of his again. He was telling her that he had once been to an Irish wake, describing how sad yet moving it was to see all those people celebrate the life of the deceased. He explained why a wake traditionally lasted three days: according to legend, there was no better way of finding out if the deceased was suffering from catalepsy, or pretending to be dead, for no Irish man or woman could listen to the sound of their friends revelling around them for three days without rising from their coffin. It was an amusing story, and as he spoke, she found herself contemplating once more the contours of his mouth, the tip of his tongue licking the whisky from his lips, the timbre of his voice, his hands cupping the glass . . .

'I never imagined you drinking whisky,' he remarked.

'While they were doing the autopsy, we waited in San Martín's office. He took out a bottle, and we all had a glass . . . I don't know, I'd never really thought about the custom of drinking a toast to the dead; it wasn't planned, but we did it. And then, at his parents' house today, more whisky. It has something, I'm not sure what, an amazing sedative quality. It allows you to remain lucid, while dulling the pain,' she said, shuddering as she took another sip.

'You don't seem to like it much.'

'I don't.' She smiled. 'I just like the way it makes me feel. And I understand why the Irish associate the taste with death. Each fiery mouthful is like taking communion, it leaves you purified, healed inside.' She lowered her gaze, falling silent for a few seconds. She hated this ebb and flow of tears; just when she thought she was in control, her grief would rise like a

311

tsunami, and as she struggled to hold back the flood she had the impression she was drowning.

She felt Markina's hand on hers, and the contact with his firm grasp, his warm skin, produced a magnetic charge that made the hairs on the back of her neck stand on end, and helped her to collect herself. She pulled her hand free, dissimulating as she picked up her glass and drained it. Markina signalled to the bartender, who came over cradling the bottle of Macallan's as one might a baby.

'Everything feels so unreal. For example, you're the last person I would have expected to end up having a drink with tonight,' she said, when the bartender had gone.

'When are you going to stop being so formal and use the familiar "tu" with me?' he said.

'I suppose when you decide whether to call me Salazar, Inspector or Amaia – the sucker who made a fool of you.' She blurted the reproach without thinking. She was tired, and probably a little drunk, but most of all she wasn't in the mood for pretence. But, when she saw the look of dismay on his face, she instantly regretted her outspokenness.

'Amaia . . . I'm sorry, I—'

'No,' she broke in. 'I'm the one who is sorry. Truly sorry.' She looked straight at him. 'Not because of Judge De Gouvenain or her complaints against me, I'm sorry because of Yolanda Berrueta, and because of you.' He was sitting perfectly still, listening in silence. 'You trusted me, you opened up to me about your mother, and I more than anyone know how difficult that is. I decided to approach De Gouvenain because I genuinely believed I was on to something. I didn't go behind your back because I thought you were indecisive or overly sensitive about the subject – even though you clearly are.'

He arched an eyebrow, grinning faintly.

He could have kissed her then and there.

'You wanted solid evidence, which I believed I would find

312

inside that tomb in Ainhoa. It turns out I was mistaken, but even so – and this is something Jonan Etxaide made me see – Judge De Gouvenain would never have issued the order unless she thought there were sufficient grounds.'

'This is behind us, Amaia,' he whispered.

'No, it isn't. Not if you still think that I intentionally went over your head.'

'I don't think that,' he said.

'Are you sure?'

'Completely,' he said, giving her that smile.

It was the calmness of his smile that enchanted her, the way he looked straight at her, the perfect beauty of the gesture, which he seemed to be performing afresh each time, and yet she could recreate every detail of it in her mind's eye. She realised this was what she feared losing, what she couldn't bear to lose. She glanced at his mouth again, then slid her gaze towards the glass, wondering as she drank from it how often a sip of whisky replaced a kiss.

She realised that she was drunk when at three in the morning the music in the bar stopped. The alcohol had worked like a soothing balm, covering her wounds with a warm blanket, putting to sleep those ferocious beasts tearing at her heart, overpowering them with the magic of eighteen years in an oak barrel. She knew this would be a brief respite, that when the beasts awoke it would start again, but for a few hours at least she had rid herself of this weight squeezing the air out of her lungs, smothering her. Most of the customers had left long ago. She spoke above all about Jonan, letting herself think tender thoughts, freed from the image of him on the floor, his hands resting in a pool of blood, his lifeless face. Remembering how they first met, how he had earned her respect. She smiled faintly as she recalled how squeamish he was about touching dead bodies, his encyclopaedic knowledge of criminal history. The tears returned, and she held them back as she talked, her tongue loosened by the whisky; even so, she turned her head slightly, avoiding the gaze of the barman, who, a seasoned professional, was standing discreetly at the far end of the bar, busily polishing glasses.

Markina listened in silence, nodding when appropriate, signalling to the waiter to refill their glasses, although his remained untouched. Later on, she would remember the mirror running the length of the bar, the strategically placed lights setting ablaze the amber tones of the various whiskies, the rows of shiny glasses, the odd word, and Markina's eyes. Gradually the fog descended over everything, and her memories became hazy. They were leaving the bar when it started to snow again, but the flakes were tiny and wet, like frozen raindrops. No, not those snowflakes the size of rose petals, those surreal-looking ones that had made the world stand still. She gazed up at the streetlamp, watching the swirling flakes swirl like a swarming mass pricking her eyes, longing for a snowfall that could bury her, smother her pain. Then, all of a sudden, those falling snowflakes roused the slumbering beasts that fed off her grief, for whom denial was no longer enough; in that moment the amber balm that had soothed them wore off, and they renewed their attack, more ferocious and cruel than ever.

Markina stood by his car, observing her. She was watching the snowfall as though witnessing a miracle. Standing beneath the streetlamp, her face wet from the flakes that turned to water as they touched her skin, while, oblivious, she gazed up at the sky with infinite sorrow. He made his way slowly to her, giving her time, waiting. After a few minutes, he placed a hand on her shoulder, and guided her to the car. As Amaia turned, he could see, mixed with the melted snow, tears streaming down her face. He spread his arms, offering her the solace she needed, and she buried herself in his embrace, as if it were the place she'd always been looking for. Then she started to sob, uncontrollably,

314

abandoning herself, letting out great gasps as he tried to contain with his embrace the grief tearing at her insides, making her tremble as if she might fall apart. Holding her tight, he let her weep, vanquished.

# 38

She could hear nothing. The world had been plunged into a deafening, dreamlike silence. She opened her eyes and saw big, crisp, heavy, snowflakes burying her, dampening every sound save for her heart, which kept beating slowly as the snow fell on her, clogging up her eyes, her nose her mouth. Then, noticing the powdery, earthy taste of raw dough, she realised this wasn't snow at all, but white powder which a remorseless killer was throwing over her to bury her alive in the kneading trough.

'I don't want to die,' she thought.

'I don't want to die!' she cried out, and the cry in her dream brought her back.

She tried to open her eyes and found the lids were sticky from crying herself to sleep. It took her a few seconds to remember the room she had just woken up in. Turning instinctively towards the light seeping through the slats of a blind someone had left tilted, she made out a tall window with a long white curtain. As she attempted to sit up, a sharp pain in her head brought her back to reality. She waited for the throbbing to subside. Throwing aside the covers, she placed her bare feet on the carpeted floor, only to realise that, apart from her boots and socks, which lay next to the bed, she was fully dressed. She looked around for her gun, and was relieved to find it on the bedside table. She stumbled over to the window, pulling up the blind and letting the dull morning light enter the room. The gigantic bed she had slept in dominated the room. Two bedside tables stood either side of it, and at the foot was a heavy piece of antique furniture, gleaming in the dim light, which served as a stand for a large painting. She climbed back into bed, running her hand through her matted hair as she remembered the events of the previous evening.

She had never cried like that before; her chest and back still ached, as if there were a hollow, an open wound between her spine and breastbone, a gash in the lining of her lung, through which both air and life had escaped. Yet she didn't care; she felt proud of the stabbing pains in her chest. She remembered that he had consoled her, embraced her when she broke down in tears, when she cursed the universe, which had singled her out once more, placing her at the centre of things, making her feel small and fearful again. But he was there. She didn't remember him saying a single word, he simply held her in his arms and let her cry, without lying to her, trying to stop her tears by promising her that everything would be all right, that it soon would pass, that the pain would go away. The vivid memory of his embrace brought back the feel of his taut skin covering his sinewy frame, holding her together as she dissolved. She remembered his scent, the perfume emanating from his coarse wool jacket, his skin, his hair. Unconsciously, she reached for the white pillows, drawing them to her face, breathing in, searching longingly for his smell, his warmth, reliving the sensation of his arms about her, his body, his hands caressing her hair as she buried her face in his neck, in a pointless attempt to hide her tears from him.

Checking her watch, she saw that it was almost seven. She replaced the pillows, cursing the smattering of make-up she had worn yesterday – enough to leave a dark smudge on the pristine white surface of the pillow. She took a quick shower, displeased by the thought of having to wear the same clothes she had slept in, and, without drying her hair, she left the bedroom.

The kitchen was open-plan, and there were no curtains at the windows; from every angle there was a view over the garden. The lawn was a dark shade of green, flattened by the previous days' snow, now melted in the light rain. Markina was sipping coffee on a high stool at the kitchen counter and browsing the newspapers. He was barefoot, in jeans and a white shirt, half-unbuttoned, and his hair was also damp. When he saw her, he smiled and folded away the newspaper, which he left on the counter.

'Good morning, how are you feeling today?'

'Fine,' she said, without much conviction.

'And your head?'

'Nothing an aspirin won't fix.'

'What about everything else?' he asked, his smile fading.

'I don't think that can ever be fixed. Which is the way it should be. I wanted to thank you for being there for me last night.' He shook his head as she spoke. 'And . . . for giving up your bed,' she added, gesturing towards the sofa, strewn with pillows and a blanket.

He grinned, looking at her in that way which always made her think he knew something she didn't.

'What's so funny?' she asked.

'I'm glad you're here,' he replied.

She glanced about, as if to confirm the fact. Yes, she was there, she had slept in his bed, she was having breakfast with him. He was half-dressed, her hair was wet. And yet, something was missing from the equation. She smiled into her coffee, cradling the cup in both hands.

'Are you going to the courthouse today?'

'Perhaps, later this morning. I have to catch up on some

reading here at home,' he said, pointing to a stack of papers on the table. 'And you?'

She thought for a moment.

'I'm not sure. I'm not working on any case, so I guess I'll do some paperwork, then check if they've made any progress on the investigation into Jonan's murder.'

'You could come back here afterwards . . .' said Markina, looking straight at her. He wasn't smiling, although there was a plaintive note in his voice.

She studied him. The half-unbuttoned shirt revealing the outline of his collarbone beneath his tanned skin, the designer stubble extending from his neck to his cheeks, his face, always youthful-looking, and his eyes, that amused determination she found so attractive. She desired him. This hadn't happened overnight. Crazy though it seemed, his game of seduction had worked; he'd managed to get into her head in a way that took over everything.

'. . . Or I could stay,' she said.

He sighed and shook his head. 'No.'

She was taken aback by his response. Only a moment ago, he had suggested that she come back later. She made no attempt to hide her confusion.

Markina gave a smile that was at once resolute but gentle.

'It's because of the way in which you came to be here,' he said. 'You were very sad last night, you needed someone to talk to, with whom to drink a toast to your friend, a shoulder to cry on, you needed to get drunk . . . And today, you're here, in my house. You can't imagine how much I've longed for that. But not like this. You know how I feel about you, you know that won't change, but I don't want anything between us to be accidental. That's why you have to leave now, and I hope you'll come back, because if you do, I'll open the door knowing you've come for me, that your being here isn't incidental.'

She didn't know what to say to this. Setting her cup down

on the table, she rose, picked up her coat and bag, which were draped over a chair, then turned to look at him. He was watching her, solemnly, and once again his eyes betrayed that peculiar determination, as if he knew things she didn't. Closing the door behind her, she made her way along the stone path leading from the front door to the street, feeling the cold air solidify her damp hair like a helmet. She hailed a taxi, buttoning her coat and rummaging in her bag for gloves, which she pulled on as the taxi took her back to her car. Afterwards, she drove through the city, the streets gridlocked at that time of the morning by delivery vans and parents making the school run, double-parking outside the school gates. Cursing, she decided to take the ring road, heading in the direction of San Sebastián.

As she drove away from the city, she began to feel increasingly lost. She remembered the times when driving had a calming effect on her; she would go out in her car at dawn, without any fixed destination, and often she would find the necessary distance to be able to think, as well as the peace and quiet she longed for. But that felt like a long time ago. This morning there was no peace. Pedestrians huddled for warmth beneath bus shelters, cursing the cars splashing through puddles left by the melting snow and rain. The motorway brought no relief. The ring road was clogged with vehicles, all of them streaked with salt and grit. She couldn't think at the wheel any more. Whenever she needed to think, she'd been in the habit of asking Jonan to drive; she'd sit in the passenger seat, staring off into space.

She pulled into the Zuasti service station and parked close to the entrance of the singular-looking building. She hurried through the rain, crossing the threshold as others were leaving. The warmth of the place enveloped her. She ordered a milky coffee in a glass and found a table by the window where she could watch the mist rolling down the hillsides as she waited for her coffee to cool so she could hold the glass in her hands.

The rain pelted against the windows, which reached halfway up the building, reminding her of an Alpine chalet. She gazed at the metal girders holding up the roof and noticed a sparrow fluttering between the rafters.

'She lives here,' explained the waitress, who had seen her watching the bird. 'We've tried to chase her out, but it's a bit difficult, what with the roof being so high. She seems to like it up there. I think she's built a nest. She's been here a couple of years – that's longer than me. When the place is quiet, she flies down and pecks at the crumbs on the floor.'

Amaia smiled at the waitress but didn't reply; she didn't want to get embroiled in a conversation. Her eyes drifted to the sparrow once more; a clever bird, or an imprisoned creature? The rain drumming on the window panes caught her attention once more, the droplets mesmerising her as they slid down the glass like oil. She wanted to think, to think about the case, about Jonan, about James, yet all she could think of was him: his naked feet, the glimpse of skin beneath his shirt, his mouth, his smile, his persistence, always wanting more. She gave a sigh, and decided to call James. Taking out her phone, she calculated the time in the States: just gone three in the morning. Frustrated, she left the phone on the table as she closed her eyes. She knew what she wanted to do, what she had to do, she knew perfectly well. He made the rules . . . yet this wasn't a game, it was so much more than that; he wouldn't settle for less. Meanwhile she was drowning in a sea of doubt. She left the remainder of her coffee on the table, together with some coins, and went back out into the rain.

Her body was trembling. She could feel the tension stiffening the muscles in her back, racing through her nervous system like an electrical current, converging in her fingertips, giving her the strange impression that at any moment they might burst beneath her nails to release this burning energy. Her stomach had clenched into a knot, her mouth was dry, and the air inside the car didn't seem enough to fill her lungs. She parked outside his house, blocking the exit, and walked back up the stone path, feeling sick with each step, as her heart hammered in her chest, pulsating in her ears. She rang the bell, resolute and remorseful in equal measure, and waited with bated breath as she tried to calm the anxiety threatening to engulf her. When he opened the door, he was still barefoot, his hair, now dry, hung tousled over his brow. He said nothing, he stood looking at her, smiling in that mysterious way. She said nothing either, but raised a cold hand until her fingers were touching his mouth, his soft, warm lips. It was as if the corners of his mouth had become her goal, her fate, her only respite. He clasped her hand in his, as though afraid to lose this connection, guiding her inside the house, as he pushed the door shut behind her. Standing before him, her fingers pressed to his lips, she paused for a few seconds, searching for words to make sense of this, but she knew that there was nothing she could say now, that she must surrender to a different voice, a language that, as an outsider, she had never been able to share with anyone. Drawing her hand away from his lips, she saw herself in his eyes, which looked back at her with the same fear, the same excitement. She stepped boldly forward, and their bodies fused, while, eyes closed, he embraced her, trembling.

Looking up at him, she knew that she could love this man . . .

She slipped off her damp coat and led him by the hand towards the bedroom. There was scarcely enough light seeping through the blind to make out the contours of the heavy furniture; she raised it, letting the overcast sky illuminate the room. As he stood beside the bed, he was watching her with that expression that drove her crazy, and yet he wasn't smiling. Nor was she. Her face betrayed her unease at knowing she was in the company of an equal. She drew closer, gazing at him, seized by a fresh anguish. She caressed him awkwardly,

322

unnerved at recognising herself in him, aware that she was there because for the first time in her life she could truly reveal herself, remove not just her clothes but the shameful burden of her existence, and in doing so she saw herself reflected in him, as in a mirror. She knew that she had never desired anyone this way, she had never experienced this intense yearning for a man's flesh, his saliva, his sweat, his semen, this desire for his body, his skin, his tongue, his sex. She realised she had never coveted a man's bones, hair, teeth, the roundness of his shoulders, the firmness of his buttocks riding her, the perfect curve of his back, the softness of his tousled hair, by which she guided him to her breasts, her loins. There had been no man before him. That day she was born to desire, all at once, she discovered a new language, a new, vital, exuberant, creative language, and she could speak; she could feel her tongue struggling to master it, then falling silent, letting him speak, feeling his strong hands clasping her flesh, holding her hips, and the vigour with which he penetrated her, the firmness of his gestures pushing, guiding, commanding her, the strength in his arms when she straddled his body to take him into her again. The fire spilling over inside her in a delayed explosion of ecstasy, pleasure verging on madness a thousand nerve endings raw and clamouring. Then the silence that leaves the body exhausted, the mind drained, the hunger sated only for a short while.

The pale sun that had blessed the city briefly that morning had disappeared completely by the time Amaia got back into her car. Although it couldn't have been much later than five in the afternoon, the leaden skies had swallowed up the light, triggering the sensors in the city's streetlamps.

She turned the key in the ignition, pausing for a few seconds as she became conscious of the changes that had occurred around her. Like a space traveller landing on a strange planet, identical to her own, but with a different atmosphere, colder, denser, obliging her to walk carefully so as not to lose her balance, giving her a new perception of things, imbuing everything around her with a dreamlike quality.

She took out her phone and checked her missed calls. First, she rang James, who explained in whispers from a distant hospital waiting room that they had just spoken with the surgeon who operated on his father, and everything had gone well. He and Ibai missed her. Then she called Iriarte. Still nothing from ballistics.

The streets in the old quarter were crowded. She decided to leave her car at the underground car park in Plaza del Castillo and walk from there to the house on Mercaderes. Approaching the front door, she noticed a bundle of junk mail jammed into the letterbox. As she pulled out the super-market and petrol station flyers, she saw that wedged into the space was a brown paper parcel tied several times with fine, dark red string. She knew instantly who it was from, but was surprised that he had sent it to that address. Agent Dupree's spidery writing covered the surface of the package, which bore her name. She clasped it to her chest as she entered the house.

She was relieved to get out of her clothes which she felt she'd been wearing for a week. After taking a long, hot shower, she emerged from the bathroom and paused to look at her dress uniform, still laid out on the bed like a memento of Jonan's funeral. It occurred to her that she ought to put it away in the wardrobe, even as a voice inside her argued that the uniform was a kind of homage to Jonan, an intangible yet powerful symbol of his honour and commitment, but also of the doubts that were assailing her, and which she was unable for the time being to put to rest.

Finally, she picked up Dupree's parcel and went into the kitchen to cut the string, pondering as she did so how very 'New Orleans' the packaging was. She unwrapped the paper, removing a piece of cotton cloth, slightly damp to the touch,

324

which enveloped a volume bound in dark, soft leather. There was no title on the front or spine of the book, which felt oddly heavy for its size. Behind the silk flyleaf was an intricate illustration, amid whose cursive flourishes she was just able to make out the title: *Fondation et religion Vaudou.*

She marvelled as she ran her fingers over the fine pages trimmed with gold leaf, wondering again at the incongruous weight of the book.

The first few chapters were devoted to the origins of the religion, which had millions of followers the world over, and was the official religion in several countries. Then she noticed a kink in the tightly packed pages. She separated them carefully until she found one that Dupree had marked with a small black feather. Amaia took it gingerly between her fingers, reading the cramped pencilled writing with which her friend had filled the margins and underlined several passages:

*Provoking death at will. The* bokor, *or witch, initiated into Lucumí, the priest or* houngan *who has chosen to use his powers for evil.*

A few pages later, Dupree had circled a couple of sentences:

*Un mort sur vous*
*Un démon sur vous*

Below he had written:

*The dead man who mounts you, or the demon who mounts you, in Latin America 'se te sube un muerto'.*

The book went on to give a detailed description of an attack by an immobilising demon, sent by a *bokor*. The demon paralysed its victim while he slept, permitting him to remain fully conscious of what was happening, as he endured, terrified, the torments of the malevolent spirit, which perched on his chest, preventing him from moving or breathing, sometimes to the point of death. Some victims claimed to have seen a hideous creature with a gigantic head crouched on top on them, still others a foul dragon.

'A Komodo dragon's saliva contains enough bacteria to cause septicaemia': San Martín's words came back to her.

As she flicked through the book, searching for further annotations by her friend, a second feather flew out from among the pages and floated ominously to the floor. She stooped to pick it up and read the passage of text, which was headed 'The Sacrifice'.

The words, placed in inverted commas to highlight their level of importance, strangeness, or repeated usage, reminded her of Elena Ochoa's account of 'the sacrifice'. She was also reminded of what Marc had said on that snowy roof terrace overlooking Pamplona only yesterday, though it seemed like years ago now: 'offering' – a word Jonan had told him she would know how to use.

The *bokor* made an offering to the devil of the most monstrous crime, the most coveted quarry, which by virtue of its pure, innocent nature remained untouchable. The sacrifice had to be carried out by the only people who had true ownership of it, who had brought it into the world: the parents themselves. A ceremony was performed during which they offered up their progeny, their newborn, and in exchange for the child's life, the demon would grant all their wishes.

An illustration showed a baby on an altar. Standing beside it were two enraptured figures, presumably the parents, and a priest who, with raised arms, was urging on a sinewy reptile that loomed menacingly over the child, covering its nose and mouth with its foul maw. Just below, Dupree had written several short sentences.

*Groups of the same gender.*
*Specific time period.*
*Precise location.*

And scrawled beneath these notes, a brief message to which Dupree had added his signature:

*Press reset, Inspector.*

She flicked through the rest of the pages, pausing to look at the ghoulish illustrations, and searching for further annotations in Dupree's handwriting. Then she closed the book, stood up, and began to pace about the house, wandering from room to room.

Still barefoot and in her bathrobe, she felt the creak of the wooden floorboards that crossed the house from end to end, resounding through the empty rooms. As she passed the sitting room, she noticed her old desktop computer, gathering dust. She searched in the kitchen dresser for the jotters she used to make shopping lists, some sticky tape, a pad of yellow Post-it notes, and a couple of marker pens, then returned to the sitting room and switched on the computer. She printed off a map of Navarre from the Internet, and taped it to the bookshelf; then she marked with a dot the different locations where the children's parents had lived. She quickly realised that she would need a bigger map, as Ainhoa was the other side of the border, France. She found one, printed it off, placed it next to the first, and added to it the children from Ainhoa. Besides the fact that most of the locations were in the Baztán Valley, there appeared no obvious connection between the various dots. She studied the pattern, aware that it made no sense to her, and recalled Dupree's words: 'Press reset, Inspector . . . Forget everything you think you know and start from the beginning.'

Her mobile rang out in the silence of the house, interrupting her musings. As she took the call, she realised that the day, with its tenuous light, had given up the ghost, yielding to night without having dawned, and that she was still in the bathrobe she had put on after her shower.

'What have you been doing all afternoon?'

She looked at the maps, which now covered a large area of the shelves, then at Dupree's book, open on the table, and felt a sudden pang of guilt.

'Nothing. Wasting my time,' she replied, switching off the light and walking out of the sitting room.

'Are you hungry?' asked Markina, on the other end of the phone.

'Very.'

'Will you have dinner with me?

She smiled. 'Of course, where do you want to meet?'

'At my place,' he replied.

'Are you going to cook for me?'

'Cook? I'm going to do everything for you.'

# 39

Oh, Jonan, Jonan. She could feel Zabalza's arms immobilising her as she dissolved into tears for her dead friend, for his spilled blood, his hands resting on the floor . . . She moaned, waking in the darkness, broken only by the faint light seeping through the doorway. She fumbled for her mobile: just gone seven. The screen illuminated the room as a call came in, and she was glad she'd put the phone on silent. It was Iriarte. She slipped out of bed and walked out of the room.

'Inspector, I hope I didn't wake you.'

'Don't worry,' she replied.

'We have some news from ballistics. According to the marks on the two projectiles recovered during the autopsy, the gun is the same one used to kill a bouncer at a disco-theque in Madrid six years ago. A gun linked to Eastern European mafias, which was found at the crime scene and then disappeared from the evidence room at a courthouse in Madrid.'

'Disappeared from a courthouse? How is that possible?'

'It seems there was an arson attack and some of the evidence was destroyed or damaged. Afterwards, when they sifted through the wreckage, they discovered it was missing. I've just emailed you a copy of the ballistics report. Also, I should warn you that Internal Affairs are likely to want to interview us again . . .'

She sighed by way of a reply.

'Are you coming into the station today?'

'Not unless you need me, I'm officially on holiday.'

There was silence on the other end of the line.

'Iriarte . . . About the gun; it doesn't mean anything, the investigation isn't over yet.'

'Of course not.'

She went back to the bedroom, gathering up her clothes as her eyes became accustomed to the darkness. She made out the silhouette of the sleeping man's shoulders and back and stopped in her tracks, overwhelmed by the intense fantasies which the sight of his body provoked in her.

She dropped her clothes on the floor and slipped back into bed next to him.


She wanted to speak to Clemos in person. She wasn't happy with the direction the investigation was taking, and although she realised that the ballistics results were what they were, she was afraid they would abandon other lines of inquiry out of apathy. She decided to go home and get a change of clothes. Pleased to see that her letterbox was still free of junk mail, she went upstairs, rehearsing in her head what she would say to Inspector Clemos. As she passed the sitting room, she glanced at the maps she had taped to the shelves, and hearing the drone of the fan, remembered she'd forgotten to switch off the computer. One by one she closed the various images of maps, until she reached the desktop screen, where a small flashing blue envelope told her she had mail. The account was an old one she had set up to browse the net, and she never used it; all her official mail went to the internal account at the station, and all her personal mail to her Gmail address, which she checked from her phone.

She clicked on the icon, and what she saw on the screen made her blood run cold. It was a message from Jonan Etxaide.

This was impossible. She had never received messages at that address from Jonan, or any of her colleagues; only James, her sisters and a couple of friends from university knew the account existed. But what puzzled her the most was that, according to the date, the message had been sent two days ago, in the afternoon, at the very time the funeral was taking place, more than twenty-four hours after Jonan Etxaide died. She trembled as she opened the message, which, far from dispelling her doubts, left her even more bewildered:

Jonan Etxaide wishes to share this file with you
File type – Documents and Images
Title – ***********
In order to gain access to this file a password is required

There were two fields that needed filling in: account name and password.

For a few seconds, she stared at the cursor flashing on the screen, pulse quickening, mouth dry, as the tremor in her finger poised above the mouse spread through her entire body. She stood up, feeling slightly nauseous, and went into the kitchen to fetch a bottle of ice-cold water from the fridge. She took a sip, then went back to the computer. The cursor continued to blink insistently. She reread the brief message a couple of times, as though hoping to find something she had missed, then looked again at the cursor flashing beside the word 'account', inexorably demanding an answer.

She typed in amaiasalariturzaeta@gmail.com, then moved the cursor to 'password'.

Marc's words echoed in her head: 'Offering' and Jonan's number.

She typed 'Offering' and paused . . . Which number? Taking out her mobile, she scrolled through her address book for Jonan's number, ruling it out even as she did so. He would never have used anything so obvious. She typed a series of zeros until the cursor indicated that the field was full. Four digits, ten thousand possible combinations, and yet he had specified *his* number. She took her phone out again.

Iriarte answered at the other end.

'Inspector, do you have Deputy Inspector Etxaide's badge number?'

'Hold on.'

She heard the clunk of the receiver on the table, and the tack-tack of a keyboard in the background.

'It's 1269.'

She thanked him and hung up.

She typed the number after the password and pressed enter.

Her palms were sweating; her heart racing as the message opened before her eyes.

There was no text, only a dozen or so files arranged in alphabetical order. She slid the cursor over them to view the titles: Ainhoa, Berasategui, Hidalgo, Salazar, Crime Scenes . . . She opened one at random. From the way the information was organised, it seemed the Cloud had merely been used to store a back-up copy. The documents inside were in no particular order; she found the warrant to search Fina Hidalgo's house, an audio file of Yolanda Berrueta's statement and Fina Hidalgo's employment history. She opened another file entitled Markina, and saw pictures of her and Markina outside the Baluarte Congress Centre.

'Jonan, what does all this mean?' she whispered, horrified.

Clicking on the file entitled Ainhoa opened a series of photographs taken inside the tomb where Yolanda Berrueta's children were buried, and included several enlarged images of specific details. Intrigued and disturbed in equal measure, she studied the tiny hands of a dead baby poking out of its coffin, and was transfixed by the blackened face of the other child. Jonan had made many enlargements. He had photographed the initials on the coffins and rotated the images, so they were legible: D.T.B. stood for Didier Tremond-Berrueta, and M.T.B. for Martín Tremond-Berrueta. Browsing the twenty-five images, she saw that Jonan had focused mainly on the metal casket, which lay open on its side. Jonan had enlarged and rotated the initials: H.T.B. He had also enlarged a corner of the plastic bag containing what she supposed were ashes, the edge of which bore a blue-and-red logo. Amaia studied the photographs, understanding why these details would have caught Jonan's attention. Placing human ashes in a plastic bag seemed odd. In the next photographs, Jonan had collected the packaging from a dozen or so different foods, including lentils, table salt, flour and sugar, all French, all made of transparent plastic with a blue and red logo. In the following photograph, Etxaide had cut and pasted the image of the bag in the metal casket and placed it next to the kilo bag of sugar; they were identical.

'Shit!' exclaimed Amaia.

She instantly thought of the sack of gravel in her sister's coffin, the bags of sugar Valentín Esparza had placed in his daughter's coffin, wrapped in a towel. Her pulse was racing at a hundred miles an hour as she studied the photographs one by one, and Yolanda Berrueta's question flashed into her head: 'Why would anyone put bags of sugar inside a casket?' She printed the images, clasping them in her hand, as she paced back and forth like a caged animal. She picked up the phone, called the Saint Collette Hospital and asked if she could speak to Yolanda Berrueta. They told her that, although Yolanda was a lot better, it would be advisable to wait a little longer. She hung up, frustrated; obviously she couldn't ask the ex-husband about this. She went into the bedroom, tipped the contents of her bag on to the bed, spilling over her dress uniform, and found Señor Berrueta's business card. She dialled the number. He picked up immediately.

'Could I stop by and have a word. It's urgent.'

The clouds moved swiftly across the leaden sky, carrying the rain away from the valley, and causing the temperature to drop by at least four degrees. Despite the cold, Yolanda's father insisted they talk outside.

'It's because of my wife, you know,' he explained. 'She's already suffering enough over what happened to Yolanda.'

In silent agreement, they moved away from the front door.

'This won't take long. In fact, I only have one question to ask you. Inside the tomb in Ainhoa, there's another smaller casket with the initials H.T.B.'

He nodded sadly. 'That's my granddaughter, Haizea.'

'You had a granddaughter?'

'Yes, a year before the twins were born, Yolanda had a little girl. I thought you knew. A healthy, beautiful little girl, and yet she died two weeks after she was born, in this very house. That was what sparked Yolanda's depression. From then on, things went from bad to worse. I always thought it was a huge mistake for her to get pregnant again so soon, but her husband insisted. The sooner she had more children, the sooner she would stop grieving the loss of her daughter, he said. But she was in no state to handle another pregnancy, and it showed the moment she conceived. She let herself go, she was a wreck, she didn't care about anything. My daughter only came alive again when the twins were born, when she held them in her arms. She was a good mother, I tell you, but she's been through a lot, her life is a tragedy. She's given birth to three children and all three are dead.'

Amaia looked at him gloomily. This was the detail that had been eluding her, the exact same thing Valentín Esparza had said to his wife: that substituting her lost girl with another

334

child would take away the pain. Esparza's wife had also said that she couldn't have another child, that she'd be incapable of loving it. But Yolanda was more fragile, more delicate, and in her case, the husband had got his own way.

'Yolanda didn't tell me about this.'

'The medication makes her confused: she gets mixed up about when things happened; the death of her little girl was so traumatic that the whole episode has become hazy in her mind.'

Amaia recalled Yolanda telling her that she got things muddled up, and she also remembered her saying in her statement at the station about the baby not being in its casket.

'Señor Berrueta, just one more question: was the little girl cremated?'

'No, she wasn't, neither were her brothers. We do things the old way, like the Tremond family. You've seen the family tomb in Ainhoa.'

'I need to know for certain,' Amaia insisted. 'It's very important, and I can't ask Yolanda's ex-husband about it.'

Berrueta pulled a face at the mention of his son-in-law.

'You don't need to ask him. The undertaker at Oieregi took care of it. I can give you his name and address; he'll confirm that the girl received a traditional burial. They drove her remains from the funeral parlour to the cemetery.'

It took Amaia ten minutes to locate the owner of the funeral parlour, who backed up Berrueta's story.

She returned to Pamplona without stopping off in Elizondo. She wanted to see her aunt, but Jonan's files were calling her. Back at her computer, she felt disheartened. Jonan had supplied no explanation with any of the documents, so she was obliged to trawl through them all to try to figure out why they were there.

She opened the file with the photographs of her and Markina again, and looked at them uneasily. Why the interest in her private life? Why was he spying on her? Why

335

was he reading her emails? She felt incredibly angry, and frustrated by her inability to understand, but she decided to leave that for later; for now, what mattered was that Jonan had sent her a message, he had given her something tangible, and she had to put her trust in him knowing what he was doing. She thought about the password he had chosen: 'offering'. The word in itself was significant, but the number he had chosen to complete it was even more important to her: his badge number, the number that made him a police officer. It brought back the memory of Marc telling her how Jonan flatly refused to entertain the notion of giving up his job.

'Damn it, Jonan, what have you been up to?'

Besides the photographs of the two of them talking that evening outside the Baluarte Congress Centre, Markina's file contained a brief biography: where he was born, where he studied, posts he had occupied before moving to Pamplona. She was intrigued by the address and telephone number of a nursing home where a woman called Sara Durán had been hospitalised. Next to it, Etxaide had written 'mother'. She shook her head, puzzled by this piece of information and its possible significance.

In the file labelled Salazar were images of her sister's empty coffin inside the family tomb in San Sebastián, and of the *mairu* bones left in the church at Arizkun, some of them hundreds of years old, but also the bleached, white bones belonging to her sister. There were several enlargements of the only photograph he had managed to take of the Puffa coat worn by Rosario on the night she fled, the one that was retrieved from the river before Markina called off the search. He had also included maps of the mountain with possible routes she could have taken to make her escape from the Ari Zahar cave on foot.

In the file named Herranz, there was a brief biography of Markina's secretary and something that took Amaia completely by surprise: more photographs, apparently taken inside a café, in which Markina's secretary could be seen speaking with Yolanda Berrueta.

The file entitled 'Crime Scene' listed the addresses of all the babies they had looked into, and which of them had succumbed to cot death; he had added Amaia's sister to the list, but not Yolanda's two boys. She went to one of the maps she had used the previous afternoon and marked the various towns and villages, including Elizondo for her sister, but leaving out Ainhoa. When she joined the dots, she saw that the line criss-crossed the N-121. Could that be it? Serial killers often perpetrated their crimes close to main roads, facilitating their escape, but that wasn't the case here.

'Press reset, Salazar,' she muttered, forcing herself to focus on what she knew. She printed out another map, marking the victims' birthplaces, including hers and her sister's. Then she noticed that, after removing the children from Ainhoa, the line was straighter. This became even clearer when, looking more closely, she saw the fine blue line marking the River Baztán. With the dots in place, the course of the river appeared to represent a crime scene stretching from Erratzu to Arraioz, through Elbete and Elizondo, and with the addition of Yolanda's baby girl, Haizea, all the way to Oieregi. She contem-plated the map. The presence of the blue line screamed out at her.

The river. 'Cleanse the river,' she thought, and as if those words had the power of a prayer to summon ghosts, the visions in her dreams appeared in her head like an echo, evoking images of the enormous white flowers and the empty coffins.

She sat down in an armchair, studying the maps from a distance, trying to understand what she was looking at. In her mind, images from Dupree's book amalgamated with Jonan's passwords, Sarasola talking about the evil nature of Berasategui's files, and the 'sacrifice' carried out by the sects in Lesaka and Elizondo in the early 1980s. She rose, and went over to mark two fresh dots on the map; she couldn't help thinking about the disgrace of not knowing their faces, of how they had been born to die, how during their short lives no one had even bothered to give them an identity, their own little place in the world.

# 40

She didn't recognise the voice on the other end of the phone.

'Amaia, it's Marc. I didn't know who else to call.'

It took her a few seconds to place him.

'Marc, of course – sorry. How can I help?'

'The police have finished searching Jonan's apartment, and this morning they brought over the key. I didn't want his parents to have to deal with it, so I came on my own, but the first thing I saw when I walked in was the bloodstain on the floor.' Overwhelmed with grief, his voice faltered. 'I don't know why I assumed they had cleaned the place, that it wouldn't be there . . . I couldn't bring myself to go in. I'm in the hallway . . . I don't know what to do.'

In less than ten minutes she was there. Marc was outside on the pavement, white as a sheet. He tried to smile when he saw her, but his mouth froze in a grimace.

'You should have called me straight away.'

'I didn't want to bother anyone,' he said, handing her the key.

She contemplated it in the palm of her hand for an instant, as if it were something completely alien. Leaning forward, Marc placed his hand over hers and gave her a kiss. Then he turned and walked away without saying a word.

It's amazing how overpowering the stench of blood can be. The tell-tale buzz of flies told her that they had smelled it too. What was once a glistening red pool had turned a brownish colour, darker at the edges, where it had started to dry. There was a sickening movement at the centre, where hundreds of maggot larvae were wriggling frenetically. Gloves used by the crime scene technicians and police officers lay strewn on the floor, together with plastic vials and paper towels. The smell of death tainted the air, and every surface was covered in the black and white powder used to lift fingerprints. She'd encountered far worse crime scenes than this; when neighbours were alerted by the stench of a body that had been dead for days or even weeks, the result could be truly shocking.

She took out her phone, searching in her address book for the number of a cleaning service specialising in trauma and crime scenes. She gave a brief description of the scene, and promised to wait until they arrived. They usually got there quickly, did the job and left, just like her.

It felt strange, being in Jonan's apartment without him, but what disturbed her most was that, despite seeing the things he had seen every day, touched every day, she couldn't feel him: all trace of his presence had vanished. Even that spilled blood was no longer his. It belonged to the flies now, and she thought about how his precious blood had become repellent.

Exhausted, she turned full circle, inspecting the room. As her gaze alighted on the sofa, she recalled the pathologist's theory about the shot fired from low down. 'Either that, or the killer was very short', she said to herself out loud. She sat down, raising her hand as though holding a weapon. Jonan hadn't been moved from where he fell, but if the assailant had been standing where she was now, he wouldn't have been able to shoot him face on. Stooping to look under the sofa, she could see that Montes was right: there were no marks where it had been dragged across the floor, and the layer of dust beneath it was undisturbed. From her kneeling position, she looked back at the dark stain, which covered a huge area of the floor. The image of Jonan sprawled on his back flashed into her mind with photographic precision. She felt the gorge rise in her throat, but managed to stifle the sensation. Standing up, she went over to the window. She realised that more flies would come in if she opened it, but at least the fresh air would get rid of the nauseating stench. She couldn't figure out how to draw back the curtains, but opened the window anyway. An icy breeze made them billow out into the room, and from the grey surface of one of them, Amaia noticed a strand of greyish fabric drift across the bloodstain to land on the far side of the room. Intrigued, she went over to it and saw that, although similar in colour to the curtains, it was clearly a different type of fabric. The threads were shiny, the scrap a few millimetres long. She glanced about, but could see no other obvious source. Selecting the camera app on her phone, she took several pictures of it from various angles. Absorbed by her thoughts, the incoming call made her jump, and she dropped the phone, which landed at her feet. Picking it up gingerly, she answered. It was Markina. His voice reached her, warm and sensual. Closing her eyes tight, she thrust aside the images that assailed her simply from hearing him speak.

'I'm at Jonan's apartment,' she said.

'Another search?'

'No, they've finished. The family was given permission to go in this morning, and they asked if I could call the cleaners. I'm waiting for them now.'

'Are you there alone?'

'Yes.'

'Are you okay?'

'Yes, don't worry, they'll be here in a minute, and then I'll leave,' she said, without taking her eye off the scrap of fabric. 'I have to go now.'

She ended the call, rummaging on the sideboard for an envelope. She found one, emptied out the junk mail, and placed the piece of material carefully inside. Then she noticed what looked like a pattern, a letter possibly, repeated at intervals along the tiny strand. Although no expert, she could see that it was clearly of fine quality. She folded the envelope, put it away in her bag, then set about inspecting the curtains and other surfaces. Besides the fingerprint powder, she found nothing. The forensic team had been thorough; the strand of fabric was doubtless insignificant, it could have been there for ages, disguised by the colour of the curtains.

She left the cleaners, shrouded in white overalls and masks, and headed for the Beloso police station.

Five minutes with Clemos was enough to confirm her worst fears. He was happy as a pig in muck. He explained briefly the information Iriarte had already given her about the gun's origins, and, despite her insistence that they should continue following other lines of inquiry, and his assurances that they would, she was convinced the investigation would now be focused in one direction.

She asked, disdainfully, whether they had found any evidence linking Etxaide with this type of criminal gang, but Clemos didn't rise to the bait, replying that it was only a question of time.

She excused herself for a moment, borrowed a sheet of paper from a printer on an empty desk, as well as a pair of scissors, and ducked into the toilets on the second floor. Once inside, she plucked some gloves from her bag and put them on, then took out the envelope containing the fabric. She cut off a tiny strand, which she placed back in the envelope, and carefully folded the remainder inside the sheet of paper. She left the toilets and went to find Clemos again.

'This morning, Deputy Inspector Etxaide's family asked me to let the cleaners into his apartment. While I was waiting for them, I opened the window, and this bit of fabric floated

342

off the curtain; I checked, and it doesn't appear to match any other material in the house,' she said, handing him the envelope.

'You should have called the technicians.'

'You're kidding me! If I hadn't been there this would have been destroyed by the cleaners. It could be evidence. I followed the correct procedure.'

'Did you take photographs?' he asked, irritated.

'Yes, I've just emailed them to you.'

Clemos snatched the envelope.

'Thanks,' he grunted. 'I'm sure it'll turn out to be nothing.'

Amaia started towards the exit without bothering to reply.

She left the building, got into her car and called Dr Takchenko.

'Doctor, are you still in Pamplona?'

'Yes, but not for long, I just finished giving my talk. I'll be leaving for Huesca around noon.'

'Could we meet? I have something for you.'

'Sure, I'm at a café in . . .' there was a pause while she looked for the name of the street: 'Calle Monasterio de Iratxe. Can you come here?'

'I'll be ten minutes.'

The meeting was hurried. Dr Takchenko was keen to get back in time to have lunch with her husband. Amaia kicked herself for not having realised that the chic café was close to the courthouse, making it the haunt of judges and lawyers.

As they were leaving, the doctor asked: 'Inspector, do you know that woman? She hasn't taken her eyes off you since you came in.'

Amaia turned around, only to encounter the furtive gaze of Inma Herranz, who was drinking coffee with two other women at the bar. She cursed the coincidence.

Dr Takchenko liked her German car. Her husband teased her about her obsession with safety, but it was true that her choice

343

had been influenced not by the luxurious appearance of the vehicle, but rather by its security features, which made it one of the safest models on the road. She loved driving on motorways, but not in cities, especially ones she didn't know. Upon leaving the café with the envelope Inspector Salazar had given her, she had intended to head straight for Huesca. And yet, she had spent the last quarter of an hour driving round in circles, finally resorting to a good old-fashioned map to find the address her satnav had been unable to locate. After avoiding by a whisker a collision with a bus, and having to put up with the horn blasts of an irate taxi driver, Dr Takchenko finally pulled up outside the offices of an express courier service. She left her warning lights on and hurried inside. Placing the envelope Amaia had given her into another, she handed it to the middle-aged man behind the counter.

'I want this delivered direct to this address.'

Then she climbed back into her German car and continued on her way.

# 41

Amaia spent the rest of the afternoon carefully examining the files Jonan had sent her. She paid special attention to the file on Inma Herranz, poring over the photographs of her and Yolanda Berrueta. In one close-up, she could see the sweat glistening on Yolanda's face. She wondered what possible relationship she could have with Inma Herranz. They didn't look like they were friends; in every single image Yolanda was talking while Herranz listened patiently. Yolanda herself had told her how she'd moved heaven and earth to find someone who would listen to her; it wasn't difficult to imagine her accosting Herranz after discovering that she was the personal assistant of a magistrate. She would have to look into it.

Her phone rang. It was him.

'I want to see you.'

As she looked away from the screen, Amaia noticed that her eyes were tired and she had a headache coming on. Even so, she smiled as she replied: 'Me too.'

'Then, come here.'

'Will you cook for me again?'

'I'll cook for you, if that's what you want.'

'Yes, that too.'

Iriarte called seconds after she had parked outside Markina's house.

'Inspector. I think you'd better come to Elizondo. Inés Ballarena and her daughter went to visit the girl's grave at the cemetery this afternoon, and they realised immediately something wasn't right. The flowers and wreaths left during the funeral were in disarray, as if someone had moved them; they informed the gravedigger, who called us. It looks as if the tomb has been tampered with. I'm on my way over there now . . .'

Markina was uncorking a bottle of wine when the phone rang. He listened as Amaia explained her reasons for not coming, apologising and adding that she didn't know how long she might be. As soon as she hung up, he hit speed-dial. His face had clouded.

'I've just been informed that the Esparza family tomb has been desecrated. The mother and grandmother noticed something wasn't right. The Navarre police are on their way there now. What have you to say about this?'

His anger mounted as he listened to the response. After hanging up, he hurled the phone across the room hitting the bottle of wine, which shattered, spilling its contents over the countertop.

Amaia parked outside the cemetery gates. Considering it was nighttime, the place was well lit. She could see Iriarte, Montes and Zabalza, as well as a couple of cemetery workers, standing with Inés, her daughter Sonia, and the old *amatxi*. Despite the cold and the late hour, the three women appeared astonishingly calm. They remained silent while Iriarte repeated what he'd already told her over the phone. Amaia looked at the tomb, which was covered in wreaths and bouquets, then addressed the women:

'What looks different? And why are you here this late? It's freezing outside.'

'We came to put candles on the grave,' explained the old *amatxi*. 'To light the girl's way.' She pointed to a pair of candles flickering at the base of the tomb.

Inés Ballarena stepped forward.

'You must excuse my mother. It's an old custom in Baztán. They light candles . . .'

'. . . to help the dead find their way in the dark,' said Amaia. 'My aunt is acquainted with that custom too, she told me about it.'

'Well,' Inés went on, 'as you can see, people sent lots of flowers. After the tomb was sealed, we arranged them in order of size, and the bouquets at the front . . . They're all mixed up now, as you can see, as if someone had taken them off and put them back any old how. Also but some of the wreaths are facing the wrong way, so you can't read the tributes. I can assure you, I was careful to place them the right way round.'

'The right way round,' whispered Amaia. Then she addressed the gravedigger:

'Have any repairs been carried out in this part of the cemetery, or has there been a recent burial in any of the adjacent tombs that might have required moving these wreaths?'

The fellow frowned at her, and shook his head slowly. She had spoken to him in the past, and knew he was a man of few words.

'Could this be a prank? Kids breaking into the cemetery and moving some of the flowers for a joke,' she suggested.

The gravedigger cleared his throat. 'Excuse me, ma'am, but I hadn't finished . . .'

She glanced at Montes, who rolled his eyes. Grinning, she gestured for the man to carry on.

'The slab has been moved, at least five centimetres,' he said, placing two stout fingers between the slab and the side of the tomb.

'Could it have been replaced incorrectly during the funeral?' she asked, introducing her own fingers into the gap.

'Certainly not. It's my job to ensure that the slabs are properly positioned, because of the rain, you see. Otherwise, all these tombs would fill up with water . . . Not only that, but the stone is more likely to get damaged if it isn't in the right place. I can assure you that after the funeral, that slab was in the proper position,' the man declared emphatically.

Montes went over to the stone and tried to move it, in vain.

'You won't get anywhere like that,' the other employee said. 'To move a slab, you need a jemmy and a couple of iron bars.'

Amaia turned to Inés Ballarena and her daughter. They both looked at the old *amatxi*, then all three declared as one:

'Open it.'

Amaia looked at the gravedigger:

'You heard what the ladies said. Open it.'

The two men took a few minutes to fetch the jemmy and the iron bars, while everyone else helped to shift the wreaths and bouquets. As the other man had explained, the method was simple. They levered the stone high enough to slide the iron bars underneath, then rolled it back. As soon as the tomb was open, they all shone flashlights inside. In addition to the little girl's casket, they saw two decaying coffins at the back. The gravedigger lowered a metal ladder into the tomb and descended, taking with him a smaller jemmy. He soon discovered he had no need of it, for the baby's coffin was wide open. And although they could all see, he looked up at them and said:

'It's empty.'

'Oh my God, in the end he took her! He came back and took our daughter!'

With that, Sonia Esparza fell to the ground.

# 42

Strangely, though she hadn't felt Jonan's presence in his own apartment, in the police station she felt his absence so keenly it was as if he were right there; she could even identify the space he was occupying. Jonan, who had vanished bequeathing her a legacy of intrigue and suspicions. Jonan and all the things around him that had driven him to conduct a parallel, secret investigation. Jonan, his reasons and motives. Jonan spying on her . . .

Had he mistrusted her? No, if so, he wouldn't have sent her the file on the day of his funeral! And how had he arranged that? She recalled Jonan's words to Marc, betraying his fear. Jonan and the mysterious password he had left for her.

'Oh, Jonan, what the hell have you done?'

She could see where Clemos and Internal Affairs were coming from; much as she hated to admit it, if she'd been in their shoes and hadn't known Jonan, she would have been suspicious. But she did; this was Jonan – even the password he had chosen to deliver his file to her was proof of his integrity. And yet this legacy was becoming too much for her to shoulder alone. Because he had sent the file to *her*, she felt she would be betraying Etxaide's last wish if she came clean about it. At the same time, not knowing whom to confide in was making her extremely anxious. She trusted Montes, she knew he would stand by her; she had her doubts about Zabalza, but the biggest headache was Iriarte. He clearly felt uneasy when confronted with things that were beyond his comprehension, such as Elena Ochoa's death. All those stories of empty coffins were a far cry from what a no-nonsense policeman like him would consider normal. For Iriarte, doing things by the book was a religion, and what she was planning to tell them, and, more importantly, to ask of them would bring them into direct conflict with the official investigation being carried out by the team in Pamplona. Gazing mournfully at the fog rolling down the mountainside, she missed Jonan more than ever, feeling his presence so intensely all of a sudden that she spun round expecting to find him there.

Deputy Inspector Zabalza was standing in the doorway holding a mug, which he raised in front of him, as if to explain himself.

'I thought you might like a coffee.'

She looked at him, then at the mug. Jonan always used to bring her coffee . . . What did this fool think he was doing? She felt her eyes prick with tears, and she turned back to the window so he wouldn't see them.

'Leave it on the desk,' she replied, 'and please tell Montes and Iriarte I want you all in here in ten minutes. I have something to tell you.'

He left the room without saying a word.

Iriarte brought a couple of files with him, and read aloud from his notes.

'We've established that the last time the Ballarena family visited the cemetery prior to noticing that the tomb had been tampered with was the previous afternoon. We don't know for sure, but anyone breaking into the tomb would probably have done so under cover of darkness, which means that night.

350

As you know, we've alerted the highway patrol and set up routine traffic controls, but so far without any result.'

Montes spoke next:

'I've talked to the family again. The young mother is still in shock, but Inés was calmer. She reckons someone knew about Valentín's intentions and carried them out for him, although she understands perfectly why her daughter believes that her husband has come back from the grave. The old *amatxi* has the most original take on it. She claims she isn't surprised; reckons Inguma took her. I quote: "She died for him, our little girl was an offering."'

Amaia looked up. 'Did she use the word "offering"?'

'She's an old woman,' said Iriarte, assuming Amaia was puzzled by the old lady's choice of words.

'We've also spoken to Valentín Esparza's relatives,' Montes went on. 'They all have an alibi for the period in question, and appear horrified by what has happened, but also somewhat indignant about being questioned. They've hired a lawyer.'

Amaia rose to her feet once more and went over to the window, as though hoping to find some inspiration in the fog now shrouding the entire valley.

'I'm sure you'll all agree with me that the disappearance of the Esparza girl reopens the case. There's something I want to show you,' she said, turning towards her desk. She removed some printed images from an envelope and spread them out on the table. 'You may remember that around the time Jonan died, I was waiting for him to send us the enlargements of the photographs he took in Ainhoa, on the night Yolanda Berrueta blew up her children's tomb. Well, that's what these are. Jonan must have left them at my house in Pamplona, I found them in my mailbox yesterday.'

Iriarte's reaction took her by surprise.

'He left them at your house? That's completely out of order. Why would he do that, why not email them to you at the police station?'

'I don't know,' she dissembled. 'Maybe he wanted me to look at the details of the enlargements—'

'We'll need to inform Internal Affairs and Clemos about this immediately.'

'I already did, this morning. However, as head of homicide, I consider these photographs to be evidence connected to the case we're working on; I don't see any reason not to resume the investigation.'

Iriarte seemed satisfied, although he looked askance at the photographs.

'What you see in front of you are enlargements of the inside of the tomb in Ainhoa. Besides the two adult coffins, there are three other coffins. As you know, the remains of Yolanda Berrueta's two sons were found inside the tomb. However, Jonan was interested in the third coffin . . .' she said, pointing to the small metal casket in the fresh batch of photographs she spread out in front of them. 'And, above all, its contents. By enlarging the photos and comparing them, he was able to establish that the bag inside the casket, which we assumed contained ashes, was in fact a bag of sugar.'

'Fuck!' exclaimed Montes. 'Who was supposed to be in there?'

'Yolanda Berrueta and Marcel Tremond's first child, a baby girl, born one year before her two sons, who died aged two weeks at Yolanda's parents' house in Oieregi. Guess what from?'

'Cot death,' breathed Iriarte.

'Cot death,' she repeated. 'And there's more. Both Yolanda's father and the funeral director in Oieregi are willing to swear that the girl wasn't cremated. That her body was inside that casket.'

'I doubt Judge Gouvenain will authorise us to look inside the tomb again, but I could speak to the police chief and ask him to check.'

'There's no point. Marcel Tremond made sure the slab was

replaced the next day. According to the priest at Our Lady of the Assumption, the Tremond family was so upset they wouldn't even allow the gravedigger to go down and clear out the rubble, or replace the upturned coffins. They ordered the tomb to be sealed without delay.'

'What a bastard!' exclaimed Montes.

'You can say that again,' Amaia concurred. 'Yolanda's father told me that after their baby girl died, his daughter sank into a deep depression. Her husband bullied her into getting pregnant again, against all medical advice.'

'Because that way she would recover more quickly from the pain of losing the girl,' said Iriarte.

'She didn't deal well with being pregnant again, but, as soon as her sons were born she devoted herself to them.' Amaia paused, giving her colleagues time to assimilate all the information. 'We've no way of confirming our suspicions, or of proving that the girl's body was removed from the tomb in Ainhoa, and obtaining authorisation to reopen it is obviously out of the question. However, this new case allows us to plot a much clearer chart in and around Baztán, in the vicinity of the river,' she said, placing a map on the table, and marking with red dots the villages close to the river as far as the border with Guipúzcoa. 'What to do next: we need to establish a profile of the suspects' behaviour and actions. Besides having lost a baby to cot death, what do these couples have in common? What do we know so far?'

The three men looked at her expectantly.

'One: they all lost baby girls. Two: before their babies died, the couples weren't well off financially. Three: afterwards they all came into money. Four: in at least four instances – the two cases investigated by social services, plus those of Yolanda Berrueta and Esparza – we know that when the little girls died they were convinced that their fortunes would change.'

She broke off.

'Any observations?'

353

'We could surmise that the couples received money or were otherwise compensated for their daughters' deaths,' suggested Montes.

'Yes, but why take their dead bodies?' asked Iriarte.

'Are we one hundred per cent certain they were actually dead?' said Zabalza. 'At least in the case of the girl from Argi Beltz, we couldn't find a death certificate, because of the story her parents concocted about their trip to England. We might be looking at illegal adoption, or they could have been sold . . . There have been similar cases involving empty tombs and stolen children.'

'Yes, I had the same suspicions about my missing twin sister, but we can rule that out in cases where autopsies were performed, and I saw the Esparza girl's body with my own eyes. But it might be helpful if you could come up with ideas about what a baby's dead body might be used for.'

'Off the top of my head, I would say for medical or forensic research purposes, but that would hardly make anyone rich. Organ trafficking, perhaps, but that would have shown up in the autopsies. And . . . well, this is a despicable practice, but because they aren't scanned or searched at airports, some drug cartels use the bodies of babies whose organs have been removed to smuggle drugs.'

'That might explain their wealth.'

'I don't think a cartel would pay that much. They would have received a lump sum at most, but these couples are seriously rich, and they all own what appear to be legitimate businesses.'

Montes broke in: 'We're forgetting something. Besides all this newfound wealth, what astonished me in at least one of the cases was that a woman diagnosed with terminal cancer was miraculously cured. There have been other such cases, but it's still incredible that a person who is dying one minute makes a full recovery the next. I looked into it, and she was given the all-clear years ago. I'm not saying it's significant, but you have to admit these people have the luck of the devil.'

Amaia sighed. 'There is another aspect of the investigation I want to discuss with you,' she said, shooting Iriarte a significant look. 'We need to proceed with an open mind; we mustn't rule out any possibility. So far, we've established the link between Dr Berasategui and these little girls' parents. We know what he did to the bodies of his victims, that he instigated their murders as the *tarttalo*. And from the remains we found in his apartment, we know that he practised cannibalism. Bearing in mind Esparza's erratic behaviour after his daughter's death, and the fact that his plan to steal her body has subsequently been carried out, I believe we should consider other kinds of practices. I have a witness who can corroborate part of Elena Ochoa's story about a sect founded here in Baztán in the seventies, at a farmhouse called Argi Beltz. A sect that practised satanic rituals, involving animal sacrifices. I also have a very reliable informant, whose name I'm not at liberty to reveal, who has confirmed that similar practices took place at another farmhouse in Lesaka, possibly led by the same man, their priest, master of ceremonies, or guru, who would have been in his mid-forties then. He moved between both groups, but lived elsewhere. My informant has also confirmed the testimony of my other witness, who claims that a little girl born at Argi Beltz died under mysterious circumstances.

'You remember the case of Ainara Martínez-Bayón, whose parents maintain she died of a brain haemorrhage during a trip abroad? Deputy Inspector Etxaide was working on this when he died. He established that the girl never left Spain, which would explain why there was no record of her death, autopsy or burial in the UK. Her parents are the current owners of Argi Beltz, a wealthy couple who hosted the meetings with Berasategui, attended by Fina Hidalgo, Yolanda Berrueta's ex-husband, Marcel Tremond, and Valentín Esparza. This can't be a coincidence, and although they described those meetings as bereavement therapy sessions, my informant assures me that the nature of these gatherings was very different.'

Iriarte rose from his seat.

'What are you suggesting, Inspector? That these people have been practising witchcraft? We can't base our investigation on unsubstantiated theories, unless of course you tell us who your informant is.'

Amaia reflected for a few seconds.

'All right, providing you all give me your word that this won't go beyond these walls. He has acted in good faith because he wants this case solved, but if this became public we'd find ourselves in hot water; he's made it quite clear that he would flatly deny it.'

The three men nodded as one.

'My informant is Father Sarasola.'

Iriarte sat down again, clearly taken aback.

'He admitted that they found a file at the clinic containing all of Dr Berasategui's research into what Sarasola refers to as "the nuance of evil". Alternatively, it could be described as a study of people suffering from psychological disturbances who present with behaviour of a demonic, satanic or evil nature, and are involved in various kinds of practices. Father Sarasola told me that, due to the toxic nature of these files, they were taken in a diplomatic bag to the Vatican. We have no way of getting them back. Sarasola will deny it, the Holy See will deny it, and the Government will come down on us like a ton of bricks if we kick up a fuss. He also told me that the contents of Berasategui's files were so dark that when he heard about Deputy Inspector Etxaide's murder he decided that we ought to know about them, in case through our investigations we have unwittingly placed ourselves in danger.'

They all remained silent, reflecting about what they'd just heard.

Once again, Iriarte spoke first.

'I see that Dr Sarasola has this nicely tied up. All I can say is I hope you have some ideas, because personally I don't see where this is going. We can check the alibis of Esparza's friends and relatives to see if any of them were involved in desecrating the tomb, but right now that doesn't seem to be leading anywhere. Berasategui and Esparza are both dead. Obtaining Judge De Gouvenain's collaboration is out of the question, and if we fail to establish a plausible link between Berasategui, Esparza, and the other couples, Judge Markina will refuse to authorise us to search the other babies' tombs. So, you tell us: where do we go from here?'

'You're forgetting Fina Hidalgo. I'm convinced she's the linchpin in all this. As her brother's assistant and a midwife, she had privileged information about all the pregnancies in the valley. We know she attended these supposed bereavement sessions at Argi Beltz. And there's something else we should remember; she openly admitted having helped parents to "solve the problem" of bringing sick children into the world. I think we should continue to investigate her.'

'I'll see to that,' said Montes.

'Also, I need you to trawl through all the information we have on cot deaths, not just in the valley but in the whole of Navarre. Pay special attention to girl babies born close to the River Baztán, and look into the parents' finances before and after their deaths: if we can establish that they profited in some way, then we've determined a pattern. Keep questioning Esparza's relatives and friends, and if you dig up anything suspicious, we'll get a warrant to search their properties, although I have little hope of finding the girl's body.'

'Perhaps Sarasola could give you some clues,' said Iriarte mockingly. 'If he's such an authority on this sort of practice, he'll know where they take the bodies.'

Iriarte had already got up to leave, but she called him back.

'I'm not done yet. First, there's something I want to say about Deputy Inspector Etxaide. During the time I worked with him, he showed unwavering loyalty and integrity. So, remember: Internal Affairs have yet to conclude their investigation; Jonan was our colleague, and we have no reason to think badly of him.'

All three signalled their agreement and began making their way to the door.

'Zabalza, wait a moment. I have a computer question for you. As you are the most knowledgeable about the subject, you'll be my go-to person from now on.' He nodded. 'It's quite simple: is it possible to programme a computer to send a message on a specific day, or at a specific time?'

'Yes. That's how spam is generated.'

'That's what I thought. Okay, so, would it be possible to programme a computer to send an email if a particular situation arose?'

'Could you be a bit more precise?' he said, intrigued.

'Say I wanted to send an email containing sensitive information, but for some reason I was unable to send it myself?'

'You could install a kind of electronic timer, which you switch on every day, and which you activate or deactivate using a password. The day you don't introduce the password, the message is sent automatically.'

She was silent as she considered this.

'Is that how he sent you those photos?'

Amaia didn't reply.

'That would have been just like him. He sent you more things, didn't he?' Zabalza paused, staring straight at her, aware that he wouldn't get an answer. 'I'm not the snitch, I didn't say a word to anyone about the search warrant, on purpose or by accident.'

Amaia looked at him, surprised by this unsolicited declaration.

'No one has accused you of being a snitch.'

'But you've thought about it. I know we don't exactly see eye to eye, but aside from any personal differences, I'd never betray a colleague or the force.'

'You don't have to defend yourself—'

358

'Trust me.'

She remembered Zabalza's distraught figure outside the apartment. His attempt to stop her from seeing Jonan in that state, and then at the wake, his expression as he listened to Jonan's friends, as if he'd been annihilated that day he walked into Jonan's apartment and found his dead body.

Just then, her mobile rang. Checking the screen, she saw that it was Dr González from Huesca. Zabalza stood up, taking his leave with a gesture, as she answered the call.

'Doctor, I didn't expect to hear from you so soon.'

'Inspector Salazar, I'm afraid this isn't the kind of news you are expecting. On her way home yesterday, my wife's car was forced off the road by another vehicle.'

'Oh my God, she's not—'

'No, thankfully she's alive. Several other drivers saw what happened; they immediately called the emergency services and pulled over to give assistance. Inspector, it took them forty minutes to free her from the wreckage. She has a broken pelvis, hip, leg, nose and collarbone, and a nasty gash on her head, but she's conscious. You know how tough she is. I didn't call you earlier, you understand, all I could think of was her.'

'Of course, please don't apologise.'

'She's still in the ICU. They won't let me see her, but I spoke to her just now, and she asked me to call you. She doesn't remember much about the accident, but witnesses at the scene say they saw the other vehicle parked on the hard shoulder. Then two men scrambled up the slope, climbed in and drove off. The police have confirmed that her car was ransacked: they emptied out the contents of her bag, opened her luggage, searched under the seats, in the glove compartment, in every possible nook and cranny. When I told her this, she mentioned that you'd given her a piece of evidence for us to analyse. Yesterday, while the police were informing me about the accident, an envelope arrived, by special delivery. I was surprised that my wife had sent me a package from

Pamplona. I believe this is what the men who searched the car were looking for.'

Amaia was struggling to collect her thoughts, but all she could conjure were images of Dr Takchenko's multiple injuries.

'My wife tells me it's a fabric sample.'

'That's right.'

'Well, you're in luck: other than verifying the exact composition, we wouldn't have been able to do much with it, but I have the ideal man for the job: Andreas Santos. He's a textile expert; I've known him for years, he's the best in his field. We once dismantled a stork's nest in Alfaro, Rioja. Among the components were vast amounts of fabric, which Santos analysed. Much to our surprise, some of them dated back to medieval times. Storks build their nests out of all kinds of material, and it seems some of them like to thieve from market stalls. Using mud and scraps of fabric, they produce solid structures that perch for centuries on top of towers. Santos has worked with various museums, and has an enormous archive of textiles and fabrics manufactured in Europe over the last thousand years. If you agree, I'd like to send him your sample.'

'If you trust him, that's good enough for me,' she replied.

# 43

The fog that had descended from the hills invaded the streets appropriating the valley, creating the illusion that it was even earlier in the morning, that moment before dawn when, if the sun refused to break through the clouds, the day would grind to a halt. As she drove slowly through the narrow streets in the Txokoto neighbourhood on her way to join La Carretera de Francia, Amaia recognised her aunt bundled up in a thick overcoat. She was sticking close to the walls of the houses as she made her way through the old quarter down by the bridge. Drawing level with her, Amaia stopped the car and lowered the window.

'Auntie, where are you off to at this time in the morning?'

'Amaia, my dear!' she exclaimed, smiling. 'What a surprise! I thought you were in Pamplona.'

'I'm on my way there now. What about you?'

'I'm going to the bakery, Amaia. I'm worried about your sisters. Flora is determined to go through with this ludicrous idea of buying the business, and they're constantly at each other's throats. I thought I'd better go because Flora called Ros last night to tell her she was going there this morning with an auditor and an evaluator.'

Amaia opened the passenger door.

'Jump in, Auntie, I'll go with you.'

Besides Flora's Mercedes, several unfamiliar cars were parked outside. The head baker greeted them with a solemn expression, mirrored on the faces of the other employees, at work behind the stainless steel counters. Ros, calm and dignified at her desk in the office, seemed determined not to abandon her post, as if it were a fortress or watchtower, or perhaps just the heart of power in that business, from which she observed the comings and goings of the two besuited men. One was busy measuring the floor space and taking photographs of the equipment and ovens, while the other sat perched beside one of the counters on an uncomfortably high stool together with Flora and the agent, who had managed the accounts for Mantecadas Salazar for years. Flora smiled when she saw them. Amaia could tell instantly that her sister was nervous, despite her attempts to dissimulate behind her habitual veneer of despotic pride. As if *she* were the owner, the Red Queen, who, with her confident manner, and strident voice, would show everyone who was in charge. But Amaia knew her sister, she knew this was a façade she presented to the public, belied by the furtive glances she kept giving Rosaura, who, impassive, watched her sister's posturing like a long-suffering spectator trying to decide whether or not to applaud at the end of a performance. And that flustered her big sister. Flora was used to her actions producing the desired effect, making people bend to her will, and she found Ros's response, or rather her lack of any response, exasperating. Amaia could tell from the way Flora took a deep breath every time she looked at Ros. But Flora wasn't the only one bothered by Ros's passivity. Amaia and her aunt had discussed it, and they agreed that while for Flora this was merely a battle of wills, yet another opportunity for her to flex her muscles, it could finish Ros. In the past year, she had made the bakery the centre of her world, she had big plans for the place, and it was undoubtedly her first major achievement in life.

'I offered to help her financially,' her aunt had admitted. 'I realise that in all fairness I probably shouldn't have, but I think the bakery means a lot more to Ros than it does to Flora.'

'James offered too, but Ros refused; she insisted she had to do this on her own.'

'She said the same to me,' her aunt replied sadly. 'Sometimes I wonder if it's a good thing that you girls are so independent; I don't know where you got the idea that you can't accept help from others.'

Reassured by the apparent calm, Amaia left her aunt at the bakery. A few minutes later she was on her way back to Pamplona.

The fog accompanied her all the way to the tunnel at Almandoz, forcing her to slow down. Each year that stretch of road took its toll of lives among the lorry drivers on their way to Pamplona and Irun, and the locals from the valley, who accepted the cruel tithe much as they resigned themselves to the rain, the fog and the periods when the tunnel was closed, forcing them to take the even more perilous old road.

She couldn't stop thinking about what had happened to Dr Takchenko, and what instinct had made her send the piece of fabric by courier. Her husband was right, she was tough, but she was also smart. On more than one occasion during their acquaintance, she had shown Amaia that she possessed not just a brilliant mind but an instinct for survival, which had kept her alive in her own country, where for reasons she had never explained, she had developed an aversion to police stations. In this instance, it was Takchenko not Amaia who had understood both the significance and the threat attached to the piece of evidence, given to her, which had put her life in danger. But if that piece of fabric was evidence that hadn't been processed, and no one had seen her pick it up, then only the killer could know that it was still there, and that it was important enough to prove guilt, or at least to cast suspicion. Sarasola's words rang in her head: 'You may have stumbled upon something extremely dangerous.'

Amaia had called Sarasola earlier, having decided that perhaps Iriarte's idea about asking him wasn't so preposterous. But there was one other thing she needed to do. She stopped off at a computer store on the outskirts of Pamplona and bought a couple of memory sticks; then she went to the house on Calle Mercaderes, where she looked again at Jonan's files on Fina Hidalgo. Besides the search warrant, and a document listing her details, there was a list of places where she had worked. She wondered why Etxaide would have been interested in that. Hidalgo herself had told them that after her brother died she had been employed by various hospitals. She went over the list again. Her last job before retiring had been at the Hospital Comarcal de Irún; prior to that, she'd worked as a midwife at two private clinics: Virgen de la Manzana in Hondarribia, and Clínica Río Bidasoa, also in Irún. Rereading the names of the hospitals, she understood what had caught Jonan's attention: Río Bidasoa. The River Baztán changed its name after Oronoz-Mugaire; in Doneztebe it was called River Bidasoa – the same river with a different name in a different province. Excited and encouraged by her discovery, she picked up her phone and called Montes.

'Inspector?'

'I think we're mistaken in limiting the search to the River Baztán. On its way to the Bay of Biscay, the river passes through Navarre and Guipúzcoa, where it's called the Bidasoa; if Fina Hidalgo acted as a recruit for the parents of these girls, it's likely that her endeavours extended to the other areas where she worked. Tell Zabalza to widen his search to include cot deaths among baby girls in Guipúzcoa, above all focusing on locations close to the River Bidasoa.'

She hung up, and inserted the memory stick into her computer. After downloading the contents of Jonan's file, she paused to reread the automatic message, which was effectively her friend's dying bequest to her. As she deleted it, she had the feeling severing something akin to a spiritual link, something that constituted a threat so great, so dangerous and imminent to someone that because of it Jonan had died, and Dr Takchenko had narrowly avoided losing her life. Before leaving the house, she put the memory stick in her bag, grabbing Dupree's book at the last moment. She drove to the car park at a shopping centre, got out of her car, greeting Sarasola's chauffeur as she climbed into the vehicle, where the priest was waiting for her.

She got straight to the point.

'You told me a witness had come forward.'

'Yes, a penitent member of the sect.'

'I need to speak to him.'

'That's impossible,' he protested.

'For me, perhaps, but not for you,' she retorted.

'He's a protected witness.'

'Yes, you told me he was protected by the police, *and the Church*,' she said.

Father Sarasola remained silent. After a few seconds, he leaned forward to give the chauffeur an address, at which the car engine started.

'Now?'

'What's wrong? Is this not a good time for you?'

She said nothing until the car came to a halt on the corner of a street in the old part of town.

'But, he's here, in Pamplona?'

'Can you think of a better place? Get out of the car, amuse yourself for a quarter of an hour, then go to number 27 in the street parallel to this one, and ring the bell to flat one.'

'Is it safe?'

'Opus Dei owns the whole block, and believe me, it would

be easier for a camel to pass through the eye of a needle than for an outsider to enter that building.'

She was shown to a magnificent apartment with high, coffered ceilings and tall windows like vast embrasures, letting in the meagre light of the Pamplona winter, which with the addition of thin white curtains gave the room a gloomy feel. Despite the central heating, or the dim yellow light bulb buried in the mouldings ten feet above their heads, together with scant, austere furnishings, created an unwelcoming atmosphere. The man wore a loose-fitting grey suit and a clean white shirt; Amaia noticed that, rather incongruously, he was wearing slippers. His cropped hair and patchy grey stubble made him look older than his age, which according to Sarasola was fifty-five.

He eyed her suspiciously, but listened attentively to the priest's words, humbly agreeing to his request.

The man, who was extremely thin, kept toying nervously with a wedding band that was loose on his finger.

'Tell me about your time in Lesaka.'

'I was twenty-five and had just left university. That summer I came to Pamplona with some friends for the San Fermín festival. I met a girl. She invited us back to the house she shared. To begin with, it was fun. Like a sort of commune, exploring the old traditions, questioning what it means to be human, and understanding the forces of nature. They grew marijuana, and we used to get high, listen to the wind, get close to Mother Earth, dance around the fire. Occasionally, the group would organise get togethers designed to encourage new members to join, people from the valley, or outsiders like me who were interested in spiritualism, magic, the tradition of witchcraft in Baztán. There was much mention of a man called Tabese, the things he said, how knowledgeable he was, but during those early days I never met him. At the end of the summer, the majority of people drifted away, but they invited me to stay on. And that's when they began to reveal to me the true nature of the group.

'I first met Tabese in September of that year. He fascinated me from the start. He drove an expensive car, he dressed well, without being ostentatious, he had the ease of a person who has always had money, you know? He was extremely attractive, his skin, his hair, his manner; he was unique. I think we were all in love with him,' he said, and Amaia noticed his smile as he spoke, entranced once more merely recollecting this man. 'We adored him. We would have done anything he asked. And we did. He was charismatic, sensual, irresistible; never before or since have I felt that way about any man, or woman,' he whispered mournfully.

'Where did he live?'

'I don't know, we never knew when he was going to come; he'd suddenly appear and we'd all rejoice. Then, when he left, we'd live for his next visit.'

'Do you remember his full name?'

'I'll never forget it: Xavier Tabese. He must have been about forty-five. That's all I know. We didn't need to know any more, then, only that we worshipped him and he gave us this power. Tabese told us exactly what to do, and how. He taught us about witchcraft, he espoused a return to the traditional ways, a respect for our roots, for primeval forces, and explained that the only way to relate to them was through the offering. He revealed to us the forgotten religion, the presence of wondrous, magical creatures that have existed in Baztán since ancient times. He told us how the first settlers erected markers in the form of megaliths and ley lines that criss-crossed the entire territory, according to Watkins's alignments dating back to Neolithic times, suggesting the presence of those spirits then; all we needed to do was rouse them by making offerings and we'd obtain everything we desired.

'He explained how for thousands of years man had enjoyed a mutually beneficial and satisfying relationship with these forces, and all we had to give in exchange were lives, small sacrifices of animals that had to be offered up in a particular way.' The man rubbed his hands vigorously over his face, as though attempting to erase his features. 'We soon received the first favours, the first proof of this power, and we felt euphoric and invincible, like sorcerers of old. You can't imagine what it feels like to know that you've brought about a change, of whatever type; it makes you feel like a god. But the more blessings we obtained from them, the more they demanded in return. I lived with the group for about a year, during which time I had access to extraordinary knowledge, powers and experiences . . .'

Here the man broke off, staring at the floor for so long Amaia began to despair. Then he raised his head again, and resumed. 'I won't talk about *the sacrifice*, I can't. The fact is we did it, we all took part, the parents themselves gave her up, took her life, according to the rules. When it was all over, they took her body away, and a few days later, people started to leave the group, and within a month everyone had gone. Tabese never came back. I was one of the last to leave. By then only the couple who had made the offering remained.

'I didn't see any of the other members for years, although I'm aware that things went well for them, at least as well as they did for me. I found a job, I started a business, and within a few years I was a wealthy man. I got married,' he said, fingering his ring. 'I had a son. When he was eight years old, he became ill with cancer. During a visit to the hospital I recognised a member of the group among the medical staff. He approached me, and when I told him about my son's fate, he said I had the power to cure him, all I had to do was offer up a sacrifice. The pain and despair of seeing my son suffer made me consider it. For better or worse, you ask yourself a lot of questions when you watch your child die. First and foremost: Why is this happening to me? What did I do to deserve this? And in my case the answer was as clear as the voice of God echoing in my head. My son passed away a few months later, and the following week I went to the police, and here I am. We did the deed, and we reaped the benefits; it's as real as me sitting here. The instant I confessed and reported the crime, everything collapsed about me. I lost my job, my money, my wife, my house, and my friends. I have nowhere to go, no one to turn to.'

'I understand that there were other groups in the area.'

The man nodded.

'Do you know of anyone else who carried out one of these sacrifices?'

'I know there was talk about one taking place immediately in Baztán. I remember once visiting the house there, one of the couples had a little girl. And that she had the chosen look.'

'What do you mean?'

'I'd already seen it in our group; the parents half-starved their daughter, and the others in the group avoided contact with her. She had been singled out for sacrifice, and any normal relationship would have complicated things. She was treated like all the other creatures chosen for sacrifice, she was nameless, without identity, ignored.'

Amaia searched on her mobile for a photograph of her mother when she was young, and showed it to the man.

'Yes,' he said gloomily. 'She belonged to the Baztán group. I don't know whether she went through with it, but she was pregnant when I met her.'

'How did they do it? What was the procedure to obtain the desired result?'

The man covered his face with his hands, speaking through spread fingers. 'Please, no, please,' he implored.

'Brother,' said Sarasola reprovingly.

The man removed his hands from his face and looked at him, transfixed by the priest's voice.

'They had to be sacrificed to an evil spirit, to Inguma, in the manner of Inguma, robbing them of air, and then as part of the offering, their dead body had to be given up.'

369

'*Un demon sur vous*,' thought Amaia.

'For what purpose?'

'I don't know.'

'Is that what happened to the body of the girl in Lesaka?'

'I don't know. That was also something the parents had to do, part of the ritual, a condition that had to be fulfilled. The child had to be female, no older than two, and unbaptised.'

'Unbaptised,' Amaia repeated, writing down the information. 'Why?'

'Because baptism is also a form of offering, a promise to a different god. They had to be unbaptised.'

Amaia couldn't help remembering her own son, stretched out on the floor of that cave, and marvelling at how the planets had aligned to keep him from dying before he was even born.

'And the age group?'

'Up to the age of two, the soul is still in transition: this makes them ripe for offering. They can be offered throughout childhood and adolescence, when another change takes place which also makes them more desirable as offerings. However, it's easier to conceal the death of a baby than that of an adolescent.'

'Why girls and not boys?'

'The offerings must belong to the same sex. I don't know why, but Tabese told us this was how it had always been. Inguma awakens and takes a number of victims belonging to the same sex, the same age group, in identical circumstances, until the cycle is completed. He explained to us the importance of doing it in the right way, and the benefits we would reap. In general, the men were keener. Parents were urged to have more children, immediately, but some of the women, even those who were committed, suffered depression afterwards, and found that extremely difficult. Others had no idea what their husbands were planning. I heard that in some cases couples split up. I didn't see what all the fuss was about back then, but having lost my son, I know I couldn't love a substitute child, and if I were forced to have one, I might end up hating it.'

'What did members receive in exchange for these offerings?'

'Whatever they wanted, although that depended on the nature of the offering: good health, riches, the removal of a competitor, revenge; in exchange for *the sacrifice*, there were no limits to what you could obtain.'

'Why was it necessary to take away the bodies after death?'

'Because that's what you do with offerings, you surrender them, you give them up, you take them to the place where they can fulfil their purpose.'

'And where is that place?'

'I already told you, I don't know,' the man replied wearily.

'Try to think, make an effort, what places did Tabese talk to you about?'

'Magical places, places that possessed powers older than Christendom, places where in bygone days women and men would leave offerings in exchange for anything from a good harvest to a devastating storm. Such powers can be used for good as well as evil. He said they were like giant magnifying glasses where the energies and forces of the universe, which modern man has forgotten, converge.'

Amaia thought about the offerings she had left on the table rock at Mari's cave, the presence she had felt the last time she was there.

'What about the forest?'

The man looked at her, startled.

'You're referring to the keeper of harmony. Not all forces possess the same nature, and that one, in particular, is benign. You must understand that this works like string theory, governing all the worlds that exist within this world; when you trigger an event that wasn't meant to happen, you must give something in return, an offering, a sacrifice. To think that an action can exist without consequence is absurd. The universe

371

must redress the balance, and the ripple effect of what you do can remain long afterwards. We awakened Inguma, through our actions, but we also awakened other forces antagonistic to Inguma.' He paused, a twisted smile on his face. 'Do you believe my son died by chance? Or that the situation I find myself in isn't a direct consequence of events in that house over thirty years ago? I believe it is. I know it is.'

'What about the members who decided to leave the group?'

'You don't understand,' he replied, with the same twisted smile. 'No one leaves the group and no one is exempt from making an offering; sooner or later, Inguma will make you pay. The group disbanded because that was part of the agreement, but we've never stopped being members.'

'I know someone who left,' she said, thinking of Elena Ochoa. 'And you seem to have succeeded.'

'I haven't finished paying the consequences. I've done what I had to do, but they'll get me in the end.'

'You seem well protected,' she said, glancing at Sarasola.

'You don't understand, this is just for now. Do you think I can stay here forever? They're biding their time, but they *will* come for me, and when they do, no one will be able to protect me.'

Amaia thought bleakly of Elena kneeling amid a pool of blood and walnut shavings.

'I met someone who said the same thing.'

As she extended her hand, the man looked at her suspiciously, folding his arms.

'Thank you for your help,' she said. He bowed his head wearily by way of reply. 'One final question: what do walnuts signify to you?'

The man's expression froze, and he shivered, his face screwing up as he started to weep.

'They left some outside my front door – I found them in my car, in my sports bag, in my mailbox.'

'But what do they signify?'

372

'They symbolise power. Within the tiny folds of the walnut's brain resides the witch's curse; it means you have been singled out, that they are coming for you.'

# 44

They had made love as soon as she arrived at his house. He had just returned from the courthouse, and was still dressed in one of the dark, elegant suits he wore to hearings. Amaia kissed him, taking her time to enjoy his mouth as she began to undress him. She had discovered the sheer delight of stripping him slowly, letting his clothes fall in a heap on the floor. She had carefully unbuttoned his shirt, running her lips over his skin, tracing a map of desire, which her hands would follow. Then she had led him over to the sofa, where she sat astride him, abandoning herself to pleasure.

Exhausted and satisfied, she stretched out, turning to watch him as he strolled naked about the house, picking up his discarded garments, pulling on some clothes, donning an apron to start making dinner.

'I love watching you cook,' she said, when he brought her over a glass of wine.

'And I love seeing you sprawled on my sofa,' he replied, running his fingers down her neck and back.

She smiled as she acknowledged that Jonan was right. Markina muddied her thinking, clouded her judgement. And she didn't care. Ever since she entered his house, ever since she went back there that morning, she had avoided having

374

that thought: she was done with thinking, done with fighting. Never in a million years would she have imagined that something like this could happen to her, but it had; he had forced her to decide, to make a choice. She'd made it and she had no regrets.

'I'd better stick to water, I have work to do.'

He frowned.

'I haven't seen you all day, I thought you'd spend the night with me.'

'I can't . . .'

'What's wrong? Is something bothering you?'

'I'd forgotten that you met her in Aínsa . . . Dr Takchenko has been in a car accident, she was quite badly hurt.'

'Oh, the Russian doctor! I'm so sorry, Amaia. I hope she recovers, she seemed like an amazing woman.'

'She will, she suffered mainly fractures, no organ damage. But it's the Esparza case that's bothering me most. Although the disappearance of the girl's body seems significant, it hasn't given us any new leads. We've spoken to his relatives and friends, but no one knows anything, no one saw anything, and there are no witnesses.'

'You shouldn't let yourself to be so affected by something that isn't going anywhere.'

'It's not just about the Esparza girl. My own sister's body was taken from her tomb, so for me this is like reliving the same nightmare over and over,' she said, avoiding any mention of the discoveries she had made based on the information Jonan had sent her.

He looked at her, smiling.

'Do you know what I think? I think one of the father's relatives or friends took the girl with the intention of burying her in the resting place he had chosen for her; the motive here is clearly an emotional one. I wouldn't be surprised if they'd moved her to his family tomb, or to another ancestral burial plot. Remember, the mother wanted her remains cremated, which some people still consider a sacrilege. Disputes among relatives over where the deceased's remains should be buried, the order of service, who attends the funeral and who doesn't, are more common than you might think. I recall one case that came to court because the family couldn't agree on whether to bury a man in his parents' family plot or the one his wife had bought them; in the end they held separate funeral services, bankrupting themselves as they competed over who could place the biggest death announcement in the newspaper.'

'To the point of stealing a corpse from a coffin in the dead of night?'

He clicked his tongue in disgust.

'You know how I feel about that: it leads nowhere, Amaia. It only causes more pain and suffering. I realise you have to investigate this, but I doubt you'll ever recover the girl's body, and I hope you aren't thinking of asking my permission to open the Esparza family's tombs. I thought the incident with Yolanda Berrueta had taught you a lesson.'

She was stung by his comment.

'I told you it had. I'm not planning to do anything that might endanger lives. Speaking of which, a witness told me they saw Yolanda speaking with your secretary in a café near the courthouse.'

'With a clerk of the court?'

'No, with your personal assistant, Inma Herranz.'

'I know nothing about that, but I can ask her, if you think it's important.'

'I do,' she said, irritated, putting down her knife and fork.

He sighed in dismay at the untouched fillet of fish on her plate.

'You're never going to stop, are you, Amaia?' She looked at him, puzzled. 'What is the true reason for your obsession with this case? The case of some wretched fool who steals his daughter's body because he wants to bury it somewhere else, or whatever you want to read into this? Can't you see the harm you're doing? You have to let this go. You have to stop it now. I love you, Amaia, I love having you in my house, I want you to be with me, but things won't work out if you continue to obsess about the past, if you insist on chasing ghosts.'

She was so taken aback by this onslaught that she could barely gather her thoughts.

'I can't. I can't do what you're asking. I won't be at peace while she's still at large. Obsession, did you say? Rosario killed my baby sister, she tried to kill my son, she has been planning to kill me all my life. This is about survival. I won't rest until she's back behind bars. I cannot rest while my nemesis is still out there. If you have never ever experienced something like this, you can't imagine what it's like.'

He shook his head, extending his hand imploringly towards hers. She folded her arms defensively.

'She's dead, Amaia, the river took her; her coat was found snagged on a branch several miles downriver. How could a woman in her state survive that? And assuming she did, then where is she?'

Amaia rose to her feet, grabbing her coat and bag.

'I don't want to continue this conversation; it's a repeat of one I've had with other people, and I don't want to have it with you. If you really love me, you must accept me as I am; I'm a warrior, a seeker of truth. This is who I am, and, no, I'm not going to stop. I think I should leave now.'

He stepped between her and the door.

'Please don't go. I couldn't bear it if you left now.'

Raising her hand, she pressed it to his lips and then kissed him.

'I have work to do. I'll see you tomorrow. I promise.'

Markina pressed his forehead against the window, fogged with his breath. He could feel the cold night through the glass. He had watched her climb into her car and drive off, and now he felt like he was dying inside. He couldn't help it, without

377

her by his side, he felt a strange hollowness, as though one of his vital organs were missing. If only he could bring her some peace. He topped up his glass with wine, and sat down on the sofa where they had made love earlier, reaching out his hand to touch the space she had occupied. For hours he pondered the question.

# 45

The instant she inserted the key in the lock she knew something was wrong. She always double-locked the door, but with one turn of the key it opened. She stepped back, looked up and down the deserted street, took out her gun, then stepped forward again, listening for any sounds inside the house. Nothing. Gingerly, she pushed open the door, scanned the hallway, where everything appeared in order, and glanced up the dark stairwell. Then she entered, switching on lights as she went, ears pricked. She opened the door to James's studio on the ground floor, then began to climb the stairs. She checked the kitchen, the spare room, the sitting room, the bathroom, the nursery kitted out by James's mother, their bedroom and bathroom, inside the empty wardrobes; there was no one. She retraced her steps, switching out lights, unable to shrug off the impression that someone had been in the house while she wasn't there. Still holding her gun, she carefully examined every surface, every object, still on the alert. She went back into the sitting room. Everything there appeared to be in order, but as she looked at the maps stuck to the bookcase, the feeling that someone had been in there was so overwhelming that she could have traced in the air the contaminated space they had occupied. She felt her gorge rise at the thought of an intruder in her house. Relieved she'd had the foresight to erase all the files on her computer, she noticed that the unused memory stick had vanished. Picking up her bag again, she went downstairs, and, as before turned the key twice in the lock as she left the house. Then she called Montes.

'I need you to do me a favour.'

'Of course.'

'Drive to my aunt's house and wait outside until I get there. I'll explain later.'

As she turned into Calle Braulio Iriarte, she saw Inspector Montes flash his headlights at her. She parked and slipped into the passenger seat beside him.

'Thanks.'

'You're welcome, but now you have to tell me what this is all about,' he replied.

'Yesterday, Jonan's family asked me to go to his apartment. While I was waiting for the specialist cleaners, I found some fibres. I gave a sample of them to Dr Takchenko, who runs the parallel tests for us in Aínsa. On her way home, someone forced her off the road and then searched her car; thankfully, she's all right. Then earlier tonight, when I stopped off at my house in Pamplona, I noticed someone had been in there. They took an unused memory stick. That's why I asked you to keep an eye on my aunt's place, in case whoever it was thought of looking here.'

'Right,' said Montes, pensive. 'You say you found fibres at Jonan's apartment.'

She nodded.

'And, naturally, you gave a sample to our friend Inspector Clemos.'

'I delivered it to the Beloso police station in person. But Clemos thinks he has the case sewn up: Eastern European mafias, drug trafficking. When I reminded him he hasn't a shred of evidence, he assured me something would turn up sooner or later.'

'Did they steal the sample from Dr Takchenko?'

'No, she's one smart lady: she had already sent it express delivery to herself.'

'Someone wants those fibres badly, what I don't understand is why they would break into your house looking for fibre samples and end up taking a memory stick.'

Amaia sighed. 'Jonan sent me a message.'

'When?'

'Well, I'm not sure. It was sent the day of his funeral, but you know what these IT nerds are like: Zabalza says it was a programmed message.'

'Yes, he told me. He also said he thinks Jonan sent you more stuff.'

'He told you that?' Amaia was surprised.

'Why wouldn't he, he tells me everything, we're friends. As I keep telling you, he's a good guy. Anyhow, it must have been a shock, getting a message from Etxaide, days after he died. Sonofabitch!' he said, chuckling. 'If it was me, I'd have had a heart attack!'

They laughed together.

'The problem is, Iriarte isn't going to like this one little bit,' Montes commented.

'I know, that's why we're not telling him.'

'Fuck, no, of course not, boss. After all, if someone sends you a message from beyond the grave, you have the right not to keep silent about it. Like someone's last will and testament. And don't worry about Zabalza, he won't say a word. As for the guy who gave us the name, so far we haven't been able to find a Xavier, Xabier or Javier Tabese.'

'Did you take into account his age?'

'Yes, seventy-five or thereabouts. He could be dead, of course. We'll keep searching tomorrow. There is some news, about cot deaths in Guipúzcoa; four cases of baby girls who died close to the River Bidasoa, in Hondarribia. We're still looking into the parents, but I can tell you now that they're all well off: entrepreneurs, bankers, doctors. The girls' autopsies were performed at the Forensic Institute in San Sebastián, and in all four cases, Sudden Infant Death Syndrome was given as the official cause of death. You'll need to tell us where to go from here; we have no jurisdiction in Guipúzcoa, so, unless you can convince Markina to forward a request to his opposite number in Irún, we're stuck.'

'It's too soon for that. Gather all the information, and we'll see. Oh, and remember to rule out any girls who were baptised.'

'That's not going to be easy. They don't specify on the death certificates, which will mean having to call up every church, parish by parish,' he said irritably.

Amaia got out of the car and said goodnight.

'Ah, I forgot, they're finally allowing Yolanda to have visitors. Ten o'clock tomorrow morning at Saint Collete Hospital.'

# 46

Yolanda Berrueta wasn't in her room. Amaia checked the door to make sure she'd been told the right number. She was on her way back to the nurses' station when she saw Yolanda taking baby steps along the corridor, aided by a nurse who was supporting her round the waist. She was shocked by her appearance. She had a few superficial grazes on her face, and a piece of gauze covered her left eye stretching back to her ear. Her hand appeared to have come off worst; her arm was heavily bandaged in a sling and grotesquely swollen. Where the hospital gown didn't quite cover her elbow, Amaia could see Yolanda's flesh poking out, the skin taut.

'Sorry about the mix-up,' said the nurse. 'We took her downstairs to change her dressings.'

Yolanda didn't want to get into bed, so the nurse helped her into a chair.

Amaia waited until they were alone, then said, 'Yolanda, I want you to know that I deeply regret what happened.'

'You weren't to blame.'

'I made a mistake, and because of that Judge De Gouvenain revoked the order; otherwise, you'd have been able to see that your sons were in the tomb, you would have had peace of mind, without coming to any harm.'

383

'It was nobody's fault, Inspector, I take full responsibility for what I did. And if things had happened as you say, then, yes, I would have seen that my sons were in there, but I'd never have known that my baby girl was missing. Everyone would have gone on thinking that I'm crazy, and they might never have listened to that poor woman in Elizondo, whose daughter has also been taken.'

She should have told Berrueta not to mention any of this to his daughter, although in his place she would doubtless have done the same. Apart from her physical injuries, Yolanda seemed vastly improved: all the muddle-headedness and lethargy had vanished, and she gave the impression of being grounded, lucid, in control.

'I was confused, you see, because of the medication. I got the coffins mixed up, but I was right, they did steal my baby. Now I have to concentrate on getting out of here, so that I can try to find her.'

Amaia looked at her, alarmed. Once again she had misjudged the woman; all that apparent self-control was merely a steely determination to continue her quest.

'What you need to do now is concentrate on getting better, and let the police do their job. I promise you that we won't stop looking for your daughter.' The woman responded with a cynical smile. 'Yolanda, my main reason for coming here was to ask you about this.' She retrieved from her bag the photograph of Yolanda and Inma Herranz, and showed it to her.

'She's a secretary to one of the magistrates at the courthouse. What is it you want to know?'

'I know who she is. I'm interested in how you came to meet her, and what you spoke about.'

'I told you I wrote to several magistrates, as well as to the ombudsman, and the President of Navarre. I wrote to everyone, begging them to let me open my boys' tomb. That woman called me and we arranged to meet at a café. I told her the whole story. She seemed genuinely interested, and set up a meeting with the magistrate.'

Amaia opened her eyes wide with astonishment.

'Which magistrate?'

'Judge Markina. He was very kind, but said he couldn't help me. He advised me to get in touch with you, he told me you were an excellent detective, and that if you thought I had a case, you'd look into it.'

Amaia listened in shock.

'He advised me to be discreet, he said to make it look like we'd met by chance, otherwise you wouldn't take an interest in the case.'

Amaia stared at Yolanda as she remembered their first meeting outside Argi Beltz. Yolanda had seemed surprised that she was so young, and said she had imagined her differently. It was a while before she was able to speak.

'Let me get this right: Judge Markina advised you to approach me as if we'd met by chance, otherwise I wouldn't take an interest in the case.'

'Yes. He told me you were very good at your job. He also asked me not to tell you that he'd recommended you, but I don't suppose that matters now. Besides, you have a right to know.'

Amaia took a stroll around the hospital gardens then returned to her car, still grappling with what Yolanda had told her, and trying to make sense of it. Markina had sent Yolanda Berrueta to her, but if he had wanted her to help the woman, why put a stop to the exhumation in Ainhoa? Had he expected her to seek his cooperation, which would have been the normal procedure? But then why, after sending the woman to her, had he dragged her over the coals when she nearly blew herself up? Perhaps because he thought, as she did, that all this suffering could have been avoided if she had gone through the proper channels.

She could make neither head nor tail of it. She climbed into her car and left the hospital grounds. No sooner had she joined the motorway than her mobile rang. It was Markina; she pressed speakerphone.

'I was just thinking about you,' she said.

'And I you,' he replied softly, 'but I haven't much time – I'm about to go into a hearing. I only rang to say that I asked my secretary, and she claims Yolanda approached her in the café one day and spoke to her. She told her about her sons, and asked if she could arrange a meeting with me. Inma listened, but dismissed the woman as crazy.'

After they said goodbye and hung up, Amaia had to pull over in a lay-by to take in the enormity what had just happened. Markina had lied to her.

The phone rang deafeningly inside the parked car.

'Iriarte.'

'Good news, Inspector. The Policía Nacional have arrested Mariano Sánchez, the missing prison guard. He was hiding out at a friend's house in Zaragoza. It seems they went out drinking last night and were involved in a collision with another vehicle. Montes and Zabalza have gone to fetch him, they'll be back in a couple of hours. We've also made some progress tracking down possible victims – I think this will interest you.'

Mariano Sánchez was still hung-over after his drinking bout. His eyes were bloodshot, his speech slurred. During the brief time he'd been kept waiting, he had asked for water three times.

'I have nothing to say,' he blurted when he saw them walk in.

'That's fine by me. In the meantime, how about I do the talking? You don't have to answer, you don't have to say a word,' said Iriarte, showing the guard an enlarged image of him passing something through the slot in the door to

Berasategui's cell. 'Despite the prisoner being in isolation, you approached his cell and, as you see in the image, you gave him the drug with which he took his own life.'

'That doesn't prove a thing. You can't see anything. All I did was shake the guy's hand, I liked him.'

'That would be a plausible lie,' said Iriarte, showing the prisoner an evidence bag containing packaging from the chemist where he had obtained the sedative, 'if the pharmacist hadn't remembered you.' Sánchez looked at the bag, annoyed, as though this small detail had wrecked an otherwise foolproof plan. 'I don't think you understand quite how much trouble you're in. This isn't just about flouting the rules, which will cost you your job, or being charged with smuggling drugs into the prison. Allow me to introduce Inspector Salazar, from Homicide. She's here to charge you with the murder of Dr Berasategui.'

The man looked at Amaia and began visibly to shake.

'Oh, shit, oh shit,' he repeated, clasping his head in his hands.

'Don't worry,' said Amaia, 'there's still a way out.'

The man looked up at her expectantly.

'If you agree to help us, I may be able to persuade the magistrate that you've been cooperating with our inquiries, and to limit the charge to supplying the prisoner with what you thought was simple medication. Perhaps the doctor had a stomach ache, and he asked you to buy him some painkillers, for example.'

The guard nodded vigorously.

'Yes, that's exactly what happened.' The man's relief was palpable. 'Dr Berasategui asked me to bring him some medicine. I had no idea what he was going to do with it. I'm sure the magistrate will understand, he told me to look after him.'

'Which magistrate?'

'The one who came to the prison that day.'

'You mean Judge Markina?'

'I don't know his name, the young guy.'

'What time was this?'

'Just after we moved the doctor.'

'And you say he asked you to look after Berasategui.'

'Not exactly. He said something about seeing to his needs. You know the weird way those guys talk.'

'Try to remember,' Amaia urged him. 'There's an important difference between telling you to see to his needs or to look after him.'

The man looked at her, confused, and took his time responding, his face contorted as he strained to remember.

'I don't know, it was something like that. I've a splitting headache – can I have some Ibuprofen?'

Amaia left the interview room and went up to her office, convinced she had been missing something, something related to what the prison guard had said about Markina. She opened Jonan's file on Berasategui, which included the images Iriarte had just shown to Mariano Sánchez, taken from the CCTV footage, showing him handing the phial to Berasategui. But Jonan had also focused on the hours that followed. She went over one by one the images of her and her colleagues entering and leaving the cell, of the prison governor talking to Markina, with and without her; in another, San Martín joined them, and then there was one of Markina on his own. She wondered why Etxaide had made several enlargements of that one, and examining it closely she saw why. In the photographs where Markina appeared in the corridor speaking to her and to San Martín, he was dressed in jeans and a blue shirt; she remembered how handsome he had looked, how nervous she had felt seeing him after her dream that night. In the others, he was dressed in a suit, no doubt the one he had worn to the courthouse that morning when she called to tell him about the incident with Berasategui.

She magnified the image to look at the time code at the bottom of the picture. It was taken at 11.59 a.m.

The prison governor had told her that Markina called to ask them to move Berasategui immediately, and because he was out of town, Markina had spoken to his deputy. The deputy hadn't mentioned that Markina visited the prison. She closed the file, removing the memory stick, which she pocketed.

Amaia hadn't made an appointment, although she called ahead to make sure Manuel Lourido was working the morning shift. She gave her name at the main gate, and noted the man's surprise as she entered the prison.

'I didn't know you were coming today, Inspector,' he said, checking the visitors list. 'Who do you want to see?'

'You won't find me on your list,' she said, grinning. 'I'm not here to see a prisoner; I came to speak to you.'

'To me?' the man replied, puzzled.

'It's about Berasategui's suicide. We've arrested Mariano Sánchez, who confesses to supplying him with the drug, as the CCTV images show, but it seems he doesn't want to go down alone. He's attempting to implicate some of his colleagues,' she lied. 'Not that we believe him, but we have to check out these allegations.'

'That bastard! I can tell you right now that it's a pack of lies – the only ones involved are him and those two pea-brains, Tweedledum and Tweedledee.'

'I need to verify that the prisoner received no other visitors that morning.'

'Of course,' he said, typing his password on the computer keyboard. 'Berasategui had no other visitors that day except you.'

'Possibly his lawyer, or Judge Markina, who ordered his transfer to the isolation unit?'

'No, only you.'

Disappointed, she thanked the man and turned towards the exit.

'But Judge Markina was here.'

'What?'

'I remember seeing him at the end of my shift. His name doesn't appear on the list because he wasn't here to visit a prisoner. He came to see the governor's deputy, and we only log visits to prisoners,' he said, gesturing at the screen.

Amaia digested this information, then said, 'Could you tell the governor I'm here? Ask him if he'd be good enough to see me.'

Manuel lifted the receiver of the internal phone, dialled a number and relayed her request.

The silence dragged on for a few seconds presumably while the governor thought it over. Considering how hard on him she had been during their last meeting, this didn't surprise her.

'All right,' said Manuel, speaking into the receiver. He hung up and came out from behind the counter.

'He'll see you now. Follow me, please.'

'One other thing, Manuel: please don't discuss our conversation with anyone; this is part of an ongoing police investigation.'

Expecting this to be a hostile encounter, she steeled herself as she entered the governor's office. They were on his territory now; one false move and he would send her packing.

He rose from his chair to greet her, shaking her hand guardedly.

'What can I do for you, Inspector?'

'It's about Berasategui's suicide. We've arrested Mariano Sánchez, who has confessed to supplying him with the drug, and I wanted to tie up a few loose ends before we close the case.' She could almost hear the man's relief. 'I understand this has been a difficult time for you. Yours isn't an easy job, and what with all these tragedies . . .'

She'd been deliberate in her choice of words: 'tragedies' made the deaths sound unavoidable, something no one could blame him for. Deep down, he wasn't such a bad guy.

'So, to wrap things up. On the day in question, I visited the prisoner in the morning. Did he receive any other visitors?'

'Well, I'd need to check, but I don't think so.'

'Shortly after he received my call, Judge Markina called to tell you that Berasategui should be moved.'

'Yes, and because I was away, I asked my deputy to take care of it. I then called him fifteen minutes later to confirm that the prisoner had been moved without incident and was told that he had.

'Would you mind if I had a word with your deputy, to double-check? It's purely a formality, for the report.'

'Of course.' He pressed a button on the internal phone, and asked a prison officer to fetch his deputy. The man entered seconds later, giving the impression of having been outside the door.

He looked a little nervous when he saw her. Beaming, she stood up to shake his hand.

'I'm sorry to bother you. I was just saying to the governor that we're closing the Berasategui case. As you're probably aware, we've arrested Manuel Sánchez, who has accepted full responsibility for supplying the doctor with the sedative. I'm writing up the report and . . . well, you know how it is.'

The man nodded sympathetically.

'The governor states that he called you at Judge Markina's request to tell you to move the prisoner, and then called you again fifteen minutes later to make sure everything had gone smoothly.'

'That's correct,' said the deputy.

Amaia turned to the governor.

'And then Judge Markina called you back to confirm that the move had taken place?'

'No, I called him.'

391

'Good,' she said, pretending to note it down. 'And did Judge Markina come here to see for himself?'

The governor shrugged, and looked at his deputy.

'Did Judge Markina come to the prison that morning in person to make sure the prisoner had been moved?' she repeated.

The deputy stared straight at her.

'No.'

Amaia smiled. 'Then that's all, we're done. Thank you both for your time, you've been extremely helpful. I can't tell you how glad I am that this case is over.'

The governor's relief was palpable, as was the barely concealed concern on his deputy's face.

She climbed into her car and called the station to summon an afternoon meeting. As she left the city for Baztán, she marvelled at that huge web of lies. The deputy denied that Markina had been at the prison, but not only had he been there, CCTV footage placed him outside Berasategui's cell.

# 47

Her aunt had cooked stewed lentils for lunch. The aroma of food and the fire in the hearth comforted Amaia, yet without James, and above all without Ibai, the house was plunged into a silence that felt alien to all three women. She decided to call James, who was surprised to hear from her. After a brief, stilted conversation, she had handed the phone to her aunt and Ros, so they could fuss over Ibai, who, according to his father, pricked up his ears and grinned when he heard their voices.

Above her the sky darkened and the first rumble of thunder reached her from the mountain. As she walked to the police station, she mulled over the conversation she'd had with her aunt when Ros left for the bakery. Engrasi had asked her:

'What's going on between you and James, Amaia?'

She had tried to evade the question. 'What makes you think something's going on?'

'Because you replied with a question, and because I overheard your conversation with him. All you talked about was the weather.'

She had smiled at her aunt's observation.

'When couples have nothing left to say to one another, they talk about things like the weather, the way you do with taxi drivers. Laugh all you like, but it's one of the signs of a break-down in communication.'

Amaia's expression clouded at the thought.

'Don't you love him any more, Amaia?'

She had left on the pretext of being late, and in her haste had left her car key behind. Daunted by her aunt's probing gaze, she hadn't wanted to go back for it. She never ceased to be astonished by that woman's ability to second-guess what she was thinking, what was troubling her.

The question echoed in her head. Did she still love James? The immediate response was yes, she loved him, she knew she did, but in that case . . . How could she explain her feelings for Markina? Dupree would have called it infatuation, Montes would have said sexual attraction. Jonan had been blunt: he thought Markina clouded her judgement, prevented her from being objective. She remembered how irritated she'd been when he said it, but in view of the latest revelations, she was beginning to think he had a point.

As she entered the meeting room, she could see that Montes had started to pin up the images and documents they'd been gathering on the white board.

'Have you made any progress?' she said, addressing the general company as she gazed through the windows at the darkening sky, thick with storm clouds. She went over and switched on the lights.

'Some, not a lot,' said Montes. 'By ruling out baby girls who've been baptised we've been able to cut down the list, but it's a time-consuming process finding the relevant parish, then speaking to the priest in person, because no one else has access to that information. And all this during office hours, which in most churches are restricted. Of the four cases in Hondarribia, we've ruled out two – one was a little German girl, who died during a family holiday, and the other was baptised.'

'Zabalza?'

'Obviously by including statistics for the whole of Navarre, the number has increased considerably. But if we limit our search to towns near the river, we can whittle them down to one case in Elizondo, another in Oronoz-Mugaire,' he said, marking them on the map, 'another in Narbarte, two in Doneztebe, and the two Inspector Montes just mentioned in Hondarribia.'

Amaia studied the line of red dots on the map as a loud thunderclap shook the building. She looked up in time to see a squall of rain hit the window.

'How far back do these cases go?'

'Ten years,' replied Zabalza. 'Do you want me to look further back in time?'

'It would be good if you could go as far back as the first cases we know about, possibly further. Use a different colour for the older cases – in Elizondo, the girl at Argi Beltz and my sister; the girl in Lesaka; the daughter of the lawyer couple, Lejarreta & Andía in Elbete; as well as that of the father who threatened the pathologist in Erratzu.'

The line clearly followed the River Baztán, or Bidasoa, as it became known, all the way from its source to the estuary, in a sinister succession of dots designating the towns or villages through which it flowed.

She wheeled round to see Inspector Iriarte standing behind her, contemplating the map with a worried look.

'You seem to have established a pattern.'

'Sit down,' she said, by way of a reply. 'I have some news. Following your advice, Inspector,' she said, addressing Iriarte, 'I sought Father Sarasola's help. To my surprise, he arranged for me to interview the protected witness who denounced the sacrifice in Lesaka. He more or less told me the same story as Sarasola: this was a spiritual sect with satanic overtones, but instead of worshipping the devil, they were encouraged to return to the supernatural traditions of Baztán. Or in the words of the witness: to the old spiritual traditions, which allowed man to commune with the powerful, mysterious, magical earthly forces around which the region's inhabitants based the religion they practised for thousands of years. They also drew on the ancient practices of witchcraft, with its potions, spells, herbalism and shamanism, learning to explore the limits of man's power.'

'Did they actually believe all this?' Iriarte looked horrified.

The rain smashed against the windows as a lightning bolt illuminated the dark sky, revealing swirling clouds, like waves on the ocean.

'I'm going to quote Father Sarasola's words when I asked him the same question: Stop thinking in these terms. Of course they believed it, faith is the driving force behind millions of people, millions of pilgrims who travel to Santiago, to Rome, to Mecca, to India; sales of spiritual books top the yearly charts, the number of sects is growing, attracting followers to the point where police forces all over the globe have set up specialised units dedicated to dealing with them. So, let's forget what we consider rational, acceptable, probable, because we're talking about something quite different here, something incredibly powerful, which in the hands of a charismatic leader can be extremely dangerous.

'This particular sect espoused a return to the old traditions, a respect for their origins, for the primordial forces, and their way of doing this was through "the offering". They adopted the old religion's belief in the existence of magical creatures associated with this part of the world since prehistoric times. The entire region is criss-crossed by ley lines – which are widely believed to be associated with paranormal phenomena – along with megalithic markers established by the first inhabitants of Baztán to designate places of spiritual significance – mountains, cliffs, rocks, ravines, caves and other places – where they could commune with those supernatural forces. One theory, espoused by a man called Watkins, suggests that such markers date back to Neolithic times, and served as landmarks during mass migrations.

'The sect leader instructed his followers in ways to summon these forces and secure their favours. Not through prayer, self-denial, obeying rules, or negotiating obstacles placed in the way of desires. The sect summoned their evil spirits with offerings of living creatures. To begin with, they sacrificed domestic animals; according to our witness, the results were so astonishing that they soon progressed to human sacrifice. But not just any old human: this ultimate offering, which they called *the sacrifice*, demanded a female child under the age of two. At that age, according to their beliefs, her soul is still between two worlds, and this makes her particularly attractive to Inguma – the demon they worship. She must also be unbaptised, and killed in the exact same way Inguma claims his victims . . .'

Another thunderclap crashed above their heads, momentarily diverting their attention to the spectacular storm brewing outside.

'By suffocating them,' said Zabalza.

'That's right, by robbing them of their breath – which is what the witness claims happened during the sacrifice. To complete the ritual, the body was then taken to a specific place, the location of which he claims not to know. Wealth seems to be the main thing the participants received in return, with the parents of the sacrificed baby being granted unlimited wishes.

'He told me a few other interesting things,' Amaia went on. 'Some of which I passed on to you yesterday: the cult leader's name, Xavier Tabese, and his age – about seventy-five, assuming he's still alive. He also said that there were occasions when only one of the parents of the sacrificial victim belonged to the sect, as seems to have been the case with Yolanda Berrueta and Sonia Esparza. There were also occasions when both parents initially consented to the sacrifice, but the mother subsequently fell prey to depression. That made me wonder: what if those couples ended up separating? If we could find mothers who separated from their husbands and whose babies are buried in their family tombs, we might be able to persuade them to consent to our opening the coffins. We wouldn't need a court order if the families themselves made the request. And to be on the safe side, they could give a pretext like wanting to check for flood damage. So I want you to check whether any of the parents of our possible victims are divorced.'

A fresh lightning bolt lit up the sky, interrupting the power supply and plunging them into darkness for a few seconds until the lights flashed back on.

She didn't mind walking in the rain, but the deafening sound of water falling on to the canopy of her umbrella made her nervous. As she came to a halt outside Señor Yáñez's house, she felt her phone vibrate in her pocket. The display showed two missed calls: one from James, the other from Markina. She deleted them both, thrust the phone deep into her pocket, and rang the bell once, imagining the old man muttering to himself as rose from his makeshift bed in front of the television. Soon afterwards, she heard a bolt being drawn back, and Yáñez's wrinkled face appeared.

'Ah, it's you,' he said.

'Can I come in?'

He gave no reply, but left the door wide open as he walked back down the corridor towards the sitting room. He was wearing the same pair of corduroys, but had swapped his thick sweater and warm dressing gown for a checked shirt. The house felt warm. She followed Yáñez, who sat down on the sofa, motioning for her to do the same.

'Thanks for calling.'

She looked at him, puzzled.

'About the boiler, thanks for calling the repair man.'

'No problem,' she replied.

The old man focused his attention on the television screen.

'Señor Yáñez, there's something I want to ask you about.'

He stared at her.

'Last time I was here, you told me that another police officer had been to see you recently. You said he'd made you a cup of coffee . . .'

Yáñez nodded.

'I'd like you to look at this photograph and tell me if this is him.' She showed him a picture of Jonan Etxaide on her mobile.

'Yes, that's him. Nice lad.'

Amaia switched off the display and put her phone away.

'What did you talk about?'

'Phfft,' replied Yáñez, with a vague wave of his hand.

Amaia rose, picking up from a side table the photograph Yáñez had shown her during her last visit.

'Your wife didn't become depressed when your son was born, did she? I think she started to feel bad long before that. Instead of making her happy, his birth was devastating for her. She couldn't love him; she rejected him because he was a substitute for the baby girl she had already lost.'

Yáñez opened his mouth but said nothing. He reached for the remote that was lying next to him and switched off the television.

'I never had a daughter.'

'Yes, you did. That other police officer suspected as much, and that's why he came to talk to you.'

Yáñez remained silent for a few seconds, before confessing: 'Having another child was supposed to make Margarita forget, but instead she became even more obsessed with what had happened.'

'What was the girl's name?'

Again, he took his time answering.

'She had no name, she wasn't baptised. She died of cot death a few hours after she was born.'

'Fuck! You killed your own daughter!' Amaia said in disgust.

Yáñez looked at her, a smile spreading over his face, then erupting into laughter. He cackled like a madman for a while, then fell silent.

'And what are you going to do, report me?' he hissed. 'My son is dead, my wife is dead, and I'm doomed to spend the rest of my days rotting alive inside this house. How many more winters do you think I'll survive? I have nothing to live for. Someone told me once that gifts from the devil turn to shit – and they were right: my life has turned into one big stinking pile of shit. I don't care if they come for me. Let them send the walnuts, I'll gladly swallow them and let the evil rip my insides apart. I gave it all up long ago. When my wife died, everything I thought was important – the money, the house, the business – lost all meaning. I gave it all up.'

Amaia thought about the words of the witness holed up in the house belonging to Opus Dei: 'No one leaves the sect.'

'Perhaps you did, but your son took your place, didn't he? A sacrifice like that couldn't be allowed to go to waste.'

Yáñez grabbed the remote and switched the television back on.

Amaia started towards the door. When she was halfway down the corridor she heard him call out.

'Inspector, the power went off this afternoon; I think the boiler is on the blink again.'

She opened the front door.

'Fuck you!' she yelled, slamming the door behind her. She headed back towards the station, went upstairs to the meeting room, and placed a fresh red dot on the map.

# 48

Ros Salazar stayed on at work later than usual. Sitting at her desk, she took the opportunity to reply to some correspondence while she waited.

The bakery door was open, and from her position, she could see Flora enter, although she pretended not to have noticed her until she placed some folders on the desk.

'Well, little sister, these are the reports and the valuation. I'll leave them here for you to study at your leisure, but I can tell you now that the business alone is worth more than the value of all your assets put together – assuming they aren't already mortgaged to the hilt. Not to mention the building and the machinery. My offer is on the last page . . . Don't be a fool, Ros; take the money and give me back my bakery.'

They were interrupted by Ernesto, the manager, who was holding up a plastic bag from the hardware store.

'Forgive me for butting in. Rosaura, I've had the copies of the keys made as you asked. Where do you want me to put them?'

'Don't worry, we're finished talking. Keep one for yourself, and put the others in the key cupboard,' said Ros. 'Thank you, Flora, you'll have my reply soon,' she said brusquely.

'Think hard, little sister,' Flora retorted, closing the door behind her as she left. Ros opened the desk drawer and placed the folders inside without even glancing at them. Then she sat staring at the cursor on the computer screen, counting the blinks: one, two, three, four, up to sixty, and then from one to sixty again.

She rose and went into the bakery. Opening the cupboard where the keys were kept, she counted the copies. There were two missing: Ernesto's and the one Flora had taken. She smiled to herself, returned to her office, switched off the computer and left, closing the door behind her.


Amaia looked at her watch, calculating what time it was in the States, then she called James. Engrasi's question had been hammering away in her head all afternoon.

'We miss you,' was the reply from across the ocean. 'When are you coming over?'

She explained to him about the investigation into Jonan's death not going in the right direction. About her friend Dr Takchenko's terrible car accident . . . Perhaps in a few days. She listened to Ibai's burbling as he played with the phone, and she felt unbearably sad, unbearably guilty.

Afterwards, she called Markina.

'I've been trying to get hold of you all afternoon. What do you want for dinner?'

'I've been busy. You'll be pleased to know that Yolanda Berrueta is doing well. I went to see her this morning at the hospital.' She paused, waiting for his reply.

'That *is* good news.'

'She told me about your meeting . . .'

Another pause, no reply this time.

'. . . The one where you advised her to get in touch with me discreetly because I was the right person to help her.'

'I'm sorry, Amaia, she was so wretched, I felt sorry for her. She reminded me of my own mother, obsessed with her dead babies, but my hands were tied. All I said was that if she could

402

get you genuinely interested in the case you might be able to help her. And I wasn't mistaken: you did.'

'You manipulated me.'

'That's precisely what I didn't do, Amaia. I didn't want her to go to you saying I had sent her; that would have been manipulative, as well as completely out of order. Okay, she went to you on my recommendation, but it was simply a piece of advice given to a desperate woman who was in a great deal of pain. You showed interest, you made the decision to help her. You can't blame me for believing in you.'

'That didn't stop you from hindering me.'

'You didn't go through the proper channels, you know that.'

'I'm referring to our conversation last night. You have a horror of exhumations, yet you sent this grieving mother to me; and then you reproached me for being obsessed with a case which you were pushing me into while at the same time not supporting me.'

'You're right, I behaved like an idiot yesterday, but you can't say that I don't protect you, that I don't defend your interests. I did when Judge De Gouvenain wanted to file a complaint, and again when the Tremond family came to my office threatening to sue you for damages. I protect you, Amaia, from everyone and everything. But in my capacity as a magistrate, my powers are limited in the same way yours are as head of Homicide. The difference is that I follow the rules, Amaia – or are you saying you didn't deviate from procedure at least once in the course of your investigation? I'm familiar with your methods, and I think you're brilliant, I'm crazy about you, but you can't expect me to behave like you. First and foremost, I have a duty to protect you from yourself, from your fears . . . No one knows better than I, what a burden it is to have a terrible family.'

She remained silent. No, she couldn't say she hadn't broken the rules. And at that very moment she was withholding information from Markina, Clemos, Iriarte, and even Montes. There wasn't a single person to whom she had revealed everything; she'd requested parallel tests to be run on that strand of fabric, and for the moment she planned to keep quiet about Yáñez's daughter – although, as the old man said, she couldn't prove anything. And it would stay that way until she discovered why the deputy governor had lied about Markina visiting the prison when Berasategui was moved; she didn't want to risk confronting Markina directly. But she had no choice.

'Did you go to the prison the day Berasategui died?'

'Of course, you saw me there,' he replied at once. This was a good sign.

'I know, I'm asking whether you went there after we spoke on the phone, before Berasategui was found dead.'

This time he paused for several . . .

'Why do you ask?'

This was a bad sign; someone who has nothing to hide replies immediately. As for answering a question with another question, that could only mean one of two things: either he was giving himself time to think up a reply, or he was avoiding the question. So either he was lying or he had something to hide.

'Did you go there or not?'

'Yes. When I learned that the governor was away, I was concerned. I've never met his deputy, and I wasn't sure he realised how serious this was, so I decided to go there and see for myself.'

'That all seems perfectly reasonable, except that when I asked him whether you'd been there, he denied it.'

'The man's a fool.'

Yes, she'd had that impression too. She breathed more easily.

'Did you speak to Berasategui?'

'No. I didn't go anywhere near his cell.'

'But you spoke to the guard . . .'

'Yes, I told him to watch Berasategui closely. Now, why don't you come over to my place, and we'll continue this conversation naked over a bottle of wine. That is if you want to.'

'I can't,' she sighed. 'I'm at my aunt's house and I promised I'd have supper with her.'

'Tomorrow, then?'

'Tomorrow,' she agreed, and hung up.

# 49

Flora considered two in the morning a prudent hour; encountering someone on the street in Elizondo at that time would be nothing short of a miracle. Besides, she had to do this that night so she could return the key before Ros noticed it was missing. Fortunately for her, the entrance to the bakery was still unlit; for years they had been asking the town council to install a street lamp, but the adjoining land was private, and the owners opposed it. She entered the bakery, only switching on the lights when she reached the office, where they could only be seen from outside by someone looking up at the eaves and who would do that. She hurriedly slipped off her shoes, climbed up on to the sofa, took down the painting by Ciga, and turned the combination lock. The door sprang open. The safe was empty. Gazing in disbelief, she thrust her hand inside feeling the back of the metal box. Her heart missed a beat when a voice rang out behind her.

'Good evening, Sister.' Flora swung round, startled, tottering slightly. 'If you're looking for the contents of the safe, I have them. The fact is, I'd forgotten it even existed until that time you came to the office when I wasn't here, and put back the painting crooked. It took me days to figure out what could be so important as to make you sneak in here like a thief in the night.'

'But you—'

'No, I didn't have the combination, but that's not a problem. When you're the owner; you call a locksmith, tell them you've forgotten the combination, and they open it for you.'

'You have no right! The contents of that safe are private.'

'I disagree: I have every right, because this is my bakery. As for the contents being private: I understand perfectly why you wouldn't want anyone to see them. They put you in a very awkward situation.' Flora was still standing on the sofa, holding on to the door of the safe to steady herself. 'If you get down from there, I'll explain what's going to happen now,' said Ros, amused. 'I've been through the contents at least a dozen times, so I practically know them off by heart.'

Flora had turned pale and was clutching her stomach with both hands, as though about to throw up; even so, she managed to collect herself enough to threaten Ros.

'You're going give it back to me right now!'

'No, Flora, I'm not giving anything back to you. But don't worry, you have nothing to fear – provided you behave. I have no desire to make things difficult for you; besides, I wouldn't want to have to visit you in prison, although I might be obliged to in order to spare Engrasi the ordeal. As I said, I've read everything, Flora. I've read and understood. I don't judge you. Unlike you, I've never set myself up as being morally superior. Much as I think you deserve to be taught a lesson, I understand why you did it. I spent years making excuses for my stupid, idle husband . . . Of course, he was no murderer; if he had been, then making excuses and covering up for him would have made me his accomplice, wouldn't it?'

Flora didn't reply.

'I understand you perfectly, Flora. You did what you had to do, and I don't judge you for that. Dying in that farmhouse was probably the best thing that could have happened to poor

Victor. However, even though I sympathise, I'm not going to let you ruin my life. I shan't report you, Flora, unless you leave me no other choice. I thought long and hard about this discovery and what to do about it, and in the end I saw the light. I think our family has suffered enough, so I put your diary and your pretty red shoes in a box and I took them to a solicitor. It has never occurred to me to make a will – I'm young and healthy, and don't intend to die any time soon – but we have to be prepared for any eventuality. So, if anything happens to me, if for some reason I drop dead, the box will be delivered to our sister Amaia. Because, Flora, whilst our morals may leave a lot to be desired, I know for sure that if Amaia found out what was in your diary, she wouldn't hesitate to turn you in. Maybe it's because of her tough childhood, all the shit she had to endure while we stood by, but she's not like us; Amaia would no more approve of what I'm doing now than she would take pity on you. So, I suggest we find another lawyer, Sister,' she said with a grin, 'to handle the gift you're going to make to me of your share of the bakery. That's all I want. You can keep your money and go on living your own life. I shan't bother you again, and we'll never mention this conversation – but if you try to mess with me, I'll finish you.'

Flora was listening intently, arms folded, a sober expression on her face.

'You seem very sure that this will work.'

'I am. In this family, we are experts at keeping terrible secrets, behaving as if everything were fine.'

Flora's face softened, and she smiled.

'Well, it seems our little Rosario has a brain after all,' she said, looking at her approvingly. 'I'll find another lawyer tomorrow – just make sure you don't let some other little shit take control of your life.'

She picked up her bag, and brushed past Ros as she headed for the door.

'Flora, wait.'

'Yes?'

'Before you go, could you please put everything back the way it was?'

Flora went back to close the safe, hang the painting on the wall and tidy the cushions on the sofa. Then she turned on her heel and left.

# 50

The small gestures, the details, all the minutiae that made up her world and that had become indispensable were highlighted by James's absence. She had been awake for a good quarter of an hour stroking his pillow with the back of her hand. The way he woke her up with a series of tiny kisses on the top of her head; the milky coffee in a glass he placed on her bedside table every morning; his big, rough sculptor's hands; the scent of his skin through his jumper; the space between his arms that was her refuge . . .

She got out of bed and padded barefoot to the kitchen to make herself some coffee, carried it upstairs and climbed back under the covers. She looked with annoyance at her phone, which started to ring just at that moment, but her irritation gave way to curiosity when she recognised Father Sarasola's number.

'Inspector . . . I'm not quite sure how to tell you this.' She was surprised: if there was one man in the world who had no difficulty articulating it was Sarasola; she couldn't imagine anything leaving him speechless. 'Rosario came back.'

'What? Did you say—'

'Less than fifteen minutes ago, your mother walked into

the clinic, stood in front of the CCTV cameras in reception, pulled out a knife and cut her own throat.'

Amaia started shaking from head to toe.

'The receptionists and the two security guards on the door immediately called for help, and our doctors did everything they could to save her, but . . . I'm sorry, Amaia: your mother died on the way to the operating theatre. There was nothing they could do, she bled to death.'

Dr Sarasola's office seemed as cold and impersonal as it had the first time she visited. He looked out of place in there; she imagined him more at home in an office like the one Dr San Martín occupied at the Institute of Forensic Medicine. Instead, the room was decorated with monastic austerity, a simple crucifix the only adornment on the vast white walls. The furniture, though of excellent quality, was as impersonal as any you might find in a bank or other institution; the cherrywood desk alone stood out, adding both personality and good taste. And yet that very starkness was conducive to thought: the absence of objects that might draw the eye encouraged introspection, meditation and enquiry. Which was what Amaia had been engaging in for the past hour. She had pulled on her clothes and driven to the clinic on autopilot as a thousand and one childhood memories flashed through her mind. Though most were painful she was nevertheless conscious of a strange melancholy – a yearning for something she'd never had.

Although she'd tried not to let her thoughts dwell on the fear she carried around with her, she must have wished a million times over that she could be rid of that burden, be rid of Rosario. She had spent the last month defending her conviction that her mother was still alive, hiding out somewhere, biding her time, waiting to strike. She had felt it in her bones, the way a sheep feels the wolf's presence; with that same animal fear and anguish driving her on, she had

411

opposed those who insisted the river had taken Rosario. Now, sitting in Sarasola's office, her initial shock had given way to a feeling of disappointment and disillusion which she couldn't explain.

Sarasola had accompanied her down a long corridor, recounting the details of Rosario's return, then ushered her into the control room. She remembered the night her mother had escaped from the clinic when she'd come to this same room to watch the CCTV footage.

'I know that you're a homicide detective, but despite your destructive relationship with Rosario, she was your mother. I should warn you that these images are shocking and you might find them disturbing to watch. Do you understand?'

'Yes, but I need to see this with my own eyes.'

'Very well.' He signalled to the head of security to replay the footage. A widescreen view of the reception area and entrance filled the monitor, from cameras located above the lift doors. There was a lot of coming and going: outpatients, medical personnel and other staff members starting or finishing their shifts. She saw Rosario enter, one hand hidden beneath her coat, the other clutching her waist. Moving slowly – not with difficulty, but like someone terribly weary, or downcast – she walked directly to the centre of the foyer, glancing up to make sure she was in full view of the camera. She was weeping, a look of sorrow on her tearstained face. She reached among her clothes, pulled out a long-bladed knife, and placed it to her throat. Amaia recognised the cruel grimace on her mother's lips as she slid the knife from left to right, slitting her own throat with one swift movement. She closed her eyes, swaying on her feet for a few seconds, then she fell to the floor. Alarms went off, people started running, nurses and medics gathered around Rosario, blocking the camera's view. The head of security switched off the screen. Amaia turned to Sarasola.

'Could you please inform my sisters?'

'Of course. Don't worry, I'll see to it.'

She hadn't wanted to speak to anyone, not her family, not San Martín, not Markina, not even the commissioner, who had called twenty minutes ago. Sarasola had taken her to his office, and she'd heard him go into what seemed like a perfect routine, putting callers off, asking them to respect her grief. But in truth she felt no grief; there was no sense of pain, no peace, no relief, not even the kind of gratification experienced by someone who sees their enemy destroyed. She had no sense of reprieve or satisfaction, and only after she had thought long and hard did she realise why: it didn't feel right, she didn't believe it, it made no sense, it wasn't logical, it confounded her expectations. This wasn't how the wolf was conquered. To destroy the wolf's power, you had to track it down, ensnare it, confront it. Wolves didn't commit suicide, they didn't dash themselves against the rocks; the wolf only ceased to be a wolf when it was killed. Amaia was haunted by the images of Rosario's despondent figure, her mournful expression, tears of despair streaming down her cheeks, the grimace on her lips as she prepared to carry out her mission. She had seen the same thing when that other wolf, Berasategui, had committed suicide, shedding tears of self-pity for the terrible loss of his own life. He had wept so much his pillow was sodden. At that instant, after watching her death, Amaia was more convinced than ever that neither Berasategui nor her mother had taken their own lives voluntarily.

A familiar sensation of revulsion overwhelmed her; the feeling she had when confronted with a lie, with the awful impression of being caught in a web of lies.

She left Sarasola's office without saying goodbye, and went straight back to the station at Elizondo.

She ran up to the second floor, searching all the offices for her colleagues. She found Zabalza sitting at his computer.

'Where are Iriarte and Montes?'

'They've gone to Igantzi, to interview a woman who filed for divorce three weeks after losing her baby girl to cot death. Then, they're seeing another woman in Hondarribia. Boss . . . I heard about your mother—'

'Don't say a word,' she interrupted, turning and heading for her office. She plugged the memory stick containing Jonan's files into her computer, and opened all the documents. She realised for the first time what she was seeing: a web of lies, make-believe and deception.

The tomb in Ainhoa from which two babies had supposedly been taken. A lie. The same tomb where a little girl's remains should have been, another lie. The meeting between Yolanda Berrueta and Inma Herranz, still more lies. Fina Hidalgo's employment history concealed a lie, as did Berasategui's relationship with the sect at Argi Beltz. The images of Judge Markina at the prison the day Berasategui died, another lie. Jonan's file was a collection of fabrications, masquerading as something else for her benefit. She opened the file containing photographs of her and Markina outside the Baluarte Congress Centre that night, wondering what they meant, what secret they might hide. She closed the file and opened another, containing the address of a nursing home in Madrid where a woman called Sara had been admitted. She wondered what the lie was behind that name.

Her phone leapt a few centimetres on her desk, emitting an unpleasant buzz like a dying insect. It was Padua, from the *Guardia Civil*. She hesitated, debating whether to answer. Padua had been one of those convinced Rosario had died in the flood; he had been personally involved in the search for her body, to corroborate his view, or for evidence that Rosario was still alive, to corroborate hers. She listened to his condolences and thanked him. As she put the phone down on the desk, it rang again. She refused the call, it was Markina again.

Deputy Inspector Zabalza put his head round the door; his face betrayed a look of anguish.

'Boss, I think we've found something important.'

She beckoned him in.

'As you requested, I made inquiries into Tabese's medical background. The College of Physicians in Madrid had a listing for a Clínica Tabese in Las Rozas, operating from the seventies right up until the mid-nineties; the man who ran it was a certain Dr Tabese. I found someone at the College who remembered him; they told me he was a popular figure in Madrid society at that time, renowned for the novel methods he imported from the States. Dr Tabese passed away, they couldn't say exactly when, although they did confirm that he's buried in Hondarribia, where he lived after he stopped working as a psychologist. The reason why we initially found no trace of him is because he adopted the name of his clinic. His real name was Xabier Markina,' he said, placing an enlarged black-and-white photograph on the desk in front of her.

'Markina?'

'Dr Xabier Markina was Judge Markina's father.'

Shocked by this revelation, Amaia studied the image. 'Dr Tabese' looked like an older version of his son.

She remembered him telling her that his father was a doctor, and that he'd died soon after his mother, consumed by grief at her repeated attempts to take her own life, for which she had been committed to a mental asylum. She picked up her phone and dialled Iriarte's number. While she was speaking, Zabalza slipped back to his office.

'Are you in Hondarribia yet?'

'Almost,' replied Iriarte.

'I need you to go to the town hall and find out where Dr Tabese is buried. The College of Physicians in Madrid has just confirmed that he was a doctor of psychology who practised from the seventies through to the nineties at Clínica Tabese, a private facility for wealthy clients. He retired and went to live in Hondarribia. Apparently he died there. He may be registered under his real name: Xabier Markina. Tabese was Judge Markina's father.'

Iriarte remained silent, while in the background she heard a long drawn-out whistle from Montes, who was presumably driving and following the conversation on speakerphone.

'Be discreet, ask to see the death certificate as well as the funeral records of the cemetery where he is buried.'

She was about to hang up when Iriarte said: 'San Martín called to tell us about your mother . . . I don't know what to say, Inspector, we were wrong and you were right. This isn't the time to discuss it, but I just wanted you to know that I'm sorry.'

'It's okay, don't worry about it,' she replied.

After ending the call, she took out Jonan's memory stick, switched off her computer, and picked up her coat. She was waiting for the lift when, on impulse, she turned and made her way to the office where Zabalza was working.

'Do you want to come with me?'

Without replying, he took his service revolver out of the drawer, slipped it into its holster and fell in behind her.

They got into her car and she drove in silence until they reached the outskirts of Pamplona. She pulled over at a petrol station, and asked:

'Do you like driving? I need to think.'

He grinned.

Four hundred and fifty kilometres without talking was more than Deputy Inspector Zabalza could endure. With the restraint of someone who has rehearsed the question a hundred times, he asked whether she'd mind if he put on some music. She nodded. Two hours into the journey, he switched off the radio, interrupting her thoughts.

'I've cancelled the wedding,' he announced.

She stared at him in astonishment. Avoiding her gaze, he

kept his eyes fixed on the road. Aware of how awkward this must be for Zabalza and not wishing to embarrass him further, she said nothing, and looked away again.

'The fact is, I should never have let things get that far. It was a mistake from the start . . . And do you know what's so awful? It was Etxaide's death that gave me the courage.' She glanced at him, then turned her eyes back to the road. 'That evening at his parents' house, I met his friends, his partner . . . Well, it was a revelation to me. Jonan's parents were so proud of him . . . And the funeral wasn't a pretence like most of them are, full of empty praise for someone because they've just died. Did you see the way they were towards his partner?' Amaia nodded. 'I listened to his friends talk about him for hours, things he had said, his thoughts . . . And it made me realise that I hadn't known him at all, probably because he stood for everything I want to be, everything I'm not. I don't care what Internal Affairs say, and I won't care about the predictable outcome of their investigation: Jonan Extaide was an honest guy, loyal and dependable. And he was brave – he had the guts to live his life.'

He fell silent. After a few seconds, Amaia asked:

'Are you okay?'

'No, but I'll be fine. Right now I'm still suffering the after-effects of dropping a bombshell, but I feel better in myself, so if you need me to put in more hours, work late, or drive to the Sahara, I'll be glad to keep busy.' She was about to speak when he added: 'And by the way, you were right. Remember what you said in Arizkun, the night of the desecration? About me identifying with that boy, his inability to face life, his feeling of being trapped. You were right, I was wrong.'

'You don't need to—'

'Yes, I do. I need to explain so that you can trust me.'

'Yes,' she grinned. 'What was it you called me? "That fucking star cop!"'

'Yes, I'm sorry.'

417

'Don't be, I like the name. I'm thinking of having it embroidered on my FBI cap – that should cause a stir among the American agents.'

Zabalza switched the radio back on.

Clínica La Luz was situated in an old building, the style of which might have been an example of Eastern Bloc architecture, but which, ironically, was all the rage during the Franco era, primarily for government offices. Its proximity to the military base at Torrejón de Ardoz gave some idea of what it had been used for in bygone days. They left the car in an over-sized car park, where a huddle of vehicles occupied the row of spaces nearest the building.

The security at the clinic lagged behind that of the psychiatric unit at Nuestra Señora de las Nieves, or the University Hospital in Pamplona, where her mother had been interned. There were no guards, just a large iron gate with an intercom panel. They pressed the buzzer and, when asked to identify themselves, replied: *Police*.

The reception area was deserted, save for a dozen trolleys heaped with towels, sponges and incontinence pads, lined up against the far wall. But what struck them immediately as they walked through the door was the smell. It reeked of urine, faeces, boiled vegetables and cheap cologne. They made their way to the counter, where they were met by a woman of about fifty dressed in a skirt suit. She walked straight up to them, extending her hand.

'Good afternoon, I'm Eugenia Narvaez. The receptionist told me you're from the police department,' she said, studying their faces. 'I hope there isn't a problem.'

'No, there's no problem. I'm Inspector Salazar, and this is Deputy Inspector Zabalza. We'd like to talk to you about one of your former patients.'

Relief flooded the woman's face.

'About a patient, why, of course,' she said, beckoning them

to follow her to the reception desk. She sat down in front of the computer, fingers poised over the keyboard, and looked up at them expectantly.

'This patient was admitted to the clinic some years ago, and I believe she died here. Her name was Sara Durán.'

Eugenia Narvaez looked at them, puzzled.

'There must be some mistake, Sara Durán has been a patient here for many years, and she's still very much alive – or she was a few minutes ago when I gave her her medication,' she said, smiling.

'Well, that *is* a surprise,' replied Amaia. 'We'd like to see her, if you have no objection.'

'None at all,' said the woman, 'although I ought to warn you that you won't get much sense out of her. Sara's notion of reality is very different from yours or mine – her mind is confused. She is also extremely highly strung, prone to crying one minute and laughing the next. Don't be alarmed if she exhibits this behaviour, just keep talking to her as if nothing's happened. I'll call one of the orderlies to take you to her,' she said, picking up the receiver.

Twenty chairs stood lined up in front of the television, which was showing a cowboy film. A dozen or so residents were seated in the chairs closest to the set. The orderly approached the only woman in the group.

'Sara, you have visitors. This lady and gentleman have come to see you.'

The woman looked at him incredulously, and then at them. A broad smile spread across her face. She stood up without too much difficulty, coquettishly linking arms with the orderly, who guided her to the far corner of the room where four chairs were arranged around a circular table.

She was painfully thin, her wrinkled face gaunt to the point of emaciation. And yet, her hair, which she wore in a ponytail, wasn't thick and shiny, not yet completely white but streaked with silver and grey. Sara was still in her nightdress, although it was past four in the afternoon. Over it, she wore a buttoned-up dressing gown, covered in food stains.

'Hello, Sara, I've come here to see you because I want you to tell me about your husband and your son.'

The smile on the woman's face vanished.

'Didn't you know? My baby died!' she wailed, burying her face in her hands. Amaia turned to the orderly, who was watching them from across the room. He gestured for them to continue.

'Sara, we didn't come here to talk about your baby. We want to know about your grown-up son, and your husband.'

The woman stopped weeping.

'You're mistaken, madam, I have no son, I only had my baby, my baby who died,' she said, pulling a sad face.

Amaia took out her phone and showed her a photograph of Markina.

The woman beamed.

'Ah, yes, isn't he handsome? But why do you call him my son? This my husband.'

'No, this isn't your husband, it's your son.'

'Do you think I'm stupid! Do you think I don't know my own husband?' she screeched, snatching the phone from Amaia and gazing at the image. She smiled again. 'Of course this is my husband. How handsome he is! So beautiful, his eyes, his mouth, his hands, his skin,' she said, touching the screen with her fingertips. 'I can't resist him. You understand that, don't you? You can't resist him either, but I don't blame you, nobody can. I've never forgotten him, I've never loved anyone the way I loved him. I still love him, I still desire him, even though he never comes to see me. He doesn't love me any more, he doesn't love me any more.' She started sobbing again. 'But I don't care, I've never stopped loving him.'

Amaia looked at her with pity. She had come across several Alzheimer's victims who didn't recognise their own children,

420

or mistook them for younger versions of people they had known in the past. She wondered if it was worth trying to explain to her that the reason her husband didn't visit her was because he was dead, or whether it was kinder to spare her the shock, even though it would last only as long as it took her to forget it.

'Sara, this is your son. I imagine he bears a strong resemblance to your husband.'

She shook her head.

'Is that what he told you? That I'm his mother? Of course, I must look a sight,' she muttered, rubbing her hands over her wrinkled face. 'They won't let me look in the mirror . . . Could you talk to them, persuade them to put a mirror in my room? I won't cut myself again. I promise,' she said, showing them her wrist, criss-crossed with scars.

Once more, the woman focused her attention on the photograph.

'How handsome he is! He still drives me crazy, I never could resist him.' She hiked up her nightdress, placing her other hand between her legs and rubbing herself rhythmically. 'I still can't.'

Amaia snatched the phone off her, motioning to the orderly to come over.

'Don't you remember your son, Sara?'

The orderly was standing beside Sara, giving her reproving looks. She stopped moving her hand, turned irately to Amaia and said:

'I have no son. My baby died, that's why I'm doomed. Because no matter how hard I've tried all these years, not a day passes when I don't think about him, even though he's never been to see me, even though I know he doesn't love me, and that he was my downfall. Despite all that, I still want him to fuck me,' she said, rubbing herself again beneath her nightdress.

'Sara!' the orderly shouted, at which she stopped. 'I think that's enough now; she's very excitable,' he said, turning to them.

As they stood up to leave, the woman turned to Amaia, a hideous, demented expression on her face.

'And so do you!' she screamed, as the orderly restrained her by the arms. 'You want him to fuck you too.' She paused, as though struck by a sudden realisation, then cried out: 'No, you don't. He's already fucked you hasn't he? Now he's in your cunt and in your head, and you'll never get rid of him!'

As they reached the stairs, they heard the woman's screams start up again. Suddenly she appeared, running towards them. When she drew level, she seized Amaia's wrist and thrust a small, hard walnut into her palm. Then she turned to face the orderly, who was coming towards her, and spread her arms in a gesture of surrender.

Amaia observed the tiny, compact walnut, glistening with sweat, or possibly something else.

'Hey, Sara!' she called out.

As the woman spun round to look at her, Amaia dropped the walnut on the floor, crushing it underfoot, the mould inside left a circle of black spores around the shell.

The woman burst into tears.

Eugenia Narvaez was waiting for them in reception.

'Oh dear, that can't have been very pleasant,' she said, noticing the way Amaia was holding her hands away from her sides.

'Don't worry. There is one other thing. We'll need to see the files covering Sara's admission; we'd also like to know who pays her fees, and if her son has ever been to see her.'

'I'm afraid that information is confidential. As for her having a son, the only child I know about is the baby girl who died.'

'A baby girl? I thought she said it was a boy . . .'

'She always calls her "my baby", but it was a girl; everyone here knows that – she tells anyone who will listen. Besides, it's written in her medical notes.'

'Do you recognise this person?' Zabalza showed her the photograph of Markina.

The woman smiled. 'No. And, believe me, I wouldn't forget a man like that in a hurry.'

'Señora Narvaez, we aren't asking to see medical information,' said Amaia. 'All we're interested in is the date she was admitted, and who pays the bill. This clinic of yours seems like a nice little business, clearly you have a lot of residents, all of whom, as far as I can see, are still in their bedclothes at five in the afternoon, and Sara doesn't appear to have had a bath for several days. I have no jurisdiction here, but I can inform my colleagues in Madrid, who will be here in an instant to turn this place upside down. Whether or not you comply with the rules, I'm sure it would be most inconvenient . . . wouldn't it?'

The woman's smile vanished. Without a word, she turned her back on them and marched off in the direction of her office. Three minutes later, during which time Amaia was able to wash her hands, the woman returned with a photocopy.

'This is a copy of her admission sheet. As for who pays, I've no idea, but the money comes out of this account,' she said, pointing to a row of figures entered in pen at the bottom of the page.

They took great gulps of fresh air as soon as they crossed the threshold.

'I think that smell will stay with me for weeks,' said Zabalza, studying the contents of the piece of paper. 'The bank account is in Navarre, the sort code is Pamplona, and the admission sheet is signed by Xabier Tabese in 1995.'

Fifteen minutes later, Amaia's phone rang. It was Markina. She took the call, but didn't put it on speakerphone.

The tone of his voice was one of regret and disappointment.

'Amaia, what's happening? I've just received a call from the clinic in Madrid where my mother is being cared for, and they told me you went to see her.'

423

*Well, well, for someone who didn't know who was paying the fees, she didn't waste much time!* Amaia thought, but didn't say.

'Amaia, anything you wanted to know, you could have asked me.'

She still said nothing.

'I've been trying to get hold of you all day. They told me this morning that you'd been at the Opus Dei hospital. I went there for the removal of the body, but you'd already left, and you're not taking my calls. Here I am worrying about you, and it turns out you're off solving imaginary mysteries, which I could have explained if you would only talk to me.' Still she said nothing. 'Amaia, answer me. I'm going crazy. Why won't you talk to me? What have I done wrong?'

'You lied to me.'

'Because I told you she'd died? All right, well, you've met her now, so you'll understand why. I've been telling everyone that she died when I was a kid. After all, I'm dead to her, so why not return the insult?' She remained silent. He was almost shouting. She could see from Zabalza's expression that he could hear what Markina was saying. 'Why is it so hard for you to understand? You told me yourself that for years you let everyone assume your mother was dead when in fact she was in a mental hospital . . . Look at your reaction today, you won't even talk about it, you're incapable of facing up to the fact that she's dead, that you're free of her. Instead, you go running off to Madrid to dig up bodies from my past. Doesn't what goes for you also go for everyone else?' You said something to me the other day, and you were right: this is who you are and I have to accept that. Amaia, I know who you are, I know the way you work, but I can't help wondering, what more do you need, why are you still looking? . . . You have your mother, and now you have mine. How many more demons must you exorcise before you are at peace? Or perhaps this is a game that excites you more

424

than you care to admit?' he said, ending the call without giving her the chance to respond.

Again he was right. She had avoided talking about her mother for years. To the point where many people close to her assumed she was dead. She had hidden her past beneath a veneer of normality, even while dreaming every night of the monster looming over her bed threatening to devour her. She understood him perfectly.

'He seems a bit pissed off,' said Zabalza after a few seconds.

'. . . And that's without knowing we're investigating his father,' she said irritably.

# 51

Iriarte's call came through an hour later. He was in a good mood. The woman from Igantzi had been extremely cooperative; she was divorced from her husband – an architect for whom things had started to look up after the death of their daughter, the only child they had together. Apparently, he remarried and had two sons; she hated him for that. She was convinced he had left her because she refused to have another child after their baby died. Their little girl was a month old at the time, and not yet baptised. Since then, the girl's remains had lain in her family vault. Iriarte and Montes had told her about the Esparza case; she didn't recall Nurse Hidalgo, but she'd given birth at the clinic in Río Bidasoa during the period when Fina worked there. They'd visited the cemetery with her that afternoon, and she had spoken to the gravedigger about opening the tomb the following day.

'As for the two women in Hondarribia, she claims she saw something strange on the day of her daughter's funeral. Unfortunately the coffin, which she suspects is empty, lies in the tomb of her ex-husband's family. The other divorcee from Hondarribia has given us permission to open her family tomb. It seems that when the girl died, a big row broke out over where her final resting place should be. Her husband's lawyers,

Lejarreta & Andía, got involved, and in the end it was agreed she should be buried in the mother's family tomb. I don't think we'll have much trouble with that one: the woman's father is a Justice of the Peace in Irún.'

'That's excellent news,' she said. 'Well done.'

'Thanks, boss. As for Tabese, we've requested the death certificate, which will hopefully arrive tomorrow. In the meantime, the cemetery showed us the funeral records, and the date matches the one on the slab, so he's been dead fifteen years. Cause of death is recorded as drowning. I've emailed you an image of the document, as well as some photos we took of Tabese's tomb, which by the way is pretty impressive.'

She opened the files to discover a rather grand, old-fashioned pantheon surrounded by four pillars and a heavy chain with links the size of fists; an abundance of flowers partially obscured the only name on the tomb.

'Apparently the doctor is gone but not forgotten. Find out who sends the flowers; they all look the same, but I can't tell from the photo.'

'Yes, they're orchids. The gravedigger told us that a florist's van arrives each week with fresh flowers from Irún. We've left a message asking the florist to call us.'

'Good. Zabalza and I will be late getting back to Elizondo, so let's aim to set off for Igantzi at ten tomorrow morning.'

She had dropped Zabalza off at the police station so he could pick up his car, and now, parked outside her aunt's house, she felt incapable of going inside, of facing Engrasi and her sisters, who had left dozens of messages telling her they would wait up for her. She sat for a while, collecting her thoughts, jotting down a few questions she wanted to ask Montes and Iriarte in the morning, until she started to feel ridiculous putting off entering the warm house that stood waiting for her with the lights on.

She pressed her hands to her face to try to ease the tension on her facial muscles. As she took them away, she remembered the sensation of the walnut Sara had placed in her palm, recalling in a flash what had been eluding her all afternoon. She started the car and drove along the Alduides road until she reached the cemetery. There was no street lighting along that stretch of road, and in the cold, night sky the stars barely glimmered. She parked facing the gates, leaving her headlights on to illuminate the cemetery. This didn't work as well as she had hoped, as the beam hit the sloping path, losing depth. Pausing to retrieve the powerful torch she kept in the boot, she entered the cemetery. The grave she was searching for was to the right of the path that ran in a straight line from the gates. She recognised it from the angel perched on top, which caught in her headlights, cast a winged shadow on to the top of the tomb. She swept the torch beam over it until she found the walnut hidden among the flowerpots. As she picked it up, she noticed that it was cold and damp from the night dew. She placed it in her pocket, and left the cemetery. She drove back to Engrasi's house and this time she got straight out of the car. She detested the hushed voices at wakes, the tone people used to speak of the recently deceased. She had encountered these atmospheres all too often recently: at the Ballarenas' farmhouse when the little girl died, in the waiting room at the Navarre Institute of Forensic Medicine when, heads lowered, her colleagues had talked about Jonan, and now she could hear the same whispers coming from the mouths of her aunt and sisters. Hearing her arrive, they fell silent. She took off her coat and hung it up in the hallway, then stuck her head round the sitting room door. Ros was the first to stand up and fling her arms about her.

'Oh, Amaia, I'm sorry, I'm so sorry! As always, you were right; how foolish we were not to listen to you.'

Rising from her chair, Flora started towards her, halting before their bodies touched. Ros withdrew, leaving her sisters facing one another.

'Well, as Ros said, it seems you were right after all.'

Amaia nodded. Coming from Flora, this was far more than she would have expected; she imagined her sister would rather die than admit that she was wrong. Ros then looked significantly at Flora, urging her to continue. Uneasy, Flora moistened her lips.

'I'm sorry too, Amaia, not just because I didn't listen to you, but because of what you've had to endure all these years. The only good thing we can take from this is that your suffering is finally over.'

'Thank you, Flora,' she said, from the heart – not because she believed her sister was sincere, but because she recognised the effort it must have taken for her to say those words.

Her aunt came over to embrace her.

'Are you all right, my dear?'

'I'm fine, Auntie. Please don't worry about me, any of you, I'm fine.'

'You didn't answer our calls . . .'

'The truth is, this has been a very strange day. In spite of everything this isn't the ending I would have expected.'

Flora sat down again, visibly relieved at Amaia's calm demeanour, as if she'd been anticipating an emotional outburst.

'I imagine they'll release the body tomorrow. I think we ought to hold some sort of ceremony.'

'You can count me out, Flora,' Amaia cut in. 'We've held more than enough ceremonies for our mother. I'm sure you'll be only too happy to deal with her remains and to ensure she has a proper funeral. Just spare me the details, please.'

Flora opened her mouth to reply, but Engrasi looked daggers at her, and said:

'Now then, girls, why not take this opportunity to tell your sister the good news.'

Amaia looked at them, expectantly.

'Flora can tell her. After all, it was her idea,' said Ros.

This drew a stern glare from Flora, but she turned to Amaia

and said, 'Well, the fact is, I've given a lot of thought to this over the past few days, weighing up the pros and cons of taking the bakery over again, and I've realised it would leave me with very little time to pursue the many other important projects I have planned, not to mention my television career. So, I've decided that since Ros has shown herself more than capable of running the family business on her own, it's best if she remains at the helm. We'll sign the paperwork in a few day's time, and from then on Ros will be the sole owner of Mantecadas Salazar.'

Amaia looked at Ros, eyebrows raised in disbelief.

'Yes, Amaia! Flora came to see me yesterday to tell me – I was as surprised as you are.'

'Well then, congratulations to you both,' said Amaia, noting the hostile glances they kept exchanging, and Ros's clear command of the situation.

'Now you must excuse me. As Amaia said, it's been a long and very strange day. I'm tired, as I'm sure you are.' Flora took her leave, stopping to kiss Aunt Engrasi on her way out.

Amaia followed her to the front door.

'Wait, Flora, I'll walk you home. I need to talk to you,' she said, gathering up her coat and bag, then telling the others not to wait up for her. 'Above all you,' she added, wagging a finger at her aunt.

'I'm too old to be taking orders from a baby like you. And don't be late, or I'll call the cops,' she replied, chuckling.

The difference in temperature after Engrasi's sitting room made Amaia shiver. She buttoned up her coat, raising the collar to keep her neck warm as she and her sister walked side by side in silence.

'What did you want to say to me?' asked Flora impatiently once they were out of sight of the house.

'Give me a chance, I've had a very tough day. I need time to think. I said I'd walk you home, didn't I?'

They continued in silence, passing a patrol car, and a couple of neighbours out walking their dog. Flora's house in Elizondo was beautiful, newly built, detached and surrounded by a tiny garden filled with flowers, which someone watered for her when she was away. They stopped outside the entrance while Flora unlocked the front door. She didn't attempt to say goodbye on the step. Amaia's resolve made it clear that she hadn't accompanied her sister out of politeness.

They went straight into the sitting room, where Amaia paused to look at the enlarged photograph of Ibai she had seen at the house in Zarautz. It was set in a slim, metal frame that enhanced the beauty of the black-and-white portrait. Could her aunt have been right about Flora's feelings for Ibai, especially given the way she pretended to ignore Amaia's interest in the picture, flinging her coat on to the armchair on her way to the kitchen. After a moment, Flora called out:

'Will you join me in a drink?'

'Okay,' she said. 'I'll have a whisky.'

Flora returned carrying two tumblers of the amber liquid. She placed one on a side table, sat down on the sofa, and took a sip from her own glass. Amaia sat down close beside her and, seizing her sister's free hand the same way Sara Durán had done to her that afternoon, she placed in her upturned palm the walnut she had taken from Anne Arbizu's grave.

Flora couldn't conceal her fright; she dropped the walnut as if it were a hot coal, spilling half the contents of her glass on to her skirt. Amaia retrieved the nut from between the two sofa cushions, held it between her thumb and forefinger, and raised it level with her sister's eyes. Flora gazed at it in horror.

'Get that thing out of my house.'

Amaia looked at her, feigning surprise.

'What are you so afraid of, Flora?'

'You've no idea what this is.'

'Yes, I have. I know what it signifies. What I don't understand is why you leave them on Anne Arbizu's grave.'

'You shouldn't have touched it, it's . . . It's for her,' she said, her voice heavy with pain and grief.

Amaia observed her sister's expression as she gazed at the walnut.

Moved, she slipped it back into her pocket.

'What did Anne Arbizu mean to you, Flora? Why do you leave walnuts on her grave? Why won't you admit that you loved her? Believe me, Flora, no one's going to judge you. I've seen too many lives destroyed by people who refuse to accept who they love.'

Flora put her glass down on the table and with a paper tissue started to rub furiously at the stain on her skirt. Then all at once, she burst out crying. Amaia had seen her sister cry like this before at the mention of her relationship with Anne. The sobs rose uncontrollably from her belly until her whole body was trembling; her breath came in short gasps. She scrunched up the tissue she had used on her skirt and tried to soak up the tears streaming down her cheeks. She sat like that for a while, until at last she was calm enough to speak.

'It's not what you think,' she managed to say. 'You're completely mistaken. I loved Anne the same way you love Ibai.'

Amaia looked at her, bewildered.

'I mean I loved her exactly the same way you love Ibai. Because Anne Arbizu was my daughter.'

Amaia was dumbstruck.

'I was eighteen when I had Anne. Perhaps you remember the summer I went to stay with our aunts in San Sebastián . . . Well, I never actually stayed with them. I had the baby and gave her up for adoption.'

'You were going out with Victor—'

'The baby wasn't his.'

432

'Flora, you're telling me that . . .'

'I met a man, he was in the livestock trade and came to one of the cattle fairs, and . . . What happened, happened. I never saw him again. A few weeks later I found out I was pregnant.'

'Didn't you at least try?'

'I'm no fool, Amaia, and I wasn't one at eighteen. It should never have happened, and it had undesired consequences. But my head wasn't filled with foolish, romantic notions. He was just passing through, a one night stand.'

'Did our parents know?'

'*Ama* did.'

'And she agreed that you should—'

'No. To begin with, I managed to conceal the pregnancy. I saved up some money; abortion was illegal in this country, so I found a doctor across the border who carried out this type of procedure. He performed the abortion, or so I believed from the amount of blood that came out of me, not to mention the excruciating pain. That butcher ripped out my ovaries, Amaia, he destroyed my insides, made it impossible for me ever to have another child. And yet, he failed to do what he was supposed to do. Despite losing all that blood, I found I was still pregnant. I was in such a bad way when I arrived home, that it was impossible to hide it from *Ama*. She took me to see Nurse Hidalgo, who staunched the bleeding. Naturally, *Ama* was in shock. Of course they didn't consider me capable of bringing up the baby myself, so it was decided we would keep it a secret until the birth, when the baby would be given away. She made me swear not to tell anyone, not even *aita*. She told me that this mishap might offer me the chance to change my fortunes. Once, when I brought up the subject of adoption, she looked at me as if I were speaking another language, and insisted that the baby wasn't going to be adopted, but rather given up.'

433

Amaia broke in, alarmed at what she had just heard.

'Did she explain what she meant by giving her up? Did *Ama* introduce you to the sect?'

'I didn't know about any sect. I only met Nurse Hidalgo, who saved my life and was going to help me give birth. They were going to take care of it, and that's all I wanted to know. And yet, there was something about Fina Hidalgo that reminded me of the abortionist who butchered me. She was all smiles and assurances: I shouldn't worry, they would make my problem go away, and afterwards my fortunes would change. I'd heard stories about midwives not tying the umbilical cord, allowing unwanted babies to die in pregnancies that had reached full term. Amaia, I don't know or care what you think of me, but you must believe that I wanted the best for that child. I wanted her to go to a good family, with prospects, as they used to say then. When I was six months pregnant, before it became impossible to hide my bump, I cashed in my savings, and went to Pamplona, to a charity set up by nuns to take in wayward women like me who had fallen pregnant out of wedlock. It wasn't so bad. I stayed there until I had the girl. The day she was born, I said goodbye to her, and agreed for her to be adopted, on condition that she went to a good family. Then I went home. I continued to go out with Victor, I carried on with my life and the matter was never raised again. But *Ama* never forgave me, and she made sure I paid for it.

'You can imagine my surprise when I heard that the Arbizus had adopted a baby girl, and I looked in the pram and there she was: Anne. I would have been able to recognise her among a million babies,' she said, the tears once more rolling down her cheeks. 'I lived all those years in resentment, watching my little girl grow up in someone else's house, afraid to give her a second glance lest I betray my feelings, tormented by her presence, which chained me to this village so that I could be close to her. And then, all of a sudden,

434

last year, she came to see me. She turned up at the bakery one evening to tell me she knew who I was, and who she was. Amaia, you can't imagine what she was like, so beautiful, so self-assured and intelligent. She had looked for her birth mother and had found me. She didn't blame me for anything; she said she understood, all she wanted was to go on seeing me without hurting the feelings of her elderly parents . . . She even proposed we announce it to everyone, after they had passed away. She gave me that picture of her when she was a baby,' she said, pointing to the photograph that took up most of the wall.

'I thought that was Ibai,' said Amaia. 'I did wonder when you'd taken it.'

'Yes, the resemblance is striking; it breaks my heart when I see your little boy, and at the same time I can't help adoring him because he looks so like her. In the brief time I knew her, she made me feel things I never thought I could feel. Anne is very special, more than you could imagine. I've never been so happy, Amaia, and I never will be again, because just when I thought I'd found happiness, he killed her, he killed my little girl . . .' Flora abandoned herself to her grief, without restraint. After confessing all her sins, she seemed no longer to care if her sister saw her in that state.

Amaia had been listening to her, speechless. Of all the relationships she had imagined between Anne Arbizu and her sister, this was the only one that hadn't occurred to her. She watched Flora weep, feeling moved and at the same time understanding many things.

'And is that why you killed him? Did you kill Víctor because he killed your daughter?' Flora shook her head, rubbing her hands over her face to dry her tears, which seemed unstoppable. 'Did you know what Víctor was up to?' Flora shook her head again. 'Flora, look at me,' she said, forcing her sister to calm down. 'Did you suspect Víctor of killing those girls?'

Flora looked at Amaia, realising she must be cautious. If Ros was right about anything, it was that Amaia would never accept her crime, no matter how she dressed it up.

'I wasn't sure until I went to see him that night at his house, and he confessed.'

'But you were carrying a gun, Flora.' She didn't reply. 'So you must have suspected. What made you think Víctor killed Anne?'

'I knew him better than anyone.'

'Yes, I know that, but when did you find out?'

'I found out, end of story.'

'No, Flora, that isn't the end of the story: he killed two other girls besides Anne, and many more, even before you and he were married. When did you find out? Did you suspect him, but you let him go on until he dared to touch Anne?'

'I had no idea, I swear,' she lied. 'It never occurred to me that Victor was responsible for the *basajaun* crimes, not until Anne's death.'

'Why? Why when he killed Anne?'

'Because of the way he chose his victims,' she said suddenly angry, her tears drying up. 'When he killed Anne, I understood how he chose them.'

Amaia remained still for a few seconds, observing her sister.

'Flora, we believe Víctor chose young girls between middle childhood and adolescence, and that his victims were random, simply in the wrong place at the wrong time: Carla got out of her boyfriend's car up in the hills, Ainhoa missed the bus, Anne led a double life, carrying on relationships her parents knew nothing about.' Flora shook her head, a bitter smile on her lips. 'What are you saying, Flora?'

'For Christ's sake! And you're supposed to be the expert,' she snapped, her habitual impatience surfacing once more. 'What did he do to their bodies?'

Amaia looked at her sister, unsure where this was leading.

'He unbuttoned their clothes, shaved off their pubic hair, removed their high-heeled shoes, cleaned off their make-up, and . . .' Amaia paused, reflecting, and looked at her sister with fresh eyes, as she went over it again in her mind. He restored them to infancy, erasing from their bodies all signs of adulthood; then he displayed them, hands upturned in an act of surrender, leaving them on the banks of the River Baztán. Like offerings to the past, to innocence. The ritualistic nature of his crimes had been obvious from the start. He had even killed them by robbing them of air. She shuddered at the thought. 'What are you saying, Flora? Explain.'

'He gave them up, he sacrificed them,' she said dispassionately.

'But . . . But, did Víctor know? Did you tell him?'

Flora pulled a face that vaguely resembled a smile.

'Me? I'd have cut out my own tongue rather than tell anyone, least of all him.'

'Then how did he find out? How did he discover that Anne was your daughter?'

'I told you, *Ama* never forgave me.'

'Rosario told him!' declared Amaia. 'She told Víctor that Anne was your daughter. Why would she do that, to break up your marriage?'

'No, we were already separated.'

'Then, why?'

'Possibly so that he would carry out what she considered her mission, the same way she planned to kill Ibai that night she disappeared, just as she tried all your life to kill you: to finish what she started with our other sister.'

'Do you think Víctor chose his victims because they were failed offerings, sacrifices that had been left unfinished?'

'I don't know how he chose his other victims, but he killed my daughter because I didn't give her up, because *she* told him to.' Amaia gazed at her sister astonished. 'Why are you looking at me like that?'

437

'Flora, I've just realised that for most of your life you hated our mother, possibly more than I did.'

Flora rose, picked up the two empty glasses, carried them out to the kitchen, and started to wash them up. Amaia followed her.

'Why leave walnuts on Anne's grave?'

'You wouldn't understand.'

'Try me.'

'Anne wasn't like other girls. In many ways she was exceptional, and she knew it; she had an extraordinary power over others, which I don't know how to explain.'

Amaia remembered the way Anne had seduced Ros's husband, Freddy, how she'd concealed her double life from her parents, the ploy she'd come up with to dispose of the mobile phone Freddy called her on, which had them scratching their heads during the investigation, and her adoptive aunt describing her as a *belagile*, a witch.

'It was Anne who told me about the walnuts, how for centuries they symbolised the power of women in Baztán, how this power could be concentrated inside a tiny walnut in the form of a desire, and that she knew how to use it . . . Silly adolescent fantasies, you know how we like to feel special at that age, but she believed it, Amaia, and when I was with her, so did I. She told me that this power doesn't end when you die, and I like to think that Anne's energy is somehow concentrated in those walnuts. They are all that unites us now, the only offering I can make to keep her soul alive.'

'And yet you're so terrified of what might be in her soul that you can't even touch the walnut?'

Flora didn't reply.

Amaia sighed as she contemplated her sister. Flora was cunning. She had opened up, probably more than at any other time in her life, and yet Amaia was convinced she had tried to slip a few lies past her. She would have to use her own cunning to identify them.

'What about that elaborate charade you and Ros performed at Aunt Engrasi's, about the bakery?'

'That was no charade. Things are exactly as we told you. Of course, Ros and I haven't resolved all our differences, but we're trying.'

Amaia looked at her sceptically. Ros and Flora had never agreed about anything in their entire lives, and the idea that they would do so overnight, just when the swords had been drawn didn't ring true. Although she couldn't prove anything, it had her wondering.

She left Flora's house and, without looking at her watch, walked up the hill to the police station. As she approached, she saw that the main gate was closed. She opened it with her security card and greeted the two officers on duty. She headed for the second floor, to where they kept the files containing information on the *basajaun* case. She devoted the next few hours to arranging on the board photographs of the crime scenes, the three victims, the autopsies they had filed away a year ago hoping never to have to revisit them. Ainhoa Elizasu, Carla Huarte and Anne Arbizu stared back at her once more. She sat down facing them, studying Ainhoa's shy expression as she looked into the camera, Carla's provocative pose, and Anne's intense, powerful gaze. She remembered their dead bodies, stretched out on San Martín's steel slab, the statements of their parents and friends, the profile of the killer they had elaborated in that very room:

*He slashes their clothes and exposes their bodies, which have not yet matured into the women they aspire to be. And he removes their pubic hair – a sign of sexual maturity – from a place which symbolises their sexuality, as well as the violation of his ideal childhood, and he substitutes it for a pastry that symbolises the past, the traditions of the valley, a return to childhood . . . The killer feels justified, sure of himself, he has a mission to fulfil, and he will continue recruiting young girls, restoring them to innocence.*

The words of the hidden witness in the Opus Dei house flashed into her mind: 'The ideal age for an offering is between birth and two years, when the soul is still in transition. After that, a child of any age will do, until adolescence when another transition occurs, which makes them desirable to these forces. But it's easier to justify the death of a two-year-old baby than a teenage girl.'

The perpetrator of those crimes, which even the press had described as ritualistic, had suffocated his victims, robbing them of air with a fine piece of cord, acting with such expertise and efficiency that he barely left a mark on their bodies, which he then carried over his shoulder to the banks of the River Baztán. There he proceeded to tear open their clothes, leaving their young bodies exposed to the moisture from the river; afterwards he shaved their pubis, combed and parted their hair, arranging it in tresses on either side of their head, placed their hands upturned in an attitude of surrender like virgins, like offerings, in a purification ceremony, a return to childhood, little girls once more, chaste once more, offerings once more. She looked up their places of birth, although she remembered perfectly. Ainhoa was from Arizkun, Carla and Anne from Elizondo. She stood up, captivated by Anne Arbizu's gaze, still fascinated by her power more than a year after her death. Disturbed, she avoided those penetrating eyes as she approached the board, tentatively placing three fresh dots on the map where the river traced its sinister course.

# 52

Early Mass at the Cathedral in Pamplona took place at seven thirty in the morning, and attendance was low. Amaia waited by the side door, the only one open at that time, until she saw Father Sarasola's chauffeur-driven car pull up outside. When she was sure the priest had seen her, she entered, making her way to one of the side altars, where she sat down in the back pew. A minute later, Father Sarasola joined her.

'I can see I'm not alone in knowing everything that goes on in Pamplona. I come here every morning, but if you wanted to speak to me, you could have called. I would have picked you up in my car . . .'

'Forgive me for turning up out of the blue, but there's something I need to talk to you about, urgently. Dr Berasategui's behaviour fascinates me as much as it does you and your colleagues at the Vatican; in fact, he probably has the most complex profile of anyone I've ever encountered. Quantico would pay good money to be able to analyse the behaviour of an instigator who commits murder by channelling other men's anger, who convinces them to take their cruelty to such extreme levels, and yet who is discriminating enough to select a particular type of victim. Until recently, profilers were so focused on the mind of the criminal that they scarcely noticed their victims, who were merely the end point of a series of actions. And yet, there's a reason why wolves attack sheep when they could just as well hunt rabbits, foxes or rats: they enjoy the taste of their flesh, their fear, their terrified bleating. All the *tarttalo*'s victims were women originally from Baztán, most of whom had left the valley, but there was a definite pattern. We know how Berasategui chose the men who would carry out the killings: as a psychiatrist, he dealt with every type of behavioural disorder. It was as easy as choosing from a menu at a restaurant. Given his expertise, we understand how he was able to manipulate those men. What we don't know is how he chose his victims. After his arrest, when I taunted him for having used such a bunch of losers to carry out his crimes, he told me he had never intended to shift the blame on to them, that they were merely actors performing his work. He saw himself as a kind of stage director. Prompting them to kill those women was Act One; Act Two was when he, the true author, collected his trophy by amputating their forearms. That also struck me as odd. I couldn't understand why a killer as meticulous as Berasategui would choose such a vulgar trophy, with all the problems that preserving it would entail. That is, until I understood the meaning of the cave where he collected them, and I realised they were offerings to the savage creature whose name he had taken.'

Sarasola listened, leaning in until his head was almost brushing her ear. She spoke in hushed tones, her voice barely more than a whisper:

'I now realise: he didn't choose those men, he chose the victims. Yesterday, someone drew my attention to a detail that had escaped me and I began to look again at his choice of victims. Women from Baztán, women who no longer lived in Baztán, women who were born there, who sometimes died many miles away, yet who ended up as offerings in a cave in the valley. Just as those teenage girls in the *basajaun* case ended up as offerings to the river.'

Sarasola sat up, startled.

'Stripped of all traces of adulthood, naked and shaved like little girls, barefoot, without any make-up, offerings to innocence, to tradition, robbed of air until they died.'

Raising his hand, Sarasola rubbed his eyes as though trying to erase the image.

'Víctor Oyarzabal was the son of a domineering mother. He started to drink at an early age in an attempt to control his murderous impulses. And for a while, he succeeded. I once asked him how he managed it, and he told me he had been in therapy. I mentioned the local AA group, but he said he preferred the anonymity of a group in Irún. I imagine I'll have no difficulty finding out who led that group, but why waste time if you are able to confirm my suspicions. Tell me, Father, did Dr Berasategui's files mention whether he treated a man named Víctor Oyarzabal, otherwise known as the *basajaun*?'

When Sarasola nodded in reply, she shook her head and leaned forward, elbows on her knees, burying her face in her hands.

'You weren't going to tell me!' she said, astonished.

Sarasola took a deep breath. 'Believe me when I tell you it's for the best.'

'The best for whom? Can't you see how monstrous this is?'

'Those men are dead; Berasategui is dead; you have the facts and you've closed the case without my help.'

'That's where you're wrong; this isn't over. While I was watching the CCTV footage at the clinic yesterday, I felt an overwhelming sense of frustration. At first I didn't know why, but then I realised that I always feel like that when I'm not satisfied with a result. Tell me something: if Berasategui was the instigator, then who made him take his own life? Because there's one thing I'm sure of: that wasn't his decision. When I interviewed him the morning he died, he sounded more like a man preparing to escape than someone about to kill himself. Who ordered him and Rosario to take their own lives? Your protected witness may be describing things that happened thirty years ago, but this sect is as alive now as it was then – and possibly even more powerful, better organised, know-ledgeable. Unlike the dark, sinister figures in Goya's paintings of witches, they're not easily identifiable as practitioners of ritual sacrifice – instead they enjoy the trappings of wealth and success, occupying positions of power and influence. Our society is riddled with them! So, stop hiding the truth, Dr Sarasola. You've read Berasategui's files, what made him choose those women?'

The priest crossed himself, bowing his head as he said a prayer. He was appealing for help. She waited patiently, eyes fixed on him.

At last Sarasola looked at her.

'Remember what the witness said: "No one leaves the sect, they always make you pay."'

'Are you saying that at some point those women belonged to the sect?'

'They, or their relatives or partners. What is clear is that they owed a debt. None of them were able to have children, except for Lucía Aguirre, but by then her daughters were too old. Those women could no longer be offered to Inguma – or produce offerings themselves – but they could be offered to a lesser god, greedy for flesh.'

'And the girls by the river?'

'Unfinished business.'

'So they used Víctor . . .'

'Víctor and others like him. You can't make someone a psychopath, but if you take their obsessions and channel them, you obtain a faithful servant. That's the way death cults operate. They identify the weaknesses in their followers, who usually share the same type of personality: they are obedient, not very bright, easily manipulated. The sect leaders begin by breaking them down, and then they recreate them at will. They are reborn within the sect, which loves, protects, respects and listens to them, it provides them with a place in the world where they feel important, possibly for the first time in their lives.'

'Damaged goods,' whispered Amaia.

'Damaged goods, invaluable to a cult leader who knows how to bend them to his will.'

She rose from the pew, leaning forward to take her leave of Sarasola.

'Pray for me, Father.'

'I always do.'

# 53

Amaia had been sitting in her car outside the Navarre Institute of Forensic Medicine for twenty minutes. It was still early, and the staff hadn't started to arrive yet. Propped against the steering wheel, she had leaned her head forward to take a brief rest. Three gentle taps on the glass interrupted her reverie. She saw Dr San Martín and lowered the window.

'Salazar, what brings you here?'

'I don't know,' she replied.

She accepted a coffee out of the machine, which San Martín insisted was his treat, and followed him to his office, holding the paper cup by the rim to avoid scalding herself.

'Are you sure you don't want to see her?'

'No, but I do have a few questions.'

San Martín shrugged, motioning with a gesture for her to continue.

'I want to know about her physical condition. I think that may give us some idea as to where she spent this past month.'

'All right, well, she was hydrated, organ perfusion was good, circulation to the limbs normal, her skin was in good condition, she presented no wounds, cuts or abrasions that might indicate exposure to inclement weather. I would rule out the possibility that she fell in the river. We have her clothes, which, although bloodstained, were appropriate to the weather and of good quality. She was wearing flat shoes, no watch, bracelets or rings, no ID. Overall, she seemed in good shape and well nourished.'

'Anything else?'

He shrugged.

'You ought to see her. This woman has dogged you for so long that she's become unreal to you, like a bad dream. You need to make her real.'

'I've seen the CCTV footage at the clinic.'

'It's not the same, Amaia. Your mother is lying dead in a refrigerated drawer, don't let her turn into a phantom.'

The morgue was located in an annexe right next to the autopsy room. San Martín switched on the lights and went over to the first drawer of the bottom tier. As he pulled the handle a trolley slid out upon which the body lay. He glanced at Amaia, who stood silently beside him. Seizing the sheet by the corners, he uncovered the corpse.

An enormous, dark seam in the customary Y incision ran from the shoulders to the pelvis. Another dark line travelled from the left ear downwards at a slight angle. Although the gash wasn't terribly deep, in the centre she glimpsed the pinkish presence of the trachea. The right hand, which had wielded the knife, was caked with blood, but the nails on her other hand appeared manicured. Her hair was noticeably shorter than on the day of her escape from the clinic with Berasategui, and her face, twisted at the moment of death, was completely relaxed now, limp, like a rubber mask discarded after a carnival.

San Martín was right. This was no demon; merely the corpse of a worn out old woman. She wished again that she could experience the feeling of liberation she so desperately needed, a sense of relief, that it was all over. But instead, a series of images invaded her thoughts, memories that weren't hers because she had never experienced them: memories of her mother giving her a cuddle, calling her 'darling', of birthdays with cakes and smiles, memories of loving hands bestowing caresses she had never received, but which by virtue of dreaming about them, imagining them, had become true experiences, cherished memories. San Martín's hand on her shoulder sufficed. She turned towards him and wept like a child.

Ibai hadn't been sleeping well since they arrived in the States, and every night he would wake up crying. James assumed this was due to the upheaval of the journey, together with the time difference and the change of habits. He took Ibai in his arms, cradled him, sang silly made-up songs, until the boy finally gave in and flopped on his father's shoulder, eyes closed. James put him down in the cot Clarice had bought, which he had succeeded in moving into his bedroom, not without some opposition from his mother. He remained for a while, watching Ibai. His face, usually so relaxed, reflected the disquiet that spread to his limbs, making his body give little jolts as it slipped willingly into oblivion.

'You miss your mama, don't you,' he whispered to the slumbering baby, who sighed, as if he had understood. Ibai's melancholy tugged at James's heartstrings. With a worried look, he picked up his mobile from the bedside table, checking for the umpteenth time his text messages and emails but finding none from her. He looked at the time, two o'clock in the morning, eight o'clock in Baztán. Amaia would be up and about. He placed his finger on the call button. As he pressed it, he felt his heart leaping in his chest, reminding him of how he had felt the first few times he spoke to her in the early days after they met. The ring tone reached him clearly, and he imagined her phone buzzing like a dying insect on her bedside table, or at the bottom of her bag. He listened until it went to voicemail. Then he ended the call, looked again at his sleeping son, his eyes welling up as he thought about how silences, unspoken words and unanswered calls can contain such a clear message.

*

Amaia took the stairs, checking the time on her phone. She saw the missed call from James, presumably from when she was in the cathedral with Sarasola. She deleted it, promising to herself that she would call him at the first opportunity. She glanced sideways at the coffee machine, acknowledging that the lack of sleep must be catching up with her, as she felt tempted by the ridiculous paper cups. She entered the meeting room to find her colleagues contemplating the whiteboard, aghast.

'What's this supposed to mean?' asked Iriarte, the moment she walked in.

She sensed his hostility, as did Montes and Zabalza, who turned towards her uneasily.

'Good morning, gentlemen,' she said, stopping dead in her tracks.

She casually deposited her bag and coat on a chair, waiting for them to return her greeting. When there was no response, she approached the board and stood face to face with Inspector Iriarte.

'I assume you're referring to the inclusion of the *basajaun* and *tarttalo* murders in the latest victim count.'

'No, I'm referring to you taking two closed cases and linking them to the current one.'

'Technically, yes, the deaths of Víctor Oyarzabal and Dr Berasategui brought both investigations to an abrupt halt. But there's a world of difference between that and saying the cases are closed.'

'I disagree. Those men were the sole perpetrators of their crimes, and the other people involved are dead.'

'Perhaps not all of them . . .'

'Inspector, I've no idea where you are going with this, but to establish a connection between those two cases and this one, you'll need something concrete.'

449

'And I have it. Father Sarasola has confirmed that Víctor Oyarzabal was Berasategui's patient; he gave him anger-management therapy, just like all the other killers involved in his crimes.'

Montes gave a long, meaningful whistle, which earned him a reproving look from both of them. Iriarte turned towards the images of the girls.

'Sarasola – a perfect witness, because he'll deny everything he has said before Judge Markina, which means we have nothing.'

'Inspector, I have no intention of taking this to Markina. And you can't deny that this information is vital to the investigation.'

'I disagree,' he said, digging his heels in. 'Those cases are closed, the culprits are dead. I don't understand why you insist on turning a case of grave robbery into a mystery of epic proportions. Stealing corpses is a simple offence against public health.'

'Is that what you think this is? Grave robbery? Have you forgotten the suffering it has caused the mothers, the families . . .?'

Iriarte lowered his eyes, offering no reply.

'. . . Apparently, you've also forgotten that Deputy Inspector Etxaide was working on this when he was murdered. Or are you going to tell me that your by the book attitude also means you've accepted Inspector Clemos's version of events?'

Iriarte shot an angry look at her. His face had turned bright red, as if he were about to have a stroke.

He stormed out of the room, slamming the door behind him.

'Come on, let's go,' she said. 'They're waiting for us at Igantzi. Something tells me that Inspector Iriarte won't be joining us today.'

# 54

A luxury four-by-four rolled up behind the police car parked outside the cemetery gates. A steep flight of steps led to a narrow path bordered by thick bushes, at the end of which was a tiny shrine. Two men and a woman stood beneath its scant eaves, huddled under umbrellas. Amaia signalled to Montes to go on ahead, while she returned to the parked vehicle.

Yolanda Berrueta lowered the window.

'Yolanda? I didn't know they'd sent you home.'

'I discharged myself. I feel much better; staying in hospital wasn't doing me any good. I'll return as an out-patient to have my dressings changed,' she said, raising her bandaged arm, which, although less swollen, still looked very cumbersome.

'What are you doing here?'

Yolanda looked over at the cemetery.

'You know perfectly well what I'm doing.'

'Yolanda, you mustn't be here; you should be in hospital, or resting at home. Fortunately for you, the magistrate accepted a bail bond – he could have kept you in prison for what you did, but don't push your luck.' She pointed at the bandages: 'In fact, you shouldn't be driving in your condition.'

'I'm no longer on medication.'

'I don't just mean the medication. Driving one-handed, and with one eye . . .'

'Are you going to arrest me?'

'I probably should, for your own good. Go home, Yolanda.'

'No,' she said resolutely. 'You can't stop me from being here.'

Amaia sighed, shaking her head.

'Okay, but I want you to call your father and tell him to come and pick you up. If I see you driving, I'll arrest you.'

Yolanda gave a nod and raised the window.

The gravediggers stood in a circle around the slab, which they proceeded to raise.

As previously instructed, the woman told one of them:

'Would you please go down to make sure no water has got into the tomb?'

Helped by one of his colleagues, the man lowered the ladder and climbed down. When he reached the bottom, the woman spoke to him again:

'From up here, it looks as if my daughter's coffin has been moved since the funeral. Could you make sure everything is in order?'

The man shone his torch at the seal as he ran his hand over it.

'This looks to me like it's been tampered with. The lid is open,' he added, raising it to reveal the empty coffin.

Amaia turned to the woman, who was leaning inside the tomb; her black umbrella lowered, partially eclipsing her face. She raised her eyes, and said dolefully:

'You may not believe me, but I knew it all along. A mother's instinct.'

Yolanda Berrueta, who was standing at a discreet distance, murmured in agreement.

*

Amaia didn't return to the police station. The last thing she wanted was another confrontation with Iriarte. Besides, she was too tired to think straight.

Montes had gone to bring the woman's ex-husband in for questioning. At midday, just as she was pulling up in front of her aunt's house, he called to tell her that, by strange co-incidence, the husband had gone away only yesterday, after his cousin, who worked for the council, tipped him off about the scheduled repairs to the family tomb.

As always when she arrived feeling particularly exhausted, the house received her in its protective embrace, with its pleasant aroma of furniture wax, which her brain interpreted as the warmest of welcomes. She refused Engrasi's offer of food, despite her aunt's insistence that she should eat something hot. Leaving her boots at the bottom of the stairs and pulling off her thick jumper, she went up, sensing the warmth of the wood beneath her stockinged feet. As soon as she entered the bedroom, she slumped on to the bed, covering herself with the duvet. Despite her fatigue, or perhaps because of it, after two hours' rest she was left with the bittersweet sensation of broken sleep, during which her brain had remained in a state of high alert. She remembered going over facts, faces, names, virtually the whole of her conversation with Sarasola, as well as the protected witness's statement, and her quarrel with Iriarte. She opened her eyes, tired, and bored of her own efforts to think about something else. Even so, she was surprised when she looked at the clock. She would have sworn that she'd been lying there for no more than ten minutes.

She took a shower, got dressed, and spent a few minutes trying to get through to a nurse who confirmed that Dr Takchenko's condition was stable. After a glance at her reflection in the glass, she went downstairs to appease Engrasi by eating something. Then she took to the road again.

Parking in Irún at that time of day was impossible. The streets were overrun with parents collecting their kids from school, people leaving work or doing the afternoon shopping. After driving round in circles for a while, they decided to leave the car in an underground car park.

Marina Lujambio and her father had arranged to meet them at a café. Montes made the introductions and, once everyone had a cup of coffee in front of them, Amaia explained the situation. She mentioned Berasategui and his relationship to the bereavement therapy group. Sparing no details when describing his cruelty, the power he had over others, his ability to manipulate his patients, she avoided mentioning the sacrifices in Elizondo and Lesaka, and the theory that this might be the work of a sect. She told them the Esparza story, from Valentín Esparza's attempt to make off with his daughter's body, to the sacking of the family tomb in Elizondo, as well as that morning's events in Igantzi. She revealed that these cases all involved baby girls who had allegedly died of Sudden Infant Death Syndrome, and mentioned the relationship between the dead girls' parents and the lawyer couple from Pamplona, as well as the therapy group at Argi Beltz to which the woman's ex-husband had belonged. The woman, aged around forty, said little. Her father, who was in his mid sixties, wore a smart suit and had a beard like a Canadian lumberjack, listened impassively. However, when Amaia had finished talking, he surprised her with his forthright response.

'Your colleague will have informed you that I'm a Justice of the Peace here in Irún. Obviously, it would be improper for me to authorise the opening of my own family tomb. But, as your colleague pointed out, and the council has confirmed, we have the right to carry out repairs on the internal structure, or to replace the slab, providing this is done after eight o'clock in the evening when the cemetery closes. There are certain stipulations: for example, the grave-digger is prohibited from opening a coffin unless it has clearly been tampered with. If my granddaughter's body isn't in the tomb, I can assure you that you'll have no difficulty obtaining an order from a magistrate here in Irún to open that other family's tomb.'

'Thank you, your honour, but that won't be necessary. This case is with a magistrate in Pamplona, and I shall be informing him shortly of your willingness to proceed. If things turn out the way you've described, he will forward us the necessary paperwork.'

Satisfied with this response, Judge Lujambio extended his hand.

'Until tomorrow evening at eight, then.'

The coastal light she loved so much had vanished by the time they arrived in Hondarribia. The evening was tranquil and warm, a foretaste of the long-awaited spring, which seemed already to have made an appearance in that beautiful region. She parked next to the cemetery where they would be opening the tomb the next day, and followed Montes and Zabalza inside. A few visitors still lingered, encouraged perhaps by the mild weather. She inhaled the warm sea breeze, mixed with the scent of fresh-cut flowers on the graves. The Lujambio family tomb was a simple, grey marble stone, laid flat on the ground, illuminated by the wrought-iron streetlamps. Amaia went over to examine the portraits set in the slab, showing the faces of the people resting inside. Most seemed to date from the sixties, the custom having fallen into disuse. On the adjacent path stood the tomb of the López family, who had refused to cooperate. Instead of flowers, two well-tended pots stood on the grave. They retraced their steps, towards the entrance, pausing close to the tomb they had gone there to visit. She recognised it from the photograph Iriarte had sent to her mobile: it stood at an angle to the other graves in the cemetery, set apart by four granite posts with a heavy chain suspended between them. It made her think of Mormon graves. At the head stood a memorial stone, with the traditional rounded shape, and below that, covering the original name on the tomb, a plaque bearing a single word: *Tabese*. She was unable to see if any other names were inscribed on the raised slab, which was buried beneath a carpet of huge white flowers. A lowish wall ran behind the tomb. They went round to inspect the back. The area was reserved for cemetery staff. Propped against the wall were two rolls of blue tarpaulin, like the one used to cover the Tremond-Berrueta tomb in Ainhoa, a thick piece of rope coiled into what looked like a sailor's knot, and a rusty wheelbarrow. Next to the far wall they saw a garden tap above an open drain. On a makeshift table covered in a wire mesh lay some soggy remains. This was the method used to separate bones from soft tissue when graves were emptied after the lease had expired. The bones were then tossed into a pit.

'Fuck, it's disgusting!' exclaimed Montes, wrinkling his nose.

Amaia continued along the wall until she found the back of Tabese's tomb, and the three steps leading down to the crypt. At the bottom stood a heavy wooden door, so low it would require anyone entering to stoop. She cursed herself for having left her torch in the car. Taking out her mobile, she switched on the flashlight app, which gave off sufficient light for her to see by. The door was weathered, making it impossible to see the type of wood, but if it was anywhere near as old as the lock, then it must have been ancient. Leaning forward, she wondered how a coffin could possibly fit through that tiny space. She noticed a pile of leaves by the wall, at right angles to the door. Lowering her mobile to the floor she saw a clear circle left by the door as it opened on the sandstone floor. Then she examined the hinges, covered in grime, except where the two leaves joined; there the light from her phone clearly detected a glint of clean metal.

'Tabese was supposed to have died fifteen years ago,' said Montes, assessing her discovery. 'And according to the cemetery register we saw yesterday, he is the only occupant.'

'Well, someone has been in there recently.'

Amaia stood on tiptoes to look over the wall, and was dazzled by a camera flash. As she walked back around the wall, she saw another flash in the distance, and heard Zabalza intercepting someone. She had an idea who it might be, but was still astonished to discover Yolanda talking to the Deputy Inspector.

'For heaven's sake, Yolanda, what are you doing here? What did I say to you this morning?'

'I came in a taxi,' Yolanda replied.

'Yes, but why are you here?'

Yolanda pursed her lips defiantly.

'That's enough, Yolanda. I've been very patient with you, but it's time you went home. I'm warning you, if I find you here again tomorrow, I'll arrest you for obstructing an investigation.'

Undeterred, Yolanda stepped forward and took another picture, her camera flash illuminating the entire cemetery.

Amaia turned to her colleagues with a look of incredulity at the woman's stubbornness.

'Come here, Inspector,' Yolanda called out.

Amaia went over to her.

'Have you noticed those flowers?' she said. Resting the camera on her bandaged arm she showed Amaia an enlarged image on the screen. 'Strange, don't you think? They look like tiny babies asleep in their cradles.'

Amaia frowned at the grotesque comparison, and yet, as she studied the image of the flower, she found herself mesmerised by its beauty. The ivory-coloured petal was furled around the pink centre, which bore an uncanny resemblance to a miniature baby with outstretched arms. Yolanda handed her the camera and, stepping over the lowest part of the chain, she leaned over the tomb and plucked one of the extraordinary flowers from its stem.

Amaia went to her aid as she stepped back over the chain

457

but Yolanda shrugged her off, putting away the camera before stalking off towards the gates without saying a word.

'Remember what I told you, Yolanda.' The woman raised a hand without turning around and left the cemetery.

'Mad as a box of frogs!' declared Fermín, shaking his head.

'Do you have the number of the florist who brings the orchids?' asked Amaia.

An assistant answered the phone, and after listening to her question, passed the receiver to the owner.

'Yes, Señor Tabese must have been a man of exquisite taste. As I told your colleague, we specialise in orchids. I grow some myself, but we import the rarer varieties from a man in Colombia, who grows the finest, most unusual orchids in the world. This particular orchid is called *Anguloa uniflora*, and, yes, it looks just like a little baby in its cradle. There's one that resembles a beautiful ballerina, and another with a little monkey face in the middle, and still another shaped like a magnificent heron in flight, so perfect you'd think it was hand-crafted. But *Anguloa uniflora* is the most astonishing of all. I read that in some parts of Colombia it was considered unlucky; if a woman received one while she was pregnant, it was a sure sign that her baby would die.'

Realising that by his own admission he could talk for hours about the fascinating world of orchids, Amaia interrupted the florist's soliloquy, thanked him, and hung up.

She followed Montes's car towards Elizondo, still chuckling to herself about the absurd discussion, only half in jest, which he and Zabalza had engaged in outside the cemetery, about which of them was the better driver. She honked her horn by way of a goodbye, as they took the turning to Elizondo. Then the screen on her mobile lit up on the dashboard, signalling a call from an unknown number.

'Good evening, my name is Professor Santos. Dr Gonzalez asked me to analyse a fabric sample for you.'

'Ah, yes, thank you, I'm most grateful.'

'We three go back a long way, and they know I take great pleasure in my work. I have some news for you about the sample. The cloth is silk satin, very fine quality, a strong fabric, which the weaver achieves by blending silk thread with other fibres to produce a perfectly smooth appearance. My immediate thought was that this might be raw silk imported from India, woven here in Europe, and I wasn't mistaken. My task was made a lot easier because the cloth bears a signature. Because it is resilient, clothiers often use it to make ties, waistcoats and other high-quality garments.'

'You said it has a signature?'

'Yes, a manufacturer will occasionally introduce tiny variations in the weave to produce a signature; but in this case the client has requested a sort of stamp, an emblem, which is visible to the naked eye. Despite having been subjected to intense heat, it has yielded some interesting information. The cloth comes from a bespoke tailor in London; naturally, I am unable to access their client list, but I imagine you will find that easier.'

'You said that the sample has been exposed to high temperatures?'

'There's no evidence of direct exposure to flames, but, yes, it has been close to a powerful source of heat.'

'And the initials on the fabric?'

'Oh, they aren't initials. Did I give you that impression? It's a coat of arms. This tailor is famous for having dressed gentlemen and aristocrats dating back to the time of Henry VIII.'

# 55

Mentally, she had gone over what she was going to say, how she would explain the progress she had made, and her urgent need for his help. And yet as she stood outside Markina's front door, she was assailed with doubts about the effect her words might have. Things had been strained between them those past few days, and the unanswered calls had been accumulating on her mobile. The conversation wasn't going to be easy.

Markina opened the door and paused for a moment, surprised. Then he smiled at her. Without saying a word, he placed his hand round the nape of her neck and drew her to his mouth.

All the explanations she had rehearsed, hoping to convince him, melted away, as he held her in an almost frenzied embrace, his warm, moist lips on hers.

He cupped her face in his hands, holding her out at arm's length so that he could look at her.

'Don't ever do that again, I've been going crazy waiting for you to come back, to call, for some news of you,' he said, kissing her again. 'Don't ever leave me like that again.'

She pulled away, smiling at her own weakness, at how such a simple action felt so difficult.

'We need to talk.'

'Later,' he said, embracing her once more.

She closed her eyes, surrendering to his kisses, to the urgency of his touch, aware of how intensely she desired him, the way nothing else mattered when she was in his arms. He still had on the grey suit he wore to the courthouse, and his briefcase and coat discarded on a chair suggested he had just got home. While they kissed, she slipped his jacket over his shoulders, feeling for his shirt buttons, which she undid, planting a string of tiny kisses along the line of stubble on his chin.

She was aware of the distant ring of her telephone, a million light years away from where she found herself at that instant. Tempted to ignore it until the ringing stopped, she stifled the voice in her head urging her to carry on, and pulled away at the last moment, to hurriedly answer the call.

James's voice reached her as clearly as if he were standing beside her.

'Hi, Amaia.'

She felt as if all the air had been sucked out of the room. Overwhelmed by a sense of remorse and shame, she instinctively turned away, straightening her clothes as if she were on view.

'James. What's wrong?' she blurted.

'You tell me, Amaia. I've been trying to get hold of you for days, but you don't pick up. Your aunt told me about Rosario.'

She closed her eyes.

'I can't talk right now, I'm at work,' she said, hating herself for lying to him.

'Are you coming?'

'Not yet—'

The call ended abruptly; James had hung up on her, but instead of feeling relief she had a sense of utter despair.

Markina had retreated to the kitchen area and was pouring two glasses of wine. He handed one to her.

'What did you want to talk to me about?' he said,

pretending he hadn't overheard the conversation, and ignoring her unease. 'If it's about your visit to my mother, then it's all forgotten; I should have known that the detective in you would be curious . . . I looked into you and your family when I met you . . .'

'This is about your father.' His expression clouded over. 'You asked me to bring you facts, solid evidence. You forced me to use subterfuge to be able to move the investigation forward, to meet your demands. This morning we opened a tomb in Igantzi.'

'Without authorisation?'

'As the owner of the plot, the little girl's mother is permitted to do so in order to carry out repairs. The girl's body is missing; all indications are that it was taken soon after she died. The father is abroad on a business trip, so we haven't been able to question him.' Markina was listening intently, his expression an amalgam of interest and scepticism. 'Tomorrow evening we're opening up another tomb in Hondarribia. In this case, the girl's mother, who has been divorced from her husband for years, is the daughter of a justice of the peace in Irún. We have his full cooperation. We have established that the fathers of both the girl from Igantzi and the girl from Hondarribia have links through their businesses to the law firm Lejarreta & Andía, as well as to Berasategui's bereavement group. We're currently investigating a similar case in the same village, as well as two others in the Navarre region. If, as we expect, tomorrow evening we find that the girl's body is missing, that makes three cases of desecration and body-snatching, all with links to the same group. Considering the crimes for which Berasategui was arrested, I believe that the logical next step is to open an official investigation.' Markina said nothing. He looked serious, as he always did when he was thinking. 'If this investigation goes ahead, your father's name is bound to come out.'

'If you've done your research, you'll know that he abandoned my mother when she went mad. Before leaving, he set up a trust fund to cover my upbringing and education. I never saw him again.'

'Did you not try to find him? Weren't you interested in what he was doing?'

'I could imagine: living the life of the millionaire playboy he was, travelling, sailing the yacht in which he would finally drown . . . I heard nothing from him until I was informed of his death. My parents' marriage was no bed of roses; I would hear them quarrelling about his infidelity.'

She emptied her lungs, then took a deep breath:

'According to our inquiries, in the seventies and early eighties while running an exclusive clinic in las Rozas, Dr Xabier Markina was also the leader of a sect with branches in Lesaka and Baztán, a sort of guru who initiated his followers into occult practices. We have a person in custody who has positively identified your father, and has confessed that he witnessed and took part in a human sacrifice performed on a newborn baby girl at a farmhouse in Lesaka. He also confirmed that they occasionally visited the group at Argi Beltz, in Baztán, who were preparing to carry out a similar sacrifice. The witness identified my mother as one of the members of that group. The daughter of two of the founding members, the Martínez-Bayóns, the present owners of Argi Beltz, died aged fourteen months, allegedly during a trip to the UK – a trip the girl never made. There is no record there of her death, nor of her burial, and no autopsy report. Nor did her name appear on either of her parent's passports, which would have been the norm at the time.

'Berasategui's father has confessed to me that he and his wife gave up their baby girl in the same way, and that his wife's subsequent depression was a direct result of that. Unable to accept what she'd done, she felt incapable of loving her new baby boy. I don't know to what extent people are born

463

psychopaths, or how much of it is down to lack of love and rejection,' she said. She omitted to mention her suspicion that Sara Durán had been driven mad by guilt rather than grief. 'I have a second witness who can confirm the link between Berasategui and other members of the group, their frequent visits to the house, as well as the photographs Yolanda Berrueta took of their cars parked outside Argi Beltz.'

Markina lowered his gaze, without saying anything.

'There's one other witness,' Amaia went on. 'He won't testify, and he enjoys diplomatic immunity so we can't force him. However, he had access to sensitive information, no longer available, which established that Víctor Oyarzabal, otherwise known as the *basajaun* killer, belonged to one of Dr Berasategui's anger-management groups, from which he recruited patients whom he instigated to murder their own wives, all born in Baztán. I have sworn not to reveal his name, although I could probably persuade him at least to confirm what I'm saying to you.'

He wasn't even looking at her.

'You've certainly done your homework,' he whispered.

'I'm just doing my job.'

'And what do you want me to do now?' he said defiantly.

'That's for you to decide. I'm a detective, these are facts, I didn't make them up,' she replied. 'Wasn't this what you wanted? I promised you I wouldn't go over your head again, and I haven't.'

He sighed as he rose from his seat.

'You're right,' he said, walking over to her. 'I never expected my career to end like this; I was the youngest magistrate to join the judiciary, and now this thing I've been fleeing my whole life is going to destroy me.'

'I don't see why; you aren't responsible for the actions of your parents.'

'What future do you think there can be a magistrate whose mother is in a lunatic asylum and whose father was the leader

464

of a satanic cult . . . Whether it's proven or not, the mere association will ruin me.'

She gazed wistfully at him, as her phone, which she was still holding, started to ring again.

'Inspector, this is Yolanda's father speaking. I'm worried about her. When she came home this evening, she started printing off pictures of flowers and she wasn't making much sense. You know she's stopped taking her medication. She didn't want dinner, and has just taken off in my car . . . I couldn't stop her, and I've no idea where she's gone.'

'I think I know. Don't worry, I'll find her and bring her home.'

'Inspector . . .'

'Yes?'

'When the police came to ask whether any more explosives were missing apart from the two hundred grams Yolanda used to blow up the tomb . . . Well, I think she may have taken a bit more – I didn't want to get her into trouble.'

'I have to go,' she said to Markina. 'Something's come up,' she added, grabbing the bag and coat she had left on the chair, next to Markina's things. The navy blue overcoat he had draped over the back slipped on to the floor. She stooped to retrieve it, and as she picked it up she felt the silky texture of the lining; she folded it neatly inside out so that she could see the faint stamp on the fabric, repeated at intervals of a few centimetres, the signature of the tailor, whose name appeared in bright colours on a label stitched on the inside pocket. She replaced the coat on the chair, letting her fingers slide over the perfectly smooth fabric.

'Do you want me to go with you?' His voice rang out behind her.

She wheeled round, startled, as she saw him slip on the grey jacket she herself had just taken off him.

'No, best not, this is more of a domestic situation.'

Overwhelmed by a rising tide of doubt threatening to engulf her, she made her way towards the door.

'Will you come back here afterwards?' asked Markina.

'I've no idea how long this is going to take,' she replied.

'I'll wait for you,' he said, smiling in that way of his.

She climbed into the car, a million and one thoughts churning in her head. Her hands were shaking slightly as she fumbled for the ignition, and she dropped the key on the floor. Retrieving it from between her feet, she sat up, only to see Markina staring at her through the driver's window.

Startled, she stifled a yell, placed the key in the ignition and lowered the window.

'You made me jump!' she said, trying to smile.

'You left without giving me a kiss,' he said.

She smiled, leaning sideways, and kissed him through the open window.

'Are you going to drive with your coat on?' he said, looking straight at her. 'I thought you always took it off when you drove.'

Amaia stepped out of the car, letting him help her off with her coat, which she placed on the passenger seat. Markina held her in a firm embrace.

'Amaia, I love you. I couldn't bear to lose you.'

She smiled once more as she got back in the car, turned on the engine and waited for him to push the door shut.

In the rear-view mirror, she could see him standing, watching her drive away.

# 56

Oh, Jonan, how desperately she needed him. Her colleague had become the precision instrument of her thinking. Without him, the facts danced about chaotically in her head. She had grown accustomed to the exchange of ideas between them, his many suggestions and observations, and his barely contained silences, as he waited for her to emerge from her musings so that he could speak. She sighed, missing his presence in a way she knew would never leave her. She divided her attention between the motorway, darkening beneath the increasingly stormy skies, her impulse to chase after that crazy woman who she feared would succeed in blowing herself up, and her need to slow down, to put the world on pause, in order to think, re-evaluate, sort out the chaos in her head. A lightning flash illuminated the peaks where the storm goddess dwelt. *She is coming.*

A tailor's signature stamp wasn't absolute proof of guilt; on the other hand, how many men in the entire country wore tailor-made clothes from London . . . As Professor Santos had pointed out, with a warrant they would be able to see the client list of the exclusive tailor. The lining, like the coat itself, was navy blue, and yet she clearly remembered having seen him wearing a matching grey overcoat with that grey suit. In fact, this combination of the grey suit and the blue overcoat had struck her as odd the last time she saw him. Had it been anyone else, she wouldn't have thought twice about it. She looked at her call register and pressed dial.

'Professor Santos? This is Inspector Salazar, I'm sorry to bother you again.'

'Don't mention it, what can I do for you?'

'I just had a thought. Could the heat damage to the fabric have been caused by a bullet being fired through it?'

'The same thing occurred to me,' replied the professor hesitantly, 'but the sample is too small to survive such a test . . .'

'That doesn't matter, we have another sample. How long would it take you to run the test?'

A succession of lightning bolts cleaved the sky, illuminating the night for a few seconds afterwards, leaving a dark imprint on her retinas that was slow to fade.

'I'll need to run a Walker test to see if there's any gunshot residue. I have the necessary equipment, but due to the size of the sample, the process of fixing and steam-ironing it will be tricky . . . I estimate it'll take about twenty minutes.'

'You've no idea how grateful I am. Let me know the minute you have the result. I'll wait for your call.' She hung up then dialled another number.

'Good evening, boss, still working?'

'Yes, as are you, Fermín. I need you to find out as quickly as possible which courthouse the weapon that killed Deputy Inspector Etxaide was taken from. Get Zabalza to help you if necessary, he may find it easier to access the information.'

The rain started to fall deafeningly on the roof of the car, and as a thunderclap shook the air, the call was cut off.

They had found a single bullet casing in Jonan's apartment, although two shots had been fired. In her mind's eye, Amaia saw Dr Hernández's diagram on which she had marked the fatal wounds, tracing the trajectory of the two bullets that could have been fired from a sitting position – a theory she had later ruled out. Now another possibility occurred to Amaia: that Jonan's killer had been facing him, and had shot him with a weapon concealed inside his pocket, or under his coat. That would explain the bullet's upward trajectory, as well as how such a small strand of fabric had flown through the air, literally propelled by the force of the explosion, held aloft by its own buoyancy, until it became enmeshed in the coarser fibres of the curtain, which, being of a similar colour, concealed its presence.

Tears pricked her eyes as she thought of Jonan, her mind returning to the moment of his death. She pictured him opening the door, overcoming his initial surprise, smiling the way he always did, inviting his killer inside . . . She felt her heart implode with anguish, reverting to the scared little girl who lived inside her mind, praying to the god of all victims, eyes shut tight. She bit her lower lip so hard that she noticed the metallic taste of blood. A flash illuminated the night sky and the roar of thunder reached her like a living creature pursuing her across the valley. *'The Lady is coming . . . She is coming.*

She recognised the four-by-four belonging to Yolanda's father parked outside the cemetery; her phone rang as she came to a stop behind it.

'Hello, Professor.'

'The test reveals a definite red stain resulting from the blast, which is consistent with gunshot residue.'

Amaia made sure she had her torch before getting out of the car and heading for the cemetery gate, which she saw was locked. She pulled up the hood of her coat, as the storm released its deluge of freezing rain. She imagined she heard a muffled blast, not much louder than a firecracker but which set the dogs guarding the allotments barking. It was instantly drowned out by the noise of thunder over Mount Jaizkibel.

She found a stone close to the wall and managed to heave herself up and over. The streetlamps that had illuminated the cemetery earlier had been turned off, plunging it into complete darkness. From behind the wall at the back of Tabese's tomb, a lone light shone out.

# 57

Inspector Iriarte was extremely agitated. He waited for the signal to turn out the lights then stood propped against the wall next to the light switch, listening to his family sing happy birthday around the lighted candles of his mother-in-law's birthday cake. He detested confrontations, but falling out with a colleague was his worst nightmare. He normally went out of his way to avoid arguments, but there were times, like that morning, when it proved impossible.

His quarrel with Salazar had left a bad taste in his mouth, and despite having finally said his piece, he couldn't help worrying that this might affect their future relationship. Salazar drove him nuts. Her unorthodox methods caused constant friction among her colleagues – a subject he had raised with her in the past, not that it had done any good. He was upset by her insinuation that being a stickler for the rules blinkered him. But what really fucked him off, fucked being the operative word, was her insinuation that he would be prepared to stand by and allow Deputy Inspector Etxaide to be crucified. The worst of it was that he too had been mulling over the question of Berasategui, and had reached the conclusion that closing the case on a man as complex as that was a risky move. Inspector Salazar's theory made sense, but how could they follow developments when he knew for a fact that she was refusing to share information?

His wife turned on the lights, frowning at him. She ushered him out into the hallway.

'Is something worrying you?'

He looked at her and smiled: she always knew exactly what was going on in his head.

'No,' he lied.

'I shouted out three times for you to turn the lights back on and you didn't even hear me. Anyway, you are worried, you can't fool me.'

'I'm sorry,' he said earnestly.

She glanced at her noisy relatives in the kitchen, and then at him.

'Go on, off with you!'

'But what will your mother say?'

'I'll take care of Mother,' she replied, standing on tiptoes to kiss him.

He had been sitting in front of the board taking notes for a while when Montes and Zabalza arrived.

'What are you two doing here at this time?' Iriarte asked, checking his watch.

Montes glanced at the board and the mound of papers spread out on the table.

'The boss asked us to check something urgently.'

'What is this about?'

'She wants to know which courthouse in Madrid the weapon used to kill Extaide went missing from.'

'I have that information, I was the one who told her about it. Why didn't she ask me!'

'Come on, Iriarte!'

'Come on, what?' he demanded, pushing back his seat, which almost fell over as he stood up. 'Or do you share her opinion that I'm prepared to put up with anything for a quiet life?'

Montes replied in a calm voice:

'This morning, you seemed to disagree with her decision to follow another line of investigation.'

'And what investigation might that be? The one you're working on now, about which I only know as much as she's willing to tell me?'

Montes didn't reply.

'Why does she want this information? What is she up to?'

With a flash of annoyance, Montes replied:

'I'm not sure . . . Jonan Extaide sent her some sort of message from beyond the grave, a timed email. It seems he had his own suspicions about where the case might be leading . . .'

'And of course the inspector kept that information to herself. Do you see what I mean?'

'Well, I wouldn't call it information; this was a private email containing a few clues, no evidence, just speculations. And possibly not even that . . .'

Iriarte looked at them, visibly angry. Then he sighed. 'It was court number one in Mostoles, Madrid. But I don't see what importance that could possibly have.'

'Judge Markina was assigned to that courthouse,' declared Zabalza. 'I read it the other day when I was looking into his father's professional background. They have the same surname, and his came up first.'

A uniformed police officer poked his head round the door.

'Boss, there's a guy on the phone who insists on speaking to you. He called earlier, and I told him you weren't here, but now that you are . . . He says he's Yolanda Berrueta's father.'

Benigno Berrueta quickly explained to Iriarte about his daughter, and how he had called Inspector Salazar. He'd heard nothing since and was getting extremely worried.

Iriarte hung up then dialled Salazar's number. It was engaged. He tried again. They heard the whip-crack of lightning striking nearby. Seconds later the emergency lighting came on and they had to evacuate the building.

'Not another fucking storm,' groaned Montes.

Iriarte hung up.

'Let's go,' he said, checking his gun as he headed for the door. Montes and Zabalza followed.

Amaia stood perfectly still for a few seconds, listening. Above the noise of the rain on the tombstone, she could hear the sound of wood being struck, and Yolanda's panting breaths. Darting behind the wall at the back of the tomb, she reached the entrance to the crypt, and saw the beam from Yolanda's torch swinging back and forth as she aimed kicks at the door.

'Yolanda,' she called out.

As Yolanda spun round, Amaia saw the look of determination in her eyes, her hair plastered to her brow beneath a rain hat. The blast had blown a hole in the door, damaging the lock, which had come loose, but was jammed between the door and the wall.

'Step away from the door, Yolanda.'

'I need to go inside; I think my daughter is in there. I didn't want to use too much explosive this time, but it wasn't enough. There's more in the car.'

Amaia went up behind her, and put a hand on her shoulder.

Yolanda swung round angrily, throwing a surprise punch that made Amaia stagger backwards. She reached for her gun.

'Yolanda!' she cried.

The woman looked at her, her expression turned to one of utter bewilderment, and then a shot rang out next to Amaia's ear, deafening her. Yolanda collapsed to the ground, a red stain spreading across her chest. Terrified, Amaia wheeled round, aiming her gun in the direction of the shot, until she saw Judge Markina's sombre face through the rain.

'What have you done?' she asked, scarcely able to hear herself speak; her right ear was ringing from the blast and everything sounded as if she were underwater. She leaned over Yolanda, and felt for a pulse, Markina still in her sights.

'I thought she was going to attack you,' he replied.

'That's a lie. You killed her, you killed her because what she said was true.'

Markina shook his head sorrowfully.

'Is this where they're buried?' she asked, standing up straight and looking towards the door of the crypt.

He didn't reply. Amaia took a few steps back, and started kicking at the lock, just as Yolanda had been doing a few minutes earlier.

'Don't do this, Amaia,' he implored, still brandishing his weapon.

She turned and threw him an angry look. Freezing rain lashed their faces.

'Are you going to shoot me?' she asked. 'If so, then you'd better hurry up, because I intend to see what's inside that tomb if it's the last thing I do.'

Markina lowered his gun, rubbing his hand over his face to wipe away the water streaming into his eyes. She aimed another kick at the door, which gave way with a loud crack. The lock fell to the floor.

'Amaia, I beg you, look all you want, but first listen to me.'

She stooped to pick up the broken lock, then tossed it aside. Pushing her hand into the hole it had left, she could feel the splintered wood dig into her fingers as she tugged the door towards her.

The unmistakable smell of death, of early stage decomposition, reached her from inside the dark crypt. With a look of disgust, she turned to face Markina, levelling her Glock at him.

'Why the stench if no bodies have been interred here in the last fifteen years?'

She took fresh aim as he moved closer.

'What are you doing, Amaia? You're not going to shoot me,' he said, gazing at her with a mixture of tenderness and

475

regret, as though addressing a child who has done something wrong.

She wanted to reply, but felt her resolve weaken as he looked at her. He was so young, so handsome . . .

'I'll answer all your questions, I swear,' he said, raising his hand. 'No more lies, I promise.'

'How long have you known? Why didn't you report them? Why didn't you stop them? These people are crazy.'

'Amaia, I can't stop this, you've no idea how powerful it is.'

'Possibly not,' she conceded, 'but perhaps the most recent ones, like the Esparza girl, could have been prevented.'

'I did my best.'

'You went to see Berasategui in prison; the governor's deputy denied it; you told me you had been nowhere near his cell. Those were your words, and yet Jonan had a photo of you right next to his cell,' she said.

'Berasategui threatened you, you were terrified,' he protested.

'You had something to do with his death?'

Markina looked away, ruffled but dignified; even in the rain he maintained that elegant aplomb that singled him out.

'Did you kill Berasategui?'

'No, he took his own life, you saw for yourself.'

'What about Rosario?'

'You said you'd never be at peace while she was still out there.'

She looked at him, surprised, not knowing what puzzled her more, the discovery that he was the grand instigator, or hearing him confess to his crimes with what seemed like a sense of entitlement.

'I can't believe this! I'm going in.'

'Please don't, Amaia, I beg you.'

'Why not?'

'Keep talking to me, but don't go inside. I beg you,' he said, raising his weapon once more and aiming straight at her.

She gazed at him in astonishment.

476

'You aren't going to shoot me either,' she said, as she spun round, stooping to enter the crypt.

It was a simple design. A central altar supported a heavy wooden coffin adorned with elaborate carvings.

Arranged in an oval shape around it lay the remains of at least twenty babies. Some were so old they were mere bones, but at her feet, Amaia recognised the bloated, decomposing corpse of the little Esparza girl. Next to her, arranged on an old shawl, lay a bleached white skeleton missing one arm. 'Like so many others.' Overcome with revulsion, she let go of the torch, dropping to her knees. Markina appeared behind her. He picked up the torch, wedging it into a crack in the wall to illuminate the grisly scene.

Amaia shed burning hot tears of rage and shame. No, this simply couldn't be happening, it was grotesque. She felt sick to her stomach, a nausea that filled her with anger and disgust. A torrent of questions broke over her like waves on the shore, each more furious than the last.

'You knew your father was responsible for all this, and yet you concealed it from me. Why? To save your career? Your reputation?'

Markina sighed, and gazed at her with that smile of his, as a flash outside lit up his silhouette against the only exit. It occurred to Amaia that she would rather be outside with the cold wind and rain whipping her face, the roar of thunder above her head. Surely the storm would provide more sanctuary, more solace than this desolate place.

'Amaia, my reputation is my least concern. This is far greater and more powerful, far stronger and more savage . . . A force of nature that existed long before we arrived.'

She stared at him, aghast.

'You mean, you're part of this?'

'I am a simple medium, the conduit for a religion as ancient and powerful as the world that originated in your valley, beneath the stones upon which your village was built, the house you live in. To a power such as you could never imagine, a power that demands to be fed.'

Amaia's eyes filled with tears as she contemplated him. How could this be? This man whom she had held in her embrace, for whom she had crossed what she thought were sacred boundaries, this man whom she had believed was a fellow victim, someone unloved by the person who should have loved him, was collapsing like some fallen idol. She wondered how much of what he had said and done was designed to throw her off the scent, to foster those beliefs. She wanted to ask him if any part of their relationship had been genuine. But she refrained, because she knew the answer, and she knew that she couldn't bear to hear it from his mouth, a mouth she still desired.

Outside, the storm raged, howling among the trees surrounding the cemetery, as the rain beat down harder and more furiously. Water was starting to flow down the steps into the open crypt, spilling over them in waves and soaking the floor.

'Is that what you believed you were doing? Feeding this power by offering up young girls so that a demon could suck the life from them?' she said, pointing her gun at the blackened remains on the ground around the altar. 'Making their parents sacrifice them? In my book, that's murder.'

Markina shook his head.

'The price is high, a sacrifice cannot be easy or simple. But the rewards are unimaginable, and this practice dates back to the beginning of time. Then Christianity came along, clothing everything in sin and guilt, making men and women forget how to commune with living forces.'

She gazed at him, unable to believe that this was the man she knew. His words belonged to preachers and prophets of doom.

'You're insane,' she murmured.

Lightning struck somewhere in the cemetery with a deafening crack.

Markina closed his eyes.

'Please don't say that, Amaia, I'll explain as much as you want, just don't call me that, not you.'

'How can you people be described as anything other than dangerous lunatics? My mother killed my baby sister!' she exclaimed, looking down at the mound of bleached bones screaming out from the dark earth. 'And then hounded me all my life . . . You were going to murder my son!' she screamed at him.

He shook his head, moving another step closer, lowering his weapon again, adopting a patient, conciliatory tone.

'Berasategui was a psychopath, and your mother couldn't see beyond fulfilling her promise . . . You understand, some people do this, not because it has to be done but out of enjoyment. But I've solved that problem, and I promise no one will ever harm you or Ibai again. I love you, Amaia, give me the chance to leave all this behind, to start a new life with you; we both deserve it.'

'What about Yolanda?' she said, looking towards the doorway. Her crumpled body lay sodden in the rain, which was descending the steps like a miniature waterfall forming a dark pool at the entrance.

He made no reply.

'Why did you send her to me?'

'When she came to see me in that confused state, spouting that absurd story about her missing boys, I saw the perfect opportunity for you to investigate the case, to see that it led nowhere, that her boys were in the tomb, and that these were the ramblings of a madwoman. It never occurred to me that you'd go over my head. I had to be part of the process, I couldn't let Judge De Gouvenain ruin everything. Her exhumation order was non-specific, and if Yolanda had seen the other casket, they would have been obliged to open it. So, I was forced to intervene. Naturally, I never imagined she would be crazy enough to blow up the tomb.'

A flash of lightning, alarmingly close, made them both duck, instinctively. *The Lady is coming.*

Trying to ignore the frenzy of natural forces converging above them, Amaia went on:

'You let this poor woman disfigure herself, you sent her like a lamb to the slaughter, and now you've killed her.'

'She had just knocked you down, for all I knew she had explosives or a weapon.'

'Why did you do this to me? Why did you pursue me?'

'If you're asking why I fell in love with you, that wasn't planned. Haven't you understood? I love you, Amaia: you were made for me; you belong to me just as I belong to you. Nothing can come between us, because, however hard it is for you to accept what you see, I know this doesn't change your feelings towards me.'

The storm roared and flashed magnificently above them, even as Amaia's head filled incongruously with statistics about the probability of lightning striking the same place twice. *She is here, the Lady has arrived.* She could all but hear their voices above the howling storm. Mari had arrived amid thunder and lightning, a spirit of the air, accompanied by the heady aroma of ozone. Markina swung round to face the door, as if he too had heard the chant of the *lamias* welcoming their lady.

'You broke into my house and stole that memory stick. Dr Takchenko's accident – your secretary saw me handing her the envelope . . .'

'I regret what happened to your friend. I like her. I'm glad she didn't die. They went too far, I never intended for her to suffer, I'm not a cruel man.'

'You're not a cruel man? But what about all those women, those young girls found dead by the river, all those babies. How much blood do you have on your hands?'

'None, Amaia. Each of us is in control of our own life, yet I am responsible for you. I love you, and I won't let anyone hurt you. Go ahead and condemn me for having protected you. Although you were right about one thing: your mother was out of control, she wouldn't listen to reason, she would have gone on until she achieved her goal, which was to kill you, and I couldn't allow that.'

'She was waiting for the final command, like Berasategui, like all the others. What power do you have over those people? Enough to control their lives?'

He shrugged, smiling in that charming, knowing way that had so beguiled her. A series of thunderclaps made the ground beneath them tremble, shaking the land of the dead, which felt like the mouth of hell when he gazed at her like that. It disturbed her deeply to admit that she loved him, she loved that man, she loved a demon, the ideal of manly perfection, the great seducer.

'Where is your grey coat?'

He gave a look of dismay and clucked his tongue: 'It got destroyed.'

'Oh, God!' she groaned.

The raging storm crescendoed outside. Like mourners expressing her pain, fresh bursts of thunder and lightning mingled with the wind howling amid the gravestones, rending the sky as the tears of Baztán gushed down in torrents, and the *lamias* cried out: *Wash away the crime, cleanse the river*.

He walked towards her, hand outstretched.

'Amaia.'

She raised her tear-stained face.

There was a catch in her voice as she asked:

'Did you kill Jonan?'

'. . . Amaia.'

'Did you kill Jonan Extaide?' she asked again in a whisper. The *lamias* were crying outside.

He looked at her, shaking his head.

'Don't ask me that, Amaia,' he pleaded.

'Did you, or didn't you?' she shouted.

'Yes.'

She gave a wail of pain, sobbing as she leaned forward, her face touching the trodden earth of the crypt. She saw Jonan lying in a pool of blood, tufts of hair ripped from his skull by the blast, his eyes which his merciful killer had closed after slaying him. She straightened up, raising her Glock, using the sights to aim straight at his chest. Her eyes were brimming with tears, but she knew she couldn't miss. Not at two metres . . .

'You bastard!' she cried.

'Don't do this, Amaia.' He gazed mournfully at her, reluctantly raising his weapon, which she saw then was Jonan's. Aiming at her head, he whispered: 'What a pity.'

The shots fired from the entrance were deafening inside the small space. Later on, Amaia would not be able to say whether she heard two or three shots above the noise of the storm. Markina looked down at his chest, surprised by the pain, which didn't register on his features. The force of the bullets fired at close range pitched him forward, and he landed face down beside Amaia. Blood flowed from his back, staining his grey suit. She saw Iriarte stooping in the doorway, drenched, the gun still smoking in his hand. He made his way towards her, and asked if she was okay. Amaia leaned across Markina's body and retrieved Jonan's pistol, looking up at Iriarte as if she owed him an explanation:

'He killed Jonan.'


First came the silence as the storm moved swiftly away, as though fleeing the scene. Soon afterwards, the ambulance arrived, and so did the forensic team, officers from the Ertzaintza, the magistrate, and the commissioner. They wore solemn, anxious faces, spoke in the hushed tones of funerals and wakes, shock and bewilderment obliging them to adopt an attitude of moderation and caution. Then it was time for words. It was midday when they completed their statements.

The lawyers Lejarreta & Andía were arrested at their offices, amidst protests and threats of legal action. The police in Elizondo took care of Argi Beltz, in Orabidea, where it seemed Rosario had been holed up since her disappearance. They arrived at Fina Hidalgo's house in Irurita only to find her dangling from her beloved walnut tree at the end of a rope. In Pamplona, true to her obsequious nature, the ugly, spiteful geisha, Inma Herranz, broke down in tears, trying to convince anyone willing to listen that she had acted under coercion. The forensic pathologist team in San Sebastián, sadly famous for their success at identifying human remains, particularly those of children, were working the case. It would take them weeks to identify and date the remains of the little girls arranged in that macabre offering around the coffin. A coffin that turned out to be empty.

An arrest warrant was issued for Xabier Markina AKA Tabese.

Considering they had shot and killed a magistrate, Internal Affairs processed the case far more quickly than expected. They gave Iriarte a bit of flak, but left Amaia alone, once she had handed in her written report. A report that included everything about the investigation, but omitted any mention of her intimate relations with Markina.

She drove herself home in her own car, as the afternoon faded into evening, observing the effects of the previous night's storm on the road between Hondarribia and Elizondo: fallen branches, trees stripped of their leaves. There was very little traffic, and she lowered her window to enjoy the calm that seemed to permeate everything, as if the valley were buried beneath a layer of cotton wool that soaked up every sound, spreading the fresh, moist aroma of clean, wet soil that was ingrained in her soul.

A thread of silvery light lingered in the sky as she came to a halt on Muniartea Bridge. Stepping out of the car, she inhaled the earthy smell of the River Baztán flowing beneath her feet. She leaned over the parapet, and saw how high the water level was after the downpour in Erratzu, at the head of the river, which had broken its banks all the way down to the coast at Hondarribia. Seeing the Baztán flowing so calmly and she had difficulty imagining the powerful force it could become. She ran her hand over the cold stone, upon which the name of the bridge was engraved, and listened to the sound of water in the weir, wondering whether this was enough, whether the river had been cleansed, the crime washed away. She hoped so, because she doubted she had any fight left in her. Her hot tears fell onto the cold stone and trickled towards the river, on that inexorable journey taken by all water in Baztán.

Engrasi was waiting to embrace her niece the moment she stepped into the house, and Amaia wept in her aunt's lap, as she had so often when she was a little girl. Hers were tears of fear, rage, bitterness and regret; she wept for what was lost, tainted, for what had died, for the bones and the blood. She cried so hard she fell asleep in Engrasi's embrace, and when she awoke she cried some more, while her aunt wished that the doors could remain closed forever, that her girl could cry away all the ills of the world. A day passed, then another, then another, until finally she had no tears left. That was the way things had to be. She needed to be ready to do what she had to do.

Afterwards she made four calls and received one.

The first was to Elena Ochoa's daughter to tell her that her mother had not taken her own life, and that the letter she had enabled them to apprehend and arrest members of that dangerous sect of child-killers currently making all the headlines.

The second was to Benigno Berrueta, to tell him that he could bury the remains of his granddaughter next to Yolanda.

The third was to Marc to tell him that they had shot the bastard who killed Jonan. She omitted to add that, as he had predicted, this hadn't brought Jonan back, or made her feel any better; in fact she felt worse.

The fourth was to James.

For the first few days, she had listened to her aunt's attempts to explain, to reassure him each time he called. Then she had simply stopped. And now, phone in hand, she felt her strength wane, as she faced the most difficult moment of her life.

He picked up immediately.

'Hello, Amaia.' His voice was as warm and gentle as ever, although she could sense his anxiety.

'Hello, James,'

'Are you coming?' he asked, his directness taking her aback. This was the same question he had asked each time they spoke since he left.

She took a deep breath.

'The seminars at Quantico begin in two days' time, and, as they've agreed for me to take part, yes, James, I will be going.'

'That's not what I asked,' he replied. 'Are you coming?'

'James, so much has happened. I think we need to talk.'

'Amaia, all I need to hear you say is that you're coming to join me, and that we'll be going home together. That's all I need to know. Are you coming?'

She closed her eyes, surprised to find the tears welling up again.

'Yes,' she replied.

It had grown dark by the time she received the call she had been expecting.

'Is it nighttime already in Baztán, Inspector Salazar?'

'Yes.'

'Now I need your help . . .'

# Author's Note

Since *The Invisible Guardian* was first published in January 2013, people have often asked me about the origins of the novel; what, if anything, influenced me to write *The Baztán Trilogy*. I invariably reply that the novels contain much of what has shaped me as a person: I grew up in a matriarchal family, and, happily, my childhood was steeped in the mythological world that lives on, under various guises, in the Baztán Valley, as in few other places. From a literary point of view, following a criminal investigation from beginning to end is something that fascinates me, and this was the genre of novel I wanted to read, and to write. The germ of the idea for this particular book though . . .

This came from a brief, disturbing news item I read filled with suffering, injustice and dread, which I couldn't shake off; it haunted my memory like an ever-present phantom. The incident vanished from the press as discreetly as it had appeared, and despite digging around I could find no further references to the shocking case. A veil of silence seemed to settle over the declaration of a repentant witness, who claimed he had participated in the ritual killing of a fourteen-month-old baby girl. The event had taken place in a farmhouse in the Navarre region thirty years before (I chose the date as Amaia Salazar's birthday). The witness claimed that the baby's parents had given her up in sacrifice then disposed of her body, and that afterwards the members of the sect had made a solemn pact of silence, which endured until that day.

"The girl's name was Ainara, and she was fourteen months old when she was murdered. Little else is known about her".

486

That sentence, taken from the original article, remained engraved on my memory, and gradually Ainara started to acquire everything that had been denied her: a face, small pale hands, the saddest eyes in the world, and her first hesitant steps. Added to the memory of this girl I never knew was the terrible realisation that the people who should have loved and protected her were precisely those who had hurt her. Not to mention the injustice of a forgotten name, the outrage of being denied a proper tomb, the violence of snuffing out a young life, and the justifying of the act as part of a ritual of faith, a sinister religion, a supernatural cult of evil worship.

This story is based on that news item, on a handful of facts and many uncertainties. My intention with the novel wasn't to offer a plausible theory as to what might have happened, but rather to emphasise the power such beliefs have to motivate heinous acts which, alas, do not belong to the world of fiction, but are all too real. Immoral creeds that feed off the blood of innocents. Evil people, not bad people, plain evil.

Ainara's memory is present on every page of my book; I visited the place where she lived out her short life, unloved from the day she was born until her death. I searched for any reference to the crime, wondering a thousand times over who the mysterious witness might be. Finally, while I was writing *The Legacy of the Bones*, I managed to get an interview with the person in charge of the investigation, which, due to the large numbers of people involved from all over Spain, has been declared secret. With the exception of the informant, all the other sect members have kept their vow of silence about their diabolical pact all these years.

At the time of writing, the investigation in to Ainara's death remains open.

# Acknowledgements

My thanks to the Navarre Police and in particular to the Elizondo Unit for being true to their motto, which I have adopted for myself: KEEP UP THE GOOD WORK!

Also to Iñaki Cía for his collaboration and kindness, and above all for his admirable hard work and dedication; and to Patxi Salvador whose advice on ballistics and explosives has turned me into a lethal weapon.

Thanks to the captain of the Guardia Civil Judicial Police in Pamplona and his team for their generous, invaluable assistance.

My heartfelt thanks to my friend Silvia Sesé for also being my editor.

Thank you to my friend Alba Fité (my 'fixer') for being so damned efficient.

To my dear Anna Soler-Pont, my agent, for being the one who takes most care of me, for being my bad cop, my advice-giver.

To José Ortega de Unoynueve for mentoring me in all things computer-related. I am starting to understand!

To Fernando from *El Casino* in Elizondo for sharing the beauty of rituals and customs that shouldn't be forgotten.

To the companies Amalur and 24/7 that specialise in trauma and crime scene cleaning for explaining to me the ins and outs of their difficult job.

Thank you to the Baztan Retailers Association, Bertan Baztan, for your generosity and your good work.

Thanks to Special Agent John Foster.

And, last but by no means least, thanks to the Lady, to Mari, for inspiring me to sow this seed, and for the bounty of her magnificent harvest.